A GOVERNESS OF GREAT TALENTS

The Governess Bureau, Book 1

Emily E K Murdoch

ARE YOU SIGNED UP FOR DRAGONBLADE'S BLOG?

You'll get the latest news and information on exclusive giveaways, exclusive excerpts, coming releases, sales, free books, cover reveals and more.

Check out our complete list of authors, too!

No spam, no junk. That's a promise!

Sign Up Here

www.dragonbladepublishing.com

Dearest Reader;

Thank you for your support of a small press. At Dragonblade Publishing, we strive to bring you the highest quality Historical Romance from the some of the best authors in the business. Without your support, there is no 'us', so we sincerely hope you adore these stories and find some new favorite authors along the way.

Happy Reading!

CEO, Dragonblade Publishing

Additional Dragonblade books by Author Emily E K Murdoch

The Governess Bureau Series
A Governess of Great Talents (Book 1)

Never The Bride Series
Always the Bridesmaid (Book 1)
Always the Chaperone (Book 2)
Always the Courtesan (Book 3)
Always the Best Friend (Book 4)
Always the Wallflower (Book 5)
Always the Bluestocking (Book 6)
Always the Rival (Book 7)
Always the Matchmaker (Book 8)
Always the Widow (Book 9)
Always the Rebel (Book 10)
Always the Mistress (Book 11)
Always the Second Choice (Book 12)

The Lyon's Den Connected World
Always the Lyon Tamer

Welcome to the Governess Bureau

You are most welcome, sir or madam.

When the nobility and gentility of England are at their wits end, they send a discrete note to Miss Vivienne Clarke's Governess Bureau. Only accepting the very best clients, their governesses are coveted by minor royalty, with every governess following three rules:

1. *You must have an impeccable record.*
2. *You must bring a special skill to the table.*
3. *You must never fall in love...*

CHAPTER ONE

July 24, 1812

T HE WAITING ROOM of the Governess Bureau was designed, in the main, to intimidate those within it. Miss Vivienne Clarke, the proprietress and owner, was of course not a cruel woman, far from it. She liked children, as far as one could tell, and she ran her business like a ship, without mercy.

That was why Miss Meredith Hubert, seated on the very edge of her seat with her reticule grasped in her hands, tried not to jump at every sound. She had met the formidable woman only once when she had been ordered to her first posting, but the interview had been brief.

Now she had returned after just two years, and Meredith knew without the reference she had been provided, there would be no second assignment. Miss Clarke had exacting standards, and only the very best governesses were given a second chance.

Not that she needed one. The Earl of Marnmouth had been pleased with her work, very pleased. Both Egerton children had learned well. There had been no complaints—none that had reached Meredith's ear, anyway—yet here she was.

Positionless. A dangerous thing for a woman of no means and few connections.

If only the earl had not decided to move to the Continent, but she had not begrudged him the decision. The Egerton children were grown now, and they had no need of a governess.

No need of her.

Meredith swallowed and looked around the waiting room. She was not the only governess with an appointment with Miss Clarke; that was clear.

All appeared respectable, likely as not the daughters of gentlemen. It was a wonder, really, that Meredith had managed to secure a position in the Governess Bureau at all. *If they had guessed…*well, she would not be welcomed to sit in this stifling room, that was for sure.

The governess opposite her looked over her book, took in Meredith's slightly creased gown, and raised her eyebrow. Without saying a word, her gaze dropped back to the volume in her hand.

Meredith rolled her eyes and then immediately chastised herself. *Rudeness in a governess was absolutely insupportable!*

Perhaps she should have brought a book herself. Everyone knew how much Miss Clarke valued reading. It was one of the safest things to do in her waiting room, while one anticipated her fate being decided.

Read a book. Show Miss Clarke how attentive you are to one's own education.

For those governesses waiting for their next posting, hoping it would be a good one, it was easy to bring a book, any old book.

Meredith hid a smile. She had never been one for attempting to impress, and she could tell by the glazed look of most in the waiting room that they were finding no joy whatsoever in…what did they have there?

Epistles on Women, Travels of Mirza Abu Taleb Khan in Asia, Wordsworth's *Guide to the Lakes…*

Meredith forced down the smile sparked by the ridiculousness of it all. *How far would one go to secure a good position?*

There was even one reading the latest edition of *The Times*. Meredith could just make out the headline, though part of it was obscured by a finger.

TERRIFYING GLASSHAND GANG STRIKES AGAIN!

"Yes, the Duke of Axwick," one of the governesses was saying in a mock whisper at the other end of the waiting room to one of her companions. It could not be more evident she wished them all to hear. "He is pleased with me, very pleased. I merely sought an appointment with Miss Clarke to inform her of my progress."

Meredith watched the flicker of eyes across the room. No one wished to give the speaker the compliment of real attention, naturally, but no one could deny their intrigue.

"Ah, we are similar, then," said another with a smirk. "I have just been released from the employ of the Duke of Mercia, your master's brother-in-law."

It could not be more evident that she wished to impress in turn, but there was a look of triumphant pity on the first speaker's face.

"Dear me," she said scornfully. "*Released* from his employ, were you? Not so similar, if you do not mind me saying so."

A trickle of fear ran down the back of Meredith's neck. And this was why she had not attempted to pay her way through life as a seamstress or maidservant. The backbiting, the catcalling, the determination to make out one's successes were another person's failures.

The sooner she could be back in another house, the better...

Further conversation in the waiting room was stifled as Miss Clarke's door opened. All the ladies stiffened, their backs as straight as rods as silence fell.

There she stood: Miss Clarke. Like a queen of her own realm, she looked out with cold eyes across the room and then spoke in icy tones.

"Miss Meredith Hubert."

Meredith swallowed. Rising to her feet, she curtseyed low,

and then stepped forward. Miss Clarke had already turned and entered her room.

It had been over two years since she had been in Miss Clarke's office, and that had only been a fleeting visit. The interview process to be admitted into the Governess Bureau did not happen here; Miss Clarke would not allow it. Only fully vetted governesses were permitted to step over the threshold, and even then, they must enter by the side door. The front door was for customers.

So it was with interest that Meredith stepped into the office and looked around. The room was beautiful. Set out quite like a gentleman's study, with a writing desk in one corner and a businesslike desk of mahogany near the window, sunlight streamed through and glinted off the gold lettering on the ledger books beside Miss Clarke's chair.

Everywhere she looked, there was splendor. A globe sat in one corner, a series of gold gilt-framed paintings, mostly landscapes, adorned the walls. There were books of all kinds in the bookcases—languages, sciences, histories, even a few Radcliffes from what Meredith could see.

On one side of the desk was a large leather-bound armchair, luxurious with brass studs. This was where Miss Clarke had settled herself, looking up shrewdly at Meredith. On the other side of the desk was a narrow wooden chair, with no cushion nor adornments.

By this chair, Meredith stood. She knew better than to merely assume she could be seated.

This was Miss Clarke's office. It was difficult not to be impressed. She was not old, probably just a little over forty, from what Meredith could guess, and in that time, she had built an empire.

The Governess Bureau.

Desired by the best in society, every duke, earl, and minor prince in Europe wished to secure a governess from the Bureau for their children. Great expectations were required from those governesses who were able to secure assignments from this very room.

Meredith found her heart beating rather quickly. No governess was guaranteed another posting once one had ended. Miss Clarke was the decider of their fate and could just as easily send them to the wilds of Scotland to a laird as send them packing with no way to pay their bills.

"Sit down, Miss Hubert."

Meredith obeyed, the hardwood discomforting and forcing her to sit slightly forward. It gave one the sensation of returning to school. There was a commanding tone in Miss Clarke's voice that every governess strove to imitate. It gave the sense of absolute power, and in this room, that was warranted.

Meredith found it difficult to meet Miss Clarke's eye as she examined her from across the desk. The silence between them continued uncomfortably.

Meredith's fingers tightened around her reticule, the soft velvet smooth against her gloves. *Dare she break the silence first—or was she supposed to wait until Miss Clarke spoke?*

"Miss Hubert," said Miss Clarke coldly. "You have finished your employment at the Earl of Marnmouth's. His decision, I take it."

In anyone else's mouth, the last sentence would have been a question, but it was so evidently a statement, Meredith did not even bother to attempt a response.

Besides, her heart was too busy sinking. Her first assignment and she had clearly failed in the eyes of Miss Clarke. Never mind that the two Egertons were absolute rascals who had needed a firmer hand than Meredith had ever expected.

Curls of panic started to tug at her heart. *What was she going to do?* Being a governess was the only respectable way she could conceive of supporting herself—she had no other skills.

Except those, her mind whispered, that dark, cruel side of her attempting to surface. *You could always go back to—*

No. She would never return to that way of life.

"I have here a report from the earl himself, in his own hand," said Miss Clarke, evidently impressed. She picked up a letter from the sheaf on her desk and unfolded it slowly.

Each second was torture to Meredith. *A report?* Surely, she had her reference, even now kept carefully in her reticule, her one piece of proof that she had served faithfully.

A report? What could the earl not have said to her directly? Would his true opinion of her now be revealed?

"My dear Miss Clarke, I write to inform you that I will no longer be needing the services of your governess, Miss Hubert," said Miss Clarke quietly, reading from the report.

Meredith swallowed. All she had to do was stay calm.

"I admit I had low expectations when Miss Hubert arrived, so young as she was," Miss Clarke continued, pausing to raise her gaze over the paper to examine Meredith, who flushed, before reading on. "Yet I have been impressed. She understands children more than I could ever claim and has taken great pains with my youngest. I have seen dramatic improvement."

Heat seared across Meredith's cheeks, though mainly from relief rather than any attempt to be coy.

Thank the Lord. The earl had always been a good man, fair and straight with her, but one never knew with these titled types. They seemed just as likely to cut one down with a smile as praise with a frown.

But the earl had written to Miss Clarke with much the same as he had written on her reference.

"—otherwise I would never be dispensing with her services," Miss Clarke read on. "We'll skip over a part of it... Please inform Miss Hubert that if I am ever in need of a governess again, then I will be writing to you to secure her. I remain, yours, etc."

The proprietress of the Governess Bureau placed the report back on her desk and examined Meredith with a sharp eye.

"How kind of the earl to share his opinions so freely," Meredith said boldly, feeling as though it was high time she contributed to the conversation.

"Indeed," said Miss Clarke.

Meredith was not entirely sure whether to attempt to speak again and decided against it. Miss Clarke hardly encouraged conversation, and besides, what more could she add? It was a relief to know one's master had not been sycophantic to one's face yet cruel in letters back to one's employer.

"This part of his lordship's report impressed me," said Miss Clarke suddenly, eyes glancing down to the paper. "Here it is—I recall in particular Miss Hubert's excellent handling of a ruffian boy on the estate, a tale which one day I will tell in full."

Meredith smiled. What a tale it was, though she would rather not be the one to tell it. *When the Earl of Marnmouth himself struggled to keep track of his illegitimate children...*

"How fascinating," Miss Clarke said curtly, raising an eyebrow. "From where did you gain such a great talent with ruffians?"

A flush covered Meredith's cheeks, and her gaze dropped from Miss Clarke's penetrating stare to her hands in her lap.

The accreditation process for joining the Governess Bureau was challenging, long, and focused entirely on the skills, experience, and wit of the woman applying to join Miss Clarke's ranks of governesses.

It was one of the reasons Meredith had chosen it. One's family, one's background simply did not matter. Miss Clarke had no interest, save that one was a lady, and she believed it possible to tell on sight when one was not.

Miss Clarke was not perfect. Meredith sat in uncomfortable silence, wondering precisely how to answer her question. But she had worked hard to keep her history a secret, and she was not about to fall at this hurdle.

"A good governess," she said in a clear, unwavering voice, "does not become intimidated by her charges, nor by anyone else."

Miss Clarke examined her closely without saying a word and then finally nodded in the approval Meredith had been desperate not to lose.

"I find myself needing to echo his lordship," she said quietly. "I, too, have been impressed by your care of the Egerton children. I had sent another governess to the earl before you, and I do not think I mentioned when I gave you this appointment. She was…lacking, I suppose one would say, in great talents."

Meredith ventured a smile. "I was honored to serve his lordship and her ladyship and their children."

"And now they are grown," Miss Clarke said. "Grown, and off to the Continent I understand, to refine their manners before they enter society."

"I will be intrigued to see how society responds to them," said Meredith, her tongue unguarded.

Miss Clarke's eyes widened. "Indeed."

Meredith swallowed. She always had a rather discomforting talent of speaking her mind, which was most unhelpful in her line of employment. Though she had trained herself, in the main, to filter out her most wild ideas, there were always a few that slipped through.

"I just meant…the Egertons are very delightful children, and I think society will be impressed," she said lamely.

Silence filled the room, and Meredith tried not to allow panic to grow. *Was it possible that her own foolish tongue had talked herself out of another appointment?*

"I believe the Egertons were very…rambunctious children, and I think you deserve a rest," said Miss Clarke finally. "There is a room above waiting for you. Good day, Miss Hubert."

Gaze dropping to her desk, she started to move the report from the Earl of Marnmouth back into the sheaf of papers.

Meredith's heart dropped into her stomach. "A-A room above?"

It was considered a reward, for she knew all governesses hoped that when an assignment came to an end, if one had impressed, she would be given the chance to take a room in the Governess Bureau and stay for a month. No bills, three hot meals a day, and nothing to do.

Paradise, for most.

Meredith, on the other hand, knew it would the end of her. *Days on end without anything to do? With only her thoughts to keep her company?*

Worse, time with other governesses, all that bickering, questioning, attempting to get to know her and her past?

Bile rose in her throat, and she leaned forward, knowing she had to say something. She could not allow this to happen. "I-I would rather go on to my next assignment, Miss Clarke."

She had not spoken rudely, but Miss Clarke stared in abject astonishment.

"Next assignment...you do not wish to avail yourself of a room in the Governess Bureau? I was always given to understand you girls sought it. A holiday, if you will. And *you* do not want it?"

Meredith leaned back slightly on her chair, attempting to control her breathing. *She had to stay calm.* She had to ensure Miss Clarke did not become suspicious.

If she were to lose her place here...

Besides, a governess of the Bureau is always polite, keeping decorum, and speaks in a calm, low manner. It had taken every ounce of her strength at times to keep in that temper of hers, but there were always fresh opportunities for her to lose it.

"I greatly appreciate the offer, Miss Clarke," she said slowly, weighing every word. "I recognize the attention, and I thank you for it. But...I like to be useful, Miss Clarke."

It was a calculated remark, and Meredith saw to her relief Miss Clarke almost smiled. The owner of the Governess Bureau liked useful girls. A girl who did not know how to be useful was not welcome here.

"Useful?"

Meredith nodded eagerly. "Yes, useful. I would much rather continue on to my next posting if you please."

Was that last bit a little thick? Meredith simply did not know Miss Clarke well enough to ascertain how far was too far, but better to go too servile than not enough, surely?

Miss Clarke's eyes glanced toward the report. "I will admit, Miss Hubert, this is one of the best reports I have received. I have said before, and I will say again, I am impressed. Perhaps there is an allowance we can make for you."

Meredith held her breath. Was she about to ensure she could move on to her next family and avoid the suspicion she had so desperately hidden from all these years?

Miss Clarke took a deep breath, and she looked slightly as though she was in pain as she said, "If you would like paid holiday instead, to see your family, then I suppose something can—"

"No!" Meredith had not intended to interrupt, nor shout so loud, and the censorious look Miss Clarke gave her was sufficient to halt her tongue.

Blast it! Meredith cursed in the silence of her own mind and wished she had the power to take back that hurried word.

All she had done now was invite speculation, the last thing she needed. Any intrigue into her family would surely ruin her. *See her family?* Meredith almost laughed at the suggestion. She had no wish to see them. She could not, even if she wished it.

Not after the life they had chosen.

"I mean," she said awkwardly, attempting to keep her voice level, "no, thank you, Miss Clarke. As I think I have mentioned before, my family travels so much, it is often impossible to know where they are going to be from one moment to the next."

Miss Clarke examined her silently.

"I...I wish to be useful, and I cannot be in a room here at the Governess Bureau," said Meredith in a low, humble tone. "Please, Miss Clarke. I wish to start my next assignment."

She fell into silence again and this time resolved not to be the one to break it. She had said her piece, made her petition to Miss Clarke. Now she waited.

She would rather leave the Governess Bureau entirely and seek out other employment than go back to them...

Miss Clarke sighed as she leaned back in her leather armchair.

"You know, Miss Hubert, sometimes you remind me of myself. I was much like you when I was your age."

Meredith looked up in surprise. It was hard to remember, sometimes, that Miss Clarke had once been young.

"In fact, I was about your age when I first started the Bureau," said Miss Clarke, with something like a smile dancing across her face.

Meredith returned the smile nervously. "I did not know you had started it at my age—and all alone? That is a remarkable feat, Miss Clarke."

For the first time in their conversation, Miss Clarke colored. "A new posting. Let me see what is currently on the books."

There were three heavy ledgers on her desk, the edges of their pages stained with the mottled colors an accountant would use, and as she pulled one toward her, Meredith stared in awe.

There were few endeavors managed by ladies. Gentlemen in Parliament said it was because women's brains were not sufficient to understand such things. Meredith had snorted when she had first been told that by a whippersnapper at a card party, when she had been waiting for her first assignment. She had assumed the whelp had been jesting.

It had become a rather awkward conversation; therefore, when it had transpired, he had been utterly serious.

For all her frostiness and aloof manner, Miss Clarke was someone to be admired.

As she flicked through the pages, Meredith could see each one was covered with neat, meticulous handwriting.

"The Axwickes, the Fitzclarences, the Mercias..." muttered Miss Clarke, eyes roving over her notes. "The Clarctons, the Astors...ah, here we are. The Carmichaels."

Meredith waited expectantly as Miss Clarke read the notes silently. *The Carmichaels.* There were no clues in that name, and she did not recall hearing about the family before. *How many children would there be? What did the parents—more importantly, the mother—think about the hiring of a governess?*

All these concerns whirled in her mind, unanswered as Miss Clarke sat in silence.

It was Meredith's impatience that gave out first. "The Carmichaels?"

Miss Clarke looked up from her ledger. "Yes. You have not lived anywhere but London, have you, Miss Hubert?"

Meredith made sure to keep her voice calm and level as she replied, "No, Miss Clarke."

A lie. One which was harmless, surely. What difference did it make whether she had lived all over England or not? Miss Clarke did not need to know about that.

"No, I thought not," said Miss Clarke. "Which is why you would not have heard of the Carmichaels. The family resides in the north. Though the head of the house is in London often."

Meredith waited for further enlightenment, but it did not appear any was forthcoming. Instead, Miss Clarke had affixed her with a rather stern look that did not invite further questions.

"And…and are there many Carmichael children?" Meredith hazarded.

Miss Clarke smiled briefly. "One. An interesting child. One unaccustomed to being told what to do, and therefore not obedient. It is…an unusual assignment. It requires a governess of great talents."

Meredith sat up straighter. "I am ready, Miss Clarke."

"Hmm." Miss Clarke continued to stare and then finally said, "Perhaps. Alfred is a nice man, as men go. A lord, naturally, the Duke of Rochdale, but 'tis a very small endowment and to be frank, Miss Hubert, I would not typically allow such a man on my books."

This Alfred Carmichael sounded fascinating, and Meredith had to fight to keep her face uninterested as she said, "Indeed."

"Not the sort of title we would accept *at all*," emphasized Miss Clarke. "But then, the world is changing. Earls, dukes, they are important, but they are not the only important people."

Meredith was utterly lost at this. She had seen the regent

once, during a parade. She had never seen more pomp and ceremony in one place, and the music, the noise, the shouts—it had caused her heart to lurch and excitement to brew in her soul.

"Not the only important people," she repeated.

Miss Clarke shook her head. "His Grace is not merely a duke, you must understand, but is also a member of Parliament. *The* member of Parliament for Rochdale. Politics, Miss Hubert, not rank is the future."

"Ah, I see." Meredith did not entirely see. Politics was so full of dukes and earls, it was impossible, in her opinion, to see much difference.

"The family dynamic is, from what His Grace has said, a delicate one," said Miss Clarke slowly. "When I say it is an unusual assignment, I mean it advisedly."

Meredith smiled. "That sounds precisely what I am looking for, Miss Clarke."

Out of London, out of the city—this was the perfect opportunity to gain a little anonymity in the rural idyll of England. London was all very well when one was terrified of recognition, of someone putting two and two together and realizing she was…

No. Leaving town suited her perfectly.

Miss Clarke was still examining her, and it was most discomforting, but Meredith did not drop her gaze.

Finally, Miss Clarke said, "Well. The duke is the eldest of the two Carmichael brothers, Miss Hubert. Different mothers, which adds a certain complexity to the dynamic, as does the twenty years difference in age between them."

Meredith nodded. She would have been surprised if a tradesman had such an arrangement, but dukes remarried all the time. *Heir and a spare, and all that.*

"So, my charge would be—"

"The younger," said Miss Clarke with a nod. "A lord in his own right, when he comes of age. Archibald. A terror, apparently."

Meredith forced down her smile. *Every young boy was called a terror.*

"His Grace is running for election again, a mere formality as far as I understand, but cannot abide the distraction of a child," said Miss Clarke. "He needs to be left alone. He will not be disturbed by a governess on a daily, nor even weekly basis. He has much more important things to be getting on with."

It was impossible to think of a greater position. A duke, far more impressive than her previous earl. Just one child, and a boy who by the sound of it, was completely ignored—and a master who would likewise leave her to her own devices.

"I accept, Miss Clarke," she said graciously.

Miss Clarke raised an eyebrow. "I have not offered you the position yet."

A flush crimsoned Meredith's cheeks. "I-I just meant—"

"This will be a challenge, Miss Hubert, and I mean that," said Miss Clarke quietly. "These political upstart types, they have high expectations. He may be a duke in name, and that will impress some, but he is not the sort of nobility we have come to expect here in London, nor at the Governess Bureau."

Meredith nodded. "Then we will show them what standards are."

She could see her words had impressed.

"Young Carmichael requires a governess of great talents," Miss Clarke said. "And I propose that you are that governess, Miss Hubert."

Meredith smiled. "When do I leave?"

CHAPTER TWO

July 31, 1812

H E WASN'T GOING to do it. Everything within him ached to, his body defying him, rebelling, refusing to obey, but he was not going to give in.

He gave in. Alfred yawned, hiding the discourtesy behind a hand.

It did not seem to matter. The conversation continued on without him, as it had done for the last twenty minutes, droning on and on about his life, as though he had nothing to contribute.

Which, in fairness, he did not.

"—rebellious voting is given as a protest, a vote against the status quo which is taken not as a disapproval of His Grace, but rather as…"

Another yawn was coming. Alfred Carmichael, Duke of Rochdale, was able to hide this one as he leaned forward to look at the paper Mr. Walker had presented him before their meeting.

Meeting. Alfred shook his head with a wry smile. *Meeting!* His father had never needed to suffer through all these meetings when *he* had been elected a member of Parliament. He had ridden out, instructed what few men who could vote that he was their only choice, and yes, rent day would still be March 31, and wouldn't it be a shame if the rents were to increase, and that was an end to it.

Meetings! Alfred felt as though he was being slowly strangled, all these endless conversations designed to ensure he would once again take the seat that was rightfully his family's.

"—you see," said Mr. Walker with a grand wave of his hand.

Alfred opened his mouth.

"And yet, we must consider the other side of the equation," started Mr. Walker again, fire in his eyes. "If one decides to ignore the original position, then enclosure is in itself detrimental to…"

Alfred closed his mouth and leaned back in his chair. Mr. Walker was back in his old flow again, his eyes bright with passion, speaking as though his very life depended on it.

The town hall where they were all seated was not large. Neither was Rochdale itself, the town from whence Alfred gained his title. But it was a pretty little place, and it was his duty, Alfred knew, to sit here and care about what everyone was saying.

Then, as future member of Parliament, he could just make up his mind.

Surreptitiously taking his pocket watch out of his waistcoat, Alfred glanced at it. *A quarter to four…the damned meeting started at two o'clock!*

He sighed as he replaced the watch and smiled at Mr. Brown. Mr. Brown looked pleased as punch to be recognized by his duke. Alfred made a mental note not to grin at the man again today. One could not permit others to get ideas above their station.

"Enclosure is not the real issue here," interrupted Mr. Hemming. "What one must consider instead is this—that local farmers are not being consulted on—"

"Consulted?" Mr. Walker laughed, and a few others chuckled with him. "I do not think His Grace requires the input of farmers and tenants in how to help run this great country, Mr. Hemming!"

Mr. Hemming's face flushed.

"As I was saying," said Mr. Walker, triumphant in his small victory over a man who, now Alfred came to think of it, had purchased the second largest house in the town recently—second only, naturally, to Mr. Walker's, "enclosure will affect our farmers in three ways. The way the first..."

Alfred tried not to smile. No matter the size of the pond, there was always someone in it desperate to be the biggest, the most important. There was no harm in Mr. Walker, not really, but the man did seem eager that his status in the world was adequately recognized.

It was not something Alfred often had to worry about. When people had to address you as 'Your Grace,' somehow one never wondered where one's place in the world was.

Besides, enclosures...Alfred cared about his tenants, knew most of them by name and, in turn, could name most of their children.

But as he had told one of them only yesterday, to the great chagrin of Mr. Walker, there was far more he could do for his tenants as a landlord than as a member of Parliament.

It was not as though he had been particularly effective in the last parliament, after all.

Chiming. The large clock over the town hall, paid for with Carmichael money, chimed the hour.

Four o'clock. This could no longer continue.

Clearing his throat loudly, the room fell silent as every eye turned to him.

"I thank you all for your thoughts and input—all of you," he said in carrying voice, inclining his head to Mr. Walker and Mr. Hemming in turn, the latter throwing out his chest with a smile. "But perhaps we can adjourn our discourse to another day?"

Mr. Walker looked scandalized. "Adjourn?" he said, placing his hands on the table they all sat around.

"Adjourn," repeated Alfred. *Dear God, the man looked as though he had suggested sacrificing a virgin to win the election!*

"Do you not wish to discuss the hustings, Your Grace?" said

Mr. Hemmings in a confused tone. "Just a few weeks away, we must write your speech—that is, support you in preparing your speech."

"How is your speech preparation going, Your Grace?" Mr. Walker raised an eyebrow.

Alfred's stomach twisted. There was that familiar sinking feeling, that sensation his bowels were about to drop out of his—

"Very well, I thank you," he said aloud, pushing the feelings away as though by ignoring them, they would cease to be. "Very well."

A member of Parliament who hated speaking in public! Alfred knew he had been fortunate to get through the last election unscathed, but it would not be possible this time.

In the last election, he had run uncontested. Who would challenge him? Carmichaels had held this seat for generations.

This year, however...

"I appreciate all of your insight, gentlemen, but I must return to the abbey," said Alfred heavily. "I have an appointment there at half past the hour, which I simply cannot miss."

All four of those who sat with him—Mr. Walker, Mr. Hemmings, Mr. Brown, and Mr. Shaw—looked around at the small clock affixed to the town hall wall. It showed six minutes past four.

"Well," said Mr. Walker, evidently discomforted.

Alfred could see his dilemma. Mr. Walker held the Carmichael family in significant regard, and it was not his place to instruct a duke on where to go and what to do.

Still, his priority was clearly the election.

"We still need to discuss where the hustings will be, and," Mr. Walker said darkly, "what do to about the Talbot boy."

Alfred sighed heavily. The Carmichaels and the Talbots. How many generations was it now that the two families had been at odds? Enemies for goodness knows how long, they were—well, not enemies exactly. Dukes did not have enemies. They had adversaries.

He could never recall being instructed to hate Talbots. His father had always believed that men such as Thomas Talbot, and now his son, were not worthy of Carmichael hatred.

"Ah, the Talbots," said Mr. Hemming, shaking his head. "An ill-wind brought them here."

"Brought them here?" added Mr. Shaw, a rather nasty smile on his face. "You don't know what you're talking about Hemming, they've been here at least two generations longer than you!"

Alfred allowed the conversation to wash over him. It was easier than attempting to interrupt.

"We cannot do anything about John Talbot," interrupted Alfred with a wry smile. "I suppose this happens in most towns when two families rise to prominence, but there is nothing for it. Both myself and Talbot are running for election, and the best man will win."

He had intended his words to smooth the rough edges of the conversation and lead to an end, but Mr. Hemming looked outraged.

"Best man will win?" he repeated, eyes wide. "But surely, Your Grace, that would mean you should win!"

Alfred sighed and glanced at the clock. Ten to five. Mrs. Martin was going to be beside herself.

"We may have to accept that I am not guaranteed to secure the seat for myself," he said. "Now, if you will excuse me gentlemen, I—"

"Not guaranteed?" It was Mr. Walker who had spoken this time, Mr. Shaw's face turned toward him in panic. "How can you say such a thing, Your Grace? Why, a Carmichael has held the seat of Rochdale for—"

"Four generations," echoed Alfred, his voice slightly sharper now. "Yes, I am well aware of that, Mr. Walker."

The man looked a little abashed, but Mr. Brown continued to look at him as though he had gone mad.

Alfred should have known it. He should never have attempted to explain it to them, and he would not be so foolish as to continue the effort.

How did one tell those who wished for nothing more than his re-election to Parliament that…well, he did not wish to be.

Member of Parliament. 'Tis an honor, his father had always said. The elder Carmichael had been too frail, too elderly at the time of the last election, and Alfred had taken on the mantle with poor grace and significant irritation.

He had done it because his father had asked him to.

The following year, his father had died. Alfred had inherited the title, the house, the fortune, the tenants—and with it all, the responsibility of going to Parliament.

That, as he had always been told, was what Carmichaels did.

"Rochdale without a Carmichael?" Mr. Shaw was saying quietly. "It could not be countenanced!"

Alfred almost laughed. "Losing the election would not require me to quit Rochdale, nor the abbey."

Mr. Shaw colored. "But to see a Talbot take your seat—*your seat*, Your Grace!"

There was a low rumble from Mr. Brown. An elderly gentleman with a beard almost reaching his waistcoat pocket, he had not said a word the entire time they had been in the town hall, and the place fell silent waiting for his statement.

"Rochdale needs Carmichaels," he said slowly and impressively.

Alfred waited, but there did not appear to be anymore. "And I will do my best, Mr. Brown, of course, but at this moment, I really must away."

"But Your Grace, there is so much more we need to discuss," said Mr. Walker in a wheedling voice. "We must resolve what is to be done if you do not win the seat!"

Alfred opened his hands expansively. "I will win, though, won't I? Carmichaels always do."

It was all he could do to keep the bitterness out of his voice. Carmichaels always got what they wanted, always drove the hardest bargain, always fought until the end. It was what they did. It was what they had always done.

"Young Talbot is proving...well, effective," said Mr. Hemming nervously. "In talking to the people, I mean."

It was impossible not to laugh at this. "As do I, Mr. Hemming—I think you will find most are my tenants!"

Silence fell in the town hall as the men stared, shocked at his levity at what they clearly believed to be a genuine disaster.

Get a grip of yourself, man, Alfred told himself. These are not men of London who understand your dry humor. They are your townsmen, and they are looking to you to provide some sort of peace!

"Look," he said quietly. "I agree, there is much more to be discussed here—more than can be reasonably covered in one sitting. I have a governess arriving for Archibald today, however, and I have no choice but to depart, return to the abbey, and greet her."

"We quite understand you have other commitments, Your Grace," said Mr. Shaw hurriedly, rising himself. "Good day to you."

Alfred bowed and, as Mr. Shaw departed, Mr. Brown followed without saying a word. Only a gentleman like Mr. Brown could get away with such indecorum, but who was to disagree with him? A man of such advanced years could do what he liked.

"I-I wanted to thank you, Your Grace."

Alfred looked up to see Mr. Hemming hovering. "Thank me?"

Mr. Hemming nodded nervously. "Yes, I-I was not involved in your first election campaign, you know, and 'tis an honor to be a small part of it now. I am most grateful to even be a part of this discussion."

Alfred blinked. Mr. Hemming...new to the town, which meant he had only lived here thirty years. A gentleman, by all accounts, though from trade rather than family wealth. A nervous man, a gentleman. A man Mr. Walker had taken a disliking to ever since he had purchased the house Mr. Walker had ear-marked for his son.

Alfred smiled. "Of course, the pleasure is all mine, Mr. Hemming."

Mr. Hemming floated away on a cloud and shut the door behind him.

"You are not taking this seriously enough, Your Grace."

Alfred turned. Mr. Walker was standing at the other end of the table, a frown on his face and a steely glint in his eye.

"I am taking my brother's education very seriously, Mr. Walker," Alfred said nonchalantly, starting toward the door.

"You know precisely what I mean," Mr. Walker snapped. "Damnit, man, if you do not pay attention, you could let this election slip through your fingers!"

Alfred halted and looked at the man, now only feet from him. He had been loyal to the Carmichaels for generations. Beside every Carmichael who had taken up his seat at Parliament, there had been a Walker behind him, cheering him on, ensuring votes were counted—or if need be, counted twice.

There were few people in the world Alfred would permit to speak to him in that way. Mr. Walker was one of them.

"I did not want to run for this damned seat last time," Alfred said quietly. "I ran, despite my better judgment, and I won. I have served in London. I do not wish to run for the seat again, and yet I am doing just that. Is that not enough?"

He could not take it anymore. Had he not sacrificed enough for his father and the family name? Striding outside into the warmth of the July day, Mr. Walker's footsteps followed him.

"Archibald is getting himself a governess, you say?" Mr. Walker wiped his brow with a handkerchief and smiled nervously. "The scamp won't be able to run amok anymore then. I suppose you will be glad of that!"

Alfred smiled. He could see Mr. Walker's words for what they truly were—an olive branch after their disagreement.

"A scamp?" he said lightly, nodding to his man waiting outside the town hall who immediately went to retrieve his horse. "I seem to remember being described that way myself once, not too long ago."

Mr. Walker's face broke into a smile. "The number of times I had to chase you off my vegetable patch, I don't think anyone would believe."

Alfred grinned. The street was teeming with people going about their business, and none of them looked twice at the two gentlemen having their conversation on the pavement.

"I think Archibald is very much cut from the same cloth," said Alfred dryly. "But nothing a good governess cannot cure, I am sure."

Where is that damned horse? The sooner he could get away, the quicker he could avoid any more mention of this election.

"Hmm," said Mr. Walker, looking skeptical. "You will have to find yourself a very good governess, if you ask me, for someone like young Master Archibald to change his ways, them's set in stone! A lady who does not put up with any nonsense, otherwise you will be managing him yourself."

One of the fascinating things about being a duke, Alfred had learned on the occasion of his father's death, was that everyone was suddenly an expert on all parts of your life. Dukes? Everyone knew what a duke should look like, stand like, dress like.

Even raising his half-brother had become a part of county concern, and it was with relief that Alfred saw Williams arrive with his horse tugging at the reins.

"I have managed Archibald since his mother died," said Alfred, not unkindly. "Please do not concern yourself, Mr. Walker. I think you will find that I have everything under control. Good day."

"Ah, yes, right," said Mr. Walker, not taking the hint as Alfred mounted his steed. "Now, about the enclosures. 'Tis an important topic, as I am sure you know and—goodbye, Your Grace!"

The last few words were shouted after him as Alfred nudged

the horse to a gentle trot. Williams would be off to the Johnsons now, helping them with some of the harvest. He could ride alone, which meant in peace, something in rather short supply at the moment.

This damned election! Rochdale Abbey was a few miles from the town, and so it was not long until the roads were left behind him and countryside beckoned, as he took the road that led to the Carmichael estate.

"Please do not concern yourself, Mr. Walker. I think you will find that I have everything under control."

Alfred laughed bitterly as his horse snorted. Everything was not under control, though he would be the last to admit it. Archibald was more than a scamp; he was a terror! No servant would agree to mind him, Mrs. Martin had vowed to leave if a governess was not found, and the undermaid was leaving today. God knows why—Mrs. Martin had made the decision, and that was her right, not that anyone had bothered to tell him.

As wind whipped through his hair, Alfred mused that it had been tempting to leave everything behind. He could just disappear and run off to America, a land where one could entirely reinvent oneself. No one could demand that the eldest Carmichael do his duty if he had a different name. No Carmichaels there ran for election. They did not serve the people in the smokey, dark, and dingy London in the south.

Alfred espied the Johnsons in the distance and made a mental note to check in on their harvest later on in the week. It was early, true, but they had enjoyed a hot summer. The sun shone down, and the bees flew up, all day, every day for weeks, and the land had responded.

He breathed it in, the unmistakable scent of Rochdale land. Just like the gorse on the moors and the trees that stood strong against the winds, he had been planted here years ago, and he would never leave it to run away.

Besides, he would never leave Archibald. Half-brother he may be, but he was a Carmichael. A Carmichael who had been permitted to run about wild for far too long.

Rochdale Abbey appeared on the horizon suddenly as he turned another corner, nestled into the landscape as though God Himself had put it there. Alfred could not help but smile. Home was home, even if it held worries and strains.

Dismounting from his horse and immediately handing the reins over to a lad who came running over form the stable, Alfred laughed to see a small scrawl of a figure sitting on the steps to the abbey.

"Hmmmph," said the figure, arms crossed and frown on its little face.

Alfred composed himself, ensured he looked sufficiently parental, though God knew what that looked like, and went to sit next to his half-brother.

"You," he said easily, "are supposed to be in the schoolroom, reading."

Archibald sighed, his dark hair, just like Alfred's, blowing upward. "You are meant to be here all the time playing with me, but you're not."

Alfred smiled wanly. *What a pair they were.*

He, the elder, the Carmichael who had begged his parents for a sibling and even cried when they had told him, sadly, it simply wasn't possible. In hindsight, he had been particularly cruel to his mother, but he had not understood, not then.

Archibald, a sudden arrival after their father remarried. Unplanned, perhaps, but desperately wanted. Just as lonely as he, Alfred, had been. Neither of them had any siblings to grow up with, to play with, to chase, and argue with and makeup with later.

Alfred had hated those lonely years, and now he had to watch Archibald go through them all over again.

"I have a governess for you," he said gently, "so you won't be so lonely. You can get an education, an education befitting your name."

Archibald frowned. "I don't want a governess."

"And neither do I," Alfred said heavily. "I do not wish to have anyone else in the house who doesn't have to be here. But there it is, Archie. We are Carmichaels. We do not make the rules. We just live by them."

The scowl his brother gave was worthy of their father. "You are the worst brother ever."

Alfred could not help but agree, though he did not say so aloud. He had not been much of a brother to him, more of a father, and by Carmichael terms, that was not saying much. But when there was twenty years between you, it was impossible for the situation not to be a little strange. Archibald could, just, have been his own son.

"Come on," said Alfred, rising to his feet. "I need to go inside. I am already late."

Archibald did not reach out for his hand, and Alfred did not offer it, though a part of him wished to. How could he understand this wild, reckless boy? Eight years old and already so far behind. The governess would see to that, of course.

"When is this governess arriving?" Archibald asked as they entered the hall.

"She is already here."

Alfred looked up. Mrs. Martin was bearing down on them with a frown, and he did not blame Archibald scampering off down the corridor. Privately, he wished he could do the same.

"You should have been here, Your Grace," said Mrs. Martin sternly, coming to a stop before him. "Half-past four, you knew that was when she would be arriving."

Alfred tried to smile. "And I am sure you did a very good job at welcoming her, Mrs. Martin."

She glared as though attempting to find sarcasm. "She is in the drawing room waiting for you—but before you go in, have you seen the small miniature of your parents? It was on the table here, and I was going to polish it but—"

Alfred had already ceased listening. Little trifles of knick-knacks and ornaments simply could not interest him. "Ask

Roberts, he will know."

"But—"

Alfred was already striding over to the drawing room. The sooner he spoke with this damned governess, the better.

CHAPTER THREE

That same day…

MEREDITH HAD NOT been idle as she waited in the drawing room for this duke, who seemed never to arrive. She looked around with interest, absorbing the place that was to be, for the time being at least, her new home.

The room was large. All Miss Clarke's talk of a minor duke was all very well, but Meredith had hardly grown up in circumstances such as this, and the plush carpet and wide bay windows overlooking the gardens were sufficiently impressive.

A number of armchairs and a few sofas were scattered around the fireplace framed with marble, and behind them, a pianoforte with an elegant velvet cover, which suggested no one in the house currently played.

There were screens, tables, and little statues of Greek gods and goddesses littering the place, all visible from where Meredith had seated herself, refusing to wait to be asked after the first thirty minutes of waiting for the duke to arrive.

Meredith raised her gaze to take in the paintings. Elderly gentlemen lined the walls, most of them stern, all with a similar frown and shade of gray eyes that convinced her she was looking at the Carmichaels past. One of them seemed to be glaring directly at her.

Yet, she was not intimidated. Meredith was not overcome by feelings of grandeur, nor did she consider the obvious wealth that had poured into decorating the room something to tremble over. The abbey itself, repurposed hundreds of years ago from a religious house, had little drama to recommend it and appeared to have been little touched in the last hundred.

And that was it, wasn't it? The thing nagging at the back of her mind as she sat, baking in the July heat, which had not let up during her almost weeklong journey to the north.

The room was beautiful, but it was strange. No personal items, no books, or favored ornaments. Nothing seemed to have been touched. It felt more art gallery than home.

Nothing demonstrated who lived here, their tastes or preferences. She could have been informed that a great duchess lived here, a family of seventeen from trade, or that the place had been shut up for a few years and cleaned periodically, and she would have believed them.

While she had had plenty of time to examine the room itself, she had no opportunity to examine her employer, who had still not arrived.

The clock on the mantelpiece chimed a quarter past five, and Meredith glanced at her pocket watch, an expensive purchase she hoped she would not regret, to check whether it was running fast.

It was slow. It was almost twenty-five past five—almost an entire hour late. Where was the Duke of Rochdale, and why did he think her so inconsequential that it did not matter whether he was here to greet her?

Meredith bit her lip. Was this a sign of things to come? She had hoped for a lack of interference, that was true, but that was far more extreme than even she could have imagined. This was disrespect. Was her charge going to be this thoroughly ignored? Was she?

Courtesy cost nothing, Meredith thought sternly, and she often found it was those with the least funds who had the most.

Rising from her seat and keeping a hold of her reticule, which contained both her reference from the earl and her appointment letter from Miss Clarke, Meredith started to meander around the drawing room.

This was intolerable. Perhaps she should go and see if the housekeeper could show her to her room? The woman was a little stern, Meredith thought with a smile as she peered at one of the paintings but surely would understand.

Ethelbert Carmichael, fourth Duke of Rochdale, said the little note underneath the painting.

She raised an eyebrow. Interesting names, these Carmichaels.

It was only when the little clock chimed half past the hour that she really lost her temper. *This was insupportable!* The clock was slow as it was, and she was tired of waiting for a man—she would not call him gentleman, he had not yet earned that right—to turn up, take a look at her, and allow her to finally take to her rooms!

It could not be clearer that the elder brother had something to learn, as well. Perhaps, amongst her lessons for the younger Carmichael, she would be able to teach them both a few manners, even if—

The door opened with a bang, and a tall, dark haired, and thoroughly irritated looking man stepped into the drawing room.

Meredith swallowed as she turned to face him. The Earl of Marnmouth had been...well, not exactly old, but past fifty and utterly besotted with his wife. There had been no awkwardness between them, no tension, just the pragmatic relationship of governess and master.

It would not be the same here, she could tell from the moment their gazes met. *This Duke of Rochdale was...*

Well, there was no other way to describe it other than handsome. Sparks seemed to fly between them as he slammed the door behind him and glared, sparks she could not see but certainly feel.

Dressed in a well-cut frock coat and tall riding boots splattered with mud, the Duke of Rochdale had that brooding, frustrated look of a man who was accustomed to getting his way and had not done so.

Meredith stared, the silence ever-increasing until she remembered herself.

She was here to serve.

Meredith broke the connection as her gaze dropped, and in that moment, she reminded herself of two things. Firstly, that she was a governess of the Governess Bureau. Falling in love was forbidden. Second, that a duke, of all people, would never look at her in that way.

She was here to be the governess to his younger brother, and that was all. She was not the sort of lady to permit her head to be turned—nor that sort of servant who would hitch up her skirts at the first opportunity.

As Meredith rose from her curtsey, it was to see the Duke of Rochdale bob his head briefly.

"Good afternoon," he said curtly.

Meredith paused to collect herself, ensuring all her frustrations were adequately removed from her tone, before speaking. "Good afternoon, Your Grace."

She waited for him to continue, giving him the responsibility of conversation, as it was his house, and she, his servant. This meant they stood in silence for a few moments, moments elongating into discomfort the longer they went on.

Meredith's aching feet begged for relief, but she could not merely sit down because she was tired. The Duke of Rochdale was before her! This was his house, and until he invited her to be seated, she would be forced to stand.

It was a full minute later, or that is what it felt like at least, of continued silence before Meredith finally broke it.

"I will sit, if you do not mind."

"What?" The duke looked utterly distracted, as though he had been so lost in his thoughts, he had forgotten not only what he was doing here in the drawing room, but who she was. "Sit? Oh, yes, sit."

Meredith inclined her head in gratitude and moved to the gaggle of armchairs around the fireplace, mercifully unlit in this heat. Seating herself, she watched the duke move across the room like an angry cat, all hackles and strides, and drop lazily into the armchair opposite.

Everything about him seemed designed to draw her in. His jaw was tight as though holding back fury, his gray eyes stormy, his whole body lounging on the armchair as if he owned the place.

Which he did, Meredith reminded herself. *This was no time to lose your head, girl!* This was a duke, yes, and a rather handsome, young one at that, which she had not foreseen. But just because his presence was intoxicating, that did not mean he had even noticed you.

Meredith cleared her throat. The sooner this conversation started, the sooner she could leave this exhilarating man and retreat to her rooms. "Will I have the pleasure of meeting the younger Lord Carmichael, too?"

It was, apparently, the wrong thing to say. The Duke of Rochdale glared, brow stern and eyes suspicious. "What do you know of him?"

It was not an unreasonable question on the face of it, but the tone was so fierce, it was as though she had suggested they sacrifice him to the sun.

Perhaps he is just overprotective, she thought to herself. It was natural for any parent or guardian, in this case, to be wary of anyone coming in close proximity with their charge and that she agreed with. Add in the complexity of brotherhood, half-brotherhood at that, and perhaps it was not so surprising that he snapped in this way.

"Nothing," she said blandly. "Save that he is your half-brother, and that I am engaged here to teach him."

At her calm and undramatic words, a change came over the

duke. He relaxed, brow smoothing and a smile now dancing on his lips.

"Ah," he said. "Yes. Excellent. I am glad to see his reputation does not go before him."

From memory, the boy was but eight years old. How much trouble could an eight-year-old boy get into that his guardian was concerned his exploits had reached London?

"You must forgive me for being so brusque Miss...Miss," said the duke. "We have a name to protect."

"We all have names to protect, even if we do not have impressive titles to go with them," said Meredith without thinking.

The moment the words had left her mouth, she clamped her lips shut, but the damage was done. The words were out, and there was naught she could do to take them back.

Meredith burned, heat rising to her cheeks and her hands twisting in her lap. Once again, that dratted temper of hers had risen to the foreground, and she had allowed it to slip through— and before a duke, before her new employer!

For years she had struggled with her self-control, always convinced that she had bettered it, that she had it under control...and then something like this happened.

"You'll always be fiery, girl," her father had said with a wry smile when she had raged at him the last time she had seen him. "Run as far as you want, change your name, lie about us...but that temper will always be there."

"Yes, indeed, we all have names to protect," said the duke, startling Meredith from her reverie. To her surprise, he was smiling. "Well put, Miss...."

Meredith swallowed. "Hubert."

It had seemed such an innocuous name, and years ago, when she had searched for a new one, it had seemed to fit.

It felt false now. For the first time in her life, she wondered why she had gone to so much trouble to hide the roots of her past. Surely he would not even recognize the name—

"Yes, the Carmichael name is one my brother and I—"

"Half-brother, is that right, Your Grace?" Meredith could not help but interrupt. It was vital she had an exact understanding of the dynamics between the two of them, and now, in this first meeting, was the time to do that.

That it required her to interrupt a duke had not occurred to her.

The Duke of Rochdale raised an eyebrow. "Yes, that is right. I am surprised you have remembered."

Meredith smiled. "The Governess Bureau only sends the very best."

It was with some pride that she spoke. In London, membership of the Governess Bureau was something to be proud of, but the more she had seen of this wild northern country, the more she wondered whether they had any sense of its import.

From the Duke's response, very little. "Ah, yes, I saw the advert," he said nonchalantly. "In truth, Miss Hubert, I have struggled to find a governess but only due to my lack of time to spend on the problem."

The problem? It was an odd way to speak of a child, and Meredith could not help but wonder whether the poor boy heard his older brother speak of him in that way. It was hardly likely to garner brotherly affection.

"Finding the right educator," Meredith hazarded, "is a serious business and should not be taken lightly."

She had not been entirely sure whether that was the correct sort of response, but it appeared that the duke was simply not interested.

With a languid shrug, he said, "I suppose it is, though I admit I do not care for it much. It was only because I am so tied up with affairs of politics, and then there's the election..."

The duke's voice trailed away, his gaze slipping past her and toward the window. Meredith waited for a moment in silence, not entirely sure whether this meant it was her turn to speak, and then cleared her throat loudly.

Nothing happened. The duke was lost in his own thoughts

and, by his frown, they were not happy ones.

Meredith frowned, too. She did not expect every parent or guardian to be devoted to their charges' study. Education, or at least the instruction of it, was not for everyone.

But this was not the Duke of Rochdale's problem. Far from only being disinterested in his brother's education, he seemed utterly disinterested in her, too—and this election that he had mentioned.

Now she looked closer, without the rush of attraction that had initially blinded her, Meredith could see lines of worry across his brow and around his eyes. Alfred Carmichael had the look about him of a man who had aged a great deal in a short amount of time.

There were even flecks of silver around his temples, Meredith realized, and the man could not be that much older than she was. The preoccupation on his face, for she could tell it was that and not rudeness now, had utterly claimed him.

There was nothing quite like having a Governess Bureau woman in the house, she had always found. *But this man?* It did not seem likely he would accept any advice or even questions from someone like her.

Meredith cleared her voice again as the silence continued. "The election, did you say, Your Grace?"

The duke blinked and started, as though astonished to find her there. "Election?"

"Yes, the election," Meredith said kindly. "You mentioned the election."

"Yes. Yes, I did." He sighed heavily. "Let us not speak of that. I can hardly escape it as it is."

The words were so unlike what she had expected, Meredith wondered for a moment whether she had misheard her new master. Escape it? He was the one running for election, wasn't he?

It was bizarre to see a man with such power have so little interest in wielding it.

"I will be frank with you, Miss Hubert, as I hope you will

always be frank with me," said the duke heavily. "I have little interest in you if I am honest. No, do not get yourself into a flap about it," he said hastily as Meredith opened her mouth. "I do not mean I have no respect for you, nor that you do not perform an essential role in my household. But I have no interest in where the beef comes for my pies, and I have just as little curiosity in your history or references."

Meredith closed her mouth. She had been ready with an elegant and almost witty retort to make him smile, and see that taking her seriously would be crucial—but how did one argue with that sort of statement?

Such blatant rudeness, and it would be considered rudeness if spoken by anyone without a title, could not be countered.

"You are here to teach my brother. Good. Teach him, and you will be well rewarded," continued the duke, with clearly no understanding of the offense he was giving. "Archie needs a firm hand and a good dose of Latin."

"Yes, I have a curriculum planned," began Meredith. "I actually thought—"

"He is a rascal," interrupted the duke darkly. "Stealing food from the kitchens. Asking impertinent questions. Playing tricks in church. Ink all over his bedclothes, I have had to discipline him more than once."

Meredith stared. These seemed like minor infractions compared to some of the horror stories Miss Clarke had shared in her warnings to new governesses.

"Give him discipline. Keep him and yourself out of the way. Out of my way."

Meredith's temper was starting to curl around the edges of her heart again. She was a servant, that was true, and she would never consider herself to be an equal with her master. Far from it, if he had any comprehension of her past...

But there were little rules within these complex households, rules she had learned to follow. One of those rules was that butlers, housekeepers, governesses... Well, they were a little set apart from the other servants. A little more prestige, certainly higher wages. Able to read and write, certainly. Not on a level footing with the master of the house, but not nearly as low as a scullery maid.

"Thank you for making my position here so clear. In equal frankness, may I inquire, Your Grace, why I was not met by you when I arrived?" Meredith asked stiffly. "I may also inquire why I was left waiting for so long with no attention."

She had never spoken so to her former employer, but then, she had no need to. Who was this man, this, this *duke*, to treat her so poorly when she came from one of the most respectable suppliers of governesses in the Empire?

The Duke smiled. "'Tis not my job to entertain you, Miss."

Meredith gaped, unable to hide her surprise.

"Anyway, my housekeeper should have given you the attention you deserve—tea, and cake, and that sort of thing," he continued blandly. "Why did she not?"

How was one to respond to such a question? She had been in his house but two hours at most, and now she was expected to tell a gentleman—nay, a duke—why his servants were not performing their duties adequately?

But Meredith knew better than to give into the temptation of a scornful remark. She would be living in this house for a long time, years, if she was fortunate. It would never do to ostracize the other most senior female servant before she had even met the rest of the staff.

No, she would need to keep the housekeeper—Mrs. Martin, wasn't it?—sweet if she was going to succeed in this house.

"I believe your housekeeper was otherwise engaged," she said quietly.

The duke sighed heavily. "Oh yes, that damned—I beg your pardon. That business with the undermaid, I still need to get to the bottom of it."

Meredith's curiosity was piqued, and despite herself, she said, "Business with the undermaid?"

"She had to leave in a hurry this morning, apparently—or at least that is what Roberts, my butler, informs me," he said, with little interest. "The house is all at sea because of it."

Meredith had never heard of such a thing. Well, maids leaving, that was hardly surprising. Some left to get married, others found positions in other households, though she could not imagine what other households there were close to Rochdale Abbey with sufficient employment for undermaids.

But did not the master of the house always know why his servants had left him? Why was the housekeeper dealing with it and yet not telling the master? Why did the butler not even know?

Questions upon questions arose in her heart, but Meredith swallowed them down.

She needed to succeed. The boy, Archibald, was twenty years younger than his half-brother, and the duke before her could be no more than thirty. That meant she probably had about five years, if she was fortunate, before the boy went to school.

Five years. It was a heady thought; five years of comfortable living, a warm place to sleep, three meals provided, and all the grounds she could wish for to explore.

It was luxury compared to London, and if she were not foolish and stopped poking her nose in where it was not wanted, she would be rewarded with what every governess, in her heart, wanted.

Comfort and security.

Meredith nodded. "I understand."

The clock on the mantelpiece chimed, and both Meredith and her new employer glanced at it. Six o'clock.

The duke sighed. "Blast—I mean...you will have to excuse me, Miss Hubert, I am not accustomed to having a lady in the house. I am afraid I have many draws on my time, and I will need to be departing in a moment for another..."

His voice trailed away, and Meredith waited for a moment before clearing her voice again. Really, he was a most easily distracted fellow.

"Yes," he said hastily. "Right. I will tell you the rules of the house, and then you can see yourself out."

It was all Meredith could do not to bristle. So rudely dismissed, and after no words of thanks, no queries about her difficult journey here, the muddiness of the roads, the weather...

All the pleasant societal niceties had been ignored. *How was this man to run for Parliament with such manners?*

"This is your house, Your Grace," she said aloud, "and I am in your service."

"Yes," he said, eyes flashing. "You are."

As their gazes met, it was all Meredith could do not to gasp. There was something there, something that crackled in the air between them: a fury, a desire, a determination to be aloof, and yet a connection between them that made little sense.

How was she going to control herself around such a man who made her at one moment furious and at the other desperate to be closer to him?

Meredith had never met many gentlemen who had...well, been attractive.

She had now, and was utterly at sea how to conceal her thoughts. Could he tell what she was thinking? He was a duke, surely far more worldly than she was.

"The rules are simple."

Meredith blinked. The moment between them had gone—unless she had imagined it.

"Rules?" she said blankly.

Alfred Carmichael, Duke of Rochdale, nodded. "The boy is not seen, not heard, and neither should you be. I am a busy man, Miss Hubert. I would like it if I could forget there was even a governess in the house."

Temper sparking but tongue, thankfully, keeping it under control, Meredith smiled. "I understand, Your Grace, and I, in turn, share my rules with you. My schoolroom, my rules. Besides, we may not want to see you. Archibald and I will be very busy. Good day."

CHAPTER FOUR

August 3, 1812

A LFRED AWOKE, SITTING upright in his four-poster bed so
violently that his pillow slipped to the floor. Forehead
beaded with sweat, his heart was racing, and he was aware of
having just departed a dream so real, he had to touch the damp
linens to assure himself of where he was.

Home. Rochdale Abbey. His bedchamber.

His heart rate slowed. He had never moved into the master
bedchamber at Rochdale Abbey when his father had died. It was
too painful. One did not simply step into the shoes of a dead man.

His bedchamber since he had come of age was pleasant
enough, and so he had remained. Now his gaze moved across the
familiar bookcases, the dresser, the window with dark red velvet
curtains blocking out what was undoubtedly another beautiful
day.

Alfred breathed out slowly, feeling the hackles on the back of
his neck calm. Whatever it was he had been dreaming about, for
he could not recall now, he had returned to the waking world.

Unsettled, he leaned back, pulling a pillow behind him to sit
up. Unsettled, that was most certainly the word for the last three

days ever since that governess had arrived.

Miss Meredith Hubert. She had sounded like a quaint little old lady when he had considered her, reviewing her merits and previous report from the Earl of Marnmouth. Good with children, a respectable educator, and no concerns from either him or the owner of the place, Miss Clarke.

She had sounded perfect.

And then that buxom, sharp-eyed, quick-tongued woman had meandered into his life, and he had been unable to account for it.

Miss Hubert.

"Besides, we may not want to see you. Archibald and I will be very busy. Good day."

In the stillness of his bedchamber, Alfred smiled, despite himself. Attempting to clear his mind of Miss Hubert was utterly impossible. Women with curves like that were made to be obsessed over, made to be courted, to be desired.

What was all the more irritating was that she had entirely taken his rules to heart. He had not seen hide nor hair of her since he had summarily dismissed her on the day she had arrived.

Miss Hubert was obedient, utterly invisible, and from what he had gathered from the chatter of Mrs. Martin and Roberts, charming.

Damn her. Alfred could hardly bear it. It was intoxicatingly intriguing to have such a woman in the house that he never saw.

But he could not think about her. Alfred pushed his dark, sweeping hair out of his face. She was here for the boy's good. He would simply have to put her out of his mind and concentrate on more pleasant things, like…

Alfred closed his eyes. *Christ alive, the election.* Every morning he woke in happy ignorance, the foolish thing having slipped his mind.

The election. It crept ever closer, threatening him with all the things he hated. Hard work. Going back down to London. Being treated like a fool because Rochdale was nothing compared to Devonshire. Away from the land, away from the people who *made him* Rochdale.

The damned election. When he had the misfortune to win again, that would be it. Years down in the south with nothing to do but write letters to his tenants and Archibald…

A wry smile crept over his face. Well, there was one potential silver lining. Now Miss Hubert was here, he would be able to correspond with her.

About the boy, naturally.

Hell's bells, he had managed to get back on the topic of that cursed governess again.

"This is your house, Your Grace, and I am in your service."

Alfred's wry smile disappeared. No, this simply would not do. He was not one of those men who believed the women in his household were his, like some sort of possession. He had never touched a servant, never been tempted to, and had never considered doing so.

That was before Miss Hubert had entered the house.

If she was anyone else, he would bed her to get her out of his system. Alfred knew it worked. How many times had he taken such a route in London?

But a serving maid in a pub who caught one's eye was not the same, Alfred told himself sternly, *as the governess to your brother!*

"Good morning, Your Grace."

Kittering, his valet, had slipped into the room so quietly, Alfred had not noticed he was there.

"Ah, morning, Kittering," he said distractedly. "What time is it?"

"A little after eight o'clock," said Kittering as he walked across the room. He pulled back one curtain but left the other closed, just as Alfred liked it. It was the easiest way to enter the day. "I believe you have a meeting with the election committee again today, so something in Carmichael blue?"

Alfred smiled dryly as he rose from his bed. "Sometimes I think you have a better handle than I on my diary, Kittering. Yes, the Carmichael blue waistcoat, and there should be a cravat to match."

The valet bowed his head. "Very good, Your Grace."

The servant knew him well. In the adjoining dressing room, there was already the blue waistcoat and cravat, along with a frockcoat and breeches in a light gray, which perfectly offset the blue.

"There has been a great stir in the kitchen this morning," said Kittering as he started to dress his master. "It appears that the butcher's order was not adequately prepared, and Cook has decided it is none other than Roberts's fault. This, as you can imagine, has been highly contested, and…"

Alfred allowed the chatter of the servants' hall to wash over him. It was one of the easiest ways to keep up with his staff, and there was never any malice in Kittering's words.

For the first time since he had returned from London at the end of the parliamentary session, however, he was tempted to ask about someone in particular.

The name of Miss Meredith Hubert was on his lips, but Alfred restrained himself as he stepped into his breeches. From the little he knew of servant dynamics, there was just as strict a hierarchy, if not more, below stairs as there was above.

"There, I think you are ready for the day, Your Grace." Kittering stood back and examined his creation. "Yes, the gray and the blue. Yes."

Alfred looked down in surprise to see he was entirely dressed, cravat and all. Kittering had even placed his pocket watch in his waistcoat. The man was getting very good, and had hardly been shabby before—a real natural. He would have to speak to Roberts about some sort of reward.

"Thank you, Kittering," he said distractedly. "Good morning."

The valet saw the dismissal for what it was, bowed, and departed, leaving Alfred alone in his dressing room.

He stepped across to the large window and looked out over the lawn. Crusting brown in the heat of the summer, the unrelenting sunshine never giving way to rainclouds, the entire Rochdale estate was looking a little worn around the edges.

Alfred smiled. There was something very comforting about the constant turning of the seasons. In London, one could hardly tell March from August, for it was always the same sticky, smoky hell. The last four Augusts, he had been trapped in town, unable to escape to where he knew he belonged.

Here, in the countryside. Alfred breathed in slowly and then let his breath out, watching a gardener stride over the baked lawn toward the greenhouses. Now he could enjoy summer as it should be. Riding, walking, eating too many ices, and wondering how the fish were doing in the lake, spending the day with a good book in a gentle breeze.

Alfred groaned. Or, sitting in election committee meetings arguing over whether the Talbots were as big a threat as everyone seemed to think they were.

Damn it, he would not be cooped up by Mr. Walker's endless meetings. He wouldn't permit it.

As he began to open the door, he caught the sound of voices—ones he recognized.

"Attend, Master Archibald," came Miss Hubert's voice with that sharpness he recognized from his meeting with her.

Alfred stepped into the corridor and looked to his left, toward the other bedchambers in the abbey—and where the schoolroom had been established, just along from the boy's room.

"I said, attend."

Alfred grinned. *Goodness, that took him back.* The tone, the forcefulness, the desperate desire to be anywhere else but the schoolroom…had they used the precise room he had been forced into every day with…what was her name? Miss Chesterton?

Miss Hubert sounded precisely how his old governess had scolded him for his inattention. Was that something all governesses were taught, somehow? Was there something in the blood of all governesses, something that drew them to the profession, which determined the precise pitch of authority, which made all boys squirm?

Against his better judgment and knowing he had a hundred other things he should be doing, Alfred crept down the corridor and saw the door to the schoolroom had been left ajar—just wide enough for Miss Hubert's voice to pour through.

"Archibald!"

"Yes, Miss Hubert."

A grin crept over Alfred's face. A strange sense of trespassing flowing through him—*trespassing, in his own home?*—in the thrill in eavesdropping on Miss Hubert.

It sounded like the boy was just as uninterested in his lessons as Alfred had been all those years ago. Alfred could remember heat-soaked days stuck up here in the eaves, algebra going in one ear and straight out of the other.

It was a mercy he was able to get through Eton, really, and it was only the name that got him through Cambridge, he was sure of it.

What did a duke need of a degree? Yes, it was pleasant to have the piece of paper somewhere…though truth be told, he had no idea where the damn thing was…

"—your book on history, please, and we will begin the lesson."

Alfred's stomach growled, but he ignored the growing hunger attempting to distract him. *History.* His least favorite subject and he was certain young Archibald was not going to be impressed by the first subject of the day either.

"History?" Archibald's whining tone, the one that grated Alfred's nerves the worst, flowed out from the crack in the door. "I have no need to study history—it has already happened! I cannot do anything about the mistakes of others!"

Alfred was forced to stifle a laugh. *The damned cheeky sod—yes, he was certainly a Carmichael!* There was the proud lilt in his voice they had both inherited from their father and a little of the determination that one's opinion was the only one worth having. The Carmichael spirit was well and truly alive in little Archie.

He listened carefully, almost jubilant to see what Miss Hubert would say next. The poor miss had cared for the dutiful children of an earl, from what he could tell. She probably had no comprehension of how to manage—

But what was this? Alfred leaned a little closer to the door, sure he had misheard what was happening in the adjoining room.

No, his ears were not deceiving him. Though he expected splutters, even perhaps a little punishment for the younger Carmichael, Miss Hubert was...laughing.

"But how else can we learn about the future, and make better decisions, if we do not know the mistakes we have already made?" she said in a cheerful voice.

Alfred blinked. It was not a response he could have given himself. It was...clever. He was impressed. Few were ever able to surprise him, let alone impress him.

The door moved slightly in the warm breeze wafting past, still keeping Alfred hidden from view but allowing him a slither of perspective into the room.

There sat Archibald, scowling. He had on his least favorite clothing, his restrictive frockcoat, and even a little waistcoat cut much in the same manner as Alfred's, and he was glaring at the other side of the room.

"Do not concern yourself though, Master Archibald," came Miss Hubert's voice in a warm, slightly patronizing tone. "It is quite alright if you do not know much history. I am not going to penalize you for your lack of knowledge. After all, not everyone knows that Henry VIII had ten wives—"

"Six wives," Archibald interrupted, a frown appearing on his young face.

There was a moment of silence. Then—

"I do not think you are correct, but excellent try," Miss Hubert continued from where Alfred assumed was the blackboard. "Now, his first wife was called Augusta, and she—"

"Wha—no, she was Katherine of Aragon!" Archibald protested.

"Really?" Miss Hubert sounded surprised. "You can name the first one?"

"I can name all of them, actually," said Archibald confidently. "Katherine of Aragon, Anne Boleyn..."

Alfred watched in amazement as Miss Hubert transformed the sullen and argumentative boy before her into an eager, contributing, and engaged child.

How did she do it? The way she had guided the boy along a conversation, transformed him into a child who had positively no interest in history and was now, from what Alfred could hear, having a debate about whether it was better to divorce one's wife than execute her.

A little concerning, true, but the boy was learning. He had brought out a pencil and was scribbling something down.

Alfred stood up straight and shook his head. Perhaps there was some value in Miss Hubert, after all. If she tamed the boy into someone resembling a gentleman, then she would be doing some good.

As he turned away from the schoolroom, Archibald had entered into a rather violent and spirited discussion about which Tudor queens *he* would have chosen to execute.

Alfred shook his head as he walked down the staircase. He had never seen such an impressive display with a child. Archibald was a little old to start with a governess; in a few years, he would be old enough for Eton, even if he did not wish to matriculate straight away.

But the boy was so behind, he had engaged someone from the Governess Bureau particularly to bring him to speed. The best education a boy could get, that was what a Carmichael deserved. Miss Hubert appeared to be a competent enough stand-in until the boy could go off to school.

It was an unusual start to the morning, and one that boded well for the rest of the day. Sadly, for Alfred, it was a false start. For a Monday, it was relatively dull.

First, after breakfast, there was the estate's paperwork. Paperwork, paperwork, there was always some sort of note to sign or bill to pay. It took until luncheon to clear the last of the bills, and when he returned to his desk, a few more had already appeared.

Then there was the letter sack brought up from London. Alfred stared in horror at the literal sack that was placed before him by Roberts.

"They can't all be for me?"

Roberts opened the sack and pulled out a handful, glancing at the addressee. "I am afraid to say they can, Your Grace. Letters addressed to you at parliament, to your rooms in London, to your club—"

"But—but I am not currently the member of Parliament for Rochdale!" Alfred stammered, hearing in his own voice the desperate plea of a man who just wanted to be left alone.

Roberts reached out a hand, and Alfred passed him the letter opener. The butler slit open one of the letters and scanned its contents.

"It appears that does not matter to them, Your Grace," the butler said matter-of-factly. "Their assumption that you will be their representative in government in a few months' time means that some are petitioning you early in order to, in the words of a Mr. Graham Hargreaves, 'jump the queue.'"

Alfred swore, using language he would never have permitted Archibald to use.

"They cannot all be requests made to me as a future member of Parliament," he said in an exhausted voice, falling back into his armchair.

After several minutes of Roberts opening a good number of the letters, however, he was forced to concede that was exactly what they were.

People always wanted something for nothing. They could not even wait until he had the power before they started demanding it for themselves!

Alfred swallowed. "Read through them, Roberts. God knows

I may have to get a private secretary if—*when* I get elected again. In the meantime, anything useful, and you know what I mean man, anything important, leave on the desk in my study. Burn the rest."

Roberts bowed and left, carrying the sack of letters with him, as Alfred shook his head in disbelief. The more he saw of humanity, the less surprised he was about people's dark and devious little ways.

And yet it was all so boring. He had received letters like that years ago when he had first taken his seat. No doubt he would be receiving letters just the same in forty years.

His gaze drifted away from his desk and toward the window. He was a duke, a member of the ruling classes. What a shame he had no actual interest in being a ruler. Members of Parliament did not have the power they once had, but Alfred had never considered himself a man on a mission. He had no injustices to fight, no demands to make. He went to London, ate too many good dinners, and slept in the backbenches, hoping no one noticed.

He was there because a Carmichael was always there, and their dukedom simply wasn't big enough to secure a place in the House of Lords.

Alfred's eyes sharpened. He had become so lost in his thoughts, he had barely noticed what had moved past the window, but now his mind prompted him that what he had just seen, he should not have been able to see.

A woman. Not just a woman, a woman on a horse. Riding across the lawn. *His lawn!*

Forced from his stupor, Alfred rose and stepped around his desk toward the window. His movement brought the woman back into sight. The horse was trotting across the parched lawn in fine fettle.

The rider turned her head, and Alfred's jaw dropped. It was Miss Hubert.

What on earth was she doing? She should be with Archibald—

was that not what he was paying her for, to take control of his brother, the child most likely to do damage to his reputation in the election, and teach him both manners and his kings and queens?

Alfred bristled. And what gave her the right to just take one of his horses and ride it? *How dare she?*

Blood roared through his veins, and Alfred stood there, fuming, at the window through which heat poured, aggravating him further. He had never been faced with such reckless behavior, such insubordination! How did she think she was going to get away with it?

Abandoning his paperwork and storming out of the study, Alfred was almost immediately accosted by Roberts.

"Ah, Your Grace, there are a number of letters which require additional clarification. If a bill is due, but there is no—"

"Not now, Roberts!" Alfred barked. Miss Hubert had so incensed him, he knew no other course of action but to confront her.

He stepped through the hallway into the drawing room, then out of the large French windows overlooking the prettiest of the gardens, bringing Miss Hubert and the horse she had taken right into view. She was clearly exercising the horse a little, trotting around in a circle.

Alfred's head buzzed with irritation. So she thought one of his mares needed exercising, did she? Did she not think he and his stable hands could care for his stables? As if one of his men could not do the job admirably well!

Words had not precisely formed in his mind before Alfred found himself shouting. "You there!"

Miss Hubert pulled the horse to a stop and turned it around with gentle expertise. A small smile appeared on her face as she shielded her eyes from the sun.

"Ah, Your Grace," she said. "What a lovely day! I just had to take advantage of it while young Master Archibald had his nap."

It was a perfectly reasonable explanation to why his brother was not here in her care, but Alfred had moved far beyond reasonable. *Three days—three days was all it had taken for this woman to arrive in his own home, and already she was taking liberties!*

"I believe I was quite clear with the rules that all have to live by when in my house and employ, Miss Hubert," he said sternly now he was closer to her, now only a few feet from the damned horse. "Yet I evidently need to list a few more because many of those I would consider obvious have passed you by!"

The smile on Miss Hubert's face faltered, and a look of curiosity replaced it. "Goodness, Your Grace, you seem rather angry for some reason. Please, explain yourself."

"Explain—explain myself!" Alfred exploded. This was too much. "Explain…explain yourself! The barefaced cheek of it!"

There was definitely coldness in her looks now, and Miss Hubert allowed the horse she was riding to take a step backward in its shock at his bellowing.

"As soon as you are able to use your words to explain why you are so upset," she said coldly, "I will be able to help you."

Alfred took a deep breath. She was right, in a way. This was beneath him, all this shouting. He had a perfectly just complaint, and he would not lose his moral high ground by shouting about it.

"My brother will be awake soon," he said curtly.

Miss Hubert nodded. "Indeed. It is generally encouraged that children have at least one afternoon off to practice sports or athletics of some kind. I thought we would play hide and seek to assess his endurance and—"

Alfred waved away her words, damned logical though they were. "That is beside the point, Miss Hubert, and you know that."

She looked as though he was speaking a foreign language. "Then you have lost me, Your Grace. I do not understand why I cannot ride after I have finished teaching for the day."

Alfred leaned forward and grabbed the reins, patting the mare's neck to comfort her from this strange woman's attentions, as he said in his most ducal and aloof voice, "Miss Hubert, please add this to your list of rules—you are not to touch my horses."

Why did she not look abashed at his words? Why, more importantly, did she raise a haughty eyebrow and look down her nose at him?

"Thank you for the suggestion," she said stonily. "And I will ask you to pay me the same courtesy."

Alfred's eyes met hers, and then the connection was broken as he looked quickly at the horse. Now he was closer and had a little oxygen in his brain, he could see quite clearly that this was not one of his horses.

He dropped the reins and took a step back, the mare nickering, as if to prove her point.

Christ alive, he had made a fool of himself. No wonder she was looking at him like that, as though he had barely enough sense to stand upright.

"I cannot bear these distractions," Alfred blustered. "I am working very hard for the election."

Miss Hubert laughed. "Why? You do not want to win the election."

Without another word, she nudged her mare into a trot and disappeared across the lawn.

Alfred stared after her, standing in the baking heat for far too long before he collected himself.

How on earth did she know that?

CHAPTER FIVE

August 6, 1812

IT WAS THE second huge sigh from Meredith that made the
chalk fly up in the air, coating her carefully pinned hair and the
sleeves of her gown. She coughed, only making the entire
situation worse as her hands moved across the blackboard with a
damp cloth, wiping away the timeline Archibald had drawn of the
kings and queens of England.

Well, she certainly could not complain about the facilities
which the Duke of Rochdale had procured for the schoolroom. It
was exactly how she needed it, with all the little details she had
come to associate with the mistress of a house.

There was no mistress here, but there were plenty of books;
the blackboard; which spanned almost the entire wall; plenty of
chalk, which wrote very smoothly; and a supply of paper and
pencils in a box by the door. It would take a great many lessons
for them to run out of that.

There was even a pair of globes near her desk at the front of
the room. One showed the earth, far more detailed than any
Meredith had seen before, and the second was one which had
taken her breath away when she had first examined it.

A celestial globe. Carefully depicting the night sky, it was beautiful.

There could be absolutely no complaints on the tools she had been given to teach the younger Carmichael brother, but none of it could balance the fact she had not seemed to make a good impression.

Here she was, putting the schoolroom to bed on Friday at the end of her first week, and what had she managed to do?

Teach Archibald a little. That was true. He was not a dull child, just a disinterested one, and she was already starting to find little tricks to engage him in actual study.

She had taken Beauty for a ride. That had not ended well—being accosted by the master of the house for what he evidently thought was stealing, despite the fact that she was riding her own horse!

Other than that, she had taken breakfast and luncheon in the schoolroom, and dinner in her own room. She had ventured down to the kitchens once, felt the inherent awkwardness of the place as the room felt silent, eyes turned to stare in wide-eyed, unhidden curiosity, and returned to her own room within twenty minutes.

And that was all. She had not seen hide nor hair of Alfred. Other than Mrs. Martin and Archibald, she had not spoken to a soul.

Meredith placed the rag down on her desk and stood back to examine the blackboard. It was ready for a new lesson next week.

She had wished to be left alone by her new master. Why should she complain now she had been entirely unheeded by the Duke of Rochdale since their altercation over her horse?

Besides, being a governess was a lonely life. Miss Clarke had warned her, had warned every lady who applied to join the Governess Bureau. One did not make friends as a governess, and one certainly made no attachments. One moved through the house like a breeze, gently ruffling some, but having no real lasting impact.

After the life she had come from, she was due a bit of peace and quiet. *What she wouldn't have given for this sort of loneliness five years ago...*

Meredith forced herself into action as she moved about the schoolroom, placing scraps of paper in the wastepaper bin, picking up a pencil where it had dropped to the floor.

She wasn't alone, was she? Archibald was her companion, but it was strange, only having a child for company. One could not confide in a child the way you could an adult. There were things she wished to share, thoughts she would like to express, jokes she would like to make—all which would be inappropriate for a child, let alone one under her charge.

She looked out through one of the large windows and saw sunshine beating down on the thirsty lawns. Yes, Archibald was not the right sort of friend for her, but who else was there?

Few servants reached the equivalent social standing of a governess. It placed her in a strange, in-between world. A servant to the family of the house, not that there was much of one here. A superior to the maids, the footmen, the boot boys, and stable lads.

It was only Mrs. Martin and Mr. Roberts who were her equals. She saw no more of one than the other. The housekeeper appeared to be rushed off her feet at the moment, with that undermaid gone and not yet replaced.

Moving over to the single desk where Archibald sat, Meredith picked up his workbook and flicked through it with a smile. His handwriting really was atrocious. They would have to spend some time on that next week, or she would never be able to mark any of his work.

He was behind for his age, but she had expected that. Most children were, without a mother in the house, and few people hired a governess for a child who was excelling.

"The Romans really were here?" he had said with a look of absolute wonder only yesterday. "Even up here, in Rochdale? Could the Carmichaels, could my father be a distant descendent?"

And Meredith had returned to her bedchamber for a moment and retrieved a favorite book from her small collection and read some of the stories from the Roman Empire, and Archibald had sat there, transfixed.

Meredith smiled. Still, there were moments of brilliance, even for an eight-year-old. He had a hunger to learn and a genuine surprise at the world, and those were two things that could not be taught.

And when he attempted to defy her...

Well, that was when she could see his older brother in him.

Alfred. Alfred Carmichael, Duke of Rochdale. He was an enigma to her, a gentleman with fury and passion but who had directed absolutely none of that into this election he kept talking about.

Meredith's smile broadened. It was clear to anyone who looked at him that the duke was no more interested in running for a member of Parliament again than taking up Mandarin.

Though perhaps it was not so obvious to everyone else. When she looked at him, the lines of worry, the frustration, the utter disinterest were written across his face like a book.

Yet from something Mrs. Martin had said when she had brought up luncheon for herself and Archibald one day, it was greatly expected that the master would win the election once more and return to London.

The duke return to London? It would certainly mean she would no longer be subjected to altercations as she had experienced already.

It had been rather wonderful, Meredith had to admit, to see him so unsettled. Yet, there was something about him. Something that made her wish to see him more often.

She and the Earl and Countess of Marnmouth had grown quite cordial to each other. The countess Sophia was so much younger than her husband, and the two ladies were able to read together, even jest together occasionally.

Meredith would never have described them as friends. She

would never have taken that sort of liberty. But still, she had seen them almost every day, dined with them once a week, and been included in their decisions for their children.

Was it too much to hope she could be so treated here?

The memory of that moment when their eyes had locked the very first day she had arrived seared her heart. There was something about Alfred, though she would never call him that to his face, naturally.

She liked him. She could appreciate a man like that, and the fact that there was no mistress at Rochdale Abbey certainly made her interactions with him a little more complicated. There could never be any accusations of impropriety when the lady of the house was present.

Meredith's smile disappeared as she returned to her tidying. She liked Archibald, which was undoubtedly the most important thing. If she was going to be here for years caring for the child, it was always easier if one liked them.

He was wild and struggled to concentrate, but it was perfectly possible to train those bad habits out of him, even if they had never been trained out of his older brother.

After another ten minutes of intense work, Meredith looked at the schoolroom with a decisive nod. The place had been put to rights, and the first week—the most difficult week in a new situation—was over. She had managed it.

It was always the hardest. To start with, one was learning your way around a new house. It was easy to get turned around with the number of corridors and rooms, especially in a place like this, where some parts of the upstairs were only accessible by the second staircase.

For now, Meredith had certainly earned her Saturday and Sunday off—something she had negotiated with Miss Clarke.

"Both Saturday and Sunday?" Miss Clarke had said, a frown appearing across her face. "How unusual. How very particular."

And Meredith had held her gaze and nodded. "Yes, a full weekend, thank you, Miss Clarke."

It had been an uncomfortable moment between them, but there had been no chance of Meredith backing down on this item of her contract. How else was she to find the time to take Beauty out as often as she wished?

Meredith's heartstrings tugged. She had not ridden Beauty since that rather awkward altercation with the duke, but she was too tired to ride today. Her bones ached in that rather pleasant way after a long day of standing up and moving about the schoolroom. She had earned a little rest, but August sunlight was still streaming through the windows.

Perhaps it was time she had a wander around the house itself. Rochdale Abbey was, from what she saw from the gardens, a large manor house, and she had seen only a few of its rooms.

And, Meredith reminded herself, the duke had left hours ago. She had noticed him depart on his horse as she had taken Archibald through the finer points of the Elizabeth succession crisis, and she had not seen the figure return.

It would be her first chance to explore her new home. Meredith smoothed down the skirts of her gown, ensured she brushed off as much chalk as possible from her sleeves, and stepped outside of the schoolroom to breathe the cooler air of the corridor.

She looked left and right. To her right were the main family bedchambers and, eventually, the main sweeping staircase, carved from marble and decked in red velvet carpet that finished spectacularly in the hallway. To the left was just a few yards of the corridor and then the door to the servants' staircase—the one she had been using.

Meredith was not entirely sure why. At the Marnmouths', she had used the main staircase like the family.

Old habits died hard, she thought wryly. In her old life, when she had been…well, it would never have done for someone like *her* to take the main staircase.

She swept down it now, pretending for a moment that Rochdale Abbey was hers. Her skirts were not as fine, true, but as she looked around the hallway, Meredith was filled with a warm sense of peace.

A new place to call home. She could use her talents here, make something of herself. Perhaps over time, she could even befriend some of the servants.

There was a corridor leading to the greater part of the house, and three doors, other than the front door, led off from the hallway. One of them was the breakfast room, she was almost sure of it—she had heard Mrs. Martin mention it when she had been left awkwardly in the hallway for twenty minutes while someone went looking for the absent duke.

Stepping over lightly, Meredith opened the door and peeked her head through.

Her gaze fell on a delightful room. Wide windows let in the sun, a little shaded now it was late afternoon, but still gloriously bright. Decorated in light blue, there were false Grecian columns all along the walls, with cherubs flying amongst rose blossoms painted on the ceiling. The place was spotless—*Mrs. Martin encouraged sufficient terror in the maids*, she thought dryly.

Meredith was almost afraid to step inside and disturb the quiet beauty of it all. Only when she turned to leave did she notice a set of three wooden tables, each with pretty ornaments on them. There was a mark on one of the tables, as though something had been removed from it after standing there for a long time. The sun mark was quite distinct.

Closing the door quietly, Meredith looked across the hallway. There was the drawing room, which she only peered into for a minute. It was a room, after all, that she had spent an inordinate amount of time in, the duke being so late.

Meredith smiled. He had not expected her to be so...well, direct, she could tell. Perhaps that was why she had seen nothing of him the last few days?

Returning to the hallway, she stepped across to the third door, her mouth falling open as she took in the sight.

A library.

Meredith had always believed every home should have a library—or at least, any home with the funds to secure a governess.

But this? This was incredible. It was beyond anything she could have ever imagined. Books lined the walls, floor to ceiling, in beautiful wooden bookcases with delicate filigree grills protecting them. A pair of mullioned windows at the other end of the room were the only walls without books, and even then, someone had cleverly designed window seats comprising of bookshelves. Several armchairs were scattered about the room, some leather, some a rich fabric with embroidery on the arms. Cushions adorned each one of them. Everything, in fact, one needed for a delightful reading experience.

Meredith stepped inside and closed the door, leaning against it to take it all in.

There was a special kind of quiet here, one that couldn't be found in any other room. Libraries somehow had this quality, and she could not put her finger on why. Was it the books themselves? The amount of sound deadening paper? Or was it the stories, their ability to transport one away from the world and into another entirely different landscape?

Meredith stepped forward, brushing her fingers across the metal filigree protecting the books as she went. She reached the window and knelt to pick up a book from the rather ingenious window seat design. She could while away many happy hours here.

"This time, I can ask you to unhand my books."

Meredith whirled around. Now she was on the opposite side of the room, and she was looking into one of the leather chairs—where her master, the Duke of Rochdale, was seated with a book in his hand and a smile on his face.

It was impossible not to blush. How could she prevent it, with their last conversation still ringing in her ears?

"Thank you for the suggestion. And I will ask you to pay me the same courtesy."

She had hardly been civil, and by the end of it, politeness was the last thing on her mind. She had been determined to give him a tongue lashing, and only her sorely tested self-control had prevented it.

It was a wonder, really, that she was still employed and not only now arriving back in London to be scolded by Miss Clarke.

Perhaps he had written to her. Perhaps his letter ending her employ in his home was almost in Miss Clarke's hand! And now she had meandered into his library, a room which was so very private and personal, and started picking up his books!

Meredith had never been one to avoid an apology if someone deserved it. "I do apologize for disturbing your peace, Your Grace, and for looking at your books. I was...I wanted to explore the abbey. I had not realized you had returned."

For some reason, there was now an even broader smile across the handsome man's lips. "Ah, so you have no qualms looking around my home as long as I am not in it?"

If Meredith had been someone else in that moment, she would have cursed and loudly—but then if she had been someone else, he would not have looked at her like that. And her body would not warm, despite the coldness of his look.

Her gaze dropped to her hands and the offending book. If only she had something clever to say, a retort which could explain herself, absolve her of her folly.

But when Meredith raised her gaze defiantly to defend herself, she saw a natural smile had crept over Alfred Carmichael's face.

"Do not worry yourself, Miss Hubert," he said more softly. "I know what you meant. Besides, this is your home now, too."

It was more the sort of response she would expect from a duke, not the unbridled anger of a few days ago. He was sitting languidly, looking up at her in such a relaxed way that she felt uncomfortable.

His gaze was...penetrating. He seemed to be looking within her, at her thoughts.

"I, myself, was looking for the family Bible," the duke continued. "I cannot find it anywhere, gone, gold leaf and all. But no matter. Any particular book you were hoping to find?"

Meredith looked down once again at the book in her hands. It was *The Theory of the Four Movements*, by Fourier. She had picked it due to the beauty of the red leather, title utterly ignored.

Still. It did not due to be overwhelmed.

"Yes," she said, looking back at her master. "*Theaetetus*. By Plato."

The Duke of Rochdale raised an eyebrow. "Yes, I know it's by Plato. Impressive. I did not expect a governess to even know Latin, let alone speak it and hunt down its classics."

Not expect a governess to know Latin? Meredith tried not to bristle too much, though a part of her glorified in the chance to show off her skills. *Time this man got a little education.*

"What kind of governess did you think you were getting?"

She paired the question with a wry smile and prayed she had not gambled. If he knew—if the Duke of Rochdale knew he had hired a woman who had grown up in a criminal gang!—she would be out of his home before the end of the day.

"You know, I had no idea what I was getting, really," said the duke idly. "I just sent a letter and a blank check to your Miss Clarke after reading your description, and you arrived two weeks later."

She could not help but smile at this. He spoke so honestly, without guile, hesitation, or embarrassment. He saw nothing strange with what he had done.

"So you purchased me," Meredith said lightly. "Bought and paid for, sight unseen."

Was that a smile?

"In a way," said Alfred Carmichael, "yes. Oh, do sit down, by the way."

Meredith sank gratefully onto the window seat. There was something about being in his presence. It did something funny to one's knees.

"The rich are indeed strange. One can buy people, something I consider in most cases to be quite abhorrent," she said. "And you knew nothing of me before you invited me into your home. It must be nice to have such faith in people."

The duke shrugged. "When you have servants, you have to trust that people are good. Even those without titles have servants of a kind. I mean, your mother must have help?"

Meredith kept calm, ensured her breathing did not alter one whit. "Oh, my parents always preferred to do things themselves. And they travel a great deal, so there is no point attempting to keep servants."

She had intended her response to be vague, to elicit no interest—and yet the Duke of Rochdale leaned forward.

"Travel? What for?"

Meredith swallowed. *This was not a safe topic.*

"You told me a week ago that you had rules. Well, I suppose the reason you could be so sure of an outstanding governess was because you hired me through the Governess Bureau," she said as matter-of-factly as she could. "We have rules, too. Rules keep people in their place. Rules keep everyone happy."

Why did his eyes seem to glint with mischief? "My word, governess rules. I am curious."

Meredith opened her mouth and closed it again. This felt like dangerous ground. She had not intended to speak so directly to her new master.

"Out with it, woman," said the duke easily.

"Rule one, you must have an impeccable record," said Meredith slowly. "Rule two, you must have a special skill, naturally. And rule three...rule three is that one must never fall in love."

She was not entirely sure what to expect, but laughter was not it.

"Dear God!" chuckled the duke. "I like Miss Clarke more and more, though I cannot say I agree with her."

Meredith smiled. "Well, no fear of anything like that happening."

Alfred Carmichael's eyes flashed.

"Yes," he said softly, gaze not leaving her face. "At least, probably not."

Was it the heat of the sunshine through the windows that was warming her? Meredith was certainly getting hotter, and realized that they were alone together. No one else was there to chaperone her.

Perhaps her discomfort was visible on her face.

"Well, as much as I have enjoyed this conversation, Miss Hubert, I must depart and continue my search for the family Bible," said the duke, rising from his seat. "The election takes up much of my time. I am sure you understand."

Meredith rose with him. "Of course, Your Grace."

He had stepped toward the door but hesitated. "I snapped at you about the horse, and I was wrong. I can, at least, admit my faults. Even though I am a little rough and ready, will you stay?"

Her eyes met his and saw the honesty there, the discomfort the apology gave him but the feeling it had to be said. Her heart fluttered painfully, the heat in her body rising inexplicably.

"Y-Yes," she found herself saying. "Yes, of course, I will stay, Your Grace."

"Rochdale."

Meredith blinked. "I beg your pardon?"

"Rochdale, 'tis often more natural," said the duke. "And I think…yes, I would like it if you called me Rochdale."

He was gone without another word, and Meredith almost fell back down onto the window seat. Rochdale. The duke. Alfred Carmichael.

How was she ever to stay away from him?

CHAPTER SIX

August 9, 1812

A LFRED KNEW CHURCHES were built partly to impress, partly
to inspire, but also partly to facilitate beautiful choral music.
Every archway, spire, and measurement was calculated for the
best musical effect, helping even the smallest voice to echo clearly
throughout the entire building.

Which was why he was trying to hide a smile, unsuccessfully,
as a loud snore from somewhere at the back of the church echoed
noisily throughout the place as the vicar continued tremulously
with his sermon.

"...which we see again in Leviticus, and I shall read that pas-
sage for us now, so we are all understanding why the relevancy of
the moment is so critical to our comprehension of..."

Poor Reverend Michaels. The elderly vicar had been a firebrand
in his day, or at least that was what his father had always told
Alfred. But the man was nearing seventy now, his grandson a
vicar somewhere in Bath, and was starting to reach the limit of
people's patience.

Alfred turned his head ever so slightly from his front pew
seat, as befitted the Duke of Rochdale, and saw old Johnson had,

once again, succumbed to exhaustion.

He could hardly blame the man. Harvest time was an exhausting season, and he had seen them himself in their droves, bringing in the hay. Every able-bodied man had been drafted. Even Roberts had been sent for and, to his credit, immediately downed his more refined tools of polish and rag to help.

Alfred smiled as he faced the altar once more. That was why he liked Rochdale. No one, not even the butler, was too important to help with the harvest.

Trouble was, the farmers were paying for their exertion now. Alfred could feel it in the church. One did not have to look around to feel the tiredness. It was hard to describe, as though a great breath had been taken in April had now finally been let out.

"...each time we see the words, we must understand the Greek and Latin roots," droned on the reverend in his monotone. "We shall begin with..."

Alfred blinked furiously. The soporific heat and general feeling of fatigue were even starting to affect him.

Alfred stifled a laugh, knowing it would be most indecorous for him to be seen laughing in church—and worse, at one of his tenants. Evidently, Mrs. Johnson was tired of being embarrassed by her husband.

"...which clearly shows us the true meaning of this verse," said the Reverend Michaels with a smile at Alfred.

Alfred returned it. There was a distant connection between the Carmichaels and the Michaels, generations back. The reverend deserved his respect as a man of the cloth—though he had certainly not earned it with his sermons.

"Unless," continued the vicar triumphantly, "we take an opposing view! If we turn to the letters of Paul to the Ephesians..."

Glancing down the Rochdale pew, as it was known due to its continuous use by the Carmichael family, Alfred saw to his dismay that Archibald had fallen asleep. *Damnit, they were meant to be setting an example!* How could he expect any of his tenants to force themselves to listen to old Michaels's nonsense if his own brother...

His heart softened. Archie looked so peaceful, his soft brown hair askew, his head leaning against Miss Hubert.

This brought his attention to the governess, who was seated on the other side of the boy. *Miss Hubert.* She was wearing a proper gown with a high neckline, a bonnet in the Carmichael blue, though he had no idea how she had found one, and matching gloves.

It did not matter that she was dressed respectfully. Many of the thoughts now flooding Alfred's mind were certainly not respectful.

Christ alive—oh, damn. He shook his head as though ridding water from his ears. *This was insupportable.* He had to remember where he was, and even if those curses were not spoken aloud, he certainly shouldn't be thinking about them in church!

He glanced at Miss Hubert again. Her eyes were still affixed on the Reverend Michaels, bright and unfazed by his monotonous tone. She appeared to be paying rapt attention.

How on earth did she manage it?

Alfred peered behind them. There did not appear to be another person in the church able to keep from dozing, or at the very least allow their attention to meander.

It was just Meredith—Miss Hubert. Perhaps it was being a governess. Her powers of focus were extraordinary. If only he had some of her skills; it was all he could do in long parliamentary sessions not to drop off occasionally, although if one was caught doing so, it was highly frowned upon.

Not that it made much difference to the older fellows. Why, James Ferguson was almost eighty, and had not made a contribution in a session for the last ten years, or at least that was what Alfred had heard.

"Sinners!"

Alfred jumped. His attention had wandered again, and he was not the only one who started as the Reverend Michaels looked out at his congregation with an unusually sharp eye.

"Those are who St. Paul refers to, in the chapter following, as…"

From what Alfred could see, Miss Hubert had not started. Of course, she hadn't. She had not stopped paying attention for a moment. Hopefully, she would be able to teach Archibald how to do it—or at the very least, to appear to be doing it. If they were fortunate, no one else in St. Matthews would have noticed that the current heir to the Rochdale duchy was asleep.

Alfred glanced over to the other side of the church, and his heart lurched. There sat the Talbots: the Right Honorable John Talbot and his sister, the Right Honorable Wilhelmina.

John noticed his glance and winked before he looked at Archibald. His rough smile broadened, and he snickered, nudging his sister, who looked over and rolled her eyes sardonically before making a point of looking back at Reverend Michaels.

Heat swept over Alfred's chest as he turned to the vicar, but he could hardly concentrate. *John Talbot.* The man was tall, handsome in that rather irritating way that seemed to take no effort and only increased when his hair was uncombed or cheeks were unshaven.

A bigger blaggard he had never seen.

Irritation rose in Alfred's chest that made his waistcoat too tight and his cravat uncomfortably knotted. The Talbot family had been looking for a way to ridicule the Carmichaels for generations. Bad blood, that's what it was. Alfred had never had it properly explained to him, and even his father did not seem entirely sure of the details.

It did not matter. John Talbot was cut from the same cloth as his foolish father, and now the idiot was running against him for his seat at Parliament.

A Talbot, in Parliament! It did not bear thinking about.

Still, Talbot was good at making Alfred look bad. It was only a few months since he had spread that rumor about the roads leading up to Rochdale. Alfred had told everyone once if he had told them a dozen times—they were not on his land, and he was not liable to repair them.

But that was not what Talbot had said.

Alfred found he was clenching his hands and slowly unfurled his fingers. He had fixed the damn—the roads in the end, anyway, and there John Talbot had been the next day, smirking away in the Town Hall, as though he had won some sort of victory!

He bit his lip. He knew Archibald meant no harm by slipping into slumber, but what would Talbot do with that information? Tell everyone at the next hustings that the Carmichaels did not respect the Church?

There was nothing for it.

Alfred nudged the boy—a little harder than he had intended.

"Wh-What?" Archibald said, roused from sleep hurriedly and evidently with no idea where he was.

It was fortunate indeed that Miss Hubert coughed loudly at that precise moment. Indeed, her coughing was so violent that the Reverend Michaels halted in his sermon and looked down at her from the pulpit in concern.

"I do apologize, sir," she said sweetly. "I am afraid a little dust caught in my throat—you were saying about the Ephesians and their difference to the Philippians?"

Alfred stared in disbelief as the Reverend Michaels smiled. "I was indeed, Miss Hubert, thank you. So, as we journey to the Philippians, who have a most different approach to..."

He should have thought of that. Why was it that Miss Hubert had all the good ideas at the moment? Alfred glared at his half-brother, who had red cheeks and a nervous expression.

"I-I did not mean to—"

"Do not concern yourself," said Miss Hubert under her breath, under the guise of passing a clean handkerchief to the boy. "Here, blow your nose."

Archibald hid his obvious embarrassment in a long blow of his nose—one that startled the vicar so entirely, he paused once again in his sermon.

"Is...is everything alright, Miss Hubert?"

Miss Hubert smiled, and Alfred saw the old man beam back. "Quite all right, thank you, sir."

"Yes, yes, well..." trailed off the Reverend Michaels. "Well, that was essentially all I had to say in the matter. If you would please rise..."

Alfred rose in relief. It was not that he had no time for the Church, far from it. He liked Reverend Michaels, always had done. It was the heat, together with the sermons.

But only one hymn later, the Rochdales followed the vicar out of the church, first in line, as befit their status. Once, John Talbot had attempted to step before them. It had not ended in a scuffle, precisely, but it was a close call.

The Reverend Michaels paused at the church door and turned to greet them as they left.

"Your Grace," he murmured. "I...well, I do hope Miss Hubert's cough is not serious."

Alfred turned to look at his brother's governess, who had the good grace to blush.

"I am sure tis just a tickle in the throat," he said stiffly.

The Reverend Michaels nodded. "So unfortunate to feel unwell during the summer months, Miss Hubert."

She smiled at the vicar, and Alfred was forced once again to hide a smile. *Well, she had made a conquest there, and no mistake.*

They moved on to allow the Talbots to take their leave of the vicar, and Alfred breathed in the heady warm air outside.

"I do believe I have given him rather a fright," said Miss Hubert under her breath as Archibald wandered off in the churchyard.

Alfred swallowed. He knew what he had to say, even if the words were momentarily stuck in his throat. His gaze raked over the rows of headstones as he spoke.

"Thank you," he said stiffly. "For covering up my brother's indiscretion. You did not need to do that."

"I was happy to, and I think in a way, it taught him a little lesson, too."

Alfred looked at her properly and saw a teasing smile on her face.

"Permit me to say, Your Grace," she continued, utterly ignoring his request to call him Rochdale, "that you did not look entirely comfortable in there. Lack of faith?"

It was such a personal question that Alfred blinked. Inquiring into one's faith was simply not something one did—or at least not in polite society. But then, Miss Hubert had a reason to ask. Understanding the family's religious ties was, after all, a core part of her role as a governess.

But it wasn't that. It was never a disagreement between himself and the Church, nor his God, not really.

How to put it into words?

"I have always found it rather strange, Miss Hubert," Alfred said, starting to walk slowly across the churchyard, "to know from a very young age where one's final resting place will be."

The words were stilted, the effort of opening up in this rather bizarre way difficult. But still, the words came, and the silence from Miss Hubert allowed him to continue.

"I even know where my plaque is going to be on the wall in the church, and out here in the churchyard," he said as lightly as he could.

Miss Hubert seemed to see right through him, however. "How macabre. And you have known this all your life?"

Alfred came to a stop before the family memorial. Carmichaels from ages past had their names and dates etched into the marble every thirty years or so.

"My father," he said, pointing out the name. "His father, his father, his father…and there. The space for me."

His finger paused at the gap below Arthur, his father. Blank space, waiting for him.

An elegant hand joined his in touching the memorial. "It must be rather strange, especially knowing it at such a young age. But of course, there is the alternate version, and I must say, I dislike it just as much."

A gentle summer breeze brushed past them, and Alfred glanced at her. Miss Hubert's mouth was set in a serious look, a frown across her forehead.

"What is that?"

Miss Hubert straightened up and smiled. "Not knowing where you will be in five years' time, let alone fifty. You are hemmed in by your family name, Your Grace, with little to surprise you in the years to come. I believe I would choose that rather than the life I lead. Never knowing what the future holds. Never knowing where your journey will take you."

Alfred stared. The thought had never occurred to him that one could go through life with no plans, no future steps marked out. He had certainly never experienced anything like it. His life had been mapped out for him before he had been born—before conception!

There were things everyone else did, and there was what the Duke of Rochdale did. No choice. No discussion.

"If you could see into the future," he said quietly as the congregation milled about in the sunshine, exchanging news and gossip, the farmers looking tired and wishing for their luncheons, "would you? Would you like to see where you were going next?"

Miss Hubert considered him for a moment before replying, "No. Even with the fear of the unknown before me, I do not think I would wish to know everything. It would be very tiring, I think, to feel as though all choice was taken from me."

It was only then that Alfred realized how close they were standing. *Why, there could only be a few feet between them.* His mouth was dry for some unknown reason, and—

"Archibald Carmichael, no!" Miss Hubert's words were spoken like a papal edict and were obeyed just as instantly.

Alfred turned to see the boy climbing down, red-faced, from a headstone. He walked sullenly back toward them.

"I think it is time we returned home," said Miss Hubert. "Do you not think, Your Grace?"

Alfred nodded, and the three of them started toward the churchyard gate.

It was only a short walk from St. Matthews to Rochdale Abbey. It was, after all, the church originally built for the abbey itself, which then became the family church. Within ten minutes, they were stepping across the lawns, and Archibald's spirits, flattened for only a moment, had risen again.

"Will you play with me, Alfred? Can we play horses? Can I go riding later, like you and Father—"

Alfred sighed heavily at the child weaving about the place as he and Miss Hubert walked sedately. "No, Archibald. I must go and prepare for the next husting."

He saw with surprise that the boy looked genuinely disappointed and was tempted to avoid the husting to spend a little time with the child—but then, the election would not win itself. Like a dark cloud on the horizon, it grew ever closer and ignoring it would sadly not slow its path.

"I cannot play in the dirt with a child," he said, a little more harshly than he had intended. "I need to win this election, Archibald, and you know that."

Archibald stopped dancing about and fell silently in step with Miss Hubert, taking her hand. Alfred saw he squeezed it and received an answering squeeze.

Heat flushed through his chest with embarrassment. His own brother was already finding refuge with a stranger! But he could not, would not apologize. He was doing this for him, for the family.

"Why do we not go to the front lawn and leave your brother to his work?" Miss Hubert could be heard saying quietly to her charge. "When we get there, you can tell me..."

Her voice faded as they took a different direction.

Alfred sighed. He had never been struck with a desire to spend time with the boy, not really, though the idea of doing so with Miss Hubert was an interesting one. But he had to do what was expected of him, and if he knew Mr. Walker, he was already inside, waiting for him.

"Ah, Your Grace!" Mr. Walker said with open arms as Alfred entered the hallway. "I was just speaking with Mrs. Martin, and she has agreed to lay out the ballroom in the style of a husting for our practice."

Alfred groaned. "You know how I hate public speaking, Mr. Walker. Can we not just sit in the drawing room and work on the speech itself?"

Rochdales were not supposed to hate public speaking. Even the thought of it made the hackles on the back of his neck rise, and Alfred could well remember the first hustings practice he had endured with his father.

"You'll never make me proud if you continue like that."

But Mr. Walker seemed unperturbed. "Nonsense, practice makes perfect!"

Allowing himself to be dragged to the ballroom by Mr. Walker's sheer enthusiasm, Alfred knew in his heart practice would not make perfect—not for him, anyway. Sometimes there were things one simply could not do, and there were but few of them.

Public speaking was one.

"Now, I have put a table up here," said Mrs. Martin impressively as they swept into the ballroom, her voice echoing. "And a row of chairs here, where you can pretend your loyal subjects are—"

"I copied out the latest version of your speech here," said Mr. Walker, thrusting a pile of papers into Alfred's hands and ignoring Mrs. Martin's glare. "All you need to do is pretend we are your audience. And…go!"

Alfred blinked at Mr. Walker and his housekeeper as they sat primly in the first row of seats, waiting for him to begin.

He swallowed, tasting the fear in his throat. This was not where he wanted to be—especially as he could hear the yells and whoops of the boy from outside.

Why was public speaking considered so important, anyway? John Talbot was a fine public speaker. *Damn his thoughts, traitorous to the last!*

Alfred swallowed again and looked down at the papers in his hands.

My dear friends, an election is not simply a vote but an enormous decision: who should represent you and your concerns in the highest house in the land.

"M-My dear...my dear friends an...an election," Alfred began, tongue twisting around the words, his chest tightening painfully.

"We cannot hear you!" Mrs. Martin shouted. "Louder, Your Grace, you need to speak more clearly!"

Visited by a desire to fire Mrs. Martin on the spot and simply do without a housekeeper, Alfred reined in his temper and looked at the speech. She was doing this to help, and he knew that. *If only it helped.*

"B-But an enormous...enormous..."

"From the beginning, if you do not mind!" came the voice of Mr. Walker.

Alfred sighed and lifted his gaze from the speech in his hands. "You know perfectly well I am not suited to this, Mr. Walker, and I do not know why we cannot..."

His voice trailed away. His gaze had moved beyond his sparse audience of two and to the French doors at the end of the ballroom. His mother had considered them an extravagance, but his father had insisted, and they now gave him a clear view of Miss Hubert and Archibald.

They were playing tig, from what he could see. Miss Hubert shrieked as she turned quickly, Archibald reaching out and tapping her on the arm, giggling furiously.

Alfred smiled. The temptation to just throw the pages up in the air and stride out to join them soared through him. He wanted to be close to her. There was something about Miss Hubert—something that calmed him, and at the same time, riled him.

He needed her in here.

"Mrs. Martin, please bring in the boy and his governess," he said curtly, hoping his tone would brook no opposition.

That was not accounting for Mrs. Martin. "Miss Hubert?" After one look from Alfred, she rose from her seat. "Very good, Your Grace."

He examined the speech. *Had he written this?* He must have done, or most of it, at least. It sounded like his words. He was excellent on paper; it was getting them out before an audience that was the trouble.

"Hallo, Alfred!" Archibald grinned as he stepped forward with Miss Hubert. "Do you want to play?"

Very much, thought Alfred. *Anything to escape this.*

Aloud, he said stiffly, "No, Archibald. Like our father before us, one day, you will be the Rochdale member of Parliament, and you will need to start learning what it takes to get there. Sit."

Alfred tried not to look at Miss Hubert as she took a seat next to the boy.

"When is the election?" said Archibald with wide eyes. "Who is voting? I heard from Christopher Walker that John Talbot—"

"Enough questions," said Alfred testily. *This was already starting to feel like a mistake.* "You are here to learn, not to ask questions."

The light of enthusiasm went out in Archibald's face.

"Your brother will be voted into Parliament in mid-October," said Miss Hubert quietly. "Everyone eligible in Rochdale will vote over three days, and John Talbot is standing against your brother."

She looked pointedly at Alfred as she finished answering the boy's questions, as though demonstrating it was possible to respond to him without getting irritated.

It was a look designed to make Alfred feel small, and it worked. The woman had a better understanding of his brother than he did, and she had only been here—what, a week and a half? Two weeks at most?

Then Miss Hubert smiled encouragingly, and Alfred's stomach lurched in a way that had nothing to do with public speaking.

He coughed. "Right. Here we go. M-My dear…friends."

Damnit, he could speak perfectly fine when it was off the cuff—why did this speech have to be so difficult!

He had thought a larger audience and Miss Hubert's calming presence would help, but all it seemed to have done was made it worse.

"An election is not simply a vote," he said in a rush and then found he had run out of breath, taking a huge gulp of air before attempting the next part. "B-But an…an…"

Miss Hubert rose to her feet. "If I may?"

Before Alfred could comprehend what was happening, she had joined him at the table and was taking the papers out of his hand. Their fingers touched, heat searing between them, magnetism pulling them together, closer, as though they were alone, as though no other people existed in the—

"I have a pencil somewhere," said Miss Hubert, pulling one out of her carefully constructed bun.

Alfred struggled to regain his equilibrium. *What had just happened? Had she been aware of it, or had the entire thing been in his mind?*

"Right, let me see," Miss Hubert said distractedly, and she leaned over the table and started marking up the speech.

Alfred goggled as Mr. Walker rose. "Excuse me, Miss, but this is politics, you can leave it to us gentlemen."

Miss Hubert straightened up with a smile. "Yes, but this is also the art of speech-making, Mr. Walker, and something I have both studied and taught. Please let me work."

Without saying another word, she bent back over the table to continue scribbling over the speech with her pencil. Mr. Walker sat down with his mouth open, and Alfred could not help but be amazed at how calmly she had spoken to him.

"Right," she said abruptly, placing the papers back in his hands. "There. You will see I have drawn marks across the words—a v is where you draw breath, n is where you breathe out, and you pause wherever there is an asterisk. Do you see?"

Alfred could barely take in a word she was saying, but he could see the little pencil scribbles across the paper.

"Try that," said Miss Hubert, taking her seat beside Archibald and looking expectant.

Alfred nodded mutely. His heart was still racing from that touch, that infinitesimal touch, which seemed to have had no effect on her at all.

Right. So, the v is where one draws breath...

"My dear friends," he said in one breath and then paused at an asterisk. *Fine so far...* "An election is not simply a vote. B-But an enormous decision. Who should..."

The marks were helping. Alfred could hardly believe it. His tongue still stuttered on a few of the areas, but he was able to get through the first page without so much as a dropped syllable. The second page was easier. By the third page, he could see the pattern of the marks, see where they were going, what they were trying to do.

"...and that is why you should vote Rochdale for Rochdale," he finished.

Mrs. Martin applauded loudly. "My goodness, that was wonderful! You...well, really know your stuff, Miss Hubert."

The last was said rather begrudgingly, but Miss Hubert took it in good grace. "Thank you, Mrs. Martin."

"You should consider running, too!" the housekeeper said, laughing at her own joke.

Miss Hubert smiled. "I am a governess, not a politician."

"No, she is right. You are a natural." Alfred almost looked around to see who had spoken before realizing that it was himself.

Miss Hubert's eyes were glittering, as though she had seen the punchline of a joke that was only just being made. "I may have great talents, but I lack one quality required."

Alfred stared, curious. There did not appear to be anything Miss Hubert could not do, and the idea that there was a quality she lacked was rather startling.

"Goodness, really? What?"

"Why, Your Grace, I am not a man," she said sweetly. "Come on, Archibald."

The two left the ballroom, leaving the three others in silence. Alfred smiled. There was something charming and yet mischievous about that woman. *He needed to get to know her a little better,* he thought, *for she was as beautiful as she was intriguing.*

"Right then!" Mr. Walker clapped his hands, causing Alfred to jump. "One more time, then, Your Grace, and with feeling!"

CHAPTER SEVEN

August 15, 1812

M EREDITH SIGHED, HER breath the only moving air in the stifling schoolroom. She had even requested Roberts to fetch her the key to the large bay windows, something he had done rather begrudgingly, but despite opening them, the hot air did not move.

The trees in the gardens were still. Not a sound could be heard, and Archibald was almost asleep over his desk.

He lifted his gaze, and Meredith looked down pointedly at the sums he was supposed to be working on. If she threw a holiday every warm day, they would never get anywhere.

"Which question are you working on now, Archibald?" she said quietly.

Archibald yawned. "I am too hot to think of math, Miss Hubert."

It was difficult to disagree with him, not when her skin was sticky with the humidity of the day.

She had always believed it was cooler up in the north. That was what she had always been told. Not today, not this summer. It was unbearably warm.

"My bedchamber was too hot last n-n-night," Archibald yawned again. "I simply could not sleep, Miss Hubert. Must I continue with my sums?"

Meredith considered it. She, too, had found her bedchamber oppressively hot the night before, though had not mentioned it to anyone else, hoping to keep it to herself. After that rather ridiculous display she had taken on herself just last week with the master of the house in the ballroom, she had purposefully kept out of Mrs. Martin's way.

Weren't these large houses supposed to be cooler in summer? She was certain she had read somewhere that they were meant to keep cool in the summer and warm in the winter. From what Meredith could see, it was quite the opposite.

There was a small sigh, and she focused on her charge—her charge who had slipped onto the desk before him and closed his eyes in the languishing heat.

"Archibald Carmichael, come here."

She allowed just a touch of the stern governess tone into her words, and Archibald awoke with a start. Sighing heavily, he rose from his chair and brought his worksheet to her.

"Speed, distance, time," she said. "Let us see how much you took in from this morning."

Glancing down the sheet, more doodles than answers, it was quite clear Archibald had taken in almost nothing. There were two half-hearted attempts to answer the first question, a complete guess for the second. The third had little stick people running around it. The fourth had not yet been reached.

Meredith tried to hide her smile. It was hardly the most riveting of subjects, true, and in this heat, it was difficult to complain.

Archibald said nervously, "Have...have I got it all wrong?"

Meredith looked up. "And why do you say that?"

The boy looked even more upset, fingers fidgeting in a ball before him. "Alfred says math is important for a future politician, to understand the budget and...and the impact on the economy of our decisions," Archibald said in a rush, as though reciting what he had been told. "Father always said I had to be the best I could be. I never knew my mother, so I do not know if she was any good at sums. Did…did I get the answers wrong?"

There was such genuine concern in his face, Meredith could not bring herself to discuss where he had gone wrong.

The poor lad. What a household to grow up in, what an example his brother was leading for him.

As a governess, one met so many different children, but they generally fell into one of two types. Either they needed to feel the weight of their mistakes before they felt any incentivization to learn and do better, or they were driven internally by a sense of fear or joy to excel.

Archibald was the latter. Punishment would not work on him, nor would the manipulation so beloved by governesses of making him feel small and powerless in her presence.

That was not Meredith's way. Archibald already had the weight of the Carmichael name on his shoulders, his life already planned for him, as it was for his brother.

How had Alfred—the duke—put it?

"I cannot play in the dirt with a child. I need to win this election, Archibald, you know that."

Archibald's gaze had dropped to his shoes, his fingers still tightly knitted together.

Meredith sighed. The duke clearly understood his weight of responsibility was too much for him to carry, so why on earth he believed it was appropriate to put that same weight on an eight-year-old boy was beyond her.

Still, she was not here to raise young Archibald. She was here to teach him.

Her gaze drifted to the window. The trees were moving now, a gentle breeze starting to bring some relief to the baking air.

"Archibald," she said gently. "I think we are finished in the schoolroom for today. It is time to get your body moving, rather than your brain."

The boy looked up, but with none of the enthusiasm Meredith had expected.

"Move? Outside?" he said plaintively. "I do not want to go outside, it is too hot!"

Meredith smiled. "You will not feel so hot when you are on a horse, riding at speed, creating your own breeze! Come on."

She rose and placed the worksheet on her desk, ready for a cooler day, but she had not even reached the door to the corridor before Archibald ran forward and grabbed her arm.

"But—but I am not allowed to ride alone!"

Meredith looked down into the innocent boy's face and felt a rush of affection for him. *Rules, regulations, and restrictions; that was all Archibald had ever known. When was he to be a child?*

"You are not alone," she said smartly as she opened the door and started striding down the corridor. "I will be with you."

Archibald did not look overly convinced as they approached the backstairs, and Meredith almost laughed. There was something so familiar in that look of distrust.

"Archibald Carmichael, I am in charge of your education," she said in a mock severe tone, finally getting a smile out of him, "and not all the education you require can be achieved in the schoolroom. Come on, keep up."

Her feet were taking her quickly down the backstairs and along the corridor that led to the backdoor. Archibald's eyes were wide, and it was only then that Meredith realized he had probably never taken the backstairs before. *Of course, he hadn't; he was the heir to the Duchy of Rochdale!*

Her thoughts were confirmed as they turned a corner and almost ran headlong into Mrs. Martin, arms full of clean bed linens.

"My lord!" the housekeeper said as she stared at Archibald. "What in heaven—what are you doing here? Miss Hubert, I did not think I would have to tell you that a Rochdale never takes the backstairs!"

Meredith attempted to keep her face straight. It was difficult not to smile at the look of outrage and indignation on the woman's face.

"I quite understand your concerns, Mrs. Martin," said Meredith smoothly, "but as this part of the house is so much cooler than the rest, I wanted to consider my lord's temperature. I know that you, as well as I, would hate for him to catch a heat fever."

Mrs. Martin's eyes snapped to Archibald, raking over his flushed cheeks and slightly sweaty brow. She bit her lip and carefully weighed up, from what Meredith could see, her desire to berate the governess and her devotion to the young master.

"Fine," she snapped irritably, shifting the heavy weight of the bed linens in her arms, herself flushed. "But do not let the master see, for pity's sake!"

Without another word, she hurried up the stairs they had just come down. *The poor woman was still very busy,* Meredith thought as she watched her go. Why was it the undermaid—Butters, wasn't it?—had not been replaced? It could not be clearer that Mrs. Martin was doing far too much.

A tug on her sleeve. "Are we really going to the stables?"

Meredith nodded. "I said we would, so that is where we are going. Come on."

The stables were easily accessible from the back door, and as Meredith and Archibald stepped out, she felt that warm breeze on her face. It was better than nothing, she supposed, but as she walked forward, Archibald held back.

She paused. "Are you quite well, Archibald?"

The boy hesitated. "I…I am not usually allowed in the stables. Only when Alfred says I can."

Meredith tried not to allow her irritation to surface. For all of Alfred's—the duke's—impressive words about how the Carmichael boys had their futures, their duties mapped out for them, he was not doing very much to help Archibald achieve them.

He was a full eight years old and was never permitted to be around horses?

Madness!

"Archibald, I repeat—I am in charge of your education," she

said calmly. "Your bother has entrusted you to me in this regard, and so that is precisely what I am going to do. We will start with tack, and a little riding experience. I will not push you to do anything you do not want to do."

She watched the sense of her words sink into Archibald's mind, watched him weigh them as only a boy could, and then he nodded.

"Come on, then," she said gently.

Henderson, the head of the Carmichael stables, gave her a knowing smile as she appeared in the doorway with Archibald's hand in hers.

"Afternoon, Miss Meredith," he said.

There were few people Meredith would have permitted to call her that. She had a position of respectability in the household and really should be addressed as Miss Hubert.

But Henderson was a man in his fifties, perhaps older, and knew horses like no one else did. He had a way with them even she did not, and Meredith had no false modesty when it came to horses. She knew them well. Better than most.

"I thought you might be coming down here today," Henderson continued with a smile, "but I did not expect you to bring young master with you."

His wrinkled face smiled at the boy, and Meredith felt Archibald step into her instinctively.

Did...did he not know Henderson? How was a boy supposed to be raised to lead if he did not even know his own servants?

"Ah, I never seen a natural like your governess, boy," said Henderson gently. "You are in good hands with her, I think."

Meredith smiled and squeezed Archibald's hand. "Practice makes perfect. That is what I always say. Now, Archibald, we are going to start with tack. Come over here and sit on a hay bale for me."

He nodded mutely and dropped onto the hay bale. Henderson winked at Meredith, who smiled as she pulled out a variety of tack from the rack on the wall.

"What do you think this is used for?" she said quietly.

Archibald's eyes lit up. "Well, I would guess, something to do with...with the horse's mouth?"

He came alive in the cool of the stables as he picked up the metal grip, staring at it in fascination.

"How do you think it would be used?" asked Meredith, seating herself opposite him. It was incredible, watching the sleepy, uninterested child perk up and engage once more.

Archibald frowned. "Well...well it looks like..."

Their conversation moved to other pieces of tack, exploring how they worked together, how they were crafted, what materials were used. Archibald took in everything she said, asking questions, becoming more intrigued as they talked.

Meredith smiled as she showed him how two parts interlocked together. She would have to remember to use more physical movement in learning when they returned to the schoolroom. He had learned more in the last fifteen minutes than all morning.

She placed the last piece of tack down on the hay bale beside her. "Well done, Archibald. That was very impressive—though I will test you in a week to see how much you have retained."

"And can I ride now?" Archibald looked eagerly down the stables, the stalls hiding the horses within but the smell surrounding them.

Meredith could not begrudge his eagerness. Anyone who loved horses had a place in her heart.

"Henderson," she said quietly, and the man appeared as though by magic. He must have been close, keeping a careful eye on them as interlopers. "Would you mind us tacking up the smallest pony you have, and my mare?"

Henderson's eyes twinkled. "You can do your own tacking, I think, Miss Meredith, but I will help young master with Polly, our pony."

"You have a pony called Polly?" said Archibald, standing in his excitement.

Henderson chuckled. "You have, master! 'Twas your brother who named him, young sir, so if you have a problem with it, you can take it up with him! But we have a new foal due any day now, and I am sure if you have a better name, we can try it out on that'n."

Wide-eyed and no longer afraid of the older man, Archibald wandered off with Henderson to go and find Polly the pony.

Meredith grinned. There was something so special about horses and the people who loved them. You could always find a friend in a stable, that was what...

Her stomach lurched. *That was what her father had always said.* And he would know. Best thief she had ever known, and horses had been his specialty. Theirs.

She shook herself and moved to Beauty, the horse whinnied in greeting. *She had put that life behind her. She was not going to even dwell on it, not for one moment.*

"Look, Miss Hubert, look!"

Meredith had just finished tacking Beauty when she turned to see Archibald on Polly, the smallest pony she had ever seen, with Henderson right behind him with a careful hand on Polly's behind to steer her.

"Very good, Archibald," she said warmly. "Give me one moment, and I shall join you."

"Polly is a good one," said Henderson quietly to her as she mounted her horse. "She'll follow you as you go. The lad won't need to do much."

It was clear Archibald could barely contain his excitement as they walked slowly out of the stables. Henderson had been right; Polly simply followed in Beauty's wake, giving Archibald all his powers of concentration for sitting correctly.

Meredith watched him. He was gentle with Polly, not tugging at the reins or pulling her mouth. *Always a good sign.*

"Now, we will not go too far," she said as she guided Beauty around the stables toward the sweeping lawn. "If it is a mile to that big oak tree, and we ride at one mile an hour, I wonder how long it will take us to get there."

Archibald giggled, his hand on Polly's mane. "An hour, of course!"

Meredith grinned. The very first question from his worksheet. Archibald had struggled to even concentrate sufficiently on what the problem was asking him when they were in the schoolroom. The stuffy, stifling schoolroom.

Yet out here, on Polly's back and with a gentle though warm breeze in the air, it had seemed laughably easy.

Onto the second question, then...

"Alright, clever clogs," she said good-naturedly. "How about if we rode at sixty miles an hour?"

"Will we?" Archibald asked eagerly.

Meredith laughed. "Not anywhere close, Archibald, but humor me. How long will it take?"

She watched him think, watched the adjustments he was making to stay steady on Polly. He was a natural.

"Why, one minute, I think," he said eventually.

"Well done, that is clever of you," she said, nudging Beauty a little to the left, so they kept along the fence at the edge of the garden. She did not want to go too close to the house. She would not want to be accused of distracting the master, not like last time. "And what about if we were riding at one hundred miles per hour?"

This one took Archibald a little longer, and Meredith waited patiently as she watched him concentrate. Seeing a child learn, watching them work it out for themselves, the sense of achievement they had when they finally battled through to the correct answer...

It was why being a governess was so rewarding.

"Good afternoon."

Meredith jumped. So focused had she been on Archibald and his mathematical problems, she had not realized that on the other side of the fence was a footpath—*a public footpath*. A gentleman was riding on a stallion at least a few hands taller than her Beauty.

He looked familiar. She recognized him from somewhere, though it was hard to place him. She had been to St. Matthews since she had arrived at Rochdale Abbey. He had to be someone from the church.

Archibald had fallen silent, and as Meredith looked at him, his cheeks flushed.

"Good afternoon," she replied quietly, in a tone that was polite and yet did not invite further conversation.

The last thing she needed was a reputation for speaking with strange gentlemen she met on public pathways—she would lose her place!

The gentleman, however, did not appear to notice her reticence. "Miss Meredith Hubert, I presume? The governess?"

Meredith watched Archibald's face turn away. He knew the gentleman, then. Why would he not look at him? *Was this a man to avoid, or was this just the shyness of a child?*

"You presume correctly," she said stiffly.

The gentleman smirked, a look that made her skin prickle. It was the look a hunter gave his prey. It was cruel to think of him in that way, she was sure, but he gave her little cause to consider him well.

"John Talbot," he said with a bow of his head.

Meredith inclined her own but said nothing. *John Talbot.* The competitor to Alfred Carmichael. But she had no reason to leave, no reason to hide. She had done nothing wrong, and her stubborn streak told her that to do so would be to retreat.

Still, she felt grateful for the thin wooden fence that stood between them.

"I am glad to see young Master Archibald out on this fine day, enjoying nature," declared Mr. Talbot.

Meredith nodded. She had nothing to say to him. Surely, he would take the hint eventually and go away?

"I do so enjoy nature," said Mr. Talbot with a grin. "What say you, Miss Hubert?"

"Yes, indeed, very pleasant."

He made a few more attempts to draw her into a conversation, but Meredith was determined. Short, sharp answers and no smiles. *That would force him to leave, wouldn't it?*

It felt like an age until he said, "Well, I will not keep you any longer, Miss Hubert, Master Archibald."

Mr. Talbot set his horse into a canter and had soon disappeared from sight.

Meredith shivered. There was something about that man, something she did not like. Her shoulders relaxed, and her breathing slowed. What a strange reaction to a man she barely knew.

Glancing at Archibald, she saw he was glaring in the direction Mr. Talbot had disappeared.

"That man," he declared in a voice that appeared far older than his years, "is my brother's enemy."

Meredith could not help but smile as she nudged Beauty to take the left path before them. "No one has enemies, not really."

"We do," said Archibald seriously. "Mr. Talbot is standing against Alfred in the election, and I overheard Roberts say he was a…a *blaggard*. Is that a rude word?"

It was all she could do to keep a straight face. "I am afraid so, Archibald, and so I will have to ask you not to use it."

"That's all right," Archibald said happily. "I know lots of others."

Meredith laughed and was about to say he should not really be using any language like that, but the words died in her throat as she saw a horse rider approach in the distance.

If that was Mr. Talbot again, she would simply turn around and take Archibald back to the stables. The last thing she wanted was for an altercation between…

And then she blinked. It was not Mr. Talbot. It was Alfred—the Duke of Rochdale.

Heat seared her cheeks. Not only were her encounters with him rather discomforting, but she was not entirely sure whether he would consider it an impertinence to take Archibald out. What had the child said? That he wasn't permitted without Alfred?

Archibald obviously sensed he might be in trouble, for his shoulders slumped, and his gaze fell onto the reins he was clutching. Meredith sat up a little straighter. She would not be reprimanded for this. She had done nothing wrong.

"My God, it's Archie!"

The duke's words were said in surprise rather than censure, and Meredith was pleasantly surprised to hear that there was a pet name between them, even if he almost never used it.

"Hallo, Alfred," said Archibald, not looking up.

"Goodness, you are riding well," said the duke as he watched his brother. "Show me a turn, then."

Meredith looked over anxiously at Archibald. They had not practiced anything like that, but then he had been riding before, just not often.

She should not have been concerned, however. Cheeks flushed with the excitement of being the center of attention, Archibald gently turned Polly around in a circle and then stopped her to a halt.

Meredith watched her master applaud, his own stallion standing resolutely still.

"I am impressed, I really am," said the duke as his younger brother glowed with the pleasure of the praise. "I had no idea you were so proficient."

"Miss Hubert is teaching me all about tack," said Archibald enthusiastically, "and about speeds, and distances, and how far I can go when I ride at a hundred miles an hour!"

The duke looked at Meredith, who smiled. "We have not actually attempted to ride at one hundred miles an hour, you understand. Just the theory, for now."

To her surprise, he laughed. "Yes, well, I had rather gathered that. Now, I think Polly looks tired. Why don't you take her back to the stables—you know the way, don't you?—and Miss Hubert and I can finish exercising our horses."

Meredith stared. *What on earth had possessed him to suggest that?* The idea of spending time with him was rather intoxicating. She could not forget that look he had given her in the library.

But this was all somewhat irregular. Unless he needed to speak to her privately—unless she had done something wrong and was about to be reprimanded?

"I will go back to the stables, and Henderson can rub her down," Archibald was saying.

"You can help him," said Meredith with a smile. "Caring for a horse is not just knowing about tack, Archibald."

"Miss Hubert is right," said the duke. "We do not just enjoy horses, we take care of them."

Archibald nodded as Meredith stared with surprise. She and Alfred watched Archibald nudge Polly back the way they had come, turning the corner before glancing at each other.

"This way, I think," said the duke and nudged his steed forward.

Meredith had no preference and so happily followed. "Of course, Your Grace."

"Now, I am almost certain that I instructed you to call me Rochdale, and even that is rather formal," he said with a wry smile. "I suppose Rochdale is too much to ask?"

Meredith swallowed. This was not the master she had come to expect. Where was the tension, the barely bottled irritation?

Perhaps, like her, he felt more comfortable on a horse, more relaxed, more himself. Assuming that this was himself. *How was she to tell?*

She should not judge him. She was still getting to know him, and if he was anything like some of the dukes she had met in London, that was an impossible task. There was always something held back.

"Rochdale, it is," she said, the name feeling a little strange in her mouth. "Yet I am not sure whether I will still use it in public."

"Use it when we are alone together, then," was his reply, and it made shivers go up her spine.

Did he think they would be alone often?

They continued to trot gently in silence for a few minutes, Meredith looking over a few times to ensure he was not bored. He did not appear to be. If anything, he appeared…well. Joyful.

"You will have to forgive me for saying so, R-Rochdale," she said, the name still feeling wrong, "if I remark that I have never seen you so at peace as now, on a horse."

He laughed. "Yes, any excuse to get out on a horse, and I will take it. I used to invent errands when I was younger, just to take out Parker here, though I have too many real calls on my time now. With each passing year, it feels as though I ride even less."

Meredith smiled. "Why allow real life to get in the way of a good ride?"

Their eyes met, and Meredith felt a shiver move up her spine. *What was that?*

"The election takes up most of my time now," he said shortly as their path took them through woodland, the dappled shade giving them relief from the heat. "It is not enough to invent errands now. I have a duty to follow, and I follow it to the letter."

There was such sadness in his voice. Meredith nudged Beauty closer, so their horses walked alongside each other.

"Why do it?" she asked quietly.

It was an impertinent question, but Rochdale did not appear to mind.

"Tradition, the name, the history of it all," he replied. "'Tis funny, before a few months ago, I had never even questioned it myself. To question it would suggest that there was another option, another choice for me."

"That does not feel very fair," said Meredith, aware she was speaking to a duke, who probably owned all the land they were riding on. *Fairness was relative.*

Rochdale laughed shortly. "Well, 'tis not as though I am the only person with responsibilities one does not care to carry out. Besides, one day Archibald will have to go through it all himself if I do not…"

His voice trailed away, and Meredith found her heart stirred in pity for the duke who rode beside her. A great name, a great family, even a great fortune did not appear to have brought the man much happiness at all.

He was a good man. She had ridden past the retirement cottages he had built on the edges of the Rochdale estate for those servants who could no longer perform their duties. He cared for people, it was clear. He even cared for Archibald, in a way.

Alfred Carmichael, Duke of Rochdale, would make a good member of Parliament. But that did not mean he would be happy. He appeared miserable, and the election hadn't even happened yet.

Meredith swallowed as they turned a corner. She knew what she was about to say was rather out of turn. A governess should not really be having private conversations with her master unless it pertained to the study and education of the child. But wasn't it? Wasn't whatever she did for the elder brother going to benefit the younger, in time?

"No one," she said quietly, "should do what they don't want to do, even if it is because of family. Even if one feels a duty."

She glanced at him and saw Rochdale smile. Something akin to affection rose in her heart, but Meredith pushed it down immediately.

She was offering advice to her employer. *That was all.* The last thing she needed was to get entangled in...in that way.

Rochdale sighed. "I am sure you are correct, for most people. I am not most people."

That temper she only ever had just under control sparked. "You are more special than everyone else?"

"I have greater restrictions than everyone else," he said, his voice low. "For example. I am enjoying this ride. I am enjoying being in the cool of the woods rather than in the bustle of Rochdale Town. I am enjoying spending time with you, Miss Hubert. Your company is...most pleasant."

Heat seared Meredith's cheeks. *Now, what precisely did he mean by that?*

"And yet despite all that enjoyment, I must away," said Rochdale, his voice rising and becoming more businesslike. "I have an appointment in less than twenty minutes with some of the townspeople to hear their grievances against each other, and I cannot be late."

Meredith was surprised to hear this. "I was not aware that was a role for a member of Parliament."

She nudged Beauty to the next right fork as he did, turning toward the main road to Rochdale Town.

He laughed. "No, it isn't. I am the magistrate here, too."

Meredith laughed. "No wonder you are tired of it all! You require a summer break, a proper one. One in which no one can demand anything of you and ices are brought to you every hour, on the hour."

Her cheeks flamed as she heard herself. That was the flirtatious suggestion of a governess to a man of her acquaintance— not to her master!

But Rochdale did not seem to think anything was wrong. To the contrary, he halted his horse, and Meredith slowed Beauty to a stop.

Rochdale's eyes found hers, and they were fierce. "Is that a governess's orders?"

Meredith's breath caught in her throat. They were alone here, right on the edge of the woodland by the road. He was looking at her like...like she had never been looked at before. There was a hunger there, a longing she did not understand.

Was he desirous of what they were speaking of, a summer during which no one made any demands, or was...was this hunger for something else?

For her?

Rochdale pulled out his pocket watch and glanced at it. Meredith found she could breathe again, now the connection was broken.

"Yes, I will be late now," he said with a sigh. "My apologies, Miss Hubert. You know the way."

He disappeared in a cloud of dust as he encouraged his horse to a trot, then a canter, then a gallop. The small figure vanished from the horizon within a minute, though it was a few more before Meredith collected herself and started back toward Rochdale Abbey.

CHAPTER EIGHT

August 20, 1812

"I F YOU DO not pay attention, then I am sorry to say, Your Grace, that I may as well leave!"

Alfred jumped. He was not accustomed to being shouted at in such a manner, and besides, he had paid attention. *Mostly.*

And who was Mr. Walker to say such things, anyway? It had been a long time since anyone had shouted at him, a duke. It was a very uncomfortable feeling.

"I am paying attention," he said defensively, hating the childish tone in his words.

It was a lie, of course, and Mr. Walker seemed eminently aware of that. They were sat, along with Mr. Hemming, in the drawing room at Rochdale Abbey. Alfred had invited them...no, actually, now he came to think about it, they had invited themselves.

No matter, they were here to discuss more about the election. It did not appear to be a proper meeting because Mr. Shaw and Mr. Brown had not been included, but it certainly felt like one. Alfred sighed as he looked down at the sheaf of papers strewn across the table before him. Party lines, official agreements, disagreements, notes of intent…

It was all so dull. Fascinating to Mr. Walker, evidently, and even Mr. Hemming had managed to stay awake during the long, warm afternoon.

They would never have to bear the mantle of this burden. It was easy to send others to war and hear their exciting exploits. *Better that than go yourself.*

Mr. Walker was examining him with a frown.

"I really was listening," said Alfred defensively. "You were speaking about…the conversation was on…"

His voice trailed away, and his gaze fell onto the papers once more. *Damn and blast it.* He should have been paying attention. How could he berate Archibald for failing to attend when he was the worst culprit of them all?

Mr. Walker sighed heavily. "Your Grace, I speak harshly as one would to a friend, and I hope you consider me such. Mr. Hemming and I are only here for your good. We have no wish to scold you."

Alfred nodded. "I know that, old friend. Your service to the Carmichaels is legend, 'tis all over Rochdale."

The man straightened up in his chair at those words, and Alfred caught sight of Mr. Hemming reddening somewhat.

Even when he attempted to be kind to one man, it somehow managed to offend the other. This was precisely the problem with politics. *One could not win!*

"Your mind has not been here all morning, Your Grace," said Mr. Hemming stiffly.

Mr. Walker nodded. "Nor all week, I would say. What has got into you, Your Grace? What important matters of state, of the election, are clouding your mind?"

Alfred swallowed. There was absolutely no possibility of him revealing what—or who—was distracting him so successfully from his duties. He would simply have to push her—it—out of his mind.

He could not permit anything to distract him. He had to stay focused.

"The election is fast approaching, and you are not taking this seriously at all," continued Mr. Walker. "What can we do to help you?"

The mere fact that he ended on a note designed to support rather than chastise made Alfred feel all the worse. These gentlemen had dedicated hours of their time to his cause, and what had he done?

Spent most of it thinking about...

"I am very sorry for my inattention, good sirs," Alfred said hastily. Anything to stop thinking about what he knew was a ridiculous distraction. "I will attempt to do better."

Mr. Walker rose from his seat to come by the table, rifling through the papers in search of one in particular.

"Please do not misunderstand us," he said, gesturing at Mr. Hemming. "We do none of this to weary you—my father served your father, and all I wish is to do the same. Why, my family has served your family for generations. All I ask is that you allow us to help you."

Alfred nodded. There was something about the way Rochdale families were intricately linked over time. Just as he belonged to the land, the Walkers belonged to the Carmichaels. It was a special sort of bond, and Mr. Walker, as the current Walker, deserved better from him.

"Let us begin again, shall we?"

Mr. Hemming nodded. "After you, Mr. Walker."

Mr. Walker had found the paper he was searching for. "Well. As I was saying, the number of gentlemen eligible to vote in this election, as opposed to the last election, has altered dramatically. If we first consider..."

He managed five minutes this time, but Alfred found he had suddenly lost track of Mr. Walker's speech and utterly forgotten to heed his words.

His damn mind wandering again! He did not do it on purpose, yet could not bring himself to listen. The topic that consumed his mind, that took him away from the election where he should be focused, was…

Miss Meredith Hubert.

It went against his better judgment, but there it was. One could not always control what, or who, absorbed one's mind, and Miss Hubert was a rather pleasant topic.

She had been here—what, a month now? Maybe a little more, and yet it was hard to tell because she had slipped into the Rochdale way of life so quickly, it was hard to remember what life at the abbey had been like before her.

Meredith was a part of his home. Alfred swallowed. *Miss Hubert, of course.* Some sort of decorum had to remain, even in his thoughts.

The difficulty was, of course, that because he felt so comfortable around her, he was beginning to allow things to slip. Feelings he had kept hidden for so long, misgivings about this cursed election, for example, had spilled out before her.

"I have a duty to follow, and I follow it to the letter."

"I disagree," said Mr. Hemming loudly, jerking Alfred from his reverie momentarily. "I think many of the young ones have a regard for His Grace and are not so easily taken in by this Talbot welp."

"That's as may be, but when I spoke with…"

Alfred nodded, for that appeared to be the only contribution either Mr. Walker or Mr. Hemming required.

He had felt so free on that ride with her. He always did when riding, as though the option still existed to ride off into the distance and never deal with the election again.

If only he had not been forced to leave her for that magistrate meeting—*or perhaps*, Alfred thought, shifting in his seat uncomfortably, *it had been a godsend.*

What would he have said to her next if he had remained in her intoxicating presence?

Alfred knew he was being ridiculous. *The boy's governess!* She was hardly a social equal, not the sort of acquaintance he should be pursuing.

There were plenty of noble or genteel families in the neighborhood, he knew, though he had never forged close bonds with any of them. Away for school, then university, and then as a bloody politician down in London, Alfred knew them by name but not many by face.

And Meredith was...intriguing. She was far more enticing than a governess had any business being, that was for sure.

"Talbot will be crushed!" Mr. Walker was saying passionately, cheeks red and whispers vibrating. "No one takes him as a serious contender. We all know he is only standing to be an irritant!"

"I am not saying His Grace will not win. I merely seek to put him on his guard!" protested Mr. Hemming.

It was getting rather heated in the drawing room, Alfred was vaguely aware, but it was nothing to the heated thoughts within his mind. Then his imagination could run wild, unheeded, and in those quiet moments, Miss Hubert was not wearing those gowns always so proper...

The election! Damnit man, concentrate!

"I think Talbot a brigand, as most do," he said in a rare moment of silence between the two gentlemen. "I believe most in the area know that though 'tis difficult. Does not his sister, Wilhelmina, have a good reputation? He could trade on that."

His remarks had been vague, unprecise, and contributed little, but Mr. Walker looked suitably impressed.

"Just what I have been saying," he said stiffly.

Mr. Hemming looked outraged. "I have said nothing to the contrary! Nay, further, I too have expressed the respectability of his family, if not John Talbot himself, and indeed I think..."

Alfred had managed to say enough to convince them he had been paying attention.

It was a shame, really. One of the few tricks he had actually learned in Westminster: the art of not really paying attention, but giving everyone the impression that you were.

Mr. Walker deserved better. Even Mr. Hemming deserved better, though it was Walker, Alfred knew, who had done far more for him and his family. Poor Mrs. Walker was quite abandoned during these election months.

"Do you not agree, Your Grace?"

Besides, for all his daydreams and pretending, Meredith—Miss Hubert, that was—was a governess. A servant, a servant under his roof, and he would be a fool to even consider attempting to cross that line.

No, he was no cad to put a female servant under his protection in that position.

And damnit all, he knew almost nothing about her. It had not slipped his notice that Miss Hubert was very quick to share ideas but slow indeed to share any information, particularly about herself.

"Your Grace?"

Was she an orphan, then? Alfred had to assume she was. From his little knowledge of these things, any young lady who could read Latin would surely come from a genteel family—and would she not be with them if she had anyone else to support her?

She supported herself, and that must mean she was alone in the world. What other option did she have, other than to be in a stranger's house?

"Your Grace!"

There was a clattering and a shout. Alfred looked up hurriedly. His gaze had fallen to his hands in his lap as he had considered the enigma that was Miss Hubert, but it appeared his inattention had once again been noticed.

Mr. Walker had dropped his notebook onto the table and rubbed his eyes as he faced his duke. "This is getting us nowhere if you cannot concentrate."

Alfred looked hastily at Mr. Hemming, who unusually was nodding in agreement with Mr. Walker. A twist of guilt turned his stomach. He was better than this; he knew he was.

"I really will try my hardest, Mr. Walker, Mr. Hemming," he

said quietly. "It is just...so many other concerns on my mind. I am sure you understand."

Mr. Hemming was nodding appreciatively, as though he could in any way comprehend the responsibilities of a duke.

Mr. Walker, on the other hand, did not look so impressed. "I do not doubt you want to, Your Grace, that is not in question. But today, you evidently cannot!"

Alfred opened his mouth but closed it again.

"Humph." Mr. Walker sat heavily down into an armchair. "I think it best to leave you, Your Grace, but before we depart, there is one decision you must make. The ball."

Alfred blinked. "Ball?"

Ball? He could not remember any of their conversation mentioning a ball.

Mr. Hemming exchanged a glance with Mr. Walker, who said, "Your Grace, it is almost as though you do not wish to be reelected!"

Guilt swam over Alfred's heart. Those were words he had never expected to hear from Mr. Walker.

The fact that this particular Rochdale had absolutely no joy in the prospect was neither here nor there, and he was certainly not going to mention it. Be the first Rochdale who did not hold onto the family seat? *Never!*

"A ball," Alfred said slowly. "A ball—here?"

Mr. Walker nodded. "An excellent way to endear yourself with the nobility and gentry in the area, Your Grace. Think of it as a way to encourage people to think well of you."

Alfred could not help but grin at this statement. "My my, you do not believe they have sufficient reasons yet?"

A flush colored Mr. Walker's cheeks, and that blasted guilt that never seemed too far away bit at Alfred's heart again. He should not tease Mr. Walker, not at his age.

"Yes, yes, a ball," he said hastily. "I will speak to Roberts and Mrs. Martin about it. A ball, I am sure that will be just the thing."

Alfred rose, a genteel signal to the two visitors that their time was over. Mr. Hemming rose quickly and bowed, but Mr. Walker took a little time to get out of his seat—*partly, Alfred thought, to demonstrate that he could just as easily decide to stay if he wanted to.*

"I wish we had discussed a little more this afternoon," he said, not bothering to hide his disappointment. "But there it is. Balls have been used for decades, Your Grace, to encourage people to vote for the incumbent Rochdale. It is the way things have always been done. Your father did it, and his father, and—"

"And I suppose my sons will do it, too," interrupted Alfred with a wry smile. "Fine, fine, a ball. As I said, I will leave the particulars to Mrs. Martin. As to the guest list—"

"I suppose we will have no choice but to invite the Talbots, too," said Mr. Hemming with a frown.

Alfred did balk at this suggestion. "Really? Talbots, in my house? I would rather not have that brigand over my threshold, if at all possible."

It was difficult to say why he had such a poor reaction to John Talbot. If the man had been any different, Alfred would feel guilty for taking such an instant dislike to him all those years ago—but then, perhaps if he had been different, he would not have been so easy to dislike in the first place.

Alfred's knuckles whitened as his hands unconsciously clenched. He had seen that damned man recently, riding past him that day he had accompanied Meredith—Miss Hubert—on a ride.

Talbot had smirked without saying a word, and Alfred had found his dislike for the man increase once again.

"I quite understand your reticence, Your Grace," said Mr. Hemming smoothly, "but it would be bad form indeed not to invite them. To leave them the only ones not invited to a Rochdale Ball? No, it simply would not be done."

Alfred glanced instinctively at Mr. Walker, but the older man was nodding.

"Besides," said Mr. Walker, "we will also invite his sister, Miss Wilhelmina Talbot, and I hear she is quite beautiful."

There was a hint there if Alfred chose to see it. He did not.

"Not now, Walker," he said, forcefully but with goodwill. "A conversation for another day, if we have to have it at all."

"Well, then, we have no more to discuss today," said Mr. Walker with a much better attempt at goodwill. "I will take my leave of you, Your Grace."

He bowed to Alfred, who returned the courtesy, and after Mr. Hemming had also given the room his bow, the two gentlemen started walking to the door.

Mr. Walker paused. "There used to be such a lovely golden pocket watch there, on the side. Where did you put it?"

Alfred glanced over but could not recall there being anything different.

"A gold pocket watch with a long chain," added Mr. Walker helpfully.

"Ah, my father's," said Alfred, the memory surfacing. "Yes, I recall it. You know, I do not know where it is. I imagine Mrs. Martin has taken it for cleaning, an excellent woman."

Mr. Walker nodded, and within another few moments, the door closed behind them, and Alfred was left alone.

In peace. Dropping onto the sofa and closing his eyes with a groan, Alfred sighed with relief and wondered whether he would be able to keep going with this sort of nonsense forever. The election was supposed to be only a month or so away, but it appeared to have taken years to get through the last fortnight.

If only he could escape. He had considered it once before, what felt now like an age ago, but it had been his duty which had kept him here. He would not abandon the family name.

And now...now there was an additional incentive to remain at Rochdale Abbey. *Miss Meredith Hubert.*

Alfred's eyes snapped open. What was he thinking? *This was madness!* She was his half-brother's governess, for pity's sake. The last thing he needed was to fool himself into thinking there was some sort of connection there!

No, he had been cooped up too long, that was his problem. He needed some fresh air. Rising decisively and moving toward the door, Alfred breathed in as he stepped into the hallway. The front door was still open, allowing a pleasant breeze to wash into the house. All he needed to do was distract himself. Do something else. Go somewhere else.

Then all thoughts of Miss Hubert could be rid from his mind.

"Ah, Your Grace." Roberts stepped forward out of nowhere, from what Alfred could tell. "I hoped to catch you."

"Roberts, what can I help you with?"

The butler sighed. "'Tis the post I am afraid, Your Grace."

Alfred blinked. "The post?"

"Yes, your letters from London. They have got as far as Peterborough, I am informed, but do not have sufficient postage to make their way up to Rochdale," said Roberts smoothly. "I require your permission to send three guineas to the Postmaster at—"

"No need," said Alfred hurriedly. *Peterborough, yes, good.* Any excuse to leave Rochdale for a few days and get Miss Hubert out of his head. "I will go myself. That way, I can deal with some of the letters there, reduce the time for replies back to London."

If Roberts was surprised that the Duke of Rochdale was happily taking such an errand upon himself, he did not show it.

"Very good, Your Grace," he said quietly. "I shall inform your valet of your trip. Leaving today?"

Alfred nodded. "Before supper, I think. I'll dine on the road."

The butler bowed and disappeared down into the servants' corridor.

Just a few hours to while away before he would be gone, Meredith out of his mind. It was only after allowing his feet to meander and take them wherever they wanted did Alfred realize the problem. They had brought him, unconsciously, right to the door of the schoolroom.

Christ and all his saints! Was he really so easily led? Was his manhood doing the thinking for him now?

The door to the schoolroom was once again slightly ajar, and Alfred could just make out the boy through the crack. He appeared to be paying close attention to the lesson, which was rather surprising. Alfred and Archibald had always been cut from the same cloth in that regard. Attention was something paid to oneself, not to others.

But look at him now.

"...the hypotenuse, here, you see?"

"Yes, Miss Hubert," said Archibald obediently, writing something down with a scratchy pencil.

Hypotenuse? That was not a word Alfred had heard in a long time.

"And so geometrically, what can we now calculate?"

Archibald looked up from his worksheet. "We...we can calculate the angle of the opposing corner, Miss Hubert."

A noise—a scraping noise of chalk against blackboard. "Well done, Archibald. So, if we take this triangle here and assume that side c is the hypotenuse..."

Alfred's mouth fell open. If he was not mistaken, and it was quite possible that he could be, this was rather advanced mathematics for a child!

Shifting to see whether he could catch a glimpse of the governess who had been intruding on his thoughts overly much that afternoon, he saw her.

Miss Hubert. She was standing by the blackboard covered in triangles of all shapes and sizes. Most of them had numbers scrawled along the lines. It was utter gibberish to him, but Archibald was replying to Miss Hubert as though he could understand all that nonsense!

A sudden warmth rushed over him. *Meredith. He liked her.*

He could not help it! Anyone would like the polite miss who had taken such pains with his brother over the last few weeks and encouraged such a change in him. The warmth spread from his stomach and up his chest, into his heart. He had never expected such impact from the mere hiring of a governess.

But these were not merely the feelings of gratitude for a pleasant and obedient servant, Alfred knew that. These were…well. The feelings a gentleman had for a lady.

And he had to ignore them. The instinct to pull her out of the schoolroom and into his arms, for example, was one best left alone. As was the one where they were alone, and suddenly all her clothes were…

No! If he knew what was good for him, and for Meredith—Miss Hubert—he would stay away from her. For her own good.

"If you would like to join the class, Rochdale, you will need to find a desk."

Alfred started. Meredith had spoken with some amusement and was now smiling—right at him!

The door had evidently moved slightly to reveal him standing outside. *Damn.*

"What are you doing out there, Alfred?" giggled Archibald as Alfred stepped into the room. "Are you joining us for algebra today? I don't think it's very useful for real life or politics, do you? Can I go riding tomorrow?"

Alfred raised an eyebrow at Meredith. The boy had a point, even if he did not wish to admit it. How was she going to explain that one?

Meredith smiled, and Alfred's heart skipped a beat.

"Actually, Master Archibald, I disagree," said the governess. "We have spent the day understanding how to calculate unknowns based on the knowledge we have. When you are in politics, you will experience many unknowns around you. Just like in geometry, you will have to attempt to decode them one at a time to see what you are left with."

Alfred had to work to keep his face straight. The last thing he needed was for Meredith to realize just how impressed he was with her.

Good God, this Governess Bureau really did send the most extraordinary women.

"Oh, I see," said Archibald, nodding. "Thank you, Miss Hubert."

Now Alfred could see the blackboard properly, he was surprised to see how complex the problems were. How was it possible the boy was learning something so challenging? Why, he was not even sure whether he could solve them!

"Listen to your governess," he said quietly, "and finish your sums while I talk with her for a moment."

"Then can I take Polly the pony and—"

"Finish your sums."

Archibald nodded happily and leaned over his worksheet once more as Alfred stepped forward and pulled Meredith into a corner.

What he wouldn't give for the boy to be gone, leaving them alone to—

"Miss Hubert," he said hastily. "May I ask why you are bothering to teach this sort of geometry to an eight-year-old? They are much too challenging!"

Despite his disapproval, Meredith smiled. "Really? Well, do not tell Archibald that. If he doesn't know he is too young to learn it, I find he just learns it."

Alfred smiled, despite himself. Meredith had an entirely different outlook on the world, one he had never encountered before. What was it that they said about different perspectives in politics? That they would always help to win elections?

Win elections…

"Miss Hubert," Alfred found himself saying impulsively, "will you dine with me?"

Meredith looked astonished, and Alfred found his stomach twisting in a most discomforting way. *Was this…embarrassment?*

"Not today," he added hastily, remembering the damned Peterborough visit he had just organized. "I must be away for a few days. But when I get back. Will you dine with me?"

Why did she hesitate? Could she sense his desire, the not altogether innocent reason for his invitation?

"To discuss Archibald, naturally," Alfred added.

Only then did Meredith smile. "Ah, I see. Of course, Your Gr— I mean, Rochdale. I will dine with you."

Alfred smiled. "Good. Good."

It took almost a full minute for him to realize he was now just standing in a corner with the governess, staring at her. After a hurried goodbye to Archibald, Alfred found himself in the corridor, and he leaned against the wall in a daze.

What was this woman doing to him?

CHAPTER NINE

August 26, 1812

M EREDITH EXAMINED HERSELF carefully in the small looking glass Mrs. Martin had deigned to give her after a third request. It was cracked down one side, had some spotting in the corners, and Meredith could only see herself properly if she stepped backward and moved from side to side, seeing half of herself at a time.

It did not matter. Even with this tiny looking glass, she could see she was not sufficiently attired for dinner with a duke.

If only she had thought about it while in London, but it had not even occurred to her that she would need to provide herself with fashion for these occasions.

The Earl and Countess of Marnmouth had not ever stood upon ceremony. They were just as likely to join her and the children in the nursery dining room.

A clean day gown had been sufficient in their dining room. Meredith bit her lip. She had no idea what to expect from this duke, and the one evening gown she owned now appeared pathetically plain.

She smoothed down the silk with her fingertips. Not anything like the best silk to be had, and the style itself was a little out of date. By some miracle, it was almost the right shade of Carmichael blue, which the footmen wore. But what if Alfred considered it an attempt to impress in a rather coquettish manner?

And what if he invited her to dine again? She could not simply wear the same gown over and over again; he would notice!

This was a mistake. She should never have accepted his invitation.

"Miss Hubert, will you dine with me?"

A smile crept over Meredith's face. She was thinking about this as though it were some sort of punishment. As though she was being forced to dine with him.

As though spending time alone with the handsome Duke of Rochdale was something to avoid.

Meredith swallowed down those thoughts and tried to ensure her sleeves were equally smooth. If only she had thought to purchase an evening gown of the latest fashion while in London. She doubted Rochdale Town had yet to see the style of gown she was wearing now, they were likely so behind with the fashions.

But what did it matter? As Meredith stepped out of the looking glass' reflection and put on the only earbobs she owned, she told herself calmly she was being ridiculous.

She had never come out into society—she had never been a part of society to begin with. Getting herself into a state about this dinner was foolish. It was quite natural for a master and his governess to discuss the charges under her care. Really, it should have occurred in the first few weeks, not after a month of service.

Meredith smiled. She had dined with the Countess of Marnmouth once a week to discuss the young Egertons. This was much the same as that.

Except it wasn't. Because she wasn't about to dine with a woman in her early forties about her children. She was dining with a gentleman who was far more handsome than any other she had known, whose jaw tightened when he thought she was not looking, who made her feel...

Meredith straightened up and stared at herself in the looking glass. A woman with dark hair and no other beauty stared back.

She sighed. *This was all wrong.* Her employer wished to know more about Archibald's education, and that was all.

"May I ask why you are bothering to teach this sort of geometry to an eight-year-old? They are much too challenging!"

Meredith recalled the way Alfred had looked in that moment. Possessive. Intrigued. As though he wished to...

"No!" Meredith found she had spoken aloud.

No, this was ridiculous. She was seeing something that wasn't there; why, she had no idea. She could never...she would not...

That was not a thing a young lady does.

She shivered. Even so. She did not need to be a woman of the world to know what a gentleman was thinking when he...when he looked at a woman like that. It was no secret, then, that Alfred Carmichael admired her.

Was it awful if she was pleased? If she found herself intrigued by the thought that she warmed him?

Meredith bit her lip again and looked away from the looking glass around her small bedchamber. She was only here because she could teach because she was good with children. If she were to risk that...if she was to put herself in a position of scandal...

She was not here to land a husband. Miss Clarke had very strict rules about such things—society had very strict rules about such things!

Meredith took a deep breath. She was here to teach Archibald. That was all.

And when she was no longer needed, when Archibald had learned all from her curriculum and probably a little more, she would return to London and the Governess Bureau and her next assignment.

Nowhere was permanent. Nowhere was home. And she would not ruin the precarious respectability that she had earned, despite her past, for a man.

After one more glance into the looking glass, she stepped out of her bedchamber. As she walked down the corridor, Meredith saw light spilling out from one room. Archibald's. It snapped shut as she approached.

Meredith smiled and knocked gently on the door. There was a pause, a scuffle, and then a small voice spoke.

"Come in."

She opened the door and saw Archibald seated on the other side of the room with a book in his hand and chest heaving. He had obviously run over from the door.

Meredith smiled. "I wished to say good night before I went down for dinner. I hope you do not mind me disturbing you."

Archibald shook his head. "I…I wanted to see what you were wearing. My mother died when I was born. I have never seen a lady dress for dinner before."

Meredith's eyes widened as she sat on the end of Archibald's bed. "Never? Your brother does not entertain the gentlefolk of Rochdale?"

It did not seem possible. What else was a duke doing all the time, when not running for elections, if not hosting and entertaining?

"A few times," said Archibald quietly, putting his book down. "But not often. Not here, anyway. I suppose all members of Parliament have dinners all the time in London. Your gown is very pretty."

Only a child who had never seen a lady dress for such an occasion could consider the old gown she had put on as pretty!

"I hear there is a ball in the next few weeks," she said instead. "Is that true?"

Archibald nodded, rubbing his tired eyes.

"Well," said Meredith quietly. "Why don't I ask your brother whether you can attend? Even just sitting in the corner and watching all the ladies and gentlemen in their finery would be something exciting, wouldn't it?"

The child's eyes grew wide. "Really? You think Alfred will

permit it? Can I go riding tomorrow with both of you?"

Meredith nodded. "Let's focus on the ball, first of all. I will ensure it. If I offer to sit with you to keep you under control—"

"I can keep myself under—"

"—then I am sure he will agree," continued Meredith with a smile. "Time for bed."

Archibald rose and quickly hugged her before clambering into bed. "I hope you have a nice dinner, Miss Hubert."

Meredith's smile broadened. You never really knew what you were going to be faced with when one was a governess. The children you cared for could be monstrous—or, in this case, absolutely delightful.

It was evident from his rapid and rather clumsy hug that embraces were not something Archibald was used to. It broke her heart.

A gong sounded downstairs.

"There, I will be late if I do not go down," said Meredith wistfully. In a way, she would rather stay here. Archibald was, by far, much the easier Carmichael brother to deal with.

"Say hello to Alfred for me," came the sleepy reply.

Archibald's eyes had already closed by the time Meredith had walked across the room. He was such a precious child. It was a privilege to care for him.

All her nerves had gone. Archibald had reminded her precisely why she was here. As Meredith swept downstairs, she knew what this dinner was for: talking about Archibald as much as possible.

That child had lost his parents. He did not even know what a lady's evening gown looked like, for goodness sake! He needed his brother, and Meredith was going to ensure Alfred knew it.

At least, that was what she had intended. Unfortunately, like all good intentions, they were swept away within a moment as she reached the bottom of the staircase and saw Alfred.

Something painful lurched in her stomach. Alfred was wearing a formal frockcoat, his silk waistcoat the precise color of her gown—that Carmichael blue again—and his cravat matched. He was standing tall, looking into the distance. He was waiting for her.

He had never looked so handsome, his appearance only improving as he smiled.

"Miss Hubert."

You will control yourself, Meredith told herself silently. You are here to give a report of yourself and your pupil and encourage the elder brother to pay more attention to the younger. That was all.

That was all she would permit, anyway, for she simply could not allow the duke anymore of herself. That was not who she was.

"Your Grace," she said. It had been a mistake to call him Rochdale. It had created...well, not exactly friendship between them.

There was too much fire in his eyes to be called friendship.

"I thought I would meet you here and take you into the dining room," he said with a smile, offering his arm.

Meredith looked at it blankly. This was not what she had expected. All these good manners...where was the gruff and businesslike duke she knew?

Well, not entirely. She had seen a different side of Alfred Carmichael on their ride together, albeit briefly. How was she supposed to know which was the real duke and which was that trotted out for ceremony?

"Miss Hubert?"

Meredith collected herself. "Yes—yes! Thank you, Your Grace, that is most kind."

She tried not to pay any attention to the heady sensations threatening to overwhelm her as she took the duke's arm. He was warm, strong. He held her close as they stepped down the corridor toward the dining room on the other side of the house.

She swallowed. This tension she felt whenever she was near him, it was not natural. Why was she so much warmer in his presence? She should say something. *But what?* What words could possibly explain the rush of emotions stirred within her if she could not understand them herself?

Thankfully, it was a short walk to the dining room, and a footman opened the door.

"Here," said Alfred quietly, helping her into a chair at one end of the long dining table.

There. She had managed it, the most difficult part of the evening. Now Alfred would step away from her, step away from the intensity of whatever it was between them, and she would be permitted to collect herself.

But instead of moving to the other end of the table, Alfred sat down beside her. *So close she could reach out and touch him.*

Meredith shivered and tried immediately to put that thought out of her mind. She was being foolish again, showing her ignorance of the nobility. It was madness to think two people could have a rational conversation seated at opposite ends of a table like this! Alfred—the duke wanted to know how his brother was doing, and for that, they would need to converse.

There was nothing more to be read into it, Meredith was sure, and she was a wanton woman indeed for even thinking there was any more to it!

"Archibald says hello," she said in a quiet voice, hoping to immediately bring some clarity and focus to their conversation.

It did not help. Alfred smiled at the mention of his brother's name, and something in Meredith's heart fluttered.

"I hope my brother is not forcing you to become his messenger," said Alfred with a wry smile as footmen stepped in silently bringing in their food.

Meredith picked up her fork, hardly knowing what she was doing. *She had to keep this business.* She was a governess, not a lady to be courted or dazzled. If Alfred was charming, that was because he was a gentleman! He was not attempting to impress her, and she would be a fool indeed to allow his courtesies to go to her head!

"Nothing of the sort," she said lightly, picking at her food.

"But I do believe it would be good for him to be more involved in your life. The ball, for example. He should attend."

She had not considered it a particularly dramatic message, but Alfred coughed and took a hasty gulp of the red wine poured for him by a passing footman.

"Ball?" he said eventually, thumping his chest. "I admit myself surprised he knew of such a thing—or you, for that matter."

Meredith laughed. "Rochdale—Your Grace, you think anything can be kept secret in a house like this? You think we do not all precisely know what plans Mr. Walker has for you?"

She winked at Miles, the footman who stood behind the duke, who stifled a laugh very poorly and was overcome with a coughing fit.

Alfred turned to stare at the unfortunate footman, who pinked and stood even straighter. When he turned back to Meredith, she was eating innocently.

"Funny," he said dryly. "I usually spend so much time in London, so little time here in my actual home, that I forget my servants know the place better than I do. Thank you, Miles. You may go."

Miles bowed low and left the room, still coughing. Meredith tried not to smile.

This was what she had missed, she thought silently. *Good conversation.* The earl and countess were both witty, and though Mrs. Martin permitted herself an occasional conversation, it was nothing like this.

"Roberts, do me a favor, would you," said the duke quietly, and the butler appeared at his shoulder immediately. "I know we prefer service à la russe in this house, but would you ask Cook whether, just for this evening, we can go back to service à la française?"

"Very good, Your Grace," said Roberts quietly before disappearing.

Meredith pinked and hoped he would not notice. This was not what she had expected. Service à la russe, or service in the

Russian style, was far more vogue in London and Paris these days; each course brought out one at a time by footmen who served onto guests' plates.

Service à la française was considered so much more old-fashioned, even if she did prefer it. All the courses out at once, covering the table, so the diners could pick and choose what they wanted at their own leisure.

But why did the duke wish to do that…if not to remove all servants from the room?

Other servants, Meredith reminded herself sternly. *Do not forget your place in all this, my girl. This was not about you. You are not special.*

Roberts had appeared again. "Cook says it would be her honor, Your Grace, and the footmen are bringing up the food now—ah, here they are."

Meredith blinked. She had not expected…well, all this. A dinner on a Wednesday was not supposed to be so grand, was it? Or were these twenty-odd platters, some piled high with sugar glazing, some adorned with flowers, what a duke always ate, even when alone?

"Thank you, Roberts, Miles, Johns, you may all go," said Alfred with a wave of his hand.

Within a moment, Meredith was left alone with the Duke of Rochdale and more food than she believed possible to fit on a table.

"There," said the duke quietly. "Now, we will not be disturbed."

Why could she not prevent her cheeks from pinking? There was nothing suggestive in there, nothing to indicate that she must be careful with her innocence. This was just a dinner.

Just a dinner.

"Please, help yourself and do not worry about mixing courses. I always preferred the French style anyway," said Alfred with a smile. "Now, talk to me about geography."

Meredith blinked. *She could not have possibly heard that correct-*

ly, could she?

"G-Geography?" she stammered as Alfred added some roast potatoes to his plate.

He nodded. "Yes, geography. What areas of geography will you be teaching Archibald in the coming weeks, particularly as we are now at war in the Americas?"

Meredith's eyes widened, and she dropped her gaze to avoid his own. Her plate was empty. Helping herself to some chicken, peas, and a funny-looking type of pie she did not recognize, Meredith could no longer avoid the question.

"I admit myself impressed," she said lightly. "I do not know many fathers—apologies, guardians, who would think of updating the curriculum."

"Well, what is the point of politicians," said Alfred bracingly, "if we cannot redraw the map a few times in our careers?"

Meredith laughed automatically. *Was that not the point of servants, to laugh at the jokes of one's masters?*

But the duke merely looked weary. "I did not intend it to be a joke, but I can see the humor."

Meredith stopped smiling and took a mouthful of the delicious food.

"'Tis strange," he said quietly. "The more time I spend around you, the more I see Archie—Master Archibald come alive. It is...intoxicating."

Meredith swallowed her food and looked at him nervously. He was not eating, and his hands...his hands were on the table, mere inches from hers, his lingering gaze warming her.

She had to get a grip of herself—of this conversation.

"Thank you," she said. "The best praise at all for a governess is praise of her pupil."

"You do not look for praise for yourself?"

Meredith took another mouthful and swallowed it before allowing herself to reply. She had to think. She couldn't just speak the first words that came into her head. That was for children, not governesses.

For it felt as though they were dancing into dangerous territory...but she could not help herself. She had to speak her mind;
she always had.

*It had been one of those qualities that had almost got her into trou-
ble last time...*

"Perhaps, at times," she said honestly, and she saw Alfred's
eyes glitter. "But when one has this station in life, one has to
leave behind the idea that one's life will have me at the center."

Meredith hoped he would understand the subtle hint to her
station. She was a governess, his brother's governess. Any
flirtation had to disappear.

Alfred nodded, his eyes fixed on her. Meredith's stomach
lurched. She was having an intimate dinner with the Duke of
Rochdale. *How had she managed to get herself into this situation?*

"In a way, I understand," he said quietly. "A politician is
meant to think of others, rather than oneself. I do not pretend it is
always easy. I think man's first inherent state is to think of
himself, to seek protection and betterment for one's own. I
suppose I hope I have, over time, risen above it."

Meredith placed her fork down and leaned in unconsciously.
It was the first real conversation she had had since arriving at
Rochdale Abbey. Mrs. Martin was civil most of the time, and the
butler, when he encountered her, was aloof but polite. The maids
held her in awe for some reason, and the footmen...well, she
knew better than to chatter with them.

This was different. This conversation was real, with depth.
He made her feel alive.

She glanced at her plate. Her food was almost entirely gone.
She had barely tasted it, her senses consumed with Alfred.

"Yet that suggests a tribalism I do not believe we still have
here in England," said Alfred nonchalantly.

Meredith smiled.

"Ah, a smile! Come now, Miss Hubert, you must explain that
to me."

There was a playful look on his face Meredith had never seen before, and she dissembled rather than explain it. "Oh, no, it was just a thought, nothing more."

The duke placed his knife and fork down. "And I request that you share it."

Meredith's heart fluttered. *What harm could it do?* "I was merely thinking that it is strange for a member of Parliament, a gentleman whose sole purpose in government is to represent a small part of England—a tribe, if you will—to disbelieve in tribalism."

Alfred stared for a moment and then chuckled, shaking his head. "I should never have doubted you, Miss Hubert."

Why did she long to have her first name on his lips? Hubert had been the name she chose, an opportunity to leave behind the ignominy of her family. Meredith was her true name, and to hear nothing but falseness from his mouth when he addressed her...it pained her more than she could have expected.

"Here, have some pudding," said the duke, oblivious to the thoughts running through her mind. "And then tell me, are you lonely here?"

Meredith had been taking a sip of wine, a luxury indeed. She managed not to splutter and did not spill a drop onto the white linen tablecloth.

Lonely? In his house? What on earth did the duke mean by asking such a thing? To be sure, if there had been a mistress in the house, it would have been a perfectly innocent question from her.

But from him, those eyes and the way he looked at her.

"Sometimes," she found herself admitting. "But I am very busy, Your Grace. Archibald and his education take up much of my time, and I have use of your library and my horse. I...I enjoy riding."

"Yes, but...but is it enough?"

As he spoke those words, he moved his hand forward as though to take hers. Meredith almost lunged for the platter of pudding to avoid him.

"My word, what a delightful dessert. I do not think I've had *gimblettes de fleurs d'orange* in ages," she gabbled.

By the time she had helped herself to a portion and replaced the platter, Alfred's hands had gone.

Meredith attempted to control her breathing. *He was being kind.* She was reading far too much into this innocent dinner, so much that she was making a fool of herself.

She could not stay any longer in this dining room. She was not to be trusted, that had been proven, and by the looks of it, neither could he. *Alfred.*

The longer she was here, the more her heart wanted her to rebel and say something that she would regret...eventually.

Meredith rose from her seat, and Alfred got up hastily. "I am so sorry, Your Grace, I am rather tired. I think I will retire upstairs and go to—"

"I wish you would not," said Alfred in a low voice. "I would encourage you to stay. I have not requested cheese and port yet, and there is much I would like to discuss with you."

Meredith swallowed. His intoxicating presence was building, and she was finding it difficult to remember why she had wished to leave. There was such honesty in his eyes and yet such desire, too. *Could one hold back the other? Was it worth the risk to find out?*

"I think I have stayed long enough," she said quietly.

Their eyes met, and Meredith almost gasped at the intensity of that look. *He knew.* He knew she found him to be most attractive, and she could see what he wanted from her.

She had to get out of this room.

"Thank you for a lovely dinner," she said quietly, stepping away from the table.

She was not quick enough. Alfred had mirrored her, moving quickly to the door and reaching it before her, thanks to his tall stride.

"Allow me," he said quietly.

Meredith nodded, trying not to look into his eyes. All she had to do was get out of the dining room.

Easier said than done. The duke had not opened the door wide, and as she moved forward to step through, he did not move away or widen it for her. Meredith's heart fluttered as she stepped closer. They were but inches away now.

Meredith could not stop herself. She paused, right before him, their noses almost touching. *What was she doing?*

All she knew was that she wanted to wait, in this perfect moment, when she could pretend that there was something real between them. That she was not merely a governess, but a lady who had been invited to dinner and was now going to test the limits of the attraction that they most certainly shared.

It would be easy, wonderful to allow herself to give in to temptation. She watched him swallow, watched him lean closer, so that she would only have to lean upward, and then their lips would meet.

Meredith stepped through the door and murmured, "Good night, Your Grace."

CHAPTER TEN

August 28, 1812

"Y̶OUR GRACE? YOUR Grace, can you hear me?"

Alfred blinked. This was starting to become a bad habit, but it was hardly his fault. He had been concentrating on what his steward had been saying as they rode slowly along the boundary between his land and the common land, but then...

He looked around. They were at least three miles from where he last remembered discussing the need for fencing. They were nearer the Johnsons' farm now, weren't they?

How had they managed to get here?

Riley, his steward, smiled bemusedly. "Are you feeling quite well, Your Grace?"

Alfred sighed heavily. His steward was a good man—another man who came from a long line of men who served the Rochdales. Why was he so incapable of treating them with the respect they deserved? *Walker, Riley...*

He needed to pay attention. *He needed to stop thinking about...*

"Quite well, I thank you," he said, heart heavy and hands patting the neck of his horse, Parker. "To tell the truth, Riley, I have not been listening. I am sorry. I have no excuse and will therefore not attempt one."

Despite his rather blunt words, Riley smiled. A man in the prime of his life, double Alfred's age and with far more experience with the land than Alfred would ever have, he was too accustomed to his master's physical absences to be upset about his mental ones.

"Ah, 'tis no bother," he said easily, pulling his stocky horse closer to his master's. "I will admit, for some reason, I did not think that the change in drainage on the outer fields had much of an interest to you."

Though the man spoke with a light, unconcerned tone, his words only served to make Alfred feel even more guilty. *The land was his.* Carmichael land. Rochdale land. It had grown him as surely as any other parent, and not only did he own it, but he represented it in the highest house in the country.

The least he could do was pay attention when someone was telling him how to take care of it.

But estate management was never something he was particularly skilled at. He had never taken to crop rotations and herd management as his father had.

Alfred smiled. One of his favorite memories of his father was the two of them stomping about the moors, his father in thigh-high boots, eyes sharp, looking for a lost lamb that had meandered away from its mother.

Every farmer and his daughter had been out looking for it. But it had been the Duke of Rochdale of the time who had found it.

Alfred's smile faded. He had always known he had never measured up to his father, not really. It was a sad day when it was so obvious.

But today was not the day to attempt to find a new vigor and passion for the way his estate was managed. Not when he had someone like Riley, so capable, in charge. Not with all his thoughts on the damned election and how it grew ever closer, inching forward like a tiger.

Not when two days ago, all that passion had been directed at a rather sensual governess, who had almost given in to temptation and kissed him.

Meredith.

Alfred swallowed. "Right then, lead on, Riley. Where to next?"

Meredith Hubert. What a temptress she was, even as a governess in that straitlaced gown.

Just the mere memory of their conversation was enough to set him alight. If only he had been braver. If she had not pulled away...if he had closed the gap between them as she had been leaving...

Alfred swallowed, his heart rate raised partly due to the effort of keeping up with Riley and partly from the remembrance of Meredith's warm body so close to his own.

In a way, it was a relief they had not kissed. Then what would he have done?

Paid her off probably. Alfred shook his head. Then he would have no governess for Archibald, and the boy would be angry, go wild, and get himself into trouble again. Bring the Rochdale name into disrepute again.

Lose him the election.

It would never do to get that close to a servant—*too close.* As Alfred and Riley jumped a stile over into the next field, Alfred knew that was precisely where the trouble came from. There were ladies one courted and eventually married, and there were women who served you.

Miss Hubert served him, served him well. Better than he could have imagined.

He would not risk that. *He would not risk losing her.*

"I suppose when you have been elected again, Your Grace," said Riley comfortably as they slowed to a trot, "official like, you will be back in London for most of the year."

Alfred nodded.

"Ah, London," said the steward wistfully. "What a sight it

must be."

Alfred glanced at him as they meandered around a field, careful not to disturb the hay that was drying. It could not be plainer that Riley wished to be in London almost as much as he wished to avoid it.

"You are not missing much," he said dryly.

It was hard to imagine why anyone would wish to spend any amount of time in the capital—except, of course, that to most of Rochdale, it was faraway and more enticing.

Alfred could not believe anyone, once they had experienced both Rochdale and London, would ever prefer the latter. London was dirty, smelly, overcrowded, and one never managed to see one's friends, even when they were in town.

Give me clean country air and a sense of duty to one's neighbors any day, thought Alfred.

The grass was always greener. He was called back to London by duty, honor, and his position. Anyone who had no choice but to stay on Rochdale land was desperate to leave it.

"I may not win, you know," he added.

Riley waved away his words. "Of course you will, Your Grace. There is always a Carmichael as the Rochdale member of Parliament."

They rode on in silence, Alfred wondering just what would happen to the people of Rochdale if he did not become a member of Parliament. The end of the world, it appeared.

All he could do was walk down the steps laid out for him. Follow the chain of events, nod at the right time, and hope he could find some fun along the way.

"Good night, Your Grace."

Alfred's jaw tightened. If he could be so brave as to have fun with Miss Meredith Hubert...

He shivered, and Parker whinnied beneath him at the sudden movement. Alfred patted his steed's neck reassuringly as they moved into another field, Riley saying something about the way the drainage fell in this field.

Alfred could not take it in. His thoughts were entirely overwhelmed by thoughts of Meredith. Her beauty. The way she smiled when she thought she had figured him out. The moment they had almost kissed, kept apart by nothing but their determination not to permit themselves that one final pleasure.

"…but we decided against it in the end, the Johnsons weren't happy," Riley was saying, though what the Johnsons had not been happy about, Alfred could not tell. "And so in the end, we had to compromise and…"

Alfred nodded. Nods seemed all that was required—except when it came to Meredith.

"I said, can you hear me?"

Alfred jerked to attention, making poor Parker take a discomforting step to the left. Getting his horse under control was easy, but facing up to the rather disappointed face of his steward was more difficult.

"I am sorry, Riley," Alfred apologized. "I just…well, as I said. Head not in it today."

Riley shook his head with a smile. "Aye, you did, Your Grace. Mayhaps I should have listened to you, then."

It was a sorry day indeed when a steward was getting the better of him. Here he was, almost thirty years of education and privilege, and yet it couldn't prevent him from making a complete ass of himself.

"I think we can safely say I am not in the right frame of mind for this," Alfred said heavily. "Again, my apologies. Can we go around the estate another day—tomorrow, perhaps?"

The steward hesitated, and Alfred felt a rather strange sensation wash over him. A tangible reminder that being the master of a great estate put him in a rather strange position—but none so strange as those who served him.

"Yes, of course," said Riley with a slightly constrained smile. "Just let me know what time, and I will meet you at Rochdale Abbey. Will you away home, now?"

Alfred sighed. "I am not sure I would be much use there

either. Come tomorrow at whatever time suits you, Riley. There is no point in me getting in the way of your day merely because of my faults. Good day."

He watched his steward canter off in the direction of his homestead and turned Parker toward the abbey. The longer he was out here, doing nothing, the better.

And he did feel better. When left alone to his thoughts, all he wanted in the first place, a weight lifted from his chest that he did not even realize there. He could disappear here, spend hours riding Parker around the county, and only return home when he wished to be the duke again.

"Archibald and his education take up much of my time, and I have use of your library and my horse. I...I enjoy riding."

Damn. What had that been? Five minutes without thinking of Miss Hubert?

Alfred shook his head irritably. He should never have attempted to kiss her; it had been madness to even consider it. The temptation had been great, but he was supposed to be a gentleman.

If Meredith had closed the gap between them, there was no knowing what he would have done. How much he would have taken from her if she had been willing to give it.

Christ alive, to hear his name cried out from her lips...

Alfred swallowed. She was intoxicating in a way he had never known before. Oh, he had known women. Had bedded a few in London; girls with no names he had picked off the street after particularly hard days. He had paid them well, and they had done their duty.

He had known ladies. Miss Wilhelmina Talbot was not the only lady of good fortune and standing in the Duchy of Rochdale, and Alfred had been to a few weekend parties.

But Miss Meredith Hubert. She was something entirely different. There was something about her...

Great talents, that was what he had asked for, and by God, he had received it. Archibald was a new boy. The way she had helped him with his husting's speech...

"*This is also the art of speech-making, Mr. Walker, and something I have both studied and taught. Please let me work.*"

If only she knew just what to do in the bedroom, too...

Alfred coughed as though that would clear the thought from his head. A governess of many talents.

"Get a grip on yourself," Alfred muttered as he and Parker leapt over a stile and onto Rochdale Abbey parkland.

It was only then he noticed there was another rider ahead of him. *These damn trespassers; they were all over the place now.* It was impossible to get rid of them. One could put up as many fences as you wanted, but it did not matter.

If Riley were here, he would have sent the man to say something. Alfred sighed. As he was on his own, and it was his damned land, after all, he supposed he had better do it.

The rider had dismounted and was looking at the scenery. Alfred couldn't blame them. It was a beautiful part of the parkland, but that did not give them the right to treat his home like their own personal view!

"Come on, Parker," he muttered, nudging his horse toward the intruder.

It was only as he got closer that he realized it was not a rider.

Well, it was. But it was also Meredith.

And she was not merely looking at the scenery. As Alfred approached, he realized there was something wrong with her horse.

"Hello," he said in a half-strangled voice.

Meredith turned to see who had spoken to her and blushed. Alfred felt his body surge with a sensation of power and importance.

So, she blushed to see him. That was worth knowing.

What was she thinking? Was she remembering the moment they had almost kissed? The memory did not leave his mind, almost overwhelming his view of her.

"Are you quite alright, Miss Hubert?"

"I am perfectly fine," she said shortly. "'Tis Beauty. She has thrown a shoe, and I have no wish to force her all the way back to the stable with me on her back. I was about to start the walk."

Alfred's mouth fell open. "But—but Meredith, it is near seven miles to the stables!"

She said nothing about his use of her first name, for which he was grateful. *He would have to be careful he did not do that again.*

"A few miles will not hurt me, Your Grace," she said. "Besides, I am a governess. I am made of iron!"

"Really? That is news to me. You did not appear made of iron when we…"

Christ alive, he almost said the words aloud. He would need to get a hold of himself if he was not going to embarrass himself entirely.

It was so delightful to see the way she blushed.

Whatever she was thinking, however, she did not mention the kiss that never was.

"A good, long walk will do me good," she said bracingly. "I would never permit Beauty to carry me if that is what you are suggesting."

"No, of course not, I am no brute to make a lame horse carry a person's weight—but this is ridiculous. Why not ride back with me?"

Meredith's eyes flickered between her horse and his own. Then her gaze met his, full of curiosity and more than a little heat.

Alfred swallowed. It had been an offer he would have made to any lady in distress, but having just made it to a woman who made him…

Well. The idea of her behind him, clinging onto his waist as he rode her to safety…

"I do not think that is a good idea," the governess said quietly.

Alfred nodded. She was right. She was always right. Had it not been Meredith who had pulled her hand away from his, who had refused to take the kiss offered to her?

Yes, she was far too sensible for any of that nonsense.

Meredith was still smiling. "I could always take your horse, Your Grace, and you could walk back."

"I thought I told you to call me Rochdale," said Alfred, moving his horse closer.

"If I do, will you lend me your horse?"

Alfred laughed before he realized she wasn't joking. *She really thought—she believed she could control Parker?*

"I am willing to be of service," he said seriously, "and you are a skilled horsewoman. I noticed that on our ride. But...Meredith, you could not control Parker. Few people can. He was bred for loyalty. Only I can control him, really."

Meredith arched an eyebrow and patted her horse's flank gently. "Oh, I don't know."

In that very slow and sultry way that ladies seemed to be taught at the age of eighteen, Meredith walked slowly over to Alfred, still atop his horse.

Alfred swallowed and kept a tight grip on the reins. Parker did not really like anyone, as many of the stable hands could attest. When it came to tacking Parker, Alfred usually did it himself. It was safer that way.

But as Meredith grew closer, she stopped about six feet away. Parker turned his head, staring with obvious disdain.

And then not so obvious. Meredith moved slowly toward the beast, breathing steadily out of her mouth, eyes never leaving him. Alfred watched, enchanted. What on earth was she doing?

She reached Parker and blew very softly on his nose. Parker took a step backward hesitantly, something Alfred had never seen him do before.

Meredith did not move. She waited, still blowing slowly out of her mouth. Alfred had a job not to allow his gaze to meander down, below her neck, to...

Well.

Parker whinnied softly and then stepped forward again, closer to Meredith. He nudged her until Meredith slowly raised a hand

and stroked his nose.

She was an enchantress. What had she done to Parker? And perhaps more importantly, was she doing the same to him? Was this why he could not stay away from her, why every step he took seemed to be just another step that led him to her?

"How...how did you do that?" Alfred breathed, almost afraid to break the moment.

Meredith laughed softly and patted Parker on the side of his neck. "I do not know what you were so worried about, Your Grace. Parker and I get along fine."

"But—that should not be possible! Parker does not like people!"

"But I like Parker," said Meredith simply, scratching his nose. "I like horses and horses like me. More than people, sometimes. In both directions. Besides, you're just a big softy, aren't you, Parker?"

Parker took another step closer. Meredith laughed and scratched him between the ears.

Alfred could not understand what had just happened. Where had this woman come from?

Finally, he found his voice again. "You really are a governess of great talents."

Meredith smiled, sunlight shining on her hair. "Yes, but that does not help in our current situation. Unless you are happy to walk back, of course."

Alfred was tempted to say he would walk back with her, though that would make no sense. Every part of him was drawn to her, and a few hours in her company, out here in the wilderness...

Who knew what might happen?

It was that damned voice of reason he had never quite been able to shrug, which reminded him of another commitment, however. Pulling out his pocket watch from his waistcoat, Alfred glanced at it.

"I am supposed to be in an election meeting at the abbey in

twenty minutes," he said ruefully.

Meredith sighed and smiled at Parker. "As I said, I am happy to walk back. It will be an excellent opportunity for me to stretch my legs, and I am sure Archibald will not suffer for having an afternoon off."

She turned away and started walking back to her horse. Alfred could not bear the sense of loss that overwhelmed him as she walked away.

"Wait!"

Meredith paused and turned, her gown displaying her figure in a most distracting way.

Alfred swallowed. "Let...let me take you. You can ride behind me. We will tie up Beauty to ensure she does not wander off. A stable lad can come and retrieve her."

"It was one dinner," she said softly. "One dinner, and we almost..."

She did not appear able to finish the sentence, but Alfred knew what she meant. If one dinner almost led to a clandestine kiss, what would such close proximity do to them? It was all he could do not to dismount and kiss her right now.

"I know I should not have placed you in that position," said Alfred quietly.

"You didn't. Not alone."

"I was sore tempted," admitted Alfred with a laugh.

Meredith laughed with him, softly, like falling rain. "I think...well. Keeping our distance from each other will help solve that. It will be easy soon."

Alfred could not imagine a world in which it would be easy. "Soon?"

She nodded. "You have an election to win, Your Grace. Once you are a member of Parliament again, you will be in London. We will hardly see each other."

It sounded like a death sentence to Alfred's ears. "You know better than anyone how little I want to win."

Meredith hesitated for a moment and then stepped toward

him. She reached up and covered his hand, still tight around Parker's reins, with hers.

"I know," she whispered.

It was an intoxicating moment. Alfred felt more connected to her then, governess as she was, servant as she was, than anyone else in the world. The rest of Rochdale faded away, leaving only them. Her eyes did not leave him, and her hand—oh God, it was warm and soft, and if anything like the rest of her, then absolutely everything he wanted.

And then she let go. "I am worried about Beauty, to tell the truth. But I suppose there is nothing for it. The longer I leave her, the more pain she is in. So...so thank you, Your Grace. I would appreciate the ride."

Alfred's jaw dropped, causing him, he was sure, to look the height of foolishness. He could hardly believe it.

"Right," he said blankly and then recalling his senses. "Right. If you can tie up Beauty there to the fence, we can have a man back with her in half an hour."

He watched Meredith carefully tie up Beauty but not, as he had suggested, by the fence but instead within the woodland.

"Fewer people will see her there," she said by way of explanation. "Beauty is my most treasured possession—more friend than possession. I would never forgive myself if someone took her."

Alfred nodded and held out an arm. *This was it.* This was the moment he had wanted, from the moment he had seen her, all fury and pent-up irritation, in the drawing room.

He almost groaned aloud to have her pressed up against him as she stepped onto Parker's back. *Oh, Christ, but she was warm.* She smelled wonderful, all honey and dew, like a summer's morning.

This was wrong, and he should never have suggested it, but it was impossible to ask her to dismount now. Not now, he had ten, perhaps fifteen minutes of riding with her.

"I am ready," came her gentle voice, and Alfred started. He had become so lost in his thoughts that he had barely remembered why she was up on Parker with him in the first place.

"Right," he said hastily. "Hold tight."

Never before had fifteen minutes departed so quickly. Meredith's obvious concern for her horse forced Alfred forward faster, bringing them closer to sending someone back for the mare—but sadly, closer to the moment when she would dismount and leave his presence.

"Woah there, Parker," said Alfred quietly as they cantered quickly into the stable yard. There was no one there. All hands must have been out with some of the farmers again, getting the last of the harvest in.

"Steady, Parker," he said, bringing the horse to a stop and then quickly dismounting, hating the distance he was putting between himself and Meredith. "Here."

He held out his hand for Meredith to take, to aid her in her dismount. She looked at him with suspicious eyes, only taking his hand hesitantly after it was clear he was not going to move Parker to a block.

"Thank you," she said softly.

Alfred moved before he was even conscious of it. As Meredith slipped down the side of Parker, Alfred moved, so she was pinned between his body and that of his horse.

"Alfred!"

It was her use of his name that did it. That was what he told himself afterward, at the very least. With Meredith in his arms and no one about to censure them, Alfred pulled her tightly to him.

"This is a bad idea," Meredith whispered. Her eyes searched his for a response, as though asking him to take responsibility for his actions, but she did not pull away.

Alfred smiled. "I know."

The kiss started slowly. Alfred did not wish to take too much from her, always seeking a willing partner—but the passion, the furious passion Meredith poured back to him was as though a dam had finally been breached.

Christ, it was wonderful. Her hands in his hair, his heart pounding, Alfred teased her lips until she gave him entrance and ravished her mouth, worshiping her.

And then it was over. Meredith had slipped through his fingers, out of his arms, and toward the stables.

"I'll find a temporary shoe," she said breathlessly, her hair a mess and her cheeks red. "And take another steed out to her."

Alfred could barely stand, let alone talk. Leaning against Parker, he managed, "Shoe? Y-You're going to shoe Beauty?"

Meredith flashed him a smile. "Governess of great talents, did I not say?"

CHAPTER ELEVEN

September 4, 1812

> *I have found during my time in the Rochdale house that Archibald has become a far more studious child, particularly in mathematics and the history of the Tudor monarchs. In accordance with the guidelines established by the Governess Bureau, I have sought ways of rewarding my pupil without spoiling him (NB: horse riding and future attendance at family events), which have been approved by the master, Alfred Carmichael, Duke of Rochdale*

MEREDITH LOOKED DOWN at her report as a prickle of heat seared her face. Even writing his name felt strange. As though she had transgressed some line.

Leaning back in her chair, Meredith examined the report she was writing for Miss Clarke. It was customary—no, expected that a governess would write monthly reports for Miss Clarke, so the proprietress of the Governess Bureau could be absolutely sure her standards were being met.

Meredith had worked on this, her first at Rochdale Abbey, for at least three days. Whenever she believed she had almost got it perfect, she would have to write his name, and her quill would simply stop.

It was impossible to complete it. She knew what Miss Clarke was expecting, of course. Insight into the child, their preferences, their challenges. Subjects they enjoyed. Rewards that were appropriate.

Meredith had wondered, in her first position, why this was all necessary—until she realized the briefing report she had been given for the Earl of Marnmouth's children had been collated information from the previous governess.

It was easy for a Governess Bureau appointee to look impressive when she had already been informed of the children's difficulties and how they liked to be praised.

But the last part of the report, which Meredith was having the most difficulty with, was the most important. The report on the parents. What was it Miss Clarke had said?

"We may be governesses to children, but it is their parents we spend the most time looking after."

Meredith smiled. It was undoubtedly true from her experience. A troublesome parent was far more challenging than a troublesome child.

Her fingers gripped her quill, turning white. What could she write about Alfred?

The Duke of Rochdale, she told herself silently. That would be an excellent place to start; though how could she consider him with that stiff, formal title after finding him so soft and warm when in his arms?

Meredith swallowed and tried to push away those memories, but it had been almost a week since their passionate kiss, and they had not faded.

How was she to encapsulate in just a few lines what she had experienced with him? *That kiss!* Her entire body shivered whenever she thought about it; a memory fast becoming the greatest distraction in the schoolroom—which, with Archibald, was saying something.

It had been foolish. Yet, she had no regrets.

"Governess of great talents, did I not say?"

The problem remained that she had a report to write, and no words made sense as she tried to write.

Meredith was not innocent of the ways between gentlemen and ladies. She had not experienced much of it, naturally. There were not many opportunities for flirtation, and even they were discouraged.

But she had heard, she had read, listened to the stories of others, and therefore knew with absolute certainty that not all gentlemen were as respectable as they liked to portray.

She had heard the misgivings of Miss Clarke, of what some gentlemen attempted to do to the female servants in their care. A housekeeper was not only there to care for the house, Meredith knew. No, she was a guardian for the women in the household.

Look what happened to so many in the past! How many girls had to leave service for a year, disappear into the country—or the towns, depending on where she hailed from—and then appear again, older, a little quieter, a little more morose.

Meredith shivered. To have a child and keep it secret, to abandon it, sell it, leave it with others...

It was never the gentlemen who paid the price.

Alfred was not like that. She bit her lip as her gaze fell onto her report. She did not know him, not really. It was impossible to tell what he would be like in that regard, though he had not knocked on her bedchamber door or made suggestions of assignations.

The mere thought made her cheeks flush. *As though she would permit such a thing!*

How was she supposed to be honest about her interactions with Alfred—with the duke—without putting herself in Miss Clarke's bad graces? Or worse, lose her place?

"Governess of great talents, did I not say?"

Meredith closed her eyes, giving in to temptation once more, unable to resist the luxury of losing herself in the memory of that kiss. That moment when she felt utterly safe, and yet at the same time on the edge of a precipice, about to fall, her heart soaring, her skin tingling wherever Alfred touched her.

"Miss Hubert, why do they speak French in British North America?"

Meredith's eyes snapped open. She was still seated at her desk in the schoolroom, her report for Miss Clarke still before her on the desk, and Archibald was looking at her curiously from his seat.

She cleared her throat. "British North America?"

It had been a mistake to attempt to write this report during lesson time, but she had found herself struggling to complete it in the few hours she had between dinner and sleep. At least here, she thought there would be no distractions.

"Yes, Miss Hubert, I am a little confused," said Archibald hesitantly. Like all children, he did not like admitting when he struggled. "I mean, did we not found British North America? Is it not right that they would speak English, as we do? My father always said that the colonies were wrong to act this way, but I...I always wondered. I wish I had known my father."

Meredith swallowed, attempting to organize her thoughts coherently. The report must be finished.

"I do apologize, Archibald. Would you mind repeating your question?"

Instead of doing so, Archibald grinned. "You like my brother, don't you?"

Heat seared Meredith's cheeks. "Yes, I respect your brother. He is a gentleman, and my employer, and the duke of this county. I...I like him."

Why did it feel so strange to say those words at all, let alone to the half-brother of Alfred, who was at least twenty years younger?

She liked him. That was all she would allow herself to think, for that was all she could allow in her heart. The idea that there was more, that her feelings for him were more complex...

Archibald's grin broadened. "That is not what I meant."

The heat of the day suddenly increased so quickly, Meredith wondered whether a cloud had moved to reveal the sun.

A child should not notice such things! Had she been so indiscreet? Worse, a child of the house. It would not have been so bad, perhaps, if it had been a stable lad who had spotted them.

If she lost this position—worse, if Miss Clarke removed her from the Bureau, she would be destitute. She would never go back to her family, that old way of life, not if it meant starving. No savings, no good name, only Beauty, who she would never sell. But how would she feed her, stable her, look after—

Wait a moment. Meredith took a deep breath and steadied her nerves.

Archibald. There he was, a grin on his face, but there did not seem to be a huge amount of comprehension there. There was no malice, no plan. How would he know what affection was, what desire even looked like?

"How do you know that I like your brother, Archibald?" she asked quietly.

It was a guileless reply she received. "Mrs. Martin told me Roberts told her Alfred only had eyes for you," said Archibald confidently. "Does that mean you're friends?"

Right. Well, it was a good thing she had inquired further before allowing her thoughts to get entirely away from her. Mostly.

That sounded merely the tittle-tattle gossip she had always experienced when entering a new residence.

"You get back to your worksheet," she said with a wry smile. "We can discuss any questions you have when you are finished."

Archibald opened his mouth to argue but then closed it and returned to his worksheet, pencil scraping across the paper.

Meredith bit her lip. It was always hard to acclimatize to a new household. She had not really made many efforts with the other servants, preferring to understand Archibald first, but perhaps she had made an error.

Chances were Archibald would forget about this and not bring it up again. Children were wonderful creatures. Seeing that innocence in Archibald was something wonderful to behold.

"Miss Hubert?"

Meredith looked up to see a concerned look on Archibald's face. "Yes?"

"Do...do you like me?"

There was such concern in his voice that Meredith could not help but smile. "Yes, I do, Archibald. But does that matter? I am your governess, a servant of your brother. I am not a parent or a family member."

The words had to be said, though it pained her to say them. Miss Clarke had always warned against it, a connection with your charge that made you more friend than an educator.

"You are there to teach the children, not befriend them," was what she often said. "Friends cannot discipline. Friends cannot teach. Governesses are not their friends."

Meredith had agreed. The Egerton children had each other.

Archibald was different. "It does matter to me. When Alfred wins the election and goes back to London, it will just be the two of us."

His despondency was obvious, and Meredith hesitated before replying. This felt like one of those important conversations that you only had the chance to respond to once.

"That is true," she said gently. "But then...it may not happen that way. From what I have seen, your brother does not wish to win the election."

Meredith held her breath. *She had either stepped across a line most drastically or...*

"I do not think he wants to win, really," said Archibald, lowering his voice in that way children did when they believed they were saying something naughty. "Alfred is always unhappy, but he is unhappiest when he was a member of Parbliamint."

Meredith hid a smile. "Parliament."

"Yes, that," nodded Archibald, unfazed by the correction. "I think the closer we get to the election, the sadder Alfred gets. What do you think?"

Meredith swallowed. It was not her place to interfere in the relationship of the brothers.

"I think we need to concentrate on your geography," she said softly.

Archibald sighed. "I wish my father was still here—or my mother. I miss them, Miss Hubert, and no one ever talks about them."

Meredith's heart twisted. She had broken ties with her parents, it was true, but that was as an adult and with the choice before her. Archibald had never had such a choice.

"I wish I had known them," she said gently. "Perhaps Alfred will speak with you about them when you are older. Until then…"

She looked pointedly at his desk, and Archibald lowered his head over his worksheet.

Meredith let out a breath slowly. She would have to be careful around Archibald. It was clear he picked up a lot more about his brother than she had expected. It was frequently the children of the house who noticed these things, but the last thing she needed was for him to start noticing how she felt about Alfred.

The Duke of Rochdale. She had to remember to call him by his proper title—, particularly in her report. She glanced back at where she had got to.

In accordance with the guidelines established by the Governess Bureau, I have sought ways of rewarding my pupil without spoiling him (NB: horse riding and future attendance at family events), which have been approved by the master (Alfred Carmichael, Duke of Rochdale)

Meredith picked up her quill and continued.

…which have been approved by the master (Alfred Carmichael, Duke of Rochdale), who is very busy with election matters. I see the duke approx. once a week and have been informed he is pleased with my progress with his half-brother.

She examined the words carefully, trying to think whether they could be misconstrued—or taken as a lie. She did not think so. Every syllable there was true; she did not see Alfred often, and he had praised her for her attentions to Archibald.

No guilt rose in her stomach. *She had not lied.*

Meredith knew there was a pile of marking still to be completed, and if she was going to introduce music in a few weeks, she would need to brush up on her sightreading. There was a piano somewhere in the house, wasn't there?

She had taken Beauty for a long ride only the day before and did not wish to overly tire her, so Meredith decided to descend downstairs and hunt down the pianoforte. If it was not tuned, she would need to speak to Mrs. Martin about securing someone to see to it.

The house was quiet, and so she was surprised to hear the gentle murmur of voices coming from the drawing room as she stepped past the door.

Meredith hesitated. If it had been Roberts, or Mrs. Martin, or even Mr. Walker, Mr. Hemming, Mr. Shaw, or Mr. Brown, gentlemen who were frequently at the house as the election grew closer, she would not have bothered to listen, but this was quite different.

A quiet medley of several voices emanated from the door, which was slightly ajar.

"—taxes do not make any sense no how, if they knew anything about cattle—"

"—will help us, won't you, Your Grace?"

There was a moment of silence, and Meredith stepped silently closer to the door.

"I will do what I can for you, as I always do," came Alfred's voice, sounding to Meredith's mind a little tired. "But I cannot pretend to have the power here, Mr. Johnson, Mr. Hastings. You must remember that Westminster is a complicated beast, and I am running to be a member of Parliament, not Head of—"

"I expect better from our elected representatives," a man said gruffly.

A spike of irritation pierced Meredith's heart. *What was Alfred supposed to do?* He had just explained he had little power at Parliament. She would not have been surprised if Alfred had responded just as irritably as she felt, but instead…

"I quite understand your frustration, Mr. Hastings, and I wish I could do more," said Alfred. "And let us not get ahead of ourselves. There are still several weeks between now and the election, and I am by no means guaranteed to win. What we must consider is—"

"You will win, though, won't you?" It was a woman's voice who spoke this time. "You're a Carmichael. We always have a Carmichael."

Meredith stepped forward. She could make out a group of townsfolk who were surrounding Alfred with their well-meaning questions and desperate requests.

He looked tired. The silver around his temples gleamed in the afternoon light, and there were a few lines around his eyes that had not been there before.

"I have always done what I can to serve the people of Rochdale," came his quiet reply. "I am fighting this election to the best of my ability, Mrs. Hastings, and I am sure you will support me in any way you can. But you must consider that John Talbot may end up being—"

"John Talbot?" A man's voice sounded outraged. "We cannot have the likes of him representing us in Parliament, Y'Grace, you have to do something!"

"Due process will out, Mr. Johnson, and we will know in a few weeks just who will be taking the concerns of Rochdale to London," came the weary response from the duke. "Now, explain to me again just what the problem is with your cattle and the new restrictions about movement. Perhaps I can find a solution as magistrate."

The conversation continued on, but Meredith had little interest in the vagaries of cattle management. No, it was Alfred she cared about.

Poor man. Despite having no interest whatsoever in being a member of Parliament, from the little he had said, he still did all he could to protect and serve the people in his care.

It was madness, really. The one person who would excel at

being a member of Parliament, and he had no wish to do so!

"—must thank you, Your Grace," was the next snatch of wording she heard, and Meredith blinked. *Was the conversation over? Were they leaving?* "We appreciate your time and your expertise."

There were murmurs of thanks and a few scuffling footsteps as they bowed. Meredith stepped back quickly, entering the library. It would never do to be caught eavesdropping!

As the drawing room door opened and people poured out, Meredith stepped forward.

"Ah, good afternoon," she said pleasantly.

A few of the farmers nodded as their wives stared curiously, but none spoke. As the last one disappeared out of the front door, Alfred stepped out of the drawing room.

"Just listening to the people," he said almost apologetically.

Meredith smiled. "I know," she said quietly. "I mean…I overheard a little. When I was going to the library."

She pointed as though that would convince him of the veracity of her words.

Alfred nodded. "They are good people. I am fortunate to have them as my tenants."

"And your constituents," added Meredith with a sense of mischief. "But I think, in reality, they are the fortunate ones. You were so good with them, so kind. I was surprised, after all your talk of not wishing to enter Parliament. I think you would be rather good at it."

Had she gone too far? It was rather forward to offer an opinion, but it was a wonder she was able to speak at all; her body was tingling all over at being just a few feet from him.

Alfred laughed. "Yes, so they tell me. I think 'tis bred into you, something that comes down in the blood. Once Archibald is older, you'll see. It will be the same for him, and we will help him prepare for this life."

We will help him prepare for this life…

Meredith swallowed. This was not a partnership; this was

business. She was a governess. It was expected that she would help Archibald prepare for his future.

"Won't...won't he go to school?" Meredith said, grasping at something to say.

Alfred stepped toward her. "Perhaps. At some point. But that is so far away. I do not wish to think about you leaving."

He was very close. Almost as close as he had been when they had almost kissed after their dinner.

"Then," she breathed, trying to make her voice stronger. "Then yes, I will help him prepare. If I am still here."

Was that a look of pain across Alfred's face? "You are thinking of leaving?"

"No, no," said Meredith hastily. "But...Alfred, you know that kiss cannot be repeated. We cannot allow...we must not."

Her words were inadequate to explain the pain within her, but she had to speak. She had to show him she knew that door was closed.

The fact that she wished to kiss him right now, in the hallway of his own home, where anyone could come across them, was neither here nor there. She had to do the right thing. She had to protect herself, her name, and her reputation.

"Even if I wish it?" Alfred's voice was low, passionate, and he took another step toward her.

Meredith backed away. "Especially then."

Alfred's jaw tightened, and she saw his self-control reassert itself. He nodded curtly and walked away, up the main staircase and out of sight.

Meredith leaned against the wall, heart fluttering. *Well, it was over with.* She had said her piece, and now she did not have to worry about kissing Alfred Carmichael ever again.

CHAPTER TWELVE

September 12, 1812

I F THERE WAS *one skill every politician needed to learn,* Alfred thought as he attempted to subdue another yawn, it was preventing oneself from yawning at inopportune moments.

Far more important than the wheeling and dealing of Parliament, he thought lazily as he tried to attend to Mr. Hemming.

"...each neighborhood in turn, as though attempting to make it clear he has any care for them whatsoever," droned on Mr. Hemming in his slow manner. "The cheek of it all! To think John Talbot believes he can convince all he truly has their best wishes in his heart—"

"Was that not what we did during the last election?" Alfred interrupted, looking at Mr. Walker. "I seem to remember walking an inordinate distance meeting several hundred people."

Mr. Hemming looked outraged. "That's as may be, Your Grace, but this is completely different! When you met with the people of Rochdale, you did so because you actually cared about them, their hurts, their hopes, their welfare! You wished to ensure they were happy, and you did so!"

Mr. Walker nodded impressively, and Alfred smiled. You

knew something had been said well when Mr. Walker had nothing further to add.

"You all believe in me so strongly," Alfred said quietly. "Your devotion to me, to my family, to this election campaign is admirable. You know I take this responsibility upon myself. But..." His voice hesitated. *How could he best explain this?* He had attempted it so many times. "But gentlemen, you must remember that there is a chance I will not win this election."

"I don't want to hear that sort of talk," said Mr. Hemming. "That breeds panic."

Alfred tried not to roll his eyes at the older gentleman. "'Tis hardly panic, sir, to speak of what may be."

"The chances are so small, Your Grace, there seems no point in discussing them," said Mr. Walker in his matter-of-fact tone. "I worry about storms, yes, but I do not concern myself with bandits stealing my corn."

There were murmured nods around the dining room table, where their current meeting was being held. The town hall, Alfred had been amused to hear, had been reserved. For John Talbot and his election committee.

"Besides, there are far more important and pressing things to review," said Mr. Hemming, scrabbling away in his notes. "The ball, for instance."

Alfred's heart sank. *The ball.* He had managed to avoid the topic for over a week, but it appeared he would not be so fortunate today.

"Is it really essential we discuss it now?" he tried, playing for more time.

Mr. Walker's heavy eyebrows met in a frown. "I know 'tis not your favorite pastime, Your Grace, but it is a very useful campaign tool and a great way to ensure people's votes. I do not believe a Rochdale Ball has been held for months. Is that correct, Mrs. Martin?"

Mrs. Martin nodded, and Alfred was astonished to find he had not noticed she was there. The dining room was packed, as it always was, with well-wishers, campaign experts, and a few of the house staff, who were serving tea and bringing fresh platters of biscuits to the table, which was why Alfred suspected Mrs. Walker was in attendance.

It was she who spoke next, cup of tea in one hand, biscuit in the other. "Oh yes, you must hold a ball, Your Grace, you know you must. Everyone who is anyone must be invited."

"It would do the place good to be shown off," said Mrs. Martin with a nod. "Though before that, we must identify what *exactly* is going on here."

Alfred's heart skipped a beat. His housekeeper was looking stern, as though she had caught him out—which of course, to some, he could have been. *Kissing one's brother's governess was, after all, hardly encouraged.*

"What is going on here?" Mr. Hemming in confusion. "I do not follow."

Mrs. Martin drew herself up in a manner reminiscent of a robin preparing for winter and looked around the room impressively before speaking. "I *mean*, Your Grace, things are being mislaid. Precious things. Two portraits of your parents, the golden pocket watch. There used to be an ivory figurine on that table there," she pointed, and everyone turned to look at the empty table, "which your dear mother purchased while on honeymoon in Rome. That's gone."

Alfred sighed, leaning back in his chair. For a moment, he had been convinced she had discovered his illicit assignation with Meredith.

"Ah, I see," he said vaguely. "Right, well, of course, let's look into it. And this ball, the one we must have. Let us name the date next week, get the damned thing over with—oh, my apologies, Mrs. Martin, Mrs. Walker."

Christ in his heavens, he had forgotten they had women present!

"Yes, we can decide on the date next week," said Mr. Hemming, making a note. "The guest list—"

"You misunderstand me, sir," said Alfred quickly. "I mean to say that the ball itself will be next week. Mrs. Martin, choose a day."

"Next...next week?" Mrs. Martin was staring as though he were mad. "One cannot simply organize a ball in a week! These things take months to plan, there is food to source, musicians to book, I will need to polish the ballroom floor at least..."

Alfred allowed her to chatter on. There was no point in attempting to slow her down when Mrs. Martin got herself into motion. *A ball!* God's teeth, he could think of few things worse than hundreds of bodies pouring into his home, his ballroom, the noise and chatter, the expense, needing to speak to each and every person to keep Walker happy...

Well, he could think of something worse. Parliament. It really was a dammed shame it looked as though he would win the election.

"It will be next week," he snapped. "Next week, Mrs. Martin. I give you full reign over the house and expenses. Bring in girls from the town if you need pairs of hands."

Mrs. Martin's mouth fell open, but no words came out.

Mr. Walker cleared this throat instead. "Is it so urgent it must be rushed, Your Grace?"

Alfred nodded. "The election isn't that far away now—only eight weeks. The sooner we can host this ball, and everyone can come here and see how I am such a wonderful member of Parliament, then they can be convinced to vote for me, and *that's all that matters.*"

He had not managed to remove all the sarcasm from his tones. There were flushed faces around the dining table, though that may have been because of the heat of the day.

"You still have not replaced my undermaid," said Mrs. Martin hotly. "I am run off my feet already, Your Grace, and there will be no let-up as we go into winter, with half the house to put to sleep and the laundry taking twice as long!"

Was that a titter of laughter coming from one of the gentlemen? Alfred felt greatly discomforted. This meeting was not intended to air his dirty laundry, even metaphorically.

"No, I am sorry, Your Grace," said Mrs. Martin dramatically. "It cannot be done."

Silence rang out across the dining room with a few awkward looks exchanged. Alfred swallowed. *How was he supposed to reply to that?*

"I can help."

Everyone turned to the doorway. The door was open, and there stood...Meredith.

Alfred stared and then hastily rose to his feet, which he regretted immediately. *Why was he rising for a governess?*

It was impossible to ignore the wave of heat spreading across his chest. Dressed plainly in a cotton day gown, Meredith was the most beautiful woman he had ever seen.

This was foolishness, idiocy! Alfred warned himself. You are fixating on this woman because she is here, because she is available. Nothing more.

However, he had, at her request, attempted to prevent another kiss, which had necessitated drastic action on his part. Namely, staying entirely away from her.

Yet his waking thoughts and sleeping dreams were full of her. *Meredith.* What he felt was not mere lust, though there was certainly a flavor of that in his thoughts. But it was more than that. *What it was, exactly...*

"I do not believe we have met, Miss...?" Mr. Hemming had also risen to his feet, and Alfred was relieved to see this prompted the other gentlemen in the room to do likewise.

"This is the governess," Mrs. Martin said in clipped tones.

Alfred frowned. It was not like her to be so unfriendly to another. Roberts and Mrs. Martin had always managed to get along quite swimmingly.

Alfred opened his mouth to say something in Meredith's defense.

"Yes, I am the governess to Master Archibald," Meredith said, curtseying and stepping into the room. "I was also the governess for the Earl of Marnmouth and helped organize his daughter's coming out ball."

There were looks of surprise around the room, Alfred saw to his satisfaction, but none so impressed as Mrs. Martin.

He tried not to laugh. *Rivalry was always something pleasant to watch at the sidelines.* He had heard the tales of Mrs. Martin and Roberts's disagreements in the past, but they had a respect for each other. This was something entirely different.

"The Earl of Marnmouth?" repeated Mr. Hemming.

Meredith's smile broadened. "I have excellent references, if you would like to have them examined."

"I suppose it was the earl's housekeeper who did the work," Mrs. Martin said icily.

Meredith, instead of arguing as Alfred expected, nodded. "Of course, and I was not suggesting that I do that here. But you have said you require help, and I am offering my services. The question is, will you accept them?"

All eyes in the room darted to Mrs. Martin.

Time to take back control, thought Alfred. "My dear Mrs. Martin, would you say it could be done next week, with Mer—with Miss Hubert's help? The sooner this ball occurs, Mrs. Martin, the sooner we can start the hunt for your new undermaid."

The housekeeper hesitated, but it was clear that faced with so many opposing her, it would be foolish to continue the debate.

"Yes, it can," she said begrudgingly.

Alfred sighed. "Thank you, Mrs. Martin."

Mr. Walker was clapping his hands. "You are a saint, Mrs. Martin, as I think you know. The Rochdale Ball will be one week from today!"

Alfred had never known a week to go so fast. Everywhere he went, no matter the time of day, there was frantic busyness. Plates washed, floors scrubbed, all the rugs from the hallway taken outside and beaten over the lawn.

Paintings which he had never really noticed before were cleaned, taking a few layers of historic dirt with them, and his dinners became wilder as Cook practiced for the ball.

What really felt strange was how utterly unrequired Alfred was in these endeavors. In most cases, he was in the way whenever he offered to help.

Two days before the ball, he had heard the most almighty clatter down the corridor from his bedchamber, and when he had raced into a spare bedchamber to see whether Archibald had inadvertently hurt himself, it was to see Meredith, her hair tied up in a handkerchief, scrubbing the floor.

"Can I help you, Your Grace?" she had said stiffly, which may have been due to her aching back rather than the tension between them.

It had hardly encouraged intimacy, however, and Alfred had retreated from the room.

Even the ballroom floor was repolished twice. Alfred had whiled away a few happy minutes watching all the maids get onto their hands and knees to scrub before the final layer of polish was added. There was one particular maid who had a rather delightful behind, and Alfred indulged in watching her surreptitiously, knowing he would never do anything about it but enjoying the view before she turned around and revealed it was Meredith.

He had been forced to step away at that point and retreat upstairs for a very cold bath.

Mrs. Martin had finally come around to the idea that Meredith was more help than a hindrance. Alfred came upon them somewhat regularly during that week, the governess following behind the housekeeper with a notepad and pen as the latter reeled off her latest demands.

"—must not leave the pie crusts out any longer than an hour, or Tom is likely to eat them. Add a note, the sideboard in the dining room not adequately polished. And here, you can see someone's boots have come in without even bothering to—"

Alfred was rewarded with glimpses of Meredith, but in most cases, the two ladies were far too busy to be paying any attention to someone as unhelpful as the Duke of Rochdale.

There did not seem anything Meredith could not do, in fact.

Great talents, indeed.

Meredith was special. He had never encountered a woman like her, and he wasn't sure he ever would. She was unique. Every time he thought he had understood her…

It was because of her that Mrs. Martin had been able to get the damned ball ready for the place within a week. It couldn't be done, that was what the housekeeper had told him.

And yet before he knew it, before Alfred had really prepared himself, he was standing in his dressing room, with Kittering fussing around him. It was time to put on the most ridiculous clothes he had ever purchased—those designed for stupid occasions like this.

He pulled his cravat.

"Is it too tight, Your Grace?" said Kittering hurriedly.

"If we had it as loose as I wanted, it wouldn't be on. You've done well, Kittering."

His valet smiled at the praise as Alfred stepped toward the looking glass. He had never been one for caring much about his appearance. There were plenty of dandies and fops to cover the streets of London, of course, but that was simply not what mattered to him.

It mattered today. For some unknowable reason, one he was ashamed of, he wanted to impress this evening—not the countless gentlemen who would soon be arriving with their all-important votes for the election.

It was Meredith he wished to impress. He wanted her to see him at his finest. She had asked him not to kiss her again, and he was not that sort of master. He did not take advantage of the women in his household who may feel they were unable to say no to him.

"You look perfect, Your Grace," said the valet stiffly. "I do not think you have looked better. Your guests await you."

Bowing, he left Alfred standing alone before the looking glass.

"Look," he said quietly. "You need this ball to win the election. Just be charming and electable. Ignore Mere—ignore Miss

Hubert."

The glare he gave himself was stern, and Alfred hoped that would be enough. *He had no one else to force him to behave, after all.*

As he swept down the staircase, Mrs. Martin appeared at the bottom of it, looking frantic.

"The carriages are arriving! They are here, the guests are here, and I haven't triple checked that the punch is—"

Alfred reached the bottom step and took his housekeeper's hands in his own. "Mrs. Martin, you have done wonders. I am most grateful for your excellent work, and I am sure the punch is fine. Now relax this evening, won't you? I would not have you exhausting yourself."

Mrs. Martin did something she had never done before and blushed. "Y-Yes, Your Grace. Perhaps I will sit downstairs with Cook and enjoy a—"

"That sounds perfect," said Alfred hastily. Out of the corner of his eye, he had seen footmen spanning out around the front door where Roberts was pulling on his white gloves. "Off you go, Mrs. Martin."

She disappeared into the servants' corridor as Roberts appeared. "Ready, Your Grace?"

Alfred nodded. "Ready for the onslaught."

And onslaught it was. Alfred spent the next hour by the front door welcoming each and every single one of his guests. It was expected, and therefore he did it.

The fact that it was dull did not seem to bother anyone. It was difficult to concentrate, however, because he could see out of the corner of his eye two figures at the end of the hall watching all of the arrivals.

Archibald and Meredith. The boy was wide-eyed, trying to take in all the glory and splendor of his guests, the ladies with feathers in their hair, the gentlemen with their intricate and ostentatious cravats.

Alfred smiled. This was the first time his younger brother had been permitted to stay up to see a ball, even at the sidelines. It was a spectacular sight, even he had to admit.

He could remember the first time his father—their father—had permitted him to remain. True, it had been about twenty years ago. The fashions were very different, and the music would be considered old-fashioned to today's ears.

"Ah, Rochdale."

Alfred started. He had not been paying attention to whom he was greeting and found to his surprise John Talbot and his sister, Wilhelmina, standing before him.

"Mr. Talbot," he said. It would not do to be seen as ungentlemanly toward the man who was attempting to oust him from his family seat.

Talbot smiled. "Ah, the old 'please elect me!' Rochdale Ball. How I have missed it."

Alfred smiled wryly in return. "Well, it has always worked before, Talbot. I suppose giving the people what they want can win elections. My family has always found so."

His remarks wiped the smile from Talbot's face, though his sister simpered.

They would have continued to converse if not for the swell of arriving guests pushing them forward. Alfred could not pretend to be disappointed. The less he had to do with that maggot, Talbot, the better.

As the guests poured in, he wished he were seated with Meredith and Archibald, rather than here playing the politician.

Besides, what he wanted Meredith for was not really acceptable in polite society.

His jaw tightened as he waited for the last straggler guests to arrive. At least here, in the quiet of his own mind, he could admit what he could never say aloud.

He wanted her. He wanted to bed Meredith, make her scream with pleasure. He wanted her to be panting under him, desperate for his touch. He had never bedded a servant before. That was a line he simply would not cross. *No matter how much he wanted to.*

"Well done," came a low voice. Alfred turned to see Mr. Walker smiling. "That was good, Your Grace. Now you will need to attempt to dance with as many ladies as possible."

Alfred groaned, speaking low so Meredith could not hear. "You cannot be serious."

"There must be some ladies here you would wish to dance with," said Mr. Walker placidly. "Start with those, and then move on to others."

Alfred swallowed, trying to prevent his gaze from moving to the one woman with whom he would greatly love to dance.

Meredith. She caught his eye and immediately dropped her gaze, leaning over to Archibald and whispering something in his ear. The child nodded, and the two of them rose.

His better judgment told him he was mad to even consider it, but Alfred had spent too long listening to his conscience. He could not help himself. Every part of him was drawn to her, and now he had the chance to be closer to her than before.

"Miss Hubert," he said clearly, his voice echoing around the hall.

Meredith and Archibald halted. She curtseyed. "Yes, Your Grace?"

Why could she not call him Alfred? "Would you like to dance, Miss Hubert?"

"No, Your Grace."

Alfred looked into the eyes of the stubborn governess before him. *No?* She was going to refuse him? *Why, he could order her to!*

But that was not in his nature, nor hers. "Why?"

The word had escaped his lips before he could stop it. Archibald was looking at them in evident confusion.

Meredith swallowed, pink cheeks now glowing. "Why? Your Grace, it would be scandalous. A duke dance with a governess at his ball?"

Her eyes darted around the hall, evidently ensuring no one else could hear them. Alfred lowered his voice so the boy would not hear his next remark.

"I would like to do more than just dance, Meredith."

"You cannot say such—"

"What more?"

Both Alfred and Meredith looked at Archibald, forehead puckered into a frown.

Alfred coughed. He needed to remember himself. *She was right.* Of course, he could not dance with Meredith; that would be ridiculous. He would invite a scandal onto his name, the last thing he needed right before the election.

"You are quite right," he said curtly. "Good evening, Miss Hubert."

It took strong willpower to step away from her, but Alfred knew it was his only choice. As he paced down the corridor and into the ballroom, applause from his guests met his ears.

"Thank you, thank you," said Alfred with a smile, raising his hand. "Now, the dancing must begin—and I know just the person to start it."

He had spotted her as soon as he had entered the ballroom. That ridiculous feather in her hair dyed a raucous pink that could be spotted a mile off.

Still, it would make Mr. Walker happy and keep the gossips away from Meredith.

"Miss Talbot," he said graciously, stepping over to her and holding out his hand. "Would you do me the honor?"

Miss Talbot, as Alfred knew she would, glanced at her brother. Talbot glared as though trying to understand why he was making such a spectacle of them and then nodded.

Miss Talbot took his hand, and the guests applauded as they moved to the center of the ballroom. Time for this damned ball to begin.

The rigor of the dance took over for a few minutes, and Alfred was not able to catch sight of her, but as he and Miss Talbot completed their move down the set, he had the time to look over at her once again—and his heart froze.

Meredith was no longer alone. A gentleman was speaking to

her, a smile on his face and a rather leering look in his eye.

Talbot. John Talbot was speaking to his—to Meredith. Alfred could not make out the words, not from here, but was that a smile on her face? Fiery jealousy rushed through him like he had never known before. *What did Talbot think he was doing, talking to his—his governess!*

"Everyone expects it, you know."

Alfred's attention was drawn hastily back to the dance. "What?"

Miss Talbot was smiling. "Us. Uniting the houses, Talbot and Carmichael."

He stared as they stepped together, hands touching. Not this old suggestion again...

"Our marriage would create a new dynasty, one without the squabbling of our ancestors," she said softly, her eyes focused on his own.

Alfred could do nothing but nod curtly. There was no response he could make to that other than 'no,' which was what he felt but knew would be an insult.

Miss Wilhelmina Talbot? She was fine, he supposed, in a bland way. Though the marriage had been suggested a number of times—first by his father, most recently by Mr. Walker—he simply could not summon up the interest in her.

The dance came to an end, with the onlookers applauding the musicians genteelly.

Miss Talbot appeared to be a little flushed. "Your Grace, why do we not—"

"You will have to excuse me," said Alfred hurriedly, bowing and walking away.

There was only one thing on his mind, and that was Meredith. Pushing past guests in his attempts to get to her, when he finally managed to reach the musicians, she was alone.

"Where is Archibald?" he snapped.

Meredith raised her eyebrows at his tone. "Why, gone to bed. It was far too late for him to be awake, but I wished him to see the beginning of the first—where are we going?"

Alfred had grabbed her hand and was pulling her none too gently out of the ballroom and down the corridor.

"Your Grace!"

Alfred ignored her. Blood was rushing through his veins, pounding so loudly he could barely hear her. Only when he had pulled her into the library and slammed the door behind him did she speak again.

"What is the meaning of this?"

Alfred saw the anger in him reflected in her eyes. "I don't want you speaking to him."

"Him?"

He had to get his temper under control. *He had to make her understand.* "John Talbot."

Meredith opened her mouth, closed it again, and then said stiffly, "I think you will find, Your Grace, that I can talk to whomever I like!"

Alfred took a step toward her. "What did he say to you?"

Clearly, there was something in his manner that made her realize this was far more important than mere jealousy, though that, too, was clouding his judgment at the present.

"He…" Meredith licked her lips, and Alfred tried not to concentrate on them but her words. "He was telling me about you."

Alfred closed the gap between them. "And what did he say?"

It was clearly something licentious, for Meredith's cheeks colored before she managed to say, "He said…well. That you bed your servants. That I should be careful of you."

Alfred swore under his breath.

"Your Grace!"

His mind was overwhelmed, utterly incapable of understanding where this rumor could have come from. It sounded to him like the sort of nonsense Talbot always came up with.

"I have never done such a thing before," he said quietly. "But then, I have never wanted to. Not until now."

Meredith stepped back. "No," she whispered. "We mustn't."

"I am determined," he said. "Unless you ask me to stop..."

"Alfred," Meredith whispered.

The kiss was deep, passionate, untamed. Alfred poured all his frustrations onto Meredith's lips, and she responded with just as much passion. All the control she had used to keep away from him was now gone.

"Meredith..."

She was warm and passionate, everything he wanted.

"No."

Alfred dropped her as though he had been burned. "I did not mean to..."

"No, you did nothing wrong," Meredith said. "No, I could not...I must not...Archibald will need tucking in."

She stepped away from him before he could reach her, before he could stop her; Alfred watched Meredith slip out of the library.

Damn. He needed to get a hold of himself.

Chapter Thirteen

September 13, 1812

W HEN MEREDITH OPENED her eyes from the comfort of her bedchamber in the eaves of the abbey, there was a smile on her face.

How could there not be? She had barely managed to fall asleep before dawn after the ball. The moment she had drifted into slumber, her dreams filled with the most wonderful scenes.

Alfred. Alfred, riding alongside her, laughter on his lips and joy in his eyes. Alfred, no longer a member of Parliament for Rochdale, but free and happy to do what he wished with his life. Alfred, kissing her passionately as they sat on the sofa in the drawing room…

Perhaps she should not indulge in such wild dreams, but they were the only place she could be as free with Alfred as she wished when she was awake.

She could not just lie here thinking such things. It was Sunday, and Alfred had already agreed with the Reverend Michaels that the Rochdale house would not be attending church today. She needed to get up and on with her chores.

Swinging her legs over the side of the bed, Meredith sensed

the early morning air. She had left the curtains open as she always did. There was something about waking up to the sunrise every morning, and as she stepped over to the window, she opened it and breathed in.

Fresh air. It was only today that a scent of autumn was in the air. The heat of the summer was gone.

"Miss Hubert!"

Meredith whirled around. It was Mrs. Martin. *She did not know about the kiss, did she?* The housekeeper had never bothered her before in her rooms, only to deliver the looking glass, and that had been with a most begrudging air.

"Miss Hubert?"

"Yes, Mrs. Martin?" Meredith said in a quavering voice. She swallowed. She must not allow anyone to think that anything was amiss.

Her bedchamber door opened to show a stern Mrs. Martin. "You are up, then?"

"Almost," said Meredith hastily, stepping toward her wardrobe. "If you let me know where you are starting, I will endeavor to be downstairs helping you in—"

"You have been a great help to me this last week." Mrs. Martin hesitated, and Meredith stared. *Had she really heard that correctly?* "I was mistaken in you, and for that, I apologize. Always happy to admit when I was wrong, as it happens so infrequently."

Meredith stifled a smile. *It was exactly the sort of apology Mrs. Martin would give.*

"That is very gracious of you, Mrs. Martin," she said. "I am always happy to be useful, and I am glad I could help on this occasion."

"Hmm," said Mrs. Martin gruffly. "I came up here especial to find you, Miss Hubert, to say that and one other thing. You should stop here, if you please, or elsewhere if it takes your fancy, but relax, is what I am saying. 'Tis much easier to tidy up after a party than prepare for one, and you've done your bit. The undermaids and I can take it from here."

Meredith blinked. *Had she really heard such words of gratitude and, most importantly, leisure from Mrs. Martin's mouth?*

The older woman smiled. "The master is pleased, and therefore so am I. You are a credit to the Rochdales. I would have you rest today."

Meredith hardly knew where to begin. "Right, well, thank you. Thank you for telling me, and thank you for saying you do not require help this morning."

"Aye, you look a little pale," said Mrs. Martin. "I dare say a day of relaxation would do you good."

Meredith smiled. "Thank you."

The housekeeper nodded and then left, shutting the door behind her and leaving Meredith to sag against the window.

She took a deep breath. Whenever the world became too confusing, and she wished to quit it, she went for a ride. Beauty had been sorely ignored these last few days during the preparations for the ball. She could do with the exercise just as much as Meredith could.

Dressing quickly in her riding habit, Meredith glanced at the gown she had laid out on the chair by her desk. It was her only evening gown. The one she had worn to dine with Alfred, and more recently, the one she had been wearing when...

But she could not think this way. Riding Beauty was the easiest way to clear her head. Hurrying down the main staircase and smiling at the two footmen carefully looking through the coats and pelisses left at Rochdale Abbey after the ball in an attempt to ascertain who their owners were, Meredith stepped into the servants' corridor and along to the stables.

Other than the footmen, she did not see a soul. A man was tacking up Parker.

"Good morning," she said cheerfully.

The man turned around, and Meredith almost fell over in surprise. *It was Alfred!*

"Meredith," he breathed.

They were alone, and the instinct to run into his arms and

allow him to kiss her utterly overwhelmed her.

"Alfred," she smiled, stepping toward him, her arms out.

She was a fool, and she knew that. Where was this going? But the temptation was too great, and it was clear Alfred had the same instinct. He pulled her into his arms willingly and bestowed a kiss on her lips which rapidly became far more passionate.

Meredith lost herself in the kiss, throwing caution to the wind and daring the world to stop her. When she was with him like this, the path ahead seemed clear.

When they finally broke apart, Alfred's breathing was heavy, and his eyes were wide with desire. And something else. Something Meredith did not recognize.

Pressed up against him as she was, she could feel the desire between his legs. Meredith shivered. He had such power over her, could say whatever he wanted to her, even order her to allow him into her bed—not that she would agree.

But she had power over him, too.

"I want you," Alfred breathed.

Meredith smiled. "I know."

What she could not bring herself to say was that she wanted him, too.

"I…" Alfred swallowed, arms tight around her. "I do not know where this is going."

This was dangerous territory, and Meredith knew she had to forestall him somehow. He could not be permitted to think about this too much.

"I do," she said lightly with a smile. "I am going down toward the lake."

Alfred laughed, finally releasing her and looking at her wryly. "I suppose I deserved that. Here, would you like me to help you up onto—"

His voice halted as Meredith leaped elegantly onto the back of Beauty—without stirrups, reins, nor saddle.

She smiled as she turned Beauty with a gentle nudge of her foot. "You were saying, Your Grace?"

"B-But...how did you...?" Alfred stared in disbelief. "I knew you were a good horsewoman, but this is beyond anything I could have expected! How did you do that?"

Meredith flushed. She was always so careful at hiding any hints of her past. It had become easier over time. Even the accent had become second nature, clipped consonants and elongated vowels now the way she spoke naturally.

But there were still parts of her background she wished would stay right there—in the background—yet they resurfaced just when she least expected.

There were still some of her great talents she did not wish the world to know.

"Practice," she said lightly. "Come on, let's go before the rest of the world wakes up."

She could tell Alfred wanted to ask further questions about her ability to ride bareback without even reins to inform Beauty of her wishes, but as she encouraged her mare out of the stables, Alfred had to hurry to finish tacking up Parker.

By the time he joined her, there were a few people moving about in the gardens. The head gardener was an early riser, and so those beneath him had learned to rise early.

None of them, however, were close enough to speak to either of them as they trotted out on the path to the lake. Meredith glanced at Alfred and saw him visibly relax. The further he was from people and their expectations of him, the calmer he seemed to be.

They rode in silence. Meredith did not wish to break the companionable quiet between them, not when she had the impression that there were few times Alfred could simply be, without having to answer questions from those around him.

Besides, what would she say? The only thing she could think of, as she guided Beauty to take the right-hand fork, was about last night—and that was hardly a safe topic.

She did not even have the words for it. How could she ask Alfred what it meant, now this was no longer an attraction they had not acted on, but a true and deep connection?

Did the duke ever marry the governess?

Meredith felt her cheeks color at the mere thought. It must occur sometimes, she was sure, although she could not think of any examples. Perhaps they kept it quiet. Perhaps it was easier if such a scandalous thing did occur, to disappear quietly into their happiness.

Could they do that? Meredith bit her lip. It seemed a bit much to hope for—

"Careful now."

Alfred's words cut across her thoughts, and she whipped around to look at him. *How had he managed to guess what she was thinking?*

But he was pointing to a fallen tree across the path.

Meredith nodded. She was getting ahead of herself. Thoughts of matrimony, of hiding their feelings—she was not even sure what their feelings were.

Could this not just be a flirtation on his side?

"You should watch out for old Rochdale there," had been the words of John Talbot. *"Can't have a woman in the house, but he wants to bed her. Achieves it most of the time, too. Did you ever meet Molly Butters?"*

"The ball seemed to have been a success," she said aloud, partly for something to distract herself from her wild thoughts.

Alfred laughed. "Yes, even Talbot was impressed by the decorations and pageantry, although that won't help me much."

Yes, the election. That was a safe topic, Meredith thought. If they could just keep to that, everything would be fine.

"And did…did you get a sense of how the people will vote?"

Alfred shrugged. "Sometimes I feel as though my win is inevitable. There does not appear to be anything I can do to prevent it."

His voice was tired, despondent. It did seem most unfair that a gentleman with such intelligence, such concern to do what's right for his people, was simply not interested in the path before him that would empower him to do just that.

"The thought fills me with sadness and regret," he said briskly. "The idea of having to return to London, of leaving Rochdale... Yet, I believe I would be even more devastated if I disappointed my father and his legacy and did not win."

Meredith swallowed. It was an impossible situation for him, and there was nothing she could say that would bring any comfort. *What did she know about the world of politics?*

"I am sure your father would not be disappointed," she said gently.

Alfred laughed as they turned the corner, and the lake came into view. "You never knew him. My father's parliamentary career was what he was most proud of in the world. Far more than his sons."

"I cannot believe that to be true," Meredith said automatically.

"Do not concern yourself. I am quite reconciled to it. I think he only had children based on what he said to me in the past so that there would be someone who could take over his legacy after he died."

He sounded so bitter that his father had not truly cared for him. Meredith nudged Beauty to walk closer to Parker.

She touched his arm gently. "You speak with such sadness, Alfred. Why run for Parliament at all if it is only going to bring you unhappiness?"

Her words had not been intended as a joke, but Alfred laughed. Then his eyes widened.

"Oh, you meant it," he said blankly.

Meredith laughed herself. "I may not be an expert in these things—as I said before, I lack the one defining quality in this whole discussion, which is that I am not a gentleman. But surely there are other things you can do with your time, with your passions, that would bring just as much comfort to the people of Rochdale?"

And to me, she thought silently. The idea of him disappearing down the London road to misery and loneliness, hundreds of miles away from her...

It was abhorrent. She could not permit it to occur.

"Paperwork is already filled out," said Alfred in a strange sort of false cheerfulness. "Filled out from birth, almost. No, I will be running for Parliament on the fifteenth of October, and if I do not win, I shall be very much surprised."

Meredith looked out over the lake. It was beautiful.

To think, he had all of this—owned all of this—and was forced to leave it.

"Well then," she said quietly, "I suppose you will have to wait and see."

"Yes, I suppose I will," Alfred said, watching her closely. "But it would be a lot easier with you by my side."

"I am by your side."

But Alfred was not smiling now, his gaze focused on her with such fierceness, she almost looked away. "I did not mean it like that," he said softly.

Meredith blinked. She could not understand what he meant. What else could he possibly...

She gasped. *No. No, he could not possibly mean—this did not happen!*

The Duke of Rochdale was asking her to marry him—or at the very least, hinting at it! *Marry him!* Cease to be governess to his brother and become the Duchess of Rochdale?

It was madness. He should not even be suggesting such a thing!

Alfred was still watching her closely, and Meredith remembered to breathe. Perhaps she had misheard him. She had made a guess, a leap at his words, and her assumption could be utterly wrong!

"I-I am just a governess," she stammered, equilibrium gone. "I teach—"

"You could still teach Archibald," he said gently. "If you wanted to."

"But I cannot be y-your..." Her voice faded away. She would not even say the word. It had to come from him.

Bride.

"I know, 'tis madness."

Meredith swallowed. *No, she was losing her head.* This would not work; it would never work! There was an attraction between them, yes, that could not be denied.

But love, matrimony, was built on far more.

You must never fall in love...

She had to put a stop to this.

"You need to take your words back," she whispered. "You cannot mean it."

"I most certainly do," Alfred said fiercely. "Right now, in this moment, I want you. I want you not just for an evening in the library but for the rest of my life."

Before Meredith could respond, he had leaned forward and captured her lips with his own. The kiss was passionate, yes, but it was different from the others. Softer. More devout. As though he was attempting, with his body, to persuade her in a way his words simply could not.

The kiss ended, and Meredith wondered how she had managed to stay on her horse.

Alfred's eyes searched hers. "I cannot deny this feeling I have for you."

Meredith hesitated. The rules of the Governess Bureau were clear. *One must not fall in love; it was absolutely forbidden!*

But was this one of those rules meant to be broken? She could not deny the sensations she felt for him, either, and they were not just of the body, but of mind, too.

"I know," she breathed. "I feel it, too."

Succumbing to the kiss she knew would immediately follow her words, Meredith and Alfred spent time at the lake talking, sharing hopes, dreams, and kisses, though never succumbing to more, though it was clear what they wanted.

And in all that time, two words were never spoken. Meredith

knew she could never be the first to speak them.

Love. Matrimony.

It was only as the sun moved across the sky that Alfred looked up at it ruefully.

"We have to go back," he said, confirming his suspicion with a glance at his pocket watch. "I was supposed to be meeting Mr. Walker and Mr. Brown for a debrief after last night's ball an hour ago."

Meredith nodded. He had requested no promises, and she had given no assurances. But something had changed between them. There was an understanding, something that had not existed before.

Before she knew it, they had returned to the stable.

"Ah, Your Grace," said Henderson with a jovial air. "Did you enjoy your ride, Miss Meredith?"

Meredith refused to catch Alfred's eye as she dismounted. "Yes, thank you, Henderson. The lake path is very pleasant."

"That it is," Henderson agreed. "And yourself, Your Grace?"

"Very pleasant," echoed Alfred with a grin. "We will up to the house now, Henderson. I have an election meeting to attend. You do not mind brushing down—"

"You leave them to us. We'll be happy to take care of them for you," said Henderson placidly, not stirring an inch from his seat and clicking his fingers at two stable lads, who immediately stepped forward.

"King of his own domain," whispered Meredith as she and Alfred left the stables to go back into the house.

"As I wish I was of mine," said Alfred in a low voice, capturing her hand in his.

They walked up to the house, Meredith's heart fluttering at the shameful display of affection between them, but it felt natural.

This was what she wanted. This was how it was supposed to be.

CHAPTER FOURTEEN

September 18, 1812

A LFRED CLOSED HIS book and looked around for the small golden carriage clock. It had been on the library mantelpiece for…goodness, as long as he could remember. A smile crept over his face. Somewhere in his mind, there was a memory of his mother smoothing down his hair and telling him that his father had purchased the clock on one of their journeys to London, so he could always tell what time it was.

The clock was gone. Alfred looked around the room vaguely. Perhaps Mrs. Martin had put it elsewhere for cleaning. Perhaps Roberts had taken it to the clockmaker to be mended. He could not keep up with these household changes.

When he was in London, he would not have to.

Sighing heavily, Alfred pulled his pocket watch out of his waistcoat and groaned. Just past ten o'clock in the evening.

It would be considered early in London, particularly when forced to entertain people, try to sweet talk them into supporting whatever bill the party was leaning on him for.

But here, in the country? When the day started with cock-crow? Time for bed.

He was starting to feel old. Not yet thirty, but he could feel each and every one of those years in his back if he sat down too long. Alfred stretched and felt something click—not painfully, but it was a shock to hear that from his bones. It must be all the riding he was doing.

Perhaps it was the campaigning. He was certainly on his feet more these days instead of stuck in an old stuffy building with hundreds of others.

Today had certainly been tiring. Alfred shook his head as he carefully placed the book he had been reading back on the shelf. Every farmer, every tenant, even a few gentlemen from Rochdale Town, each one of them had to be spoken to, had to be listened to.

It was not that he minded. Alfred had always considered that his role when his father had been in government. The old duke had gone to London, and his son had remained at the abbey to care for the people. He had enjoyed it, then. *When it had been a choice.*

He would always have checked on them, ensured tenants had what they needed, that tools were replaced as they should—but it felt so false now.

"Not false," Mr. Walker had said as they had left the house, and Alfred had shared some of his misgivings. "Just…carefully timed."

Alfred picked up the lamp on the table and blew out the others, leaving the library in darkness as he stepped into the hallway. Only then did he realize he was thirsty.

A quick trip to the kitchen, he thought, rather than disturbing Roberts for such a trifle. A glass of water would not be difficult, he was sure—though admittedly, it had been many years since he had last been down to the kitchen.

Then bed. Alfred stretched, feeling his back tighten. Yes, he was ready for slumber.

He was unable to reach the kitchen, however, because as he stepped toward the door to the servants' corridor, it was opened rather abruptly, and an irate Mrs. Martin appeared.

"Your Grace," she said sternly, and Alfred stepped back. It was almost a malediction.

"Yes, Mrs. Martin," he said, trying not to hold the lamp as a protective shield.

The housekeeper glared, and he hastily put the lamp down on a small table.

"I am glad I have caught you," she said quietly, "particularly as we are alone. 'Tis a sensitive matter I must discuss with you."

Alfred privately thought it felt more as though he was being accosted, but he was too polite to say so. Besides, Mrs. Martin had served the Rochdales for years. He could barely remember the housekeeper before her, and she had always performed excellently. The recent ball was just one example of that.

He cleared his throat but kept his voice low. "Anything you wish to say to me, Mrs. Martin, will be treated in the strictest confidence—but perhaps you would like to converse in the drawing room?"

Mrs. Martin looked around them, and Alfred felt a prickle of foreboding creep up his neck. *What on earth did she need to speak to him about that was so vitally important?*

"I think that would be best, Your Grace," she said, stepping over to the drawing room without waiting for him.

Alfred followed, picking up the lamp for a little light, but he needn't have bothered. The fire in the drawing room grate had died down but still gave sufficient light to the two armchairs nearest for them to easily converse.

He sat down in one and then stared at the hovering Mrs. Martin before he remembered himself. "Oh, sit down, Mrs. Martin, do."

The housekeeper sat down and smoothed her skirts nervously.

Alfred smiled, then forced a more serious expression. He should take whatever Mrs. Martin said seriously, he knew, but it was difficult to get worked up about petty household affairs.

Whatever it was, Mrs. Martin would be able to sort it out if she put her mind to it.

"I...I am glad to have caught you, Your Grace, private like," said Mrs. Martin in a low voice. "'Tis not a pleasant topic of which I have to speak to you, and...well. I would not be saying it, coming to you, if I was not sure."

"And I am glad you have caught me in turn, Mrs. Martin," Alfred said easily. "Now. How can I help you?"

"'Tis more a case of how I can help you, Your Grace, if you permit me to say so," said the housekeeper in a hurried voice. "You see, I have long had my suspicions, yet I have kept quiet for fear of rousing the culprit afore my time, but things are still going missing."

Alfred could not entirely follow. "Missing? Are you sure things are not being moved to other places? I, myself, often find if I cannot find a thing, I just—"

"No, Your Grace," interrupted Mrs. Martin, concern across her face. "No, I have looked everywhere for some of these items, and they have been missing for...well, almost two months! Some of them are quite valuable. I first noticed it when..."

Alfred sighed. *Silver spoons and the like, he supposed.* Well, those were the affairs of others, though he would rather swap this little problem for his own—that damned election and what it entailed—for something as small as this.

Besides, he was never one for trifles and material possessions. He had been like his mother in that regard. They had never noticed pretty new things or adequately thanked his father for any of his treats. One of the reasons they had so frequently angered him.

"—no wish to apportion blame onto anyone, but something must be done, Your Grace, for I fear we are not safe in our beds if—"

"My dear Mrs. Martin," Alfred interrupted. This had gone on too long, and he was starting to tire. "I really do not mind where things are put back. There is no need for items to be placed precisely from where they were taken."

Mrs. Martin bristled. "That is not what I am saying, Your Grace! I am trying to tell you I think they've been stolen! There is a thief in the house or coming into the house and—"

"A thief?" Alfred blinked. It was quite an accusation, particularly from his steady and otherwise unruffled housekeeper. "If you are concerned, Mrs. Martin, and I can see you are, then I recommend speaking to Roberts. At the very least, I think we can assume if there is a thief," something he privately highly doubted, "then we can agree it is none of the staff. No servant would do such a thing."

His housekeeper was still smoothing down her skirts anxiously, not entirely meeting his gaze. "Well, that is the thing, Your Grace, you see. It all started when—"

"I am sorry, Mrs. Martin, I am most fatigued," said Alfred with a weary smile. *It was time to shoo away this complaint.* It did not seem to have any relevancy to him. "I was off to bed when we started to speak, and I must continue on there now. Good evening, Mrs. Martin."

He rose, and she rose with him, her lips pursed as though preventing all the things she wished to say from spilling out.

Alfred sighed heavily as he stepped into the servants' corridor. *What a thing to get upset about!* Besides, Mrs. Martin was hardly a young woman. Was it possible she was losing her memory, starting to forget where she had put things or what was put away?

He would have to speak to Roberts about that. The butler would undoubtedly have noticed if there was something amiss with his housekeeper.

As Alfred stepped down the corridor, he turned a corner and heard a voice. It was low, gentle, and unless he was mistaken...

Meredith.

Alfred stopped. She was speaking quietly to someone he could not see, but as he tried to slow his breathing to allow his ears to hear anything other than the frantic pulse of his heart, he guessed it was Archibald. Who else could it be?

"—and that is why, whenever a child goes to sleep," came her gentle voice down the corridor from the kitchen, "a special fairy is sent down by the king of the fairies."

"The king of the fairies?" That was Archibald.

"Yes," said Meredith quietly. "And there is a special fairy for each child, and you have the same one every night, so she knows you well. She is there to protect you from nightmares, you see? Even if you cannot see the fairy, she is there."

"But...but I still have nightmares," came the quiet concern of the child.

A clatter. A movement of crockery, perhaps a cup.

"I know, Archibald," Meredith's voice was low and warm. "But you see, your special fairy is there, even if you cannot see her. And that is why, no matter the nightmare, no matter how frightened you are, nothing can hurt you."

"Because...because of my special fairy?"

"Because of your special fairy. Now, drink up that hot milk."

There was silence as Alfred's heart melted. A beautiful story cleverly done. Archibald must have had a nightmare, and instead of chastising him for disturbing her as Alfred might have done, Meredith had taken him downstairs, warmed some milk, and told him that tale.

She was caring for him, really caring for him. Alfred had never expected a governess to do anything of the sort, but Meredith...she was special.

"Are you sure?" came Archibald's voice, still quiet but without the tension Alfred had first heard. "Did I really have a special fairy protecting me?"

Alfred smiled. *Ah, to be young again, with all the myths and legends before you.* What it was to believe something so completely. The innocence of a child.

"Sometimes," he heard Meredith reply, "that special fairy lets someone else in the house know she is there. 'Tis only polite, after all, for she is a guest here. Your fairy informed me of her presence a few hours ago, just as you were going to sleep."

Alfred could only imagine how wide-eyed Archibald must be. "Truly?"

"Truly," came Meredith's voice. "She is a flower fairy, you know. Her name is Rosemary, and she has a friend called Lavender, another flower fairy."

"I am glad Rosemary came to visit."

"And she will return every time you go to sleep," added Meredith in a soft voice. "You know, tomorrow we could go down to the kitchen gardens and ask one of the gardeners there if we could cut little sprigs of rosemary and lavender to make sure your fairy feels welcome."

Alfred smiled. *She really was a governess of great talents.* Of course, the rosemary and lavender would help the boy sleep and give him the confidence that his—what did Meredith call it?— special fairy would be welcome.

Meredith. She would be the most incredible stepmother to—

Alfred jerked his head slightly. He must be tired. Archibald was not his son, though at times, it felt like it. He had helped care for him and then been his guardian for so long, it was as though Archie was his own.

Stepping forward quietly, he gently pushed the kitchen door open.

There they were, facing away from him. Meredith was seated at the wide oak kitchen table with a cup of warm milk, and Archibald, dressed in his little nightclothes, was in her arms grasping his own cup.

Despite thinking himself inobtrusive, Meredith immediately looked up to see Alfred, and smiled. She was dressed in what could only be described as a nightgown, though it was lighter than he had expected. Autumn nights were still warm.

"You see, Archibald," she said softly, continuing on with her story, "the flower fairies particularly like to come indoors as autumn draws near because it's colder outside. When they choose a child to care for, they are loyal to that child all year round. You are very fortunate."

"I-I wasn't afraid, you know," said Archibald quietly.

Alfred could see his fingers white against the cup, his face pale.

"I know," said Meredith gently. "But your special fairy, Rosemary, wanted to make sure you knew she was there, so if you spotted her out of the corner of your eye, you did not shout at her. She's very gentle, and sometimes you can catch sight of a flutter of their wings, just as you start to drift off to sleep."

Archibald nodded solemnly. "I wouldn't shout at a fairy."

Alfred could not help it. His heart, already softened at the story she had been telling, was now overflowing. *How quickly childhood was over.*

"Are you ready to go to bed now, Archibald?"

The boy nodded, slipping off Meredith's lap and placing his cup on the table. Meredith rose, too, and offered her hand to the child, but Archibald shook his head.

"With Rosemary upstairs, I am quite happy to go up on my own," he said, with a little of that old Carmichael cheek returning. "I want to see if I can spot her, and she might hide if both of us go up."

Alfred saw Meredith smile. "I quite understand. Off you go—I will tidy up here, so Mrs. Martin does not come for us in the morning!"

Archibald giggled and started walking toward the door at the other end of the kitchen.

"And do not consider this an excuse not to do your Latin work tomorrow morning," Meredith called after him, but the door had already closed.

Alfred stepped into the kitchen. "You spoil him, you know."

Meredith did not look around as she picked up the two cups and took them over to the sink. "He has not been spoiled enough, I think."

There was no malice in her words, so Alfred did not take the comment personally. The Rochdale family was not one for being pampered, at least not in his experience.

"Is that my fault?" he teased.

Meredith glanced over her shoulder as she poured a little water into the basin. "No, I do not think so. I think you have had many other calls on your time, and you have done your best for him. Not all children can boast a steady and dependable home."

Nine times out of ten, Alfred would not have noticed. He was not really the noticing type, but because the words were spoken by Meredith, they had added meaning.

Her words were brisk, but her tone was sad. Almost as though she knew what it was to experience the opposite. Almost as though she had suffered in the past.

"You...you did not have that?"

Meredith was too busy washing the cups to reply, though Alfred wondered whether that was just a rather convenient excuse to collect herself and consider her words.

When she had placed the cups on the side to dry, she turned to him with a smile that looked rather brittle to Alfred's eye.

"He should really be in school in a few years," she said quietly. "He will be a man before you know it. The more time with others, the better. He is alone here."

Alfred sighed, stepping around the kitchen table. "The future is set for him, Meredith. There was a place waiting for him at Eton from the day he was born. I know, I helped with the paperwork."

Helped with the paperwork? He did the entire thing. His father—their father—had been too busy with his red box. Parliamentary paperwork came before family every time.

"However, I agree that making some friendships with the right people would be beneficial," he added.

Meredith smiled. She stepped forward and kissed his cheek. "You mean alliances," she said gently. "I meant friendships."

She had started to step back, but Alfred did not let her. His arms quickly found their way around her waist and pulled her closer. *A kiss on the cheek?* Was that all he would be given?

"Not so fast," he murmured, before bestowing a passionate

kiss on her lips. *Christ, she felt wonderful—and what was even more wonderful was the very slight amount of fabric between his hands and her skin.*

It was all he could do not to push her onto the kitchen table and take her right here. Meredith returned the kiss, her arms around his neck, but when the kiss ended, there was a wry smile on her face.

"Do not think you can get around me with your kisses, delightful as they are," she said.

Alfred laughed, keeping her in his arms. "I have said before, and I will say again—Archibald's life is already mapped out for him. He is a Carmichael. It has hardly hurt me."

Should he be worried by the hesitation on her face, that look of concern?

"Well, not much," he amended with a laugh. "And I speak the truth when I say that some of those friendships, or alliances as you would call them, are already set for him. One has to look at the world head-on, Meredith."

She pulled away from his arms and leaned against the sink as she examined him.

"I wish…" she said finally. "I wish it could be different."

"Different?"

Alfred had never considered different to be a possibility. *Different?*

It had never occurred to him. *What would his life be if not…this?* It was impossible to imagine the trajectory of a Carmichael's life in any other way. They were the Dukes of Rochdale. They were members of Parliament.

To change it in any way would be to leave behind decades, nay, centuries of tradition.

"Goodness, different," he said jovially as he sat down at the table and gestured that Meredith should sit. "I am not sure I would even know where to start. You mean to tell me Archibald may not be a member of Parliament?"

Meredith moved to sit beside him as indicated, but Alfred

pulled her toward him and onto his lap. She laughed as he kissed her neck.

"Whether or not he will be a member of Parliament in the future, he is a child now," she said. "Any child should be what they want when they grow, not hemmed in by tradition."

Alfred laughed, but then caught sight of Meredith's face. *There was no jesting there. She was serious.*

"By God, you cannot mean that," he said slowly.

Meredith shrugged, her nightgown slipping slightly and almost giving Alfred a most delicious view before she most irritatingly rearranged it.

"Why not?" she said. "I was never destined to be a governess until—I mean, I chose it, and here I am."

Alfred smiled. It was almost funny, the way she thought she could compare a simple choice to hundreds of years of tradition. "But you won't be a governess forever, will you?"

The words had slipped out before he could stop them, and as Meredith looked at him shyly, he saw she knew what he was attempting to suggest. It was just like the conversation at the lake. Alfred knew the words he wanted to say but could not bring himself to say them.

What was he thinking? Having a beautiful woman in his arms did not mean marriage. So many other gentlemen in his position would have bedded her by now, pensioned her off somewhere— or kept her in the house for a ready supply of comfort.

And Rochdales did not treat servants that way, whatever that damned Talbot said, Alfred thought savagely.

But...marriage? Why was he even considering it?

Alfred knew why as soon as he looked into Meredith's eyes. Here was a woman beyond compare. A governess, true, but the great talents she possessed were more valuable than beauty or dowry—and she had one of those anyway.

Alfred swallowed. He had known the woman a few months. *Did he really think offering his hand was a good idea?*

"I suppose I will not be a governess forever," said Meredith, cutting into his thoughts. "But I like being a governess, and I like Archibald. I would not want to disappear from his life with-out...without great cause. Not unless a better offer came along."

There was just a hint of mischief in her words, and Alfred tightened his grip around her. He did not want to let her go, not ever, but that did not mean marriage was the solution.

What had she said, down at the lake?

"You need to take your words back. You cannot mean it."

It was all so damned confusing. If only he knew his own heart, his own mind, it would not be so difficult, and he knew her heart even less.

Meredith felt something for him, he knew she did. She accepted his kisses—but she did not want him to propose marriage, that was certain. *Or was it?*

"Not unless a better offer came along."

What did she want from him? What did he want from her?

Meredith slipped off his lap as Alfred groaned. "We agreed—"

"Agreement be damned," said Alfred passionately. "I know you want me to kiss you. You do, don't you?"

For one heart-stopping moment, he thought he had misread the signs. But there was no mistaking that look. Meredith's gaze raked over him, finishing at his mouth, and he saw her lick her lips. He almost groaned aloud with the self-restraint.

"Yes," Meredith whispered.

In an instant, she was in his arms, and Alfred's lips were on hers. Pushing her back, he pinned Meredith between his chest and the sink, his hands around her waist, keeping her there as she moaned in his mouth.

Alfred pulled away, passion clouding his eyes but not his intentions. He had to give in. He could not stand it any longer.

"I...I want to please you," he said in a jagged voice. "It won't harm you. It won't take any of your innocence from you. Will...will you let me?"

Meredith looked up in wild confusion, her lips bruised by the violence of his passion. "Please me?"

Alfred moaned as his head dropped. *It was too much; she was too precious.* "Yes," he said quietly, raising his head to look into her eyes once more. "You can ask me to stop at any time, and I promise I will do so. Let me...let me please you, Meredith."

It was almost a plea, and he could tell she heard the longing in his voice.

"Yes," she breathed. "Yes, I want—"

She was not permitted to continue. Crushing her mouth with his own, Alfred tried to steady himself. He could not rush this. *It had to be perfect.*

Still worshipping her mouth with his, he gently moved his fingers down the length of her nightgown and then hiked it up.

"Oh!"

His fingers stopped as he broke the kiss and looked at Meredith. Her eyes were full of desire, her body only still upright thanks to the support of the sink behind her.

"Can I keep going?" he whispered, kissing her neck and feeling her shiver under him.

"Yes," whispered Meredith in return. "Oh, yes..."

He moved slower this time, achingly slower as his fingers gently stroked the stockinged thighs that quivered at his touch. God, it was all he could do not to pull down his breeches and enter her, take the pleasure he was painfully denying himself.

No. That would not do. He did not bed servants.

"Meredith," he breathed, moving from her neck to those lips once more at the same instant that his fingers brushed across her secret place.

"Oh!" she gasped, eyes wide.

Here she was, utterly at his mercy. He was stronger, more worldly, master to her. He could take what he wanted but never would. He would never countenance such a thing.

And she did not ask him to stop.

"Trust me," he breathed, and she nodded, unable to speak and eyes fluttering as he gently moved a finger within her. "Christ alive!"

She was perfect. Alfred gloried in the feel of her, almost groaning at how welcoming she was, how wet she was. It was all he could do to concentrate on kissing her, keeping her upright with one hand as the other slowly teased her, stroking the fires of her pleasure.

"Alfred," she moaned, and hearing his name on her lips as she twitched with pleasure almost made him cry out with joy. "Yes, oh, yes, more…"

More? Alfred swallowed and allowed a second finger to tease her, and as he bent his head to kiss her decolletage, he felt the change within her. She was close.

"Almost there," he whispered, capturing her mouth once more with his to ensure her shouts of ecstasy did not raise the whole house.

When she came, shuddering and wonderful under the rapid rhythm of his clever fingers, Alfred closed his eyes and almost wept. *It was beautiful. It was everything he wanted.*

Almost.

Meredith's hands had clutched his shoulders as the ecstasy overwhelmed her, and then she leaned back.

"I…I could never have imagined such pleasure."

Alfred smiled. *He had never known such torture.* "And that's just a taste…"

He leaned forward to kiss her again, his fingers moving to the buttons at the front of his breeches.

It was the wrong decision.

"And—and you'll not be getting any more," said Meredith hastily, her voice still weak. "Not from me."

Alfred knew what she needed to hear. *Had he not said it a thousand times to the ladies of London streets?* "'Tis not just about wanting, Meredith. I…I care about you. I have feelings for you."

And it was true this time, though it felt strange admitting it. What had this governess done to him?

Meredith looked up, her hair disheveled, her eyes piercing him as though attempting to understand what he had done to her, what he meant.

"Alfred," she whispered. "I…I think I am starting to fall—"

"Your Grace? Is that you?"

They froze. The voice was just outside the kitchen. It was Roberts, damn him. Alfred was not sure whether he would ever be able to forgive him.

"Your Grace?"

Alfred groaned quietly and hung his head. "I…I have to go."

Meredith nodded, taking her hands away. "I know."

Bloody hell! The last thing Alfred wanted to do was leave her, especially after giving Meredith her very first taste of what a man could do to a lady.

But he had no choice.

He stepped away, the connection broken, and he hated it. "We will finish this conversation another time," he promised her.

"Christ," swore Alfred as he turned away, unable to look at her. *He would have her, one way or another.* "I am confused."

Meredith nodded. "I know. So am I. This…this sort of thing, it usually ends in tears."

He knew she was right. Masters and servants kept their distance for so many reasons. When the lines were blurred, no one knew how to retreat back to those old niceties.

"I promise not to weep over you," he quipped.

The last thing he wished was to give Meredith—Miss Hubert—false hope. He had to try to keep away from her, or he would say or do something that he would, in time, regret.

Now how could he get out of this sticky situation he had created for himself—without hurting her or himself?

CHAPTER FIFTEEN

September 20, 1812

"**A**RE YOU ABSOLUTELY sure you want to go ahead with this?" Meredith had not intended her question to be offensive. Nor was she doubting Alfred. There were few gentlemen so proficient.

As the carriage rocked around a corner, she kept her arm closely around Archibald to ensure he did not slip out of his seat. His elder brother, on the other hand, looked as though he would be quite happy to throw himself off the nearest cliff to escape the carriage.

Meredith looked closely at him. Alfred's face was pale, his smile gone, his expression anxious.

He nodded.

Meredith bit her lip. They had all entered the carriage five minutes ago, and he had not appeared so nervous then.

They were going to the husting.

She did not say any more. It did not appear Alfred could answer any questions as it was, and she did not wish to pile any more pressure on him than he was always experiencing.

Meredith's mind took her back to that practice speech she and

Archibald had listened to a few weeks ago in the ballroom. The usually so eloquent Duke of Rochdale had...

Well. Fallen to pieces was not the most pleasant way to describe it, but it was at the very least accurate.

Some people were just not suited to public speaking.

In just an hour, Meredith told herself, *this would all be over.* If she thought saying those words to Alfred would bring him any comfort, she would, but there was no point. Alfred knew as well as she did that he would have to make his speech before all the potential voters of Rochdale, and that was something he considered quite impossible.

"Oh, yes, the Duke of Rochdale is an elegant speaker," Mr. Walker had assured her only the day before. "Yes...a little stilted, at times, but he speaks from the heart."

Meredith glanced at Alfred. *Today, it looked as though he was more likely to speak from the stomach.*

It had been only two days since their encounter in the kitchen.

Alfred had touched her, had teased her, had made her...

She had permitted him to...

What had she been thinking? What had Alfred been thinking? He had been so riled up that he seemed to have taken leave of his senses.

She must never speak of it. Who would she ever be able to confide in? That was not something ladies did. Meredith flushed. *It was something harlots did, women with no dignity and no honor!*

At the very least, she consoled herself as she leaned back into the carriage, she could take refuge in the fact that she had kept her maidenhead.

Yes, no matter what pleasure had rocketed through her body, and it was far more than she had ever believed possible, she was a virgin still. That was important. Not that she would ever be getting wed.

"'Tis not just about wanting, Meredith. I...I care about you. I have feelings for you."

What he had meant was certain. He wanted her, exactly how he was not sure, and besides, matrimony was absolutely off the cards. Marriage to the Duke of Rochdale?

Miss Clarke would never let her hear the end of it.

Archibald looked up. "What happens if someone shouts during Alfred's speech?"

Meredith frowned. "Now, do not worry about such a thing, Archibald, I am sure—"

"Or someone throws something?" Archibald said eagerly, looking over at his half-brother, who had closed his eyes as the carriage rattled on. "Or what about if—"

"Archibald!"

Meredith rarely had to raise her voice. It was one of her talents she was most proud of. There were governesses forced to shout at their charges every day to keep them in check.

Not her. This was probably the first time she had to really glare at Archibald, and her glare was another fine characteristic of being a governess.

Archibald sighed. "It was only a question, Miss Hubert."

He turned to look out of the window, thankfully falling silent so Meredith would not have to field any more questions.

It also gave her the opportunity to examine Alfred without Archibald guessing there was something more to it.

He looked dreadful. Meredith would never say it, of course, but it was hard to ignore the pallor of his cheeks or the frantic look in his eyes. Alfred was not made for this sort of life.

Yet he clung to it. Tradition, family, honor, duty…whatever he called it, Alfred was stuck in a rut, life mapped out for him.

The carriage came to an abrupt halt, and Meredith looked hurriedly out of the window. So lost in thought, she had not noticed they had arrived at Rochdale's town hall.

"You are going to be brilliant, Al—Your Grace," she said hurriedly.

She reached out and squeezed his hand. Alfred smiled weakly but did not speak.

Meredith hesitated. There was so much she wished to say, so much that could help—but with Archibald right beside her, there was no possibility of being so honest. She attempted to communicate through another squeeze of her hand.

"Alfred," she began quietly.

"We're here! Can I get out? Can I sit at the front?"

Archibald's enthusiasm entirely distracted Meredith, who quickly turned to her charge.

"We are, you can, and not a chance," she said breezily, opening up the door and seeing the driver there ready to help Archibald. "Carefully, now."

The boy scrambled down and disappeared from sight. This was it; the only moment that she and Alfred would have together before the husting. Perhaps the last time they would be alone for a long time if their last parting words were going to mean anything.

"Even if...if there were a question I would like to ask you. I...I cannot. Not tonight. I am sorry, Meredith."

"Alfred, I—"

"There he is! The man of the moment—good morning, Your Grace!" Mr. Walker had appeared in the doorway beaming. "Let me help you out, no, no trouble at all, take my hand."

There was nothing for it. Alfred nodded at Meredith and released her hand before stepping out of the carriage, assiduously ignoring the hand proffered by Mr. Walker.

By the time Meredith had gathered her skirts and was ready to descend, there was no hand to help her down. She was left to descend the carriage alone. She was only the governess, after all. The only reason she had been included in the invitation was because Archibald—now running about the pavement excitedly—would need someone to keep him in line.

"I want to go to the front!" Archibald was saying impatiently as Meredith stepped out of the carriage and over to him. "Can we sit—"

"No," said Meredith decidedly. She and Archibald—especially

Archibald, in this mood—would be more hindrance than help. He was moving about most distractingly. "We have no wish to divert your brother's attention, do we? Now, let's find seats near the back."

The town hall was rammed. It appeared that the whole of Rochdale had turned up to hear the two candidates speak, *even those who,* she thought ironically, *did not even have a vote.*

Near the front of the hall, where two chairs had been set out to face the rows, was John Talbot. Meredith tried to keep her gaze averted. The last thing she needed was to catch his attention. *Not today. Not here.*

Mr. Talbot was surrounded by a group of well-wishers, however, and Meredith was able to shepherd Archibald to the back row of seats and nudge him along to the end.

"There," she said quietly. "We will sit here and encourage your brother with our smiles. And I am expecting you, Archibald Carmichael, to sit still like a grown-up."

Archibald looked up with wide eyes and immediately sat stiffly.

She smiled. "Just sit and watch, Archibald. I am sure your brother would like you to take in as much as possible."

As she said this, Mr. Walker stepped to the front. "Please, ladies and gentlemen, take your seats—please, we are about to begin. Each candidate will share their thoughts on the election and the issues that matter most to you, the people of Rochdale. First, we have..."

She was interested to see what the people made of John Talbot. From the little she had seen of him and the little more she had been told, she did not have a high opinion of him.

His speech did not improve that estimation. He spoke well, clearly, without hesitation, and with a great deal of self-satisfaction, which did not endear him to Meredith at all.

It was the content of his speech, however, that was most repellent. She had expected to hear his story, family history, and passion for the area, and then dive into some of the concerns of the people he would seek to rectify if elected their representative for Parliament.

That was what she knew Alfred would be speaking of, anyway.

John Talbot, on the other hand, took quite a different view.

"I am not precisely saying that I am the best candidate for your votes," he said, that horrible smirk once again appearing on his face. "Though I do not believe I would be telling a falsehood if I said I was the only candidate who *deserved* your votes!"

That statement received a few laughs from the gaggle of people seated at the front right—most of them, Meredith saw, those who had surrounded him before the speeches had begun.

Meredith frowned. It was not very noble of him to speak that way about Alfred, even if that was what he believed. Wasn't there supposed to be some sort of honor in politics?

"These Carmichaels have taken too many liberties for too long," Talbot said to gasps from some members of the audience and cheers from others. "They just assume they will have your votes, so they do little to secure them! When I was speaking to a Mr..."

Meredith could not believe he was getting away with speaking like that! To say such things at all was abhorrent, but in a public platform—nay, as a speech to the populace!

He was a fool if he thought people would be impressed, she thought dryly. The people of Rochdale were not fools. They would not be taken in by such a vicious and unprovoked attack.

She looked around. Other than those who were quite clearly his supporters—Meredith spotted Miss Wilhelmina Talbot nodding her head—no one else seemed to agree with him.

Her spirits lifted.

Meredith clapped politely as John Talbot came to the end of his speech.

Archibald was outraged. "What are you doing?" he whispered. "He is against Alfred!"

Meredith nodded. "But just think what people would say if

they thought we were not being sporting?"

She watched the child's brow furrow as he considered this and then clapped politely.

Surely there would be a better reaction to Alfred's speech. Meredith was sure there would be; it came from the heart, and he was a better man. The best man she had ever met. She could not allow her emotions to be too visible on her face, not here in public. *It would never do for anyone to guess.*

Alfred clutched at the papers in his hands and did not look up at his audience.

Meredith tried to send him all her courage, all her bravery, all the gumption that had got her from there to here.

As though he could feel her thoughts, Alfred glanced up and caught her eye. Meredith beamed, and a small smile flickered across his face. He shifted his feet, standing a little taller, and the look of imminent nausea faded away.

"Ladies...ladies and gentlemen," he said hesitantly. "Ladies and gentlemen."

Meredith found her mouth going dry. This was the moment he had to prove himself a politician, not just the son and grandson of one. *He needed to read her marks.*

Alfred took a deep breath, but nothing more came out.

Archibald looked at Meredith as mutters began. "Is he going to keep going?"

"Of course. He just needs a moment."

She had not taken her eyes from him, and Alfred met her gaze once more. From this distance, there was nothing she could say to hearten him, but she took a big theatrical breath.

Alfred mirrored her, taking a deep breath before launching into, "Ladies and gentlemen. It is a great honor to be standing here before you t-today, as a man who wishes to serve...to serve the community I so greatly love."

Meredith breathed out a sigh of relief. Even in that short opening statement, she could hear the confidence return.

He could do this.

He made no snide comments about the Talbots at all. Meredith knew Mr. Hemming had been a big proponent of such things, but Alfred had put his foot down, and she was relieved to see none had made their way surreptitiously into the final version of his speech.

Her heart soared. He truly was the member of Parliament the people deserved.

She was proud of him. She knew she shouldn't be; she had no right to be, other than as his servant. But she loved him. Perhaps she had not known it quite as she knew it now, but it was impossible to ignore. She loved Alfred, and even if he never loved her, never shared the feelings she wished she could openly express, he would always have her heart.

It was something she would never speak of, and no one else could know. What a scandal it would be if anyone knew how they felt about each other…what he had done to her in the kitchen…

Meredith's cheeks pinked. It would be mad enough, the governess and the duke—but a thief? For that was what they would think of her, if her true history ever came out.

No, she would never permit that to happen. Alfred deserved better. *He would never win the election with her by his side.*

"—this great county," Alfred was saying, smiling now. "I have known it and loved it for all my…"

A thought struck Meredith, making her chest tighten. *Perhaps that was it.* Perhaps Alfred knew it would be impossible to win the election with her by his side.

But what about after the election?

It was a heady thought and one she struggled to push aside. It was delightful, the idea that he was waiting until he had been declared the Rochdale member of Parliament, and then he could declare himself to her.

Then he could sweep her up in his arms and declare his undying love. Or perhaps on a ride by the lake—or even…

Meredith's smile disappeared slowly. *She was getting far too ahead of herself*, she chided gently. If indeed that was Alfred's plan—and she had absolutely no indication it was—the election had to come first.

"—which is why you should elect me, Alfred Carmichael, Duke of Rochdale, to be your member of Parliament in the forthcoming el-election," finished Alfred with a broad smile.

Applause rang out across the town hall, and a few people even rose from their seats. Meredith mirrored them, and Archibald, evidently unclear why she was doing so but believing anything she did was the proper thing, rose, too.

"Wasn't he good?" he said enthusiastically.

"He was indeed," said Meredith, and then added, "You know, Archibald, we should probably add some public speaking practice into your curriculum—if you are, indeed, to follow your brother into politics."

Archibald flushed in the same way his brother did when irritated. "Do I have to?"

Meredith felt a pang of guilt as they sat down, the applause dying away. They were so similar. Archibald, like his brother Alfred, clearly had no interest in following the family tradition and entering into politics.

His future was mapped out, just like Alfred's, and it could not be clearer that he did not want it any more than his half-brother.

"We will see," she said quietly.

There was no need to lower her voice, however. There was a rumble of chatter growing from the crowd as people started to discuss the two speeches. John Talbot had risen to join his sister and other supporters, and Alfred stood there as though unsure what to do next.

"Come, let us go and congratulate your brother," she said.

Archibald nodded, and the two of them made their way toward him—but before they reached him, Meredith put a hand on the child's shoulder and made him stop.

"But first," she added, "we need to allow the people to speak to him. 'Tis their votes, you understand, that Alfred needs to secure."

Several people had risen and approached Alfred immediately, many of them with smiles, a few nodding, and one man had extended his hand.

"What an excellent speech, Your Grace," he said gruffly. "It put me in mind of your old father, I don't mind telling you. Actually, now I think on it, your father was to help me with a dispute I have with..."

Meredith smiled. He was a born leader, even if he did not wish to take on the mantle. The way he listened to people, heard their stories, tried to think of how he could help them...the people of Rochdale had an excellent future member of Parliament.

Then her heart twisted. Breaking away from her brother's group, Miss Talbot stepped toward Alfred. The townspeople melted away, allowing her through as a lady.

Alfred smiled and took her by the hand.

The twisting of Meredith's heart became truly painful, and it took a few moments for her to understand what it was.

Jealousy!

It was absurd, but she could not pretend it was any other emotion. She was jealous! Jealous of the instant respect Miss Talbot claimed from the people around her. Jealous of the way Alfred could take her hand, and in public! And no one would censure Miss Talbot or chastise her. The world would see flirtation and nothing more.

Alfred said something in a low voice Meredith did not catch, and Miss Talbot giggled.

Meredith's mouth fell open, and she closed it hastily. *They were flirting!*

Miss Talbot replied in a quiet voice, and Alfred nodded, chuckling as he continued to hold her hand before him.

Meredith swallowed. He had to be polite to anyone he spoke to. As soon as he could relinquish Miss Talbot's hand and move on to speak to someone else, he would.

But he did not. Alfred placed his hand on the small of Miss Talbot's back with a smile and moved her away from Meredith and Archibald to start a conversation with Mr. Walker.

She hated that she felt this possessive over him. He was her master, not her husband, nor anything else that would give her permission to complain about who he spoke to.

She could not claim ownership of him any more than this woman could. She had received no promises from him—it was she who stopped him from offering in the first place!

"Who is Alfred speaking to?" Archibald's voice was quiet, so only she could hear.

Meredith ensured her voice was calm. "Miss Talbot. John Talbot's sister."

Her eyes did not move away from her as she spoke to Alfred and Mr. Walker.

"Isn't she pretty?"

"Very pretty," said Meredith.

Alfred leaned closer to Miss Talbot to whisper in her ear, and Meredith bit her lip.

How well did she know the Duke of Rochdale? She had been in his house…what, a few months? Already she had given him more of herself than she could ever have imagined.

The chatter and general noise of the husting continued around her, but Meredith could not attend to any of it. Her mind was flooded with memories of what she had permitted Alfred to do to her in the kitchen.

"I…I could never have imagined such pleasure."

"And that's just a taste…"

Heat seared her cheeks. *Even thinking about it here, in public, felt wrong!*

Alfred was suave, persuasive. More handsome than any gentleman she had ever met. She had been born to thieves and escaped to become a governess. Yet she had allowed Alfred as many kisses as he wanted, save that first moment they had almost embraced at his dinner.

There was another laugh from Miss Talbot, and Meredith's gaze sharpened. When one loved someone, as she loved Alfred, seeing him with anyone else was painful. The idea she may not be as special to him as he was to her was even more painful.

What could she do?

Before Meredith could think, Archibald slipped from her fingers and ran forward.

"Alfred, that was great! You were spectacular!"

Alfred, Mr. Walker, and Miss Talbot all laughed, and Meredith stepped forward, too, glad to be given an excuse to approach them. Being far from him was painful.

She smiled at Alfred, and he looked at her briefly.

"Ah yes, Miss Talbot, the governess," Alfred introduced swiftly. "Now tell me, you were saying about…"

His words continued, but Meredith's ability to take in his words had utterly vanished.

The governess? This was intolerable, it was rude, it was…

Exactly as it should be. Despite all her pain, her frustrations, her desire to be close to him, it was Alfred and not she who was remembering their proper place toward each other.

It was almost an hour later that Meredith found herself helping Archibald back into the carriage.

"Do you think there will be another husting? Can I do a speech? Can we sit at the front next time? Do you think I will be allowed to visit London when Alfred is a member of Parliament? Can I—"

"Hush, Archibald," Meredith said wearily. "In you get."

She followed him into the carriage and tried not to look at Alfred. Thank goodness it was only a twenty-minute carriage ride back to Rochdale Abbey. It would not be long to sit in silence. Then she could retreat to her rooms, claim a headache—not that it would be a lie.

Alfred was laughing. "Perhaps you can visit me in London, yes Archibald, but you must first attend to your governess. I will see you back at the house, Miss Hubert."

"You are not returning in the carriage?"

Alfred looked behind him before answering, and Meredith saw Miss Talbot waiting for him. Another spark of jealousy fanned the flames in her heart.

"Alas, no, I need to stay here and finish a few things," Alfred said lightly, not quite meeting her eye. "You two go on without me. Do as you're told, Archibald."

Meredith nodded. She should have expected this. She was a fool not to have seen it coming. She was a fling, that was all. Skirt available at the house. Convenient. Nothing more.

As the carriage started to pull away, Archibald started chattering again. "I think I like hustings," he said in a matter-of-fact way. "Everyone preferred Alfred, didn't they, Miss Hubert? Don't you think?"

Meredith nodded dully. She certainly preferred Alfred over John Talbot, but it did not seem to matter. There was no chance she would ever be more to Alfred than someone to kiss and fondle whenever he chose. Well, that was what he thought.

She took a deep breath. *You must never fall in love…*

She would keep to what she did best. She would be the best governess to Archibald Carmichael as she could, and that was all.

"Can I have an ice when we get home?"

"Yes, Archibald. Now let's have some quiet."

CHAPTER SIXTEEN

September 25, 1812

"——eND OF TODAY'S sermon. Amen."

"Amen," chorused Alfred, with some relief the service had come to an end.

Alfred cleared his throat as the congregation stood for the final hymn. If only the Reverend Michaels could consider more interesting topics for his sermons. He was sure the vagaries of canon law were very interesting to some people. He was just not entirely sure that the people of Rochdale Town were those people.

To make it worse, Alfred had a far more interesting distraction right beside him. Meredith.

She was a temptation he had never known before. No other woman had caught his eye like this, caught his heart up in knots whenever he tried not to look at her.

The more Alfred attempted to avert his eyes and concentrate, the more difficult it became. Meredith's arm was warm against his. Her legs, covered demurely by the skirts of her gown, were mere inches from his own. Every part of her body was just a hand away, and Alfred had to fight hard, even amid this hymn, not to reach out.

St. Matthews was not the place for that sort of thing. *He needed to behave himself.*

A smile spread over Alfred's face. She was so good, so restrained. After their frankly confusing conversation in the kitchen, he had vowed he would do nothing to tempt her.

How could he keep to that when every inch of her caused him to be tempted?

Before he knew it, Alfred was seated once again, and the vicar was closing the service.

"Go in peace, to love and serve the Lord," he said, smiling out at his congregation.

"Amen," Alfred chorused with the rest of the congregation.

The Reverend Michaels bowed to the altar and processed out with the choir. Alfred rose and bowed along with everyone else as their vicar passed and then sat down heavily.

Well, this was it. One of the last Sundays before the election. That meant he had to stay and talk to as many potential voters as he could. That was what Mr. Hemming had said, anyway, and Mr. Walker and Mr. Brown had agreed with him.

Still, it was with some trepidation that Alfred waited to see who would approach him—and with some surprise that he saw…no one.

Not a single person. Instead, there were a few people gravitating toward…

"Ah, Mr. Johnson, Mrs. Johnson, all the Johnsons," said John Talbot loudly with a broad smile that did not quite reach his eyes. "And how are we all today?"

Alfred swallowed. What did it matter to him if people wished to speak with Talbot? The fact the crowd around the Talbots was starting to grow, however, did irritate him. *After all he had done for them! After all his family had done for them!*

"Let's go home," he said gruffly, rising to his feet and stepping out of the pew.

"I wanted to play with—"

"Now, Archibald," he snapped without looking around. He could not face Meredith, not like this. For all his talk about not wishing to be a politician—*which was all true!*—it was still strange to see people move toward the other man on the ballot sheet.

"Ah, Rochdale!"

Alfred stopped dead and sighed, carefully arranging his face into a pleasant expression as he turned around. "Talbot. Miss Talbot."

The two Talbots had managed to extricate themselves from their adoring masses, Alfred thought bitterly as Meredith and Archibald paused by his side.

"I must say, I was impressed with your speech," said Talbot with a wicked glint in his eyes. "Hardly any hesitations at all, *this time*. I suppose next time you run, trying to claim the seat off me, you may even be good at all these little speeches."

Alfred swallowed. It was very much his intention not to punch Talbot in the face, particularly halfway down the aisle in St. Matthews, but if the man kept up like this...

"Miss Talbot," said Meredith hastily, curtseying low. "Mr. Talbot. Bow, Archibald."

The boy bowed nervously, and Alfred could see the back of his neck was red. The boy would have to get used to it. *Plenty of enemies in the spires of Westminster.*

"Thank you," he said stiffly to Talbot's words. "And you were charming, as ever."

He said no more. *Better left at that.*

"Good luck with the election in a few weeks," Talbot continued cheerily. "What will you do when the results are announced?"

Alfred's jaw tightened. "Go down to London, of course."

Talbot laughed, that irritatingly, self-satisfied, smug laugh of a man who had caught another man out. "No, no, I mean when I win."

"His Grace doesn't want to hear any of that, John, hold your tongue," Miss Talbot interrupted. "Do you, Alfred?"

Alfred barely noticed the use of his first name. He was so relieved to move on from the subject of the election. "Yes—no, thank you, Miss Talbot."

He was not entirely sure how to escape this conversation; it would be damned rude if he just decided to leave, but the longer he stood here, the hotter his waistcoat seemed to become.

"You will excuse us."

Alfred looked in surprise at Meredith, who was curtseying again. "Excuse you?"

"Yes, I'll get Archibald back into the carriage," said Meredith, not meeting his gaze.

"Carriage," said Alfred blankly. "Yes, carriage!"

He turned to the Talbots with relief. *Of course, Meredith was a genius.* The perfect excuse. They would go back, and then he would need to join them in just a few minutes.

"Probably nothing worse than an early autumnal cold," he said to the Talbots as Miss Talbot watched Meredith and Archibald leave the church. "Nothing to worry about but got to keep the heir to the title safe."

"Poor chap, I hope he feels better soon," said Miss Talbot, reaching out and squeezing his arm. "'Tis so sad to see one's child so unwell."

"Brother," corrected Alfred.

"Whatever," said Miss Talbot.

Alfred smiled. It really was incredible how sometimes it was easy for one to see Miss Talbot's beauty and nothing else. And then she opened her mouth.

"Well, you will have to excuse me," he said, bowing hastily. "I really should attend to my brother and Me—Miss Hubert, in the carriage. Good day."

He had almost reached the church door until Talbot's voice stopped him.

"Nonsense, you need to escort my sister home."

Alfred turned and looked at the Talbots with surprise. "Your sister? Home?"

"Naturally," said Talbot as his sister simpered. "Girl can't walk back on her own, that would be criminal! She needs a chaperone, and no one better than you to do it. I've got to go canvassing. Secure those votes."

Alfred swallowed. Everyone expected it. That had been clear from Mr. Walker, and Miss Talbot had repeated those exact words to him at the ball, hadn't she?

"Our marriage would create a new dynasty, one without the squabbling of our ancestors."

He had no wish to marry Miss Wilhelmina Talbot. She was not the sort of person who could make him happy, but that did not seem to matter. Social decorum dictated that he offered his protection to her on the way home. *Damn and blast it.*

"Of course," he said stiffly. "Let me just advise the governess of my change of plans."

It was highly tempting to simply step into the carriage himself once he had reached it.

"There you are," said Archibald with a wide grin. "I feel fine, by the way. I don't know why there is all this fuss!"

Meredith smiled. "And that is how we intend to keep it, Archibald. Now sit back and let your brother take his seat."

She looked up expectantly at Alfred. "I...no, I need to walk Miss Talbot home."

Meredith's smile disappeared. "Oh. I see."

"As soon as I return home, let's go for a ride," Alfred added hastily. "Or a walk. Or we could read in the library, or—"

"Can I come on the ride?" piped up Archibald.

"No," said Meredith and Alfred together.

Her cheeks pinked, and she dropped her gaze. "Because your brother and I are not going on a ride. I am sure I shall be far too preoccupied keeping an eye on you and planning lessons for anything like that."

Alfred leaned forward. "I am sure those things can wait, and Mrs. Martin could sit with Archibald if—"

"I will be busy all afternoon," Meredith said coldly.

Alfred did not know what to make of it. "Busy."

What on earth could she be playing at? Yes, they had agreed—well, he had said he could not offer his hand. But that did not mean they would never spend any time together...

"Yes, busy," Meredith said, leaning forward to close the carriage door. "It may have escaped your notice, Your Grace, but some of us have to work for wages. Good morning."

She tapped on the roof of the carriage, and it moved forward. Alfred was forced to step back to prevent his feet from being run over.

Well! What was all that about? He knew perfectly well she worked for wages—he was the one who paid them, wasn't he? Surely lessons and all that nonsense could wait if they wished to see each other?

Meredith had been so cold. Was it possible something else had occurred to make her so distant? Or was she ensuring Archibald did not suspect there was anything between them?

"There you are!" A giggle erupted behind him. "I cannot wait forever, you know, Your Grace—or may I call you Rochdale?"

Alfred turned on the spot to see Miss Talbot standing outside the church and her brother nowhere to be seen.

"Yes, fine," he said distractedly, unaware of what she had said. "Shall we go, then?"

Miss Talbot stepped forward and took his arm. "Thank you, Rochdale. I always feel so much safer when I am with you."

Alfred frowned. "Strange, I never considered the paths around here unsafe. Has something occurred when I was in London perhaps?"

They had taken the footpath that led to the bridle path, which spanned most of the Johnsons' farm. The Talbot house was on the other side of it, a two-mile stretch Alfred never considered long.

"You silly man," said Miss Talbot in what she evidently thought was a flirtatious manner. "That is not what I am afraid of. 'Tis what I want from you. Your presence, if you will."

Alfred nodded, not really paying heed to her words. The sooner he got this walk over and done with, the sooner he could be home.

It was the longest sixty minutes he had endured. Miss Talbot chittered loudly about who so and so was marrying, and what sort of dowry they had, and wasn't it a shame it wasn't larger like hers, and other such nonsense. Alfred merely allowed the words to wash over him.

"Though when I marry," she said, squeezing his arm in a most alarming manner as they came to the gates of her home, "I hope I will not be settled too far from John and the rest of Rochdale. If only there was someone nearby with whom I could share my heart."

Alfred grunted in a non-committal fashion. He was not going to be drawn into such nonsense by ridiculous hints such as those.

Propose to Miss Wilhelmina Talbot, simply so she would not have to move out of the neighborhood? What utter rot. Propose to a woman merely because everyone expected it? Because it would align the two households who were most prominent?

"Well, here we are," he said bracingly. "Good day, Miss Talbot."

"Oh, no—you must walk me up to the house," said Miss Talbot with a smile.

It was simply not in Alfred's power to say no. How could he? The drive was not long, only a few hundred yards. Only a few minutes, and he would be rid of her. Then he would be back on his way to Meredith.

"And this is where I leave you," he said, trying not to sound too cheerful, removing Miss Talbot's arm from his own.

She pouted, looking up at the manor house in some surprise. "You...you do not wish to come in and—"

"No," said Alfred, perhaps a little too quickly.

Miss Talbot's eyes narrowed. "You are taking your time in offering for my hand, you know. I'm giving you as many opportunities as I can, Your Grace, but really!"

Alfred managed to keep his jaw from dropping.

"Miss Talbot," he said heavily. "I am sorry to say I will not be proposing to you. Not today, not ever."

Miss Talbot blinked as though attempting to understand. "I beg your pardon?"

How was he supposed to say this more directly without giving offense? "Miss Talbot, I do not love you."

"Oh, you are funny, Rochdale. As if that mattered! What has love got to do with it?"

Alfred smiled dryly. *At least that was honest.* "I know our kind usually weds for alliances, but I have all the alliances I need. What I want is a wife, a partner in life."

"I can do that," Miss Talbot said eagerly, evidently sensing the wind had changed. "I can be that for you, Rochdale. I really can."

Alfred looked at her. She had been born and raised as he had, told from a young age what her destiny was supposed to be. How could he blame her for clinging onto that as tightly as he clung to this foolish notion of him becoming a politician?

It was not her fault. She had never had someone like Meredith dropped into her life, forcing her to recognize everything she had ever been told.

"You...you cannot, Wilhelmina, you must see that," he said more gently. "I have not fallen in love with you, and so I cannot marry you."

"Who have you fallen in love with?"

Alfred hesitated. "Good day, Miss Talbot."

He felt lighter as he strode down the drive and along the bridle path back to Rochdale Abbey. That was a conversation he should have had a long time ago—at the ball, perhaps. But it was done now and would end that thinking from her, or her brother, or Mr. Walker, too.

Yes, he would have to remember to tell Mr. Walker. It was essential everyone stopped attempting to force him toward Miss Wilhelmina Talbot. Especially when...

Alfred swallowed as he stepped over a stile, taking a slight shortcut. Never before had he noticed just how...*cloying* was the only word he could think of. How cloying Miss Talbot and other ladies were.

Not until he had met Meredith had he known what it was to feel comfortable around a lady.

She had shown him a new way of what a woman could be— what a lady should be. He smiled as his feet took him rapidly closer to her.

"Meredith," he said as he caught her arm just outside the French doors of the ballroom around the back of the house. "I am sorry about that, I had no wish to walk Miss Talbot home, but I was given no choice. Now, how about that ride?"

He had expected her to smile. To laugh, to show relief he was home. Perhaps even say she had been hoping he would suggest that, and she was ready to tack up her horse.

Meredith said none of those things. "I told you, I have no wish to ride."

Alfred's temper flared. He had not put up with Miss Talbot all that time just to be pushed away by Meredith when he finally had the chance to spend time with her!

"No, you told me you were busy," he said, trying to keep his temper in. "I do not see how you are busy at all."

Meredith's cheeks flushed, but she said nothing, just tried to pull her blanket into her arms more completely. The book was slipping from her grasp, but still, she held her head up high and refused to say anything to him.

Alfred was at a complete loss. *What had he done?* Surely they had both understood each other when he had told her he simply could not offer for her hand?

"Is...is there something wrong?" he asked carefully. "Have you received...I don't know bad news from your family?"

Meredith glared and turned around, striding toward the kitchen gardens.

"Wh-What?" Alfred called after her, stepping forward hurriedly in an attempt to keep up with her.

"No, I have not heard anything from my family," she said, refusing to look at him as she paced down the gravel paths. "It is just that I can decide whether or not I wish to go for a ride. I may still be your servant, but I can make my own decisions!"

There was a heated fury under her words, but Alfred was at sea. He had never ordered her to go on a ride with him, had he? He had hardly ordered her since she had arrived!

"Please," said Alfred, taking her arm and forcing her to stop and look at him. "Please, I have offended you in some way though I know not how, and I am sorry for it."

He was astonished to see tears in Meredith's eyes, though she blinked them away. "I have no right to be upset."

Alfred stared. He had never seen Meredith like this, so upset. At the same time, she appeared furious—and not with him, he could see that now. No, she was furious at herself.

Meredith glanced up at the house. "We must not—someone will see. They will see us conversing."

Alfred pulled her further into the walled kitchen garden where they would not be overheard. "I did not realize privacy would be required for this conversation. But now that we have it…why do you not tell me precisely what is going on here?"

There was a wry smile on her face as Meredith dropped the rug and the book down onto the gravel, right by the last of the summer carrots.

"You know, I never thought I would be one of those women to get upset about this," she said quietly. "It is stupid and foolish, and I knew at some point you would marry, but—"

"Marry?" Alfred interrupted in shock. "What—marry? I am not getting married!"

"Tell that to Miss Talbot."

Alfred blinked, unable to understand where this was coming from. "Miss Talbot—Miss Wilhelmina Talbot? I am not marrying her, nor have I ever said such a thing!"

"Are you sure?" she shot back. "For everyone I speak to expects it. Why, it could not have been clearer today that *she* expected it!"

Alfred opened his mouth but paused. It was starting to come together now. He would never have guessed it of her, but then he supposed there was still much to be learned about Miss Meredith Hubert. There were depths to her he had not quite reached.

"If I did not know any better, Meredith," he said slowly, "I would say you were jealous."

She was! She was jealous!

"Well, why should I not be?" Meredith said defiantly. "There is no understanding between us, Alfred, and I know there never will be. But you know I...there are feelings on both sides, I thought. And there you are, with Miss Talbot. Dancing at balls, walking her home from church...you do think I am the only one to come to such a conclusion?"

Only then did Alfred see it all from her perspective and realized she was exactly right. What else could be taken from such actions—*except, of course, the truth.*

"Yes, a marriage between myself and Miss Wilhelmina Talbot was proposed by our families," he said gently, taking her hands in his, her gaze finally rising to meet his own. "But I have no interest in her. Truly, Meredith. Miss Talbot is a lady of the town, and I wish her well in finding someone to marry her. Because I am not that person."

Meredith examined him closely. "She is...Miss Talbot is a very pretty woman."

"Really?" said Alfred with a grin. "I had not noticed. I was too busy looking at you."

She laughed, and at that moment, the ice melted.

"You probably think I am very foolish," she said ruefully.

Alfred chuckled, her hands in his. "No, but I admit it has done wonders for my ego!"

Meredith laughed and dropped his hands to pick up her rug and book. "I really do have to go in soon and start planning next week's lessons."

Her voice sounded wistful, and Alfred wondered whether she was just waiting for a different kind of invitation.

"Well, in that case," he said gently, "why don't I walk you back to the house—the long way round, though. I am desirous of a little time with you."

She nodded, and they walked slowly down the gravel path to the other side of the kitchen garden, towards the orchard. They continued in silence until Alfred laughed.

"My apologies," he said with a grin. "I was just thinking of something Miss Talbot once said to me. It made me realize there was no possibility that we would ever be married."

Meredith looked at him curiously. "What did she say?"

Alfred laughed again at the mere memory. "She said—and you will not believe this—but she said she was convinced that one day, women should vote!"

"I do not understand," said Meredith quietly. "What is the joke?"

The dappled shade from the orchard gave them some relief from the sun, but it was no protection from the serious look that Meredith gave him.

Alfred gaped. "Well, you—you cannot really think that women should vote?"

"Why not?" shrugged Meredith as they stepped into the more formal gardens on their way back to the house. "In Sweden, women can vote if they pay taxes. That seems a rather good idea to me. If one is paying for the country one lives in, it is only right that one gets a say in how it is run."

It was news to Alfred, though he had to admit that it made sense, of a sort.

"Well, the Swedes can be strange if they wish," he said magnanimously, "but I do not believe we will ever have a system like that here!"

"Why not?"

Alfred stared. "Why not?"

Meredith nodded. "I actually agree with your Miss Talbot. I

do not believe it will be long before women can vote."

It was impossible not to laugh at these words, and Alfred continued to chuckle as he held open one of the garden gates for her.

"But Meredith, women are simply too emotional!"

It was a striking glare she gave him now, and Alfred hastily ceased speaking.

"Emotional is not always a bad thing," she said fiercely. "Should we not be emotional about poverty? About education? About protecting ourselves?"

These were thoughts he had never had before. Such radical ideas!

They had reached the back door now, and Meredith hesitated. "I do not mean to be divisive, I only share what I think."

Alfred pushed away his concerns. He was falling in love with her, and all other problems could be solved later. *After the damned election.*

"Not at all," he said before opening the door for her and watching Meredith disappear into the kitchen. "Good day, Miss Hubert."

CHAPTER SEVENTEEN

September 27, 1812

I T WAS NO good. No matter where she looked on all the shelves, she couldn't find it.

Stepping down the library steps, Meredith sighed. She had seen the leather-bound copy of *The Theory of the Four Movements* weeks ago. Just when she needed it to explore the theme of utopia with Archibald, she could not lay her hands on it.

Meredith leaned against the armchair and wondered how much time was worth spending, looking for the book. Perhaps it had been lent to another—Mr. Walker, perhaps.

She smiled at the thought of the gruff man reading the Frenchman's theories and looked at her pocket watch. Still early. She had time before lessons were to begin again.

Besides, she had seen Mrs. Radcliffe's latest novel. Meredith pulled it gently from the shelf. Sometimes a novel was far more interesting than reality.

Each time she thought she understood Alfred, knew where this was all going, comprehended that he had a plan for her, for them—he did something to confuse her. The ball, that encounter in the library, the rides, the moment in the kitchen when he showed her true pleasure...and then nothing.

Meredith did not believe she was a fool. She knew matrimony was unlikely for her at all, let alone with a duke! But then why did he continue to return to her?

"Miss Talbot—Miss Wilhelmina Talbot? I am not marrying her, nor have I ever said such a thing!"

Meredith shook her head as she slipped into the welcoming embrace of the armchair, with Mrs. Radcliffe's novel in her hands. His protestations that he was not in love with Miss Talbot made sense, she supposed. She had certainly seen no stolen kisses or looks of love between them.

Well, not from Alfred's side.

But the way he had acted, the poor Talbot girl could be forgiven for thinking she would receive a proposal! Walking her home—why did he not just refuse Mr. Talbot's request?

She simply could not imagine being a duke, having that much power, and not choosing to use it in the way he wanted.

Just as she started to read the first line of her book, the door opened.

Meredith closed the book. Whether it was Roberts or Mrs. Martin, she was certain to be criticized. Being a part of the household for almost two months did not seem to matter.

"Do not concern yourself, I only came to look for a book for Master Archibald's lesson," she said automatically as she rose from her seat.

"I should think so," came Alfred's reply. "That is what a library is for, isn't it?"

Meredith smiled. There he stood in the doorway, a broad smile on his face. The gentleman who had invaded so many of her thoughts over the last few weeks.

Almost since the moment she had arrived here.

"Alfred," she breathed.

The duke stepped into the library and shut the door behind him. "Just the woman I was looking for."

Meredith raised an eyebrow. "Really, at this early hour? If you have a query about Archibald's education, then I would be more than happy to take you through the lesson plan I have orchestrated from now until Christmas. We will be focusing on—"

It rapidly became clear, however, that Alfred was not interested in understanding the minutiae of Archibald's education. Firstly, because he did not permit Meredith to finish her sentence; and secondly, because of the manner in which he did this.

Stepping across the room, Alfred pulled her into his arms and stopped her words with a passionate kiss.

Meredith melted into his arms and gave herself over. *All she wanted was Alfred.* She wanted to spend her life in his arms, right here, being worshipped by him.

It did not feel like much to ask. Losing herself in the pleasurable sensations he sparked across her entire body was all Meredith could do—standing up alone was taking too much concentration. The world was better whenever she was in his arms. This was where she belonged.

Alfred broke the kiss and released her from his arms. They could not keep doing this.

This was getting out of hand.

He examined her with a look of concern. "Something is not right, Meredith. I can always tell with you. What is it? You can tell me anything."

Meredith thought there were a great deal of things she would never tell him. What duke would want to hear their younger brother had been placed in the care of a woman who had grown up in one of the worst thieving gangs in all of England?

She almost smiled. Sometimes she wondered how she managed to keep it all in, the sadness, the disappointment, the lies.

"You can tell there is something wrong?" she deflected with a smile. "Just like that?"

Alfred looked serious. "I am starting to become an expert in you, Meredith, and I know when you are not happy. Something is wrong, and I wish to change it. Talk to me."

Meredith was tempted to simply say her sadness could be

kissed away. Those fingers could bring such pleasure. Perhaps they could repeat their previous encounter in the kitchen.

Footsteps echoed in the hallway, and a footman was scolded for having mud on his shoes. Meredith almost laughed. *No, it was madness to think that they could get away with such a thing. Not today.*

Stepping away from him to ensure she was not tempted to throw herself back into his arms, she looked along a shelf as though hunting for a book.

"I came in here looking for a copy of *The Theory of the Four Movements*," Meredith said calmly, hoping her frantically beating heart did not betray her. "I was sure you had a copy, and I was hoping to discuss utopia and dystopia with Archibald in the coming—"

"You are not despondent because you cannot find a book," interjected Alfred. "Come now, give me some credit."

Meredith turned to glare, temper rising, before allowing it to wash away. "I truly came in here to look for that book."

"I am not saying you did not," Alfred countered. "But that is not what ails you."

Meredith had never noticed just how tall Alfred was. With such a serious look, his jawline tight, and eyes focused on her, it was like standing in the sun on a brilliantly hot day.

She did not say a word. *How could she trust her voice?* It was far too likely to spill out her hopes and dreams, her wild expectations for a future she knew she could never have.

She should have written to Miss Clarke. Sunday evening, she had sat at her desk and wondered whether writing to the proprietress of the Governess Bureau was the best idea. *Request a new place. Say that nothing had gone wrong, but she wished to be closer to London.*

Half of the letter had been written before she had screwed it up.

No, she could not leave. Not after such good progress with Archibald. There was no knowing who would come after her to care for Archibald, and she felt...well. *Responsible for him.* As though she would be betraying him if she decided to leave because she could not control her feelings for his half-brother.

"You cannot hide from me forever, Meredith. I am your master."

Meredith bit her lip. She had to say something. She would always regret it if she did not, and now Alfred had spoken those words, she did not have much of a choice.

"Yes," she said calmly as she turned to face him. "Yes, you are, and that is precisely what is on my mind."

Alfred's forehead puckered. "What, that I am the master of this house? I would have thought you would have been well aware of that fact the moment you accepted this position."

"And yet I did not know that... When I accepted this position? Alfred, can you not hear it in your own words?"

He looked genuinely confused, and Meredith realized she would need to spell it out. "Alfred—or Your Grace, as I should address you—you are the master of this house. You are the master, and I," she swallowed, "I am just a servant within it. I am your brother's governess!"

She had expected him to look abashed, nod, or say he had not considered that.

Instead, a broad smile crept over his face. "I know, 'tis a little saucy, isn't it?"

A little saucy? Did he have any idea what she was risking? How the entirety of society, not to forget the *ton* and Parliament, would judge them from what they were doing—what they had already done?

Perhaps he did not care. *Perhaps this was merely something he had done before.*

Meredith pushed the thought aside. She could not permit that John Talbot to influence her. She knew Alfred better than that.

The important thing was to stay calm. This was a conversation they had avoided. Usually, they were so distracted by...well, kissing, that they never managed to talk about it.

But they needed to talk about it.

"Alfred," Meredith said quietly. "When I came here, when I was chosen for this appointment by Miss Clarke…I thought I would spend a little time discussing with you which Roman senators you thought Archibald should learn about. Whether a trip to the nearest city would be beneficial for his study of the English church. In short, all the questions that a governess should be asking her master."

Alfred nodded, taking a step toward her. Meredith retreated. She could not permit her emotions to get the better of her.

"But here we are, talking about…about…."

"Love?" Alfred said softly.

Meredith swallowed. It was not a word she had ever spoken to anyone. Even her parents had been reticent to discuss emotions, that sort of thing considered a weakness.

When you cared too much about a person, they could betray you.

That was what it had been like in the cut and thrust world of thievery, and Meredith had never seen anything in the rest of the world to suggest it was any different.

Fixing her gaze on Alfred firmly and trying to ignore how handsome he was, Meredith knew she had to say something.

"This…this cannot continue."

Every syllable in that sentence hurt to say, and it was with some relief that Meredith came to the end of it.

Because it was true. It was not as though she could do anything to change their situation! No, as she had said to Alfred in the kitchen garden…

"There is no understanding between us, Alfred, and I know there never will be. But you know I…there are feelings there, on both sides, I thought."

Alfred considered her closely. Meredith felt discomfort settle in her chest. She was not accustomed to being examined in this way.

"What do you want?" Alfred said finally.

Meredith swallowed. *Did she have the bravery to say what she really wanted?*

For what she wished more than anything was for Alfred to…to propose to her. There, she could admit it in the quiet of her mind. It would be the culmination of the wave of desire he had stirred in her the moment he had invited her to dinner—no, before then, when he had accosted her on the lawn when riding Beauty.

She had thought him so rude then, so condescending. He had not bothered to know her, yet made so many assumptions about her—but had she not done the same? Even now, when she knew him better, there was still so much to discover.

Alfred leaned against an armchair, still examining her closely. "I do not think there is an easy answer to that question, is there, Meredith?"

Meredith swallowed but knew no words were coming.

"In that case," Alfred said in a low voice, "why cannot we just enjoy this for…for what it is?"

Meredith had always been a woman who knew what she wanted. She had wanted to leave the Glasshand Gang, and eventually, she had managed it. She had wished to find some sort of respectability, and eventually, she had managed that.

The day she had been accepted into the Governess Bureau had been one of her happiest. *Why, there was even a pension scheme, Miss Clarke had said!* She would not have to work all her days merely to end up in the workhouse. The Governess Bureau had given her the stability she had so desperately craved…but was she about to lose all of that? It was a risk she took by accepting Alfred's words.

"Why cannot we just enjoy this for…for what it is?"

An arrangement. That was what Miss Arabella Smith had entered into with her employer, Lord Hastings.

It had been her last employer because when Miss Clarke had discovered the details of the arrangement, something Miss Smith had always refused to reveal, she had removed Miss Smith from the Governess Bureau.

Meredith had never heard of Miss Smith again. There had

been rumors, of course. *There were always rumors.* Most of them sounded incredible, but there was no knowing what could happen.

There had been a few others, though not at the Governess Bureau. Other governesses did not have the rules of the Bureau to live up to, as Meredith did, and she knew the rule was there for two reasons.

Firstly, to protect the Governess Bureau.

Secondly, to protect the governesses.

Because that was what an arrangement with your master did. It removed all your protection as a woman of the household. The masters simply took what they wanted, and whenever they wanted, with the promise of a good reference at the end of it all.

"Tell me...tell me about Molly."

Alfred frowned. It was quite clear that the question, in his mind, had no bearing on the rest of their conversation.

"Molly?" he said slowly. "I do not believe I am acquainted with anyone called Molly."

Meredith's heart sank. It was hardly an auspicious start. If he could not even recall her name, it was unlikely Alfred had cared about her very much.

"Molly Butters," she said softly. "She was the undermaid here. She left the day I arrived. You...you do not remember her?"

Alfred had a blank look. "What has a Molly got to do with us?"

"Just answer the question, Alfred," Meredith said in a firmer tone. The concerns she had been unable to ignore needed to be addressed. She owed herself that, at the very least.

Alfred sighed heavily as he rolled his eyes. "Fine, we will play this little game. Molly, I cannot even recall her face."

Something cold and sharp slipped down Meredith's throat and into her stomach.

"I...I cannot believe that you do not remember her," she said finally, trying to keep the tone of accusation from her voice. "She was here for almost three years, from what Mrs. Martin has told me. You do not recall her at all?"

Alfred shrugged with something like a smile on his face. "Meredith, I think you forget just how many servants there are in my house—and for the garden and the grounds. And all my tenants! You think I have the capacity to remember the name of an undermaid?"

Was this a sign of things to come? Meredith's ice-cold stomach was now twisting in knots most painfully. If that was how Alfred treated a servant he had bedded and then swiftly, it appeared, forced to leave…well. *How would he treat her?*

Would she receive the same treatment?

"What is this all about, Meredith?"

She did not reply. *How could she?*

"I do not understand why you are so interested in her," said Alfred, rising from the armchair, "when it is *us* I wish to speak of."

Meredith nodded without saying anything. She had made a lucky escape, then. It would have been so easy for her to allow him to bed her. Alfred was persuasive, certainly, and he had proven what pleasure he could bring her.

Yet she had held out, thank God. Meredith tried not to let her disappointment show. Alfred was not the man she thought he was.

Taking a deep breath, Meredith said quietly, "I think…I think it is best we stop this. This, between us."

Alfred grinned. He evidently believed she was joking. "What, caring about each other? Wanting each other?"

If only he had said love again. Until that point, Meredith was almost certain that if he had just professed his undying love for her, she would have succumbed. How would it have been possible for her to resist?

But he did not. It was all physical for him, all about getting under her skirts.

Alfred stepped toward her. "My goodness, are you trying to tell me you don't like my kisses?"

Before Meredith could respond, Alfred pulled her into his

arms once more and kissed her neck, trailing a line of kisses down to her décolletage. It was heady, wonderful, forbidden, and that made it all the more delicious—but Meredith pulled away.

Not today. Not again.

"No," she said quietly.

She was being taken advantage of; she knew it. Meredith wanted to trust him, wanted to believe the hurt look on his face—but how could she, when he had given her no indication of serious intentions?

Meredith stepped away from his embrace, though with some regret. She had to speak seriously to him, she had to make him understand.

"I am in earnest, Alfred. Where is this, this assignation going?"

Meredith looked closely into his eyes. This was Alfred's moment to impress.

The smile faded from his face. "I do not know."

Pain like nothing else entered Meredith's heart. Even as she had asked about Molly and found the answer she had feared, a small part of her had been convinced there was a plan in Alfred's mind that would bring them together.

Now it was clear Alfred had no great intentions for her— other than to relieve her of her innocence. He was not thinking of the future. He was far more interested in the here and now.

Meredith stepped toward the door to the hallway. "Well, until you know that, I think it best if we do not meet like this."

"Meet like—Meredith, we live in the same house!" Alfred protested.

"I cannot do this," she said, her voice breaking. "I cannot give you what you want with no idea of the future. You must not ask me, Alfred. Please, leave me alone."

Meredith's scrabbling fingers found the door handle, and she almost staggered into the hallway. She had to be quick, for she could hear Alfred's footsteps following her—but she stepped lightly across the hall and up the stairs.

"Meredith—Miss Hubert, come back!"

Alfred shouted after her, but she ignored him, focusing on keeping her feet quick up the stairs as her heart raced.

"Meredith!"

She did not look back.

When Meredith slammed her bedchamber door, she leaned against it with a frantically beating heart.

How long could she stay in this house?

CHAPTER EIGHTEEN

October 1, 1812

"AND THAT," ALFRED said heavily, with a great sense of relief, "brings our campaign to a close."

Applause rang out across the drawing room, Mr. Walker in the lead. Mr. Brown had not bothered to bring his hands together, and Mr. Hemming looked a little disgruntled and was clapping just as loudly, if not more so, than Mr. Walker, as Alfred tried to hide his smile.

If he were not very much mistaken, there would now always be a Walker and a Hemming involved in a Carmichael victory.

"Please, please," said Alfred, holding up his hands in an attempt to slow the applause, but it only succeeded in the opposite.

"Three cheers for His Grace!" called out Mr. Walker.

Alfred grimaced. "No, Mr. Walker, please don't—"

"Hip, hip, hooray!" began Mr. Hemming determinedly.

Alfred allowed his hands to fall to his sides and listened with a careful smile on his face as all those who had supported him offered congratulations for a race well run.

It was ridiculous, really, but there was nothing for it. The more he attempted to calm them, to demonstrate that he had done very little, the more they tried to congratulate him.

Embarrassment flooded his veins, but Alfred was not new to this sensation of taking credit when it was not due. He had been applauded on his first day in the House of Commons. Some old gentleman who had known his father forever, it appeared, had orchestrated it.

"*A new Carmichael in the House!*" someone had shouted all those years ago. "*Three cheers for the future Duke of Rochdale!*"

And here he stood, the current Duke of Rochdale, about to, once again, enter that dreaded though hallowed hall. At least, when the results were announced in a fortnight.

What a long fortnight it would be. He would have to start packing. Kittering would need to start laundering and putting aside his formal wear, and a new Season in London would require a few more waistcoats and cravats.

"Mr. Hemming," said Mr. Walker stiffly, offering his hand for the younger man to shake. "A clean run. I commend you."

Alfred once again hid a smile. It took a tremendous amount of effort for Mr. Walker to say that, he knew. If only one had a daughter and the other a son. There could have been a natural merger there if ever there was one.

"I cannot believe we have done it again," said Mr. Hemming, taking the older man's hand and shaking it vigorously. "All thanks to your guidance and leadership, Mr. Walker."

A rapprochement, Alfred thought wryly. One that would undoubtedly be increased once he won the damned election.

For he *would* win. A Rochdale always won, and Alfred was not so pigheaded as to believe it was anything to do with him, his charms, his wit, or his popularity.

"There we go, a smile on our member of Parliament's face!"

Alfred looked up to see Mr. Walker beaming. "I beg your pardon?"

The older gentleman was seating himself beside the duke by the fire with a wide grin. "We need you to be positive, Your Grace! In a few weeks, we'll be waving goodbye!"

Alfred almost laughed. Mr. Walker spoke as though that was to be celebrated rather than mourned! Rochdale Abbey was his home, but it was his duty to leave it.

"Yes, yes," he said with a nod. "Something like that."

Mr. Walker looked at him carefully, the noisy chatter masking their more intimate conversation. "You know, Your Grace, we are very proud of you. I can see in your heart that you fear some of the responsibility your father gave you, but you bear it well. I believe he would have been very proud of you."

"You are too kind, Mr. Walker."

The older man rose stiffly and bowed. "I am minded to think that many people around you give you false praise, Rochdale, if you pardon the informality. I think you, like your father, despise it. So I will say only this. You are a credit to him. Good day, Your Grace."

Alfred's respect, already high for the veteran campaigner, rose as he stood to bow in turn. Mr. Walker certainly saw more than he gave him credit for, and as Alfred bowed to each of the gentlemen in turn as they left the abbey, it was with a strange sense of sadness.

Mr. Walker had guided him through the maze of campaign rules and regulations the first time he had run, five years ago now. Alfred could not have guessed then just how complex the whole damned thing was. As he watched the man get into his carriage and back to Rochdale Town, he sighed heavily. In the next election, Mr. Walker would undoubtedly bring his son with him to start him off on his own journey of commitment to the Rochdale cause.

And around and around it went...

As Roberts stepped forward to close the door, Alfred put out a hand to stop him. "What is that?"

What had caught his eye was certainly not something he would have expected to see in Rochdale Abbey grounds.

At least, not for years.

"Is...is that a kite, Roberts?"

The butler peered out of the front door with a serious expression and examined the sky where the duke was pointing. "I do believe it is, Your Grace."

Alfred blinked against the bright blue sky. The autumnal winds were moving it about so quickly, it was hard to see it clearly, but it was a kite. Flapping about in the air and with ribbons pouring off from all sides, it had that rather careworn feeling of a kite made by a child, rather than one of those impressive silk ones, which could be purchased in London.

A long string, barely visible against the sky, trailed down from the kite as it fluttered, twisting around the side of the house.

"How curious," Alfred said quietly as he stepped outside for a better look.

"Your Grace, I have some important papers for your review," said Roberts hastily. "Up in your study, you will find them—"

"There will always be important papers for my review," Alfred said. *Who had the end of that kite?* He was prepared to bet it was Meredith. "I am sure they can wait."

"They cannot wait, Your Grace, one of them in particular—"

"Good, good," said Alfred vaguely, taking another step forward.

Meredith. After that row in the library two days ago, she had assiduously avoided him. He had gone to the schoolroom and been made to feel so entirely unwelcome that he had backed out immediately.

"Your Grace!"

Alfred turned to see Roberts frowning. "I am sorry, Roberts, but I need to go outside for a bit. All that sitting down in the drawing room, very stuffy. I need...I need fresh air."

He strode away before his butler could say another word. He did not wish to be reminded just how many papers there were piling up on his desk in the study. *Contracts, bills, disagreements, requests for his judicial input...*

The whole of Rochdale assumed he would be disappearing to London in a few weeks, and was desperate to get his input—or at the very least, his seal and signature—before then.

They had no interest in *him*. On the other hand, neither did Meredith.

Alfred's footsteps crunched on the gravel as he walked around the house, silently chastising himself for this fool's errand. As he turned the corner of the drawing room and a new vista of lawn came into view, a smile crept over his face.

It was not Meredith but Archibald who had ahold of the string, eyes brightly shining with excitement as he looked up at the kite. The cheeky, mischievous nature was still there, but the rambunctious, destructive elements were gone. What stood before him, facing away so unaware of his older brother's presence, was a Carmichael, a future Duke of Rochdale, and Alfred beamed with pride to see him.

"A little more slack, and watch the wind!" Meredith's voice rang out in the blustery day, and Alfred's gaze flickered to her. She was seated underneath the wide oak tree, watching her pupil carefully. "Remember what we learned about wind and currents!"

Archibald nodded and tugged a little at the string in his hands, giving it more slack.

Alfred could not help but smile. Meredith was a fine woman, something his body could not forget, but she was first and foremost an outstanding educator. What other woman—what other *tutor* would use flying a kite a way to teach a child about the vagaries of the wind?

He had never known a governess to take this much interest in a child before. Certainly, none of his had. They had never worked to draw him out of himself, to find ways of engaging him beyond the dreaded textbook.

He really must reply to that letter from Miss Clarke at some point. She had been desirous of understanding how Miss Hubert was progressing about two weeks ago, but Alfred had ignored the letter. It was probably half-buried on his desk by now.

"I'm doing it. I'm doing it!" Archibald's cry of joy was almost lost on the wind as a particularly strong gust whirled past Alfred, but he did not need to hear the precise words.

The boy was starting to become a rather interesting character, Alfred thought. The more he came out of his shell, the more he liked him. The more Carmichael he saw.

Not wishing to disturb them, and mindful Meredith was not interested in discussing anything with him beyond the purchase of string—*which,* Alfred realized in the haze of hindsight, *now made sense*—he stepped along the side of the house and sat on a bench just to the left of the French windows of the ballroom. From here, he had a perfect view of his brother and his governess.

Truth be told, Alfred's gaze was more often drawn to the lady than the child. She sat supremely comfortably, like an empress. Her blanket was adorned with a few cushions, and she sat regally with her legs tucked to the side.

Alfred's heart twisted. The conflict between them was crushing him slowly. His stomach lurched as she laughed, watching Archibald closely.

He loved her. Though he could only admit this within the quiet of his heart, Alfred knew it to be true like he knew the moors out beyond Rochdale Abbey. They were there, and he could take or leave them, but he could not ignore them.

Everything about Meredith was what he would have looked for in a partner if he had been so inclined to marry. Caring, intelligent, far wittier than he was. An ethic of strong, hard work, even when unappreciated or unthanked. And beauty. *Christ alive, she was beautiful.*

And here she was, most disobligingly slotting into his life, his family, demonstrating just what a wonderful wife she would be.

Alfred's hair was ruffled by the wind. *It felt as though she had been made for him.*

He had never given much thought to the woman he would marry. Miss Wilhelmina Talbot had been mentioned a few times when he had been growing up, but he had never considered her seriously.

When he had been in London, the title of duke had opened doors for him, including Almack's, but when ladies heard his duchy was not only in the north, but tiny compared to that of Lancaster, Cornwall, or Axwick, they had turned their noses up at it. At him.

Besides, he had always had other things to do. He was young, and the duchy already had an heir. Finding a wife had never been a priority.

But he knew what would be required of him. As Alfred watched Archibald skip about in pure joy, watching his kite spiral up in the air under his careful maneuvering, he knew he would one day choose a wife. A woman of good breeding, good education, beauty if possible, but most importantly, a partner, someone he could go through life with, who would make each day better simply because she was within it.

Alfred's gaze was drawn once again toward Meredith. She fitted the bill, of course. He knew nothing of her family, but it could not be more obvious they were gentlefolk. How else could they afford such travel as Meredith had mentioned?

His jaw tightened. Yet she was a servant, by definition below him—worse, a servant in his household. She was supposed to be protected by all the social niceties a female servant could expect in the house of a great gentleman like himself.

Alfred swallowed. The voting for this damned election had not started yet. It was still his to win—or lose. If he was foolish enough to announce he had engaged himself to a servant...

It would be the end of him. Not just his career in Parliament, that he could not care two figs for. No, it would be the end of the Carmichael reputation. Who would associate with a gentleman who, it would be assumed, had seduced his own brother's governess?

No, it could not be done. Yet Alfred could not help the way he felt about her.

At that moment, a sudden gust of wind blew past him and hurtled upward, pulling the kite in an unexpected direction.

"No!" Archibald's cry of frustration was almost lost in the wind as his kite spiraled out of control—until it became lodged in the oak tree under which Meredith was sitting.

"Careful, Archibald!" Meredith warned as the child hurtled toward the trunk.

The kite was entirely tangled in the branches near the uppermost of the oak tree. Even from this distance, Alfred could see Archibald's face had fallen, though he had not succumbed to tears.

Alfred sighed. Why was it that there always needed to be a man to sort things out? For all Meredith's talk about women voting, it was quite clear men were needed to solve half the problems that women and children—

He had been halfway out of his seat, but he fell back onto the bench in shock at what he saw. *It didn't make any sense. What on earth was she doing?*

Meredith had risen from her blanket. She had not looked around for a gardener nor stepped toward the house to ask a footman for his assistance.

All of these responses would have been acceptable, and Alfred would not have been surprised by any of them. What had shocked him, however, was the strange thing she was doing with her skirts. Meredith seemed to be…well, pulling them up in a very odd way. It almost looked like…well, like she was tucking her skirts into her…

Alfred swallowed. It was very odd behavior at the best of times, but how it was supposed to help with—and then he gasped.

Meredith had reached out a hand to touch the trunk of the old oak, examined it for a moment, and then lightly, as though it was as simple as taking a walk down the lane, clambered up to the first branch.

She did not stop there. Not looking down and advancing upward with no fear, the governess ascended the tree.

Alfred's jaw dropped. Archibald was laughing and clapping as she rose higher.

Alfred rubbed his eyes, half thinking the vision of the young lady climbing a tree like a ten-year-old boy would disappear—but no. When he looked again, Meredith had reached the kite and was gently starting to untangle the string.

"—not as high as before," Archibald was saying. "Higher, Miss Hubert, higher!"

Alfred could barely contain his astonishment. *Higher—she had done this before?* Was this a regular occurrence, his governess climbing up trees? If he had not heard Archibald's words, he would still have wondered whether he was seeing things.

But instead, he watched. Meredith eventually had the entire kite string untangled from the branches and dropped the kite down into the waiting arms of Archibald at the foot of the tree.

"Now you mind...wind it up careful...not tangled," she said.

A swell of wind moved across the lawn, and Alfred's stomach lurched. *Meredith—she was still in the tree!*

It swayed most alarmingly, but she merely clung on until the swell was over and then carefully climbed down.

"No, like this," Alfred heard her say as she dropped lightly onto the ground, untucked her skirts without any ceremony, and moved to the child to show him how to wind up the string.

Alfred was surprised he could hear her at all over the thundering of his pulse in his ears. Partly from shock, partly with relief that she had come to no harm, but partly in anger.

What on earth was going on? Tucking up skirts to show her legs, climbing up trees, so easily able to jump down what must have been almost ten feet...

English ladies simply did not do such things! They could not do it; it wasn't in their nature!

What sort of life had Meredith had before she had come to him?

"No one should do what they don't want to do. Even if it is because of family. Even if one feels a duty."

Alfred swallowed, eyes not moving from the giggling child

and his governess but seeing them no longer.

Now he saw the pattern. Meredith had utterly avoided telling him anything about her family, or indeed herself. What did he know of her? She was a governess. She liked riding. That was all.

Alfred tried to calm himself, but the evidence—or lack thereof—was there now he came to think about it. He had assumed her father was a gentleman because he traveed, but it meant nothing!

What she could do was astonishing and certainly not something a gentlewoman did. *Great talents indeed!* Alfred was sure he could not climb up that tree, so how could she?

And then a terrible thought swept through his mind as the words of Mrs. Martin echoed in his memory.

"I am trying to tell you I think they have been stolen! There is a thief in the house or coming into the house and—"

Items were going missing in Rochdale Abbey. He had dismissed Mrs. Martin's fears, considered her foolish to worry so—but what if she was right? What if…

It was awful to even think it, but what if it was…*Meredith?*

Alfred hated himself for even allowing the thought to enter his head.

What if the thief was Meredith?

A twinge of fear crept around Alfred's heart. The very thought sickened him, but he would have to raise it with her. There was nothing else for it. This could not continue, this questioning within his mind.

A seed of doubt about her had been planted in his heart, and he had to root it out—if it was false.

CHAPTER NINETEEN

October 5, 1812

MEREDITH'S HAND MOVED slowly and carefully over the blackboard, removing all evidence of the Latin lesson which had ended the afternoon. Not one of Archibald's favorites, and not one in which he excelled.

I wonder, mused Meredith. *He has such an aptitude with history—perhaps there was a link there, a way we could make Latin itself more palatable.*

She resolved to consider this later. It was only a Monday, after all, and she would need to ensure they got through a few more days before she started changing the way the lessons were planned out.

Her careful eye swept over the schoolroom. Archibald had been obedient enough, she supposed when she asked him to carefully put away his schoolbooks. Well, they were put away. The haphazard pile of books in the corner was no longer on his desk, but it could not be said that they had been stacked neatly. Far from it.

With a small sigh, she stepped over and started straightening them. She knew the cost of books, and some of these had gold leaf. *Only the best for the heir of a duke.*

A gentle cough, accidentally ignored for she knew not how long, only disturbed her when Meredith straightened up to consider her handiwork—books now neat and tidy.

She turned and saw, to her surprise, Roberts in the doorway, looking uncomfortable.

"Why, Roberts," Meredith smiled. "Come to brush up on your geography?"

The butler did not return her smile. He was certainly a man who kept to himself. In truth, Meredith had hardly seen him since she had joined the Rochdale Abbey household.

Still, there was no reason to be suspicious of him—other than she had never seen him anywhere near the schoolroom in that time, and on the rare occasion that he had a message for her, it typically came to her through Mrs. Martin.

"No, I have not come to…ah, brush up on my geography," said the butler stiffly. "I have a message for you."

Meredith waited, but Roberts seemed unwilling to continue. She folded her hands demurely before her, as Miss Clarke had taught all governesses.

"When speaking to a butler, or at times, a steward," she had drilled her governesses, *"it always does to look a little more retiring than one actually feels. No one wishes for the gentleman to feel inferior, does one?"*

Meredith had never understood those words until now. Roberts certainly did look as though he felt on the back foot, not quite meeting her gaze.

"A message?" she ventured after another minutes of silence. *Really, it was most odd. If he had a message for her, why not give it?*

But the butler's gaze was moving around the schoolroom searching for something—as though assuming something would be here and finding, to his surprise, it was not.

Well, rude butlers were not a new phenomenon to Meredith. As the Egertons had grown, she had become part governess, part chaperone really, and the Right Honorable Miss Egerton had taken tea with a number of notables in London. Many of those butlers did not consider a governess a worthwhile companion to the daughter of an earl.

Meredith was overwhelmed with the sudden panic that the butler would be able to see a difference in her because of...well. What she and the master had shared in the kitchen all those nights ago.

She waited. She had attempted to draw out the message from the man, and he had not permitted it. All she could do in the meantime was wait.

It felt like an age, but eventually, Roberts said stiffly, "You are formally requested to attend to the master in his study."

"Formally requested?"

The butler nodded.

It was the way the butler was looking at her...or not looking at her, which gave Meredith reason to pause. The poor man looked quite unhappy.

Meredith picked up a book on Roman history almost idly, her mind whirring frantically. "Requested?"

Roberts nodded, his gaze still not meeting hers. Meredith had expected him to pull a face, wink, or even say something comforting. Perhaps the master wanted a report on whether French or German would be an appropriate second language.

But if Meredith was not mistaken, Roberts looked, instead, a little cold. There was a lack of warmth even Miss Clarke would have been proud of.

"Very well," Meredith said slowly. "Thank you for relaying the message, Roberts. I will be down as soon as I have finished here."

She turned away, expecting him to depart as quickly as he could, so obviously desirous of leaving her presence.

"No, you must go down now."

She swallowed. *What was this about?* She could not think of anything she had done recently, nor anything Archibald had done, to elicit such treatment. *Or was it perhaps*—and her heart fluttered at the mere thought—*that Alfred wished to see her privately and had concocted this ruse to allay suspicion?*

Roberts coughed and dug something out of his waistcoat pocket. "I have been given this instruction, Miss Hubert, and all I do is follow it to the letter."

Meredith took the scrap of paper handed to her. Written in a bold hand were just a few words.

Bring the governess to the study immediately.

Meredith turned it over; it was so brief, she assumed she must be missing the second part of the message. But that was all.

This made no sense! After all, they had experienced together, all they had shared, Alfred could not merely step upstairs and ask her himself to come to the study—or even better, have the conversation, whatever it was, in the schoolroom without all this pomp and circumstance!

Unless…unless her initial estimation was correct, and he wished to restart their…well, *romance* was the only word she could think of, though she was not entirely sure if there was a name for what they had shared.

Those kisses, those words of affection—did Alfred merely wish to resume them, to ignore the concerns she had voiced so clearly?

She handed the note back to the butler with a wry smile. "Will my day gown suffice, do you think?"

For the first time since his cough to announce his arrival, Roberts spoke more directly. "Your apparel does not concern me. *Now*, Miss Hubert. His Grace expects you immediately."

And with that, he left and stepped along the corridor, footsteps fading out of hearing.

Meredith raised an eyebrow. It had been another long day on her feet, attempting to guide Archibald through the joys and pitfalls of declining nouns in Latin. The last thing she wanted was to explain to Alfred again just why they could not—why they should not…

It was too much to hope, then, that she could enjoy a quiet evening in her bedchamber with nothing but a good book and the privilege of solitude.

A few weeks ago, she would have wished for nothing more than an evening with Alfred, would have relished it, would have considered it a great honor.

Now? Her heart was conflicted. She knew he had no serious designs on her. She would remain here as his brother's governess, but that did not mean she was open to his overtures.

Meredith stepped down the staircase lightly, then across the hallway and down the corridor, past the ballroom, and around the corner to the study. The door was shut.

She took a deep breath.

She straightened her gown and pushed all assumptions from her mind, needing to be calm.

Fighting the temptation to just walk in and find out what all this nonsense was about, Meredith knocked on the door.

"Come."

Alfred's voice, even through the door, sounded stern. Meredith entered the study.

She had never been inside the study before. It was much like Miss Clarke's in many respects, though much larger. Alfred was seated behind a mahogany desk with brass fittings, the room curving around in an L-shape, bookshelves, and cabinets everywhere, packed with things that caught the eye. An elephant's tusk, a huge seashell, a—

"Miss Hubert." Alfred's voice was just as cold inside the study as outside it.

Meredith's gaze snapped over to him, though she struggled not to continue glancing around the room curiously. There were so many parts of Rochdale Abbey she had not explored.

"Please be seated."

It was not his words that sparked Meredith's rebellion. She always had a defiant air, but it was the way Alfred spoke without looking at her, gesturing at the chair before him on the opposite side of the desk. It was the complete lack of attention he was giving her, his gaze focused on the paper in his hands.

Fiery defiance sparked around her heart. "I would rather

stand."

She was being contrary just for the sake of it, she knew, but she could not help it. She could not bear this stuffiness, this formality. *What on earth had he brought her here for?*

"Well, that's fitting," he said finally.

His words did not make sense. Meredith frowned. *What was he talking about now?*

"I am sorry, Your Grace, I do not quite understand your meaning," she said quietly.

"Like a criminal in the dock," Alfred said curtly. "You will stand."

Meredith's mouth fell open, utterly bewildered at his words. "Like a criminal in the—what exactly am I accused of?"

This could not be happening, Meredith thought wildly. This was a joke, a bad jest. Stand like a criminal in the dock?

She had worried herself thinking he would want to kiss her, and instead, here she was, standing like a fool, about to be accused of something she had not done!

For she had not done whatever it was. She did not need to know what it was; she had done nothing of ill-repute since stepping into this house. She had left that part of her life behind before she had been welcomed into the Earl of Marnmouth's home as a governess.

So it was not a typical crime then, she thought hurriedly, racking her brains. Was it something she had done in the schoolroom, had she taught Archibald something she should not have?

It appeared, however, that she no longer had to wait to find out.

Shaking his head, Alfred said quietly, "I cannot believe that I trusted you, Miss Hubert. Did I not welcome you into our home? Did I not give you sufficient bed and board? Were your wages not what you had expected?"

Meredith swallowed, throat dry, but she could not leave her fractious temper behind. "And I, in turn, cannot believe you are not informing me of the supposed crime I have committed!"

Her eyes sought his out, but Alfred would not meet her gaze.

"Your Grace," she began again, trying to inject a little reverence into her voice. Perhaps she could lighten the mood, make him laugh? "'Tis a strange trial, this one, if that is indeed what it is. Why, I believe criminals are meant to be told what they are accused of!"

She laughed, but it sounded hollow and strange in the large room. Alfred did not join her in her false merriment. Instead, he shook his head.

"With each passing word, you further convince me of your guilt," he said slowly.

Meredith's eyes widened. This was going far beyond a joke now. What could he possibly believe she had done? It was quite clear now by the way he refused to look at her, the tightening of his jaw, the way his hands were clasped painfully before him on the desk—he truly believed she had acted wrongly.

What on earth could he have misunderstood?

"I cannot incriminate myself for a crime I have not committed," she said.

Alfred did laugh at that, though it was bitter. "Oh, so you know what to expect? I should have guessed you had been through a trial before."

Meredith's heart turned cold. "Of course not!"

Her employer had gained a completely incorrect view of her—from whom, she was not sure, but it would be a disaster if she was to be formally accused. Why, who would believe her? The word of a governess against a duke—more, against a past and future member of Parliament?

Taking a step forward, Meredith said, "I am certain this is just a misunderstanding. I would hate for you to have a false impression of me due to a misunderstanding, so if you can just tell me what it is, I can tell you the truth."

"Theft," spat Alfred, anger pronounced across his face. "*Theft*, Miss Hubert. What do you say to that?"

Meredith's heart went cold. *No, it was not possible.* She had been so careful to hide her ties to the Glasshand Gang. No one would have recognized her, not here in the north. Even Miss Clarke had no idea of her true parentage, of what life her family had chosen. She had been careful to lie just enough.

No, this was mere coincidence; Meredith was sure of it. All she had to do was keep calm and demonstrate that she had done no such thing.

"I have done nothing of the sort," she said. "You may search my rooms if you—"

"*My* rooms!" interjected Alfred with a fierce glare. "You are here on my good graces, Miss Hubert, and I cannot believe I was so easily taken in! Madness, utter madness! To think, I was starting to consider…"

He swallowed, discomfort showing in his face as he shifted in his chair.

Meredith's heart was now thumping heavily against her chest like an iron weight. *He was starting to consider…what?* Had he been about to offer her his hand? Had he finally come to a decision that would make them both so happy?

"After much consideration, I have decided," Alfred continued, his eyes transfixed on her own, "to terminate your employment. You may return to the Governess Bureau. I will supply you with a reference of sorts."

It had all happened so quickly it was difficult for Meredith to take it in. His last words rang in her ears, echoing and merging with each other, so it was difficult to discern his meaning.

"After much consideration, I have decided to terminate your employment. You may return to the Governess Bureau. I will supply you with a reference of sorts."

Terminate her employment? Theft? It was all wrong. This could not be happening! She would not leave Rochdale, nor return to London—the Governess Bureau would hardly accept her back with the charge of theft on her record, even if it was unproven!

For it could not be proven. Meredith thought wildly about

the books she borrowed from the library—all were still in Rochdale Abbey, or at the very least in the grounds.

"I am not a thief," she said quietly.

Alfred did not look at her. "Forgive me if I do not believe you."

"I do not forgive you!" Meredith said, her temper rising. "After all we have—after I let you—why would I lie to you, Alfred? Why would I steal from you—what could I possibly steal from—"

"That's *Your Grace*, I thank you!" Alfred cut in, and Meredith's words halted.

Your Grace. He had asked her to call him Rochdale, all those months ago. She had called him Alfred for weeks, knowing her heart was utterly compromised and that she loved him most ardently.

Now to stand before him, accused of a crime she had not committed but could not prove to the contrary, and have him demand the correct address…

Meredith swallowed. She was allowing her emotions to get the better of her. It was clear that someone had been telling lies about her, attempting to discredit her not only with her employer, but with the man she loved.

The question was, who?

She had few friends in Rochdale, but she had not believed she had many enemies.

Mrs. Martin? No, she was perhaps not a close acquaintance, but after the support she had given the housekeeper for the ball, she had at least been respectful.

Roberts? Meredith could not see the butler concocting such a tale. It was not his style; he was simply not flamboyant enough to make up such a thing.

Miss Wilhelmina Talbot, perhaps? Meredith almost smiled at the thought, even in her misery. No, Miss Talbot would not consider her, a governess, an actual threat. There were much easier ways to get Alfred's attention than encourage him to dismiss his brother's governess.

Meredith sighed. She could not conceive of anyone who would gain by her departure from Rochdale Abbey.

"I have done nothing wrong," Meredith said slowly, forcing down her anger and ensuring her words were calm. "Your Grace, I am not even aware of anything missing! What could I have possibly stolen?"

"There are plenty of things missing, and the disappearances started just as you arrived at this house," Alfred said sharply. "The valuable family Bible with gold leaf, my father's old pocket watch, two family miniatures, the list goes on!"

"I would never steal from you!" she said, outrage at the accusation finally overspilling into her words. "How can you think that of me, Alfred? You know me better than anyone!"

"Do I?" Alfred shot back. "Who are your parents? Why have you become a governess? Why does no post arrive for you, you have no friends, no correspondents? Your talents are great, but where do they come from?"

Meredith tried to think, her mind so full of confusion it was difficult to untangle the hurt from her thoughts.

What did those items have in common? There must be a pattern, a reason that the real thief—whoever they were—had chosen those items. *It had been one of the rules of the Glasshand Gang,* she thought ruefully. *Never leave a pattern, never leave a trace.*

"I welcomed you into my home," said Alfred softly. "I allowed you free rein with my brother, I even...and this is how you repay me?"

Meredith could not take in his words.

"I just want to know where the items are," he said. "They...much was my father's. Please, I just want them back."

But Meredith was not listening. His father's pocket watch, the family Bible—miniatures?

"Who were the miniatures of?"

Alfred waved a hand. "'Tis no importance, you could not have chosen them because of the people they depict!"

"Your Grace," said Meredith, taking a step forward. "Who were the miniatures of?"

Perhaps it was her governess training, but Alfred swallowed and then said, almost against his own better judgement, "My father and his second wife. The boy's mother."

The boy's mother. It was all to do with his parents, or at the very least, his father and his two wives.

What was it Archibald said, as she attempted to make him focus on his geography?

"I wish my father were still here—or my mother. I miss them, Miss Hubert, and no one ever talks about them."

"Have…" She hesitated, but knew she had to ask. "Have you asked Archibald about the missing items?"

The question was right, but outrage did not adequately cover his expression. "How—how dare you blame my brother!"

"I am not blaming," said Meredith hastily, "I was just wondering if—"

But Alfred had risen from his chair and strode around the desk. "You go too far, Miss Hubert, even for you. Goodbye."

He had opened the door into the corridor, and Meredith stared. "This conversation is not over!"

"It is over when I say it is over," snapped Alfred.

Meredith opened her mouth to retort but closed it again. He was not interested in hearing her thoughts, nor the truth. Alfred had made his decision, judged her falsely—and, it appeared, without even knowing her past. Anything which could have grown between them, any love…it was all over.

She stepped toward the door but was halted by Alfred's one word.

"Meredith."

Her gaze raked over his face, wishing she could kiss away the pain so obviously transfused through his face.

"Why did you do it?" he whispered. "We had something, something I believed far more precious than pocket watches."

Meredith took a deep breath. "We have something, Alfred.

We still have it. I have not stolen a thing, though…though I believe you have stolen my heart."

Their gazes met for a fraction of a second, and in that moment, Meredith's heart leapt. There was a desire to believe her there, she knew it—if only she could get him to—

"I wish I could believe you," he whispered.

Meredith smiled wryly. "I wish you could believe me, too. I was falling in love with you—or at least, the man I thought you were. Good luck in the election."

CHAPTER TWENTY

October 6, 1812

ALFRED TOOK A long, deep breath before raising his fist to knock on the door before him.

The sleepless night he had just spent had been riddled with panic, despair, and even a little doubt. Could he have spoken differently to Meredith—*no, Miss Hubert, he must consider her with her full title now.* Now any potential bonds between them were broken. Now he had revealed he knew her secret, her crime, and she had given no evidence to the contrary.

"Your Grace, I am not even aware of anything missing in the house! What could I have possibly stolen?"

Alfred's jaw tightened and his stomach gave a horrendous lurch once again. Pain, yes, regret, but something more. He had lost something so precious he had not realized its value before he had seen Miss Hubert, for who she really was. For *what* she really was.

She could have cost him the election!

No, he had been right to dismiss her. It was only a shame she had not been able to leave the house that moment, but he was no cad. He would permit her a few days to collect her things and make arrangements for her return to London.

The very thought of her leaving, never to be seen again...he hated that. He hated the weakness it revealed in him. So besotted with her, so desperate to please her, to be pleased by her, he had almost been entirely taken in.

But no longer. Now he had to have another difficult conversation, one he wished could be delegated—he was the head of this household. It was only right Archibald heard the news from him. He would not be like their father, keeping truths close to his chest and never trusting those around him with information. Withdrawn, removed from the life of his family. His sons.

No, despite the awkwardness of the conversation's content, it had to be done. He wanted to be better than the man who had gone before him. Even if he had no wish to be a member of Parliament, he could desire to be a better man.

Taking another deep breath, Alfred knocked gently on the boy's bedchamber door.

"Miss Hubert?"

Alfred's heart sank as he opened the door. "No, it's me. Alfred."

Archibald was seated by the window, a book in his lap and a toy soldier in his hand. The look of disappointment on his face was blatant, and caused a tug of remorse on Alfred's heartstrings, but the boy quickly covered.

"Oh, hullo," he said with a forced brightness that made Alfred wonder whether he had already taken on so many of their father's bad qualities.

"Can...can I come in?" Alfred said with a smile.

Archibald blinked, obviously a little confused by the question. His older brother had never asked permission to enter his bedchamber before. "I suppose so, if you want."

This response did not exactly bode well for the conversation that he was about to have, but there was little he could do about that. He did not wish the boy to live in a house of secrets. Their father had always been determined to avoid discomforting topics, and Alfred was not going to fall into that trap.

Shutting the door behind him, Alfred looked around the room. The walls and ceiling had been painted to resemble a tent when he himself had been a boy, and though the decoration was peeling in parts, it was still there. So, too, was the wooden castle Roberts's predecessor had made him, soldiers scattered about the room.

It had been years since he had last been in here. He had already vacated the room by the time Archibald had been born, naturally, and had never had much of a reason to return. It was strange to see it, both his and not his. He could still see the scuff by the window where he had tripped as a boy, attempting to move the castle on his own.

"This...this used to be my room, you know," he said lamely.

Archibald nodded without saying a word, his solder still in his hand.

Alfred took a deep breath and stepped over to him, dropping awkwardly to sit on the floor beside the boy. "And who are you today?"

"William the Conqueror," said Archibald promptly. "Did you know William the Conqueror had four sons, and two of them ended up being king? His wife was Matilda. Matilda was often called Maud, it gets very confusing."

"Is that so?" said Alfred vaguely.

Archibald nodded vigorously. "I like Matilda, not that one, but his granddaughter. She wanted to be queen, but her cousin Stephen didn't want her to, so they fought a war."

Alfred smiled. He forgot, sometimes, just how wondrous it was to discover the history of one's country for the first time. There was only one first time you learned about these things, and there was a sense of wonder on the boy's face he had entirely forgotten. He had never had much time for history, but it was clear the toy soldiers were getting far more use by his brother.

He swallowed. How easy it would be to permit the boy to chatter on, then leave. He could simply talk with him, instead of relaying news he knew would pain the child.

Alfred's heart hardened. *It was Meredith—Miss Hubert's fault.* She was the one who had gained the boy's trust, and she was the one hurting him now. If she had not stolen, how different this could all have been.

"Miss Hubert says she has to go back to London," said Archibald conversationally, eyes still affixed on his soldier.

Alfred's mouth fell open with astonishment. *How dare she!* Knowing she would be dismissed from her post, her employment terminated due to her own folly and greed, she had told Archibald first—worse, she had told him a lie!

Going back to London? Poppycock, what nonsense! She wasn't 'going back to London,' as though she wished for a holiday! She was being sent away in disgrace!

Alfred swallowed. If he had been a different man, perhaps he would have made it known to the world just what she had done. Everyone would know Miss Meredith Hubert was a thief and not to be trusted in the homes of others.

But it would be a stain on his character if the truth got out. How could anyone trust him if his judgement were so poor, he permitted a crook into his own household!

Besides, Archibald needed to be able to trust a governess again, and though she had her faults, Miss Hubert had gained his trust. The last thing he needed was for Archibald to think all future governesses were thieves.

"Yes, Miss Hubert is going away," Alfred said stiffly, hoping she would be gratified by his restraint. "I have decided she isn't a good governess for you, so she is returning to London, and you will be getting another one. Another governess, I mean."

The toy soldier dropped to the floor. "I do not understand."

Alfred saw the confusion in his brother's eyes. "I know, but you will have to trust me when I say that she is not good for you, Archie."

Even the pet name was not enough to make Archibald smile. Instead, his eyes narrowed. "But...but Miss Hubert is the best governess. You will not be able to find another like her, so you must let her stay. I think she is marvelous! You are not to send her away!"

He should have seen this coming. It was the danger of introducing a stranger into the household, of course, but he had thought the Governess Bureau was a secure choice.

If only he had spent a little more time with his own brother. It was clear, given a choice between his governess and his own brother, Archibald was quite happy to turn against his kin and stand by the woman who had so quickly tamed his heart.

Alfred's own heart quickened. *As she had done with him.*

"She has done something wrong," he said gently, "and for that reason I cannot permit her to stay here. Her punishment is that she has to leave us, Archie. 'Tis for the best."

Archibald blinked in only that way a child could do, with such innocence and confusion. "What has she done wrong?"

Alfred hesitated. How could one explain the whole situation to a child? For it was not merely the theft which had turned his heart against her, though it had instigated the re-examination of his feelings.

No, it was the fact—*if he was honest*—that he had entirely trusted her. More, he had succumbed to emotions he had never experienced before. He had taken some of her innocence, had wished to bed her—had restrained from doing so with her character in mind.

Yet, she had not hesitated to sully that character with the crime of thieving. It was a betrayal like no other he had ever experienced. The more Alfred attempted to explain it, the more pain he felt.

"She acted wrongly," was all he managed to say.

His brother did not look convinced. "But what did she do?"

His heart contracted as he thought about the family Bible. No one had been harmed, yet she had taken things which simply could not be replaced. Candlesticks, silver, even jewelry, most could be replicated or replaced. But not the things Meredith had stolen.

"Miss Hubert knows that what she has done is wrong," he said aloud, "and the trouble is, Archie, she cannot admit she is in the wrong. That means she cannot ask for forgiveness, and we should always own up when we do something wrong, shouldn't we?"

"But what if she didn't do it?" Archibald said earnestly. His small fingers had reached to pick up the dropped soldier, but his eyes never left his brother's. "She helps me to ride, and she knows an awful lot about history, and...and I like her. Does she have to go?"

Alfred sighed heavily. His younger brother had voiced many of the thoughts he himself had experienced over the last few days.

She was wonderful, Meredith Hubert. He wished for nothing more than for her to be innocent, to stay with them and continue to make the Carmichaels' lives better.

But he could not ignore the evidence. However much he wished to, there was no way around the fact that items only started to go missing while she was here, and there had been no other change of staffing during that time.

It was Meredith.

"She must have been a thief before she came here," Alfred said, forgetting himself.

Archibald's eyes widened. "Thief?"

Damn and blast! He had told himself he would not reveal anything about the sordid affair to the boy—it wasn't fair to bring him into this. He had only started the conversation because the boy would need to know she was going.

"What has she stolen?" Archibald persisted. "It was her horse you know, you got that wrong. You were so sure you were right, and you were wrong. What if you're wrong now?"

Alfred carefully bit down his frustration.

If he could not trust her around his possessions, what made him think he could trust her with his heart?

"We had an argument," Alfred said heavily to put the whole conversation to bed.

"Friends argue sometimes," said Archibald solemnly, "but they make it up again, if they are true friends. I would do that, if I had a friend."

His brother's words cut through Alfred like a knife. *Christ, he had never quite realized just how isolated the boy was*—it wasn't until his sad little face looked wistful at the thought of having a friend, any friend, that he realized how alone he was.

The governess had been to change that. It had been one of the reasons he had hired a damned governess in the first place. *Someone to be a companion to the boy.*

The memory of the two of them flying kites whirled through his mind, and Alfred smiled, despite himself. That should have been the continuation of a wonderful friendship.

"What has she stolen?" said Archibald.

Alfred hesitated before responding. *He was just a child.* It was the principle of the thing, and the fact that they were family items which had hurt. What had Mrs. Martin said, before he had accused Meredith?

"I've gone through all of Miss Hubert's belongings, Your Grace, and I cannot find hide nor hair of them," she had said smugly.

And Alfred had looked at her blankly. "You speak as though that proves her guilt, Mrs. Martin. I would suggest it rather proves the opposite."

"Well, makes her an expert, doesn't it?" Mrs. Martin had retorted. *"She had already sold it all, surely?"*

Alfred wondered where the family Bible was now. It was no use to most people, the covers inscribed with all Carmichael births for four generations. But the gold leaf was valuable. It had probably been stripped away by now, ripped from the binding.

There was a sniffing noise. Alfred saw, to his horror, that Archibald was close to tears.

"There, now," he said, rising and bringing the boy into an awkward hug. "There, now."

Strangely, Alfred felt better after the embrace. He was not one to typically hug his brother. Perhaps that should change.

When they finally pulled apart, Archibald's eyes were red but there was no sign of tears.

"Come on," said Alfred bracingly. "Why not dine with me this evening, Archibald? Won't that be a treat?"

Archibald nodded and looked hesitantly at his soldier. "Can…can William the Conqueror come?"

Alfred smiled. *There it was, that childish innocence that his brother still had. Long may it last.*

"Of course he can, but he will not have his own plate, he will have to eat from yours," he said seriously. "Come on, the dinner gong will be going any moment."

Alfred really thought he had managed to pull off the impossible as they walked down the corridor together. He had not entirely told Archibald the truth, and the boy seemed reconciled to the fact his governess was leaving. Precisely when, he would have to discuss with Meredith—Miss Hubert—in the morning.

But as they reached the top of the staircase, Alfred's heart skipped a beat. Down in the hallway, right by the front door, was Meredith.

This was unexpected. He had believed her to be restricted to her bedchamber, but instead, she was here and looking just as beautiful as ever.

If he could ignore the theft, and the subsequent lies which had attempted to cover it up, he could have kept loving her. He would have loved her forever. They had shared moments which had been special. Moments he would never forget. But he could also not forget the theft, the lies, the attempts to conceal her treachery.

"Miss Hubert!"

Before Alfred could reach out and restrain his brother, the child leapt forward with a smile on his face, flinging his arms around her and burying his face in her pelisse.

"Miss Hubert, I don't want you to go!"

Alfred kept his mouth tightly closed as he continued to sedately descend the stairs. If he had as little self-restraint as the boy, he would probably have done a similar thing.

He had no wish for her to leave. When he watched her gently stroking Archibald's head and murmuring comforting words, it was easy to pretend she had done no ill, and was only dressed in her coat because she was visiting a friend...

A friend a long way off. Now Alfred had reached the bottom of the stairs, he could see a trunk beside her in the hallway.

She was leaving to go somewhere overnight, then. Though it pained him, it was for the best. The last thing he needed in the week before the election was a thief in the house. They could come to an arrangement when she returned—what *was her notice period? A month?*

"Archibald, go into the dining room," Alfred said quietly.

Archibald did not move but looked up instinctively at Meredith.

Just in time, then. He could not have the heir to the duchy of Rochdale so enamored with a servant—*a thieving servant at that!*— that he would not obey an order from his brother.

"Go on," Meredith said gently, removing Archibald's hands from around her. "You do not have to worry, Archibald. Good friends are not always together, but they can remain good friends, even over immense distances."

Archibald looked as though he wished to say a great deal more, but at a glance to his older brother, he merely nodded and walked toward the corridor that led to the dining room.

Alfred waited until his brother was out of earshot before rounding on Meredith.

"How dare you speak to him like that," he snapped. "Do not speak to him that way! He is not your friend, and you are no longer his governess!"

The desire to protect his brother from any further harm pounded through his veins, mingled and conflicted with the passion he still felt for her and the hurt she had caused him.

Christ alive, but he would need a stiff drink after this conversation.

Meredith did not look impressed nor cowed by his harsh

words. Instead, she said coolly, "I am the only friend that boy has in this house, so please don't tell me what I can and cannot say to him. You have already apparently decided what I have and haven't done."

Alfred found his hands had clenched into fists and worked hard to unclench them. He needed to keep his temper. She was far sharper than he ever gave her credit for.

"How," he said, swallowing to strengthen his voice. "How dare you say that to—"

"You?" interrupted Meredith with an innocent face. "A duke? A past and future member of Parliament? My master? Or the man I thought cared about me?"

This was precisely how Alfred did not want the conversation to proceed. He could not bear to have his affection thrown in his face like that; it was abhorrent! She evidently did not care for him; so easily referencing the passion they had shared. But it was not so easy for him.

As he stepped closer, another two trunks moved into view. Alfred looked more closely. Yes, it was not just a pelisse, but a traveling cloak. She was not going elsewhere for the night. *She was leaving.*

Meredith noticed his gaze, and said with supreme calmness, "Yes."

"You are leaving." Alfred said, rather unnecessarily. "Where are you going?"

"I have taken rooms in the King's Head, in Rochdale Town," said Meredith quietly.

Evidently his surprise was visible on his face.

She hesitated, then said, "I would rather be there than under a man's roof who does not believe me."

Well, if she wanted to throw that graciousness back into his face, so be it. Alfred could see nothing but confirmation of her guilt in her sudden decision to leave the house. If she were innocent, would she not wish to stay to attempt to prove it?

But the pain in his heart was great, and Alfred could not help but breathe, "To think, we could have been married."

"We were never even engaged," said Meredith curtly. "You never bothered to ask for my hand. Just like all the other ladies who went before me."

Now Alfred was entirely lost. "The other ladies?"

"I only know one by name," said Meredith quietly. Two red spots had appeared on her cheeks, the topic evidently discomforting her. "Molly Butters."

Irritation sparked across Alfred's chest. "Do...do you think I fall in love with every female servant who crosses this threshold? Do you think me some sort of cad who just goes about seducing young ladies in my care and keeping, and then just throws them away?"

The words rang out in the hallway, far louder than he had intended. Was this the depths of depravity she believed him capable of? Did she not know him at all?

"Th-That is what you think of me," Alfred managed, his old stutter creeping back due to the violence of his thoughts. "Well, off you go then. Go."

"You could not have stopped me even if you wished to," snapped Meredith. She picked up her trunks and moved toward the front door, saying over her shoulder, "And I will be taking my horse from your stable, so don't think I am stealing from you again!"

It was a low blow but before he could respond, Meredith had disappeared from sight, around the corner of the house.

Alfred took a deep breath. She was gone. He had to put this whole debacle behind him and concentrate on the election, only a week away.

Taking care not to look out again in case she had come back into view, Alfred closed the front door and locked it for good measure.

CHAPTER TWENTY-ONE

October 7, 1812

> *Dear Miss Clarke,*
>
> *I hope this letter finds you well, and the Governess Bureau is continuing successfully.*
>
> *I wished to inform you, before my current employer sends word, that I have been falsely accused of a crime I most certainly did not commit. The Governess Bureau would never tolerate a thief, Miss Clarke, and you know me to be a most trustworthy and honest soul.*
>
> *You must believe me, Miss Clarke. I would never betray you and the Governess Bureau, nor risk my place at*

Meredith looked at the progress of the letter she had been attempting to write to Miss Clarke for the last twenty minutes. It was difficult to encapsulate her despair adequately, and now she read the words, they did not exactly sound promising. On the contrary, they looked instead as though she was attempting to protest too much.

Meredith crumpled up the paper, dropped it to the floor, and sighed as she examined a blank, white page. Dipping her quill into the ink, she started again.

Dear Miss Clarke,

I hope this letter finds you well, and the Governess Bureau is continuing successfully.

I wished to inform you personally that my employment in the home of the Duke of Rochdale has been terminated. This is due to a false accusation of theft which I have not been given the opportunity to refute. You know I would never

Meredith heaved a sigh. No matter how she attempted to relay the information, it always ended the same way: a desperate plea to be believed, as she had not at Rochdale Abbey.

If she was unable to convince Miss Clarke of her innocence, she would not only lose her place in the Carmichael family, but in the Governess Bureau itself.

True, there may be a few families who would accept a governess who had been delicately let go by another. There were always differences in temperament to be considered, after all, and accounting for taste.

But by a duke? Returned to London in disgrace, forced from the Governess Bureau?

Only families who had no other options, would pay poorly, and likely leave her unprotected from some of the male servants would consider her.

Meredith bit her lip. Miss Clarke knew nothing of her family background, nothing about the Glasshand Gang, nothing about her connection to them. There was a chance, though small, Miss Clarke would believe her against the word of the Duke of Rochdale. Alfred had no proof of her guilt—how could he, when she was innocent?

But that may not matter to Miss Clarke. Any stain on one of her governesses was a stain on the Governess Bureau itself, and that would not be tolerated. Meredith knew she would be off the books, forever.

She leaned back in the wooden chair in the small room she had taken in the King's Head. This was why she had changed her name. This was why she had removed every blot of that family name from her history, why she had lied about her past whenever necessary.

The prejudice. She had lived with it all her life as Meredith Glasshand, and with the emergence of Meredith Hubert into the Governess Bureau, had been sure she had escaped it.

But obviously not. *Perhaps it was in her very nature,* she thought dully. *Blood would out, that was what her father had always said.* It could not be mere coincidence that the only crime she had ever been accused of was theft.

Her gaze fell to the third letter attempt which now lay on the small desk before her. It had been good, until that last sentence. She could not defend herself, it seemed, without sounding as though she was begging for forgiveness.

She could not send a letter like that; it would undoubtedly incriminate her in Miss Clarke's mind, rather than convince anyone of her innocence. And she would never go to prison, not after how hard she'd worked. She had escaped that life, and she would never return.

It was getting dark in the pokey room she had taken for just three shillings a night, and Meredith glanced at the window. The nights were drawing in so much earlier now. She would have to go downstairs to get a candle or a lamp, if they had one. It would undoubtedly cost more than the room, but there it was. *Light was a luxury.*

Just as she had risen to make her way downstairs, there was a knock on the door.

Meredith's stomach lurched. It would not be Alfred, no matter how much her heart secretly wished it would be so. He would not demean himself to see her in a public house. Not after being so convinced of her guilt, with no cause.

"Come in?" she said hesitantly.

The door opened and revealed a maid. She bobbed a nervous curtsey. "Came to light t'lamps, Miss."

Meredith blinked and then noticed the lamps in her hands.

Her heart sank. She had only a little money saved, and the last months' worth of her wages was, as yet, unpaid.

"Right," she said. "How much…"

"Included in y'room, Miss," said the maid with a look of astonishment that anyone would be charged extra for light. "Here, let me."

The maid placed one of the lamps on the small desk and one on the bedside table. She took out a tinder box, lit both lamps, and moved to the doorway.

"Anything else I can get you, Miss?" The maid bobbed another nervous curtsey.

Meredith almost smiled, though a flush tinged her cheeks. She knew precisely what the maid was thinking—what everyone in Rochdale was probably wondering.

The duke had got rid of his governess—why? What had happened in Rochdale Abbey?

Notoriety was something she had left behind a long time ago, when she had finally broken with her family and tried life on her own, yet there was something about it that never quite seemed to leave you. There was something about her that attracted it, no matter how respectable she became.

"That will be all, thank you," she said quietly.

The maid closed the door behind her.

Meredith glanced at the two lamps as she pulled the curtains closed over the window. Well, every time she forgot she was miles from London, she was given further proof of it. *Two lamps, and absolutely no additional charge?* She had been robbed before, that was for sure.

Returning to her seat, Meredith closed her eyes and lost herself in the memories of the last few months which had given her such joy but were naught but painful now.

The kiss in the library. The way Alfred had made her feel, the joy he had given her in the kitchen. Their many rides together. It was astonishing, really, how easily she had been swept up it in all, despite knowing she should not be doing anything of the sort.

You must never fall in love…

It was wicked to dwell on such memories, particularly when she had been risking so much creating them in the first place.

But Meredith could not help it. All she had was memories now, and though they pained her, she would treasure them still. Treasure the moments she had believed, perhaps, that things could have ended differently.

That she could have married Alfred…

Meredith opened her eyes. He had not even broached the topic. The gulf between them, of class, of occupation, of honor, had been too great. Even their great attraction to each other could not bridge it.

The room she had taken at the King's Head was small, it was true, but it was no smaller than the bedchamber allotted to her at Rochdale Abbey, and neither were different from her chamber with the Marnmouths. *Governesses it appeared*, Meredith thought ruefully, *did not require much space to breathe.*

Though she was but ten miles from him, Meredith felt she could have been a million miles away.

She cared about him. She had thought he had cared for her— but that could not be, or Alfred would have believed her when she had said she was not the thief.

"I have done nothing wrong."

Meredith looked back at her letter to Miss Clarke. Where had she got to?

I wished to inform you personally that my employment in the home of the Duke of Rochdale has been terminated. This is due to a false accusation of theft which I have not been given the opportunity to refute. You know I would never.

She almost laughed. *Never what? Never steal?* She certainly had in the past. *Never fall in love with her employer?* She could not write that with any integrity either. She had already broken one of the Governess Bureau's most sacred rules. Why would Miss Clarke believe her?

Meredith's stomach rumbled. She had not eaten yet that day,

saving her pennies for a large, stodgy, evening meal she was certain the King's Head would provide.

But before she went downstairs, she had to decide how to continue with her letter. How could she convince Miss Clarke of her innocence?

Picking up her quill, Meredith wrote:

You know I would never do anything to bring the Governess Bureau into disrepute. I have been most grateful of the trust you have placed in me, and I would not.

She hesitated. She had no wish to lie, but every time she approached the truth, her quill stopped and she was unable to continue.

Meredith could never have predicted meeting a man like Alfred. The titled gentlemen she had interacted with were few, to be sure, and most of them had been happily—or unhappily—married, and at least two decades older than her.

Yet despite her place, she had never felt inferior when speaking to Alfred. He had always treated her as…as someone to be desired. She had never felt more at home than when in his arms—nor felt more betrayed until he looked at her so coldly, as if he did not know her.

"Do…do you think I fall in love with every female servant who crosses his threshold? Do you think me some sort of cad who just goes about seducing young ladies in my care and keeping, and then just throws them away?"

He did not know her. Not entirely. She had lied, kept her history a secret from him, never revealing the whole truth of who she was.

She had not felt able to at first, and now Alfred had proved to her beyond any doubt that *he* could not be trusted. He did not trust her, and she did not trust him. *How had she managed to convince herself that was the appropriate beginning to a marriage?*

Meredith's stomach rumbled a little more urgently, and she looked down at the letter and sighed before screwing it up and dropping it on the floor.

She had but two pieces of paper remaining from the small supply she had brought with her to Rochdale Abbey. There had been copious amounts in the schoolroom, and she had been tempted. It would have been far easier to just take it. *Who would know?*

She would. Meredith was not a thief, not anymore. But the fact of the matter was that paper was expensive, and undoubtedly difficult to procure in a small town such as Rochdale. She needed to write to Miss Clarke soon, for it would not be long before Alfred did so, and she had to tell her side of the story first.

She could not merely turn up outside the Governess Bureau in London, with no appointment and no assignment!

Dipping her quill into the ink pot that was now looking perilously low, Meredith tried to concentrate as she wrote another letter to Miss Clarke.

Dear Miss Clarke,

I regret to inform you that my appointment with the Duke of Rochdale has been unfairly terminated due to

There was no way for her to explain it, no way to prove she had not taken those things.

Losing her employment at the Governess Bureau would mean losing everything. She could not, would not permit it to happen.

"You are leaving?"

Meredith sighed as she recalled the words spoken by Archibald. She had not wished to go, but she could not stay that house after being accused falsely of such wrongdoing.

All the servants knew, she was certain. She was almost sure someone had been in her bedchamber at the abbey, though that too would be difficult to prove. Her riding habit, however, had been quite crumpled when she had returned after putting Archibald to bed one night, and she would never have left it in such a state.

Well, there was nothing she could do about that. *The servants of Rochdale Abbey could go on thinking whatever they liked about her,* Meredith thought viciously as she laid her quill down for the final time that night. *She knew the truth, much good it would do her.*

Leaving the letter where it was, abandoning it for the certain knowledge that unless she ate soon, her brain would be useless anyway, Meredith smoothed down her skirts and looked for a shawl to place around her shoulders.

Perhaps after a plate of whatever was being cooked this evening, she would have the strength to return to her letter. It at least could not get any worse than it was at the moment.

The staircase was full of noise and chatter as Meredith stepped down it, noise echoing up from those eating and drinking and from the numerous rooms that opened out on the landing.

She had never been in the King's Head before. It wasn't right for a young woman to enter it alone but she had no choice now. Heads watched her as she entered the dining parlor.

Most appeared to be farmers she recognized from St. Matthews. The elder Mr. Johnson even inclined his head to her. *So. It appeared that the rumor of her thievery had not yet reached the townspeople.*

"Good evening, Miss Hubert!"

Meredith turned to see the beaming innkeeper, Mr. Morgan. "Good evening, sir."

"You have everything you need?" asked Mr. Morgan jovially, coming around the bar to greet her.

Meredith politely thanked him for all he had done to make her stay so enjoyable. It could not be more obvious the man was fishing for clues as to why she was staying at his inn in the first place, but she was not going to fuel any rumors, save her mere presence alone.

"And how long do you think you will be staying with us?" Mr. Morgan asked.

Meredith hesitated. She had not entirely formed her plans, but knew she could not remain for long. Every day increased the chances Alfred would let slip his accusation to someone outside the household, and write to Miss Clarke with the false allegation.

"At least one more day," she said slowly. "Perhaps two."

The temptation to stay longer was a strong one. The moment she left Rochdale, there was no coming back. It would mean accepting that it was all over between her and Alfred—whatever it had been, or could have been.

She should really return to London. Then she could make her case to Miss Clarke in person, which would surely improve her chances of being believed.

But she was a coward. Meredith knew this about herself. If she was not so fearful of facing Miss Clarke, she would have left straight away, rather than taken a room here in the inn.

Just a few more days, and she would have sufficient time to think of the right way to word that letter. Assuming she could purchase some paper.

"Just a day or two more?" Mr. Morgan did not bother to hide his surprised expression. "Well, that's fine, Miss Hubert, that's fine. You just tell me or my missus the day you wish to leave, and we will ensure your room is perfect for you until then."

Meredith smiled weakly. "Thank you, Mr. Morgan. I actually was thinking about some dinner."

The innkeeper spread out an arm. "Say no more, Miss, say no more—sit where you like, and I'll bring out some of the stew our Betty has cooked up. Sorry 'tis not something more fancy, like you would have up at the big house."

He looked a little discomforted at these words, as though remembering she would be accustomed to much finer fare.

But Meredith sought to put him at ease. "I do assure you, Mr. Morgan, stew is quite my favorite and I am sure your Betty has created something delicious."

The man beamed, and Meredith escaped his presence without revealing any more.

The inn was bustling but not busy, and Meredith had a great deal of choice as to where she could sit. After scanning the room for a moment, she chose a quiet corner relatively distant from everyone else. The last thing she wanted was to answer any more questions. The last few days had already been an ordeal.

Farmers stood around the bar, buying each other half pints and continuously saying to each other that they must only have one more, or their wives would have their guts for garters. This did not seem to slow down their consumption of the half pints, nor prompt any of them to make their way to the door.

Meredith hid a smile. *Some things never changed.*

There was a table crowded with people who appeared to be the inhabitants of a mail coach. One lady there looked most unhappy to be seated alongside a clerk, from what Meredith could make out, but they were eating away happily and the scent of the food wafted over to her, making her mouth water.

"Here you go!"

Meredith started. So interested had she been in those around her, she had not noticed Mr. Morgan approach with a large bowl of stew and an almost clean spoon in the other hand.

"Thank you, sir," Meredith said with a smile. "That...that is all I require."

Mr. Morgan bobbed a little bow, and returned to the bar.

Meredith wiped the spoon surreptitiously on her skirt, and started to eat. The stew was heavenly; packed full of flavor, with plenty of meat which was not always guaranteed. It was just the sort of meal she would have had on the road with her parents when she was younger, and her great appetite meant she had eaten almost a third of the bowl before forcing herself to slow down. *A stomachache would be quite the way to end the day.*

Partly in an attempt to slow herself down, Meredith looked out again at the inhabitants of the inn. The mail coach party had been brought a rather large pitcher of red wine, from what she could see, and the lady and the clerk were getting along famously now.

Meredith hid another grin. *It was amazing how alike people were, when the trappings of society were removed.*

There was a pair of gentlemen in one corner playing chess, or something that looked similar to chess. Meredith recognized the younger Mr. Hemming, and hoped he had not seen her enter. It would not do for him to inform his father and cause a panic before the election.

Meredith sighed as she swallowed another mouthful of the delightful stew. After all that he had accused her of, she was still concerned about Alfred's election campaign. *He did not deserve her.*

Then her eyes fell onto someone far more interesting, a woman about Meredith's age, seated alone. It was such an unusual sight in an inn or tavern that Meredith's gaze lingered on her for a moment, and the woman looked up and caught Meredith's eye. She smiled.

Meredith smiled back. *Well, she could see no harm in it.* There was naught wrong in being polite—but her courtesy had an effect she had not predicted. The woman picked up her bowl of stew, rose from her seat, and started toward her.

Meredith groaned internally. It was a mistake to catch someone's eye! All she wanted was peace and quiet. She should have asked Mr. Morgan to take her stew in her room.

"May...may I join you?" the woman said, a little breathlessly. "I would rather do that than have a man ask to sit with me."

Meredith had not considered this. Sitting together would certainly prevent anyone else from wishing to speak to her, and the woman looked harmless.

"Of course," she said as graciously as she could. "Please, sit down."

The woman did so, almost dropping her bowl of stew in her nervousness. Meredith could not begrudge a woman like that.

"I'm Molly," she said with a smile.

The name rang a bell in Meredith's tired mind. "Meredith," she said. "I am—I was the governess, up at Rochdale Abbey. With the Carmichaels."

Whether it was at the mention of Rochdale Abbey, or the Carmichaels, Meredith could not tell—but Molly suddenly flushed. Meredith looked down at her stew. *Perhaps the gossip had travelled far faster than she had imagined.*

"And...and what about you?" she asked, curiously.

Molly coughed. "Well, as it happens, I was an undermaid there myself."

Meredith's mouth fell open. Of course, why had she not put the two things together—Molly Butters! The undermaid who left on the day she herself arrived at the abbey.

"Goodness," said Meredith, trying to cover her moment of surprise. "To think, in another lifetime, we may have known each other up at the abbey!"

Molly nodded. It could not be more evident to Meredith that the undermaid did not wish to speak any more about her time at the abbey, and though it was impolite to merely ask outright, she could not help it. *She had to know.*

"And...you left hurriedly?" she asked quietly.

Molly nodded. She placed her spoon down and took a deep breath, as though about to admit to something awful. "I had to, in the end. I could not stay."

Meredith worked hard to keep her face impassive. *This was it; she was finally getting to the bottom of the mystery of the undermaid.* Why had she left? Why had it been so impossible for her to remain there—close to Alfred?

"Do you..." Meredith swallowed. "Do you mind if I ask you why?"

Molly did not answer immediately. She looked around as though to ensure no one else could overhear them before answering. "I...I had a baby."

Meredith's mouth dropped, and she hastily closed it to ensure Molly was not offended.

She could hardly believe it. *She had been right!* She had not precisely accused Alfred of seducing and then abandoning Molly Butters, but her instincts had been right. *The man was a menace!*

She and Molly could surely not be the only ones. The Duke of Rochdale preyed on his servants, and really, she should be grateful she was able to escape with her innocence intact.

Just about.

Her instincts had been true, and in hindsight, the sullied reputation of a thief was a far better outcome than poor Molly Butters. Having a child...

"Did...did you ever get money from him?" Meredith asked quietly. "From His Grace?"

Molly frowned. "I don't understand."

Of course, she didn't, Meredith thought bitterly. *A mere undermaid wouldn't consider Alfred needing to do anything of the sort.* She knew his type, the men who thought they could just dispose of a woman after they got a little bored of her.

"Money," she repeated. "From His Grace, Alfred Carmichael. The duke. For you and your baby to live on," she spelled out.

A strange look flooded Molly's face. "Oh, no. No, it wasn't—His Grace never touched me. He was too much of a gentleman to even consider it!"

The very thought seemed to give Molly a fright, and she shivered.

Relief, sweet relief tinged with a little guilt, swept through Meredith's soul.

She had jumped to the most likely conclusion.

But not here. Alfred had not seduced Molly Butters, and that was why he had almost no memory of her.

"Molly Butters. She was the undermaid here. She left the day that I arrived. You...you do not remember her?"

"What has a Molly got to do with us?"

But now she knew it had not been Alfred who had seduced Molly and abandoned her with child, so Meredith was filled once more with curiosity. Who could it have been? *Roberts, perhaps?* There was no knowing with some people...

Molly could obviously see the question on her lips before she spoke it, because she sighed and said, "I thought everyone in Rochdale knew by now, so there's no reason why you should not. It was...it was John Talbot. Him's as running against His Grace in the election."

Meredith's mouth fell open. "John Talbot?"

"You should watch out for old Rochdale there. Can't have a woman in the house but he wants to bed her. Achieves it, most of the time, too. Did you ever meet Molly Butters?"

Why had she not seen it before? She had felt something was off about Mr. Talbot the first moment she had met him, and she had never heard a kind word spoken of him. Even Alfred had not been able to find anything nice to say about him, and...

Alfred. Oh, she had accused him falsely just as he had accused her. She had been so sure he had been the one to seduce and abandon Molly Butters. Now she thought about it, there was just as little evidence as there was proving her to be the thief at Rochdale Abbey.

She should not have shouted at him. She should have believed him, as he should have believed her.

They should have believed each other.

CHAPTER TWENTY-TWO

October 9, 1812

"——And though of course, it will be a great loss to the people of Rochdale itself, in time we will recognize the great advantage it is to have you in London," continued Mr. Walker in an unbroken stream since he had first arrived at Rochdale Abbey just before dinner had started.

After the cook had ensured there was enough food for two, Alfred had received him in the library, in the vague hope that here, rather than the drawing room, would indicate his interest—or lack thereof—in a long conversation. That had been two hours ago.

"Why, having a Carmichael back in Parliament is what this duchy needs," Mr. Walker said as he sat comfortably in an armchair by the roaring fire. "Though I will of course miss you, my boy, just as I missed your father whenever he went to serve us in the big town. But then, I said to my own boys…"

Alfred's eyes were glazing over, and he was managing to nod at all of the right times, as far as he could tell, as Mr. Walker continued on quite happily.

"But when you win the election, we will have to accept…"

Alfred's stomach, full of good food and even better wine, was starting to make him soporific. It was pleasant to sit with Mr. Walker and be unrequired to contribute in any way. The last few weeks had been exhausting, and it was a relief to simply allow another to take the burden of conversation. The election was soon and with each passing day, there was a greater knot in his heart, tightening, growing ever heavier.

"—though it is fascinating how quickly these things change," said Mr. Walker, hiccupping slightly, his eyes unfocused as he poured himself another glass of red wine. "Take Hemmings, for example. Rapscallion in many ways, only just arrived in Rochdale!"

Alfred tried not to smile. *The Hemmings had arrived almost thirty years ago.*

"Blasted ingrates," muttered Mr. Walker. "Like those Talbots—aye, I know you do not wish to hear about them, but the man fair gets my blood boiling and no mistake!"

He would not be here much longer. He had already instructed Kittering to start packing, and Mrs. Martin's questions about hiring new servants had increased before he left.

Within a few weeks, he would be gone. He would have to be content with having Rochdale as a distant memory. A memory of home. No one could call the rooms he took in London 'home'. Not compared to the abbey. Not compared to the home he had wished for, had dreamt about with…with her.

Meredith. Miss Hubert. Governess she may be, but that was no reason why he had not hoped that one day, she could be much more to him.

That was all over. As Mr. Walker's voice continued, Alfred attempted to both listen closely to ensure he nodded at the right times, and ignore him completely. It was far more pleasant and yet more painful to lose himself in thoughts of Meredith. Two days, or perhaps three, and no sign of her. Alfred had been certain she would return.

There were still some belongings of hers upstairs. Mrs. Martin had told him there was one trunk remaining, and Alfred had instructed her, without explanation, to leave it.

Leave it? A small part of him was obviously convinced Meredith was coming back. Alfred hated that part of him; it was weak, pathetic. *Did he really believe that?*

Yes. He desperately wanted her to provide proof she had not stolen those things. But if she had such evidence, why had she not presented it at the moment of her accusation?

Because, thought Alfred dully, *it did not exist. She was the thief.*

"—Walkers in these parts for five hundred years!" Mr. Walker said, and Alfred nodded. "Carmichaels in these parts for nigh on the same amount of time!"

"Yes, indeed," said Alfred, finding it amusing that his family was only just accepted to be on a par with the Walkers.

Mr. Walker pointed at Alfred. "Y'see! You see what I mean then!"

There was a pause before Alfred realized he was required to input at this point. "I-I do indeed, yes, Mr. Walker. Most elegantly put."

This seemed to appease the older man, who sipped his red wine and looked at the fire before he started speaking again. "I don't know, you think the old ways will continue forever and then before you know it, another decade has passed and half the people around you cannot even remember what the old ways were…"

Any other year, Alfred would have had great sympathy for the old man. It could not be pleasant, seeing the traditions of life that you loved so much disappear. One could cling onto them as much as possible, but that did not mean they disappeared any less.

If only he could turn back time—but what difference would that make? Meredith would still choose to steal, and Alfred would be presented with the same difficulty; confronting her with her own thievery, and watching her lie about it.

The library door opened, and Roberts entered with letters on a silver tray. "The evening post, Your Grace."

Taking them from the butler's tray, Alfred could see a letter from Talbot, which he put in his pocket—*no point in opening that now, not in the state Mr. Walker was in*—something that looked like another bill, and a letter addressed to...

"Miss Hubert, Your Grace," said Roberts delicately. "I shall forward it to Miss Clarke at the Governess Bureau, if I may?"

Alfred nodded. He did not trust his voice. How long would post arrive for the governess? How much longer would he be reminded of her absence? *Not long.* In a few weeks, he himself would be gone from the place, away from the land he loved and to the town and duty he despised.

It was only then that he realized the butler was still hovering by his chair. "Yes?"

Roberts swallowed. "I have been requested to ask you, Your Grace, as a favor to Mrs. Martin...she wishes to know whether she can go through the governess's room and clear it out."

"No," said Alfred hastily, as nonchalantly as he could.

The butler raised his eyebrows, and even Mr. Walker ceased his monologue.

Alfred tried to keep his face straight. He wished for neither his old friend nor his butler to have any comprehension of the pain he was feeling. It was simple enough.

"I believe Mere—Miss Hubert is still at the King's Head in Rochdale," he continued stiffly. "She may request that trunk to be sent to her. I wish it to be left."

Roberts' eyebrows rose—if possible—a little higher.

Irritation flared in Alfred's heart. *Well, really. Who was the master here? Did he have to explain his every wish and desire to those who were supposed to serve him? What next, an explanation as to why fish was chosen for Fridays?*

"I know the servants are surprised at my decision to let Miss Hubert go, Roberts," he said in his most authoritarian voice. "But I had good reason, and I would ask you and the others to trust me."

Roberts' gaze flickered over to Mr. Walker, who despite the great amount of red wine he had imbibed, was not entirely immune to the temperature of the conversation. He had evidently plucked a book from the bookshelf beside him, and was now assiduously concentrating on the third volume of Mrs. Radcliffe's *The Mysteries of Udolpho*.

Alfred and Roberts's gaze returned to each other.

"No question of trust," said the butler quietly, "just surprise. Is that all, Your Grace?"

"Yes," snapped Alfred, his bad temper not receding. It was only after Roberts had quietly shut the library door behind him that he regretted his tone.

He was not that sort of person. *He was not that sort of master!* He could not remember the last time he had shouted, really shouted at a servant.

This whole kerfuffle had left him unsettled. He had never been forced to terminate the employment of any servant before, and now he had.

And worse, it had been Meredith.

Alfred swallowed and looked over at Mr. Walker still hidden by his book. It was only now she had gone that Alfred realized just how much Meredith…*grounded him.*

Like lightning to earth, she had anchored him. Surprising, shocking, challenging, yes, but he had never felt more safe, more accepted. Now she was gone, he was…well, all at sea.

Alfred closed his eyes and tried not to recall the numerous encounters which had built up, slowly but surely over weeks, the close connection they had enjoyed. Why, it had been in this very library that he had first kissed her. In the kitchen where…she had allowed him to…

His eyes snapped open. *Careful, man*, he counselled himself. *The last thing you want to do is lose control.*

Mr. Walker turned a page, the noise deafening in the quiet.

Perhaps he was overthinking this because Meredith was close by, Alfred wondered, shifting uncomfortably. The King's Head was not far on horseback. He certainly was not considering riding over there and telling Meredith that it did not matter she was a thief, that if she loved him, and he loved her…

Alfred sighed. *No, it was a foolish dream. How could a member of Parliament declare his love for a thief? How could a duke wed a governess?* Idle thoughts.

Besides, Roberts had hinted just yesterday that there may be a far more sinister reason why Miss Hubert had not yet departed for town. *Was she waiting for the master of the house to leave the abbey, leaving it vulnerable to additional thefts?*

It was an excruciating thought, but not one Alfred could discount. After all, she knew the house. If her climbing abilities are anything to go by based on what he had seen with the kite, she had the ability to get through a window even two floors up, if she wanted.

Alfred reached for his glass of wine, hardly touched since he and Mr. Walker had entered the library. *Perhaps going to London wouldn't be a burden after all, but a relief.*

"Mr. Walker, please return home as soon as you wish," Alfred said delicately. "I am sure Mrs. Walker is waiting for you. I would not wish to deprive her of your company."

Mr. Walker, unfortunately, did not take the hint. Lowering the book, he said with a bright smile, "Oh, no, she is not expecting me until long after dinner. And what an excellent one it was, too. I must thank your cook. You know, it has been years since I enjoyed…"

A clock quietly chimed ten o'clock as Alfred returned to nodding at whatever Mr. Walker said. That was all the input required, apparently, as the old man just continued on.

"Not that our cook is particularly bad, of course," Mr. Walker's voice cut into Alfred's thoughts. "I had to tempt her away from London with much higher wages than I had initially been prepared to pay, but the custard tarts, Your Grace! Never before nor since have I tasted…"

Talbot. *Blaggard.* He had organized the last-minute husting to toy with him, and the blasted thing was, it had worked! *If only he'd had Meredith to assist him with the—*

Alfred caught himself just in time. He could not go through life wishing he had Meredith by his side. He would be back in Parliament before he knew it.

Still, the misery of the husting had cast a shadow over his election campaign Alfred simply had not needed.

Miss Wilhelmina Talbot had been there, too. Alfred had looked for a friendly face in the crowd as he had spoken, wondering whether Miss Talbot would give him a smile.

She had not. If ever the phrase 'cold shoulder' was employed, it was for Miss Talbot.

Perhaps that would have upset him another time, in another life. He was more distressed that Meredith had not been there. It had been a slim chance. Just because she was still in Rochdale Town that did not mean she was likely to attend the husting, even though a small part of him had wondered whether she would hide at the back.

But she had not. *Alfred had been forced to do the damn thing alone.*

"Your Grace."

Alfred started. Mr. Walker's voice was low, quiet, companionable. He looked up to see the older man smiling with a gentle and understood expression.

"Your Grace, I know the hustings weren't what you wanted them to be…"

Alfred nodded, not trusting his voice. Sometimes it was easy to forget Mr. Walker, though a social inferior to the House of Rochdale, had known Alfred since the day he was born.

"Archibald refused to come," said Alfred bleakly. "I tried to impress upon him the importance of his attendance, both for my sake and for his own, but he didn't agree."

"Children can be most troublesome," Mr. Walker said. "I would know. I have five."

"I would have liked him to be there. Someone by my side,"

Alfred said. "But then I think I expected too much of Archibald. He has been impossible since…"

He could not bear to finish his sentence. He would not think about Meredith.

Damn. He had depended on Meredith far more than he had realized over the last few months, more than he could possibly have known until she was taken from him.

"Well, I think you are doing a fine thing, a very fine thing indeed, if you do not mind me saying so, Your Grace," said Mr. Walker with a smile. "Following your father's footsteps. Continuing on his legacy, and that of your grandfather, and his father afore him."

Alfred nodded, but the man's words did nothing to assuage his heart. He had never been truly honest with Mr. Walker, not really. He had never told the man that running for election was not his preferred choice. He had never revealed the panic that speaking in Parliament elicited in him, how he hated London, hated the duty his life was dedicated to.

Perhaps he should have been more open. Perhaps of all people, Mr. Walker would have understood. It would certainly have saved him heartache. Maybe that honesty would have helped Mr. Walker understand why Alfred did not wish to run for this election.

Or perhaps not. Mr. Walker was looking with such pride, Alfred was not sure what would happen if he was finally honest with the man.

"Well, Mrs. Walker will be waiting to lock up," said Mr. Walker, glancing at his pocket watch and eyes bulging as he saw the time. "I had better be off, Your Grace, I hope you can forgive me."

Alfred rose. "Oh, so soon? What a shame, but thank you for your company, Mr. Walker. I have greatly enjoyed our conversation."

"No need to see me out," said Mr. Walker as he started to walk to the door.

But Alfred would not permit that. "No, no, I insist."

Roberts was by the front door, having predicted in that impressive way only butlers could that a guest was leaving. Alfred shook Mr. Walker's hand, promised he would ask his cook to send around to Mr. Walker's cook exactly how the ham had been prepared, and sighed heavily when the door finally closed behind him.

"Right," said Alfred with a sigh. "I think I will—"

"Your Grace, a moment?"

Alfred worked hard to ensure Mrs. Martin could not see the frustration on his face as he turned to greet her. Out of the corner of his eye, he saw on the grandfather clock that it was near eleven o'clock. *No wonder he was so tired.*

"Your Grace," said Mrs. Martin with an unusually stern face.

Alfred knew precisely what she was going to ask. "The answer is no, Mrs. Martin."

"I cannot abide to leave it!" she said. "I want to clear out the rooms where that woman was, Your Grace, and I do not understand why I am to leave things as they are!"

Alfred could no longer answer that question himself anymore. *He had to let go.* He had to accept that Meredith Hubert was not coming back.

"Fine," he said, his temper showing then adding, "Fine, Mrs. Martin, I understand. Please go through the room tomorrow."

The housekeeper was evidently expecting more of a fight and appeared wrong-footed by his reply. "I mean to say, I—oh. Right. Thank you, Your Grace."

"I do apologize, Your Grace," said Roberts quietly. "I was under the impression you had told me—"

"Yes, I know what I said," said Alfred wearily. "And now I am saying something else. Please, sort this out between the two of you. I…I am tired."

Roberts and Mrs. Martin exchanged glances before walking away. Alfred was left alone in the hallway with only his bitterness and contrariness to keep him company.

God's teeth. How was it possible to feel a stranger in his own home?

It was time for bed. Alfred dragged his weary feet up the staircase and along the corridor to his bedchamber, but his mind was so on other things he did not notice at first that he had stepped right past his own chamber and along the corridor and toward...

The schoolroom. The door was ajar, as it had been the first time Alfred had walked past it and espied Meredith teaching Archibald. The memory was so clear, it was as though it had happened yesterday.

It was almost inevitable where his feet took him next, and Alfred had no ability to chastise himself. *Meredith's bedchamber.*

Pushing the door open, Alfred stepped inside. Despite Mrs. Martin's concern that she had not cleaned it after the governess had vacated it, from what Alfred could see, Meredith had left the place in relatively good order.

The bed had been stripped, linens carefully folded. There was not a scrap of evidence that anyone had lived here, other than the trunk pushed up against the wall. There was almost nothing left of her.

Knowing how foolish he was acting, but unable to prevent himself, Alfred picked up the pillow and brought it to his face, breathing in. It smelled exactly like her. The last bit of her that he had left—other than a piece of paper scrunched up in the wastepaper bin.

Alfred knew he should not look at it. For all he knew, it was private correspondence between Meredith and...*who?* The only two people she could possibly have been writing to were Miss Clarke and...and whoever she was involved with in this thieving malarky.

Reaching down, Alfred picked up the paper. His guess had been correct. It was a letter from Meredith. There were quite a few ink splotches and even areas that appeared to be...tears.

Dear Miss Clarke,

~~I regret to inform you~~ *I know one of the most important rules of the Governess Bureau is not to fall in love. I have* ~~always believed~~ *never been tempted to do so before.* ~~but I must tell you~~

I am writing you this letter to give up my employment at the Governess Bureau, for I have fallen in love with ~~my employer~~ *the Duke of Rochdale, and I* ~~believe hope~~ *believe he returns my affections.*

~~I don't know what to do, Miss Clarke. Help me to understand Should I Can you~~

Alfred bit his lip. *Christ, she seemed so lost when she had written this letter, so unsure of herself. So unsure of him.*

Meredith had been something truly special. And he had lost her. Or had she lost him? It was her actions which had separated them. *If she had just not stolen—how hard could it be?*

A governess could not become the Duchess of Rochdale. A servant couldn't marry the master. A member of Parliament couldn't marry a thief.

Crumpling the letter and dropping it into his pocket, lest Mrs. Martin saw it tomorrow, Alfred left her bedchamber and was on his way to his own when a thought occurred to him.

The missing items, those which had been stolen. They had searched her bedchamber, and it was quite clear that they were not there. Mrs. Martin had even done so before Meredith had been confronted, so there was no chance they were secreted into her locked trunk.

But the schoolroom. They had not searched the schoolroom.

Heart beating frantically, Alfred hastily stepped over to her desk and opened it slowly, half hoping he would find the stolen items, half hoping that he would not.

The desk was empty.

Alfred's shoulders slumped. *Well, it was too much to hope.* She was evidently far cleverer than he gave her credit for. It certainly would have been a foolish place to hide them.

It was only as he walked back toward the door that Alfred noticed Archibald's desk was slightly open. There was something preventing it from closing. A strange impulse to open it overwhelmed him, and it was with horror and surprise that Alfred lifted the lid to find...

The golden pocket watch. Two miniatures. The large family Bible, and countless other small things which Mrs. Martin had not even noticed were missing.

Alfred sagged onto the small chair by the desk. *Archibald.* It was Archibald. He was the thief—his own brother!

"Have you asked Archibald about the missing items?"

Oh, it all seemed so obvious now. Archibald was always asking about his parents, hadn't he? Alfred had brushed off the questions as not important, not worthy of his time.

Yet they had been for Archibald. A mother who had died giving him life, a father who was older, distant, and had died when he was so young. It was natural for him to have questions, and for him to go about the house finding artifacts of their existence, all for himself.

"Oh Christ," Alfred moaned, a hand moving to his temple.

Meredith had seen it. She had at the very least suspected, and what had he done when she had voiced that suspicion?

"How—how dare you blame my brother!"

Why would Meredith—*Meredith!*—have stolen from him? She loved him.

And he loved her. Alfred found with rising joy that not all, but many of his problems were about to solve themselves. Meredith was not the thief, and they loved each other. Now the truth had been discovered there was no reason, after he had won the election of course, that they could not be together.

He would offer her his hand in marriage. They would be happy.

All this information and rush of emotion made Alfred feel giddy. It was hard to know what to do first—until it became clear as he looked down into the desk of stolen treasure.

Archibald. He needed to speak to Archibald, explain he was not angry nor upset, and that they would be asking Meredith back to the abbey not as Archibald's governess, but as Alfred's wife.

Alfred rose hurriedly and checked his pocket watch. *Past eleven o'clock.* True, it was late to be waking the boy, but it was such a joyous piece of news, he would surely not mind. Opening Archibald's bedchamber door quietly, Alfred tiptoed over to the bed, and reached out to wake his brother.

That, however, proved impossible. The bed was empty.

Alfred looked around the room in the darkness, as though expecting to find Archibald inexplicably out of bed playing with his soldiers. He was not there.

This did not make sense. *Where else would the boy be at this time of night?*

Perhaps in the room assigned as dining room for Archibald and his governess. It took Alfred a few steps along the corridor to peer his head in, but the place was empty. He knew Archibald wasn't in the schoolroom, nor Meredith's bedchamber, he had been in both of those.

So, where was he?

"Your Grace, goodness!"

Alfred whirled around to see Mrs. Martin clutching her chest.

"I did not expect to see you still up, Your Grace," she said. "You will forgive me for saying this, but you look troubled."

"I cannot find Archibald," said Alfred blankly.

Mrs. Martin nodded. "Yes, it was strange he wasn't at his dinner, wasn't it? I assumed he ate too many autumn apples, out in the orchards where he's been playing all day. I hope he's sleeping soundly now."

Alfred's heart went cold. "You...you mean to say he hasn't been seen all day?"

"Well, no, but little boys run about, don't they?" said Mrs. Martin heartily. "He'll be tired in the morning!"

Alfred attempted to keep his voice calm. "Mrs. Martin, I do not believe we understand each other. I cannot find Archibald *now*. He is not in his bedchamber, nor anywhere else."

Mrs. Martin's smile vanished. "Not…not in his bed?"

"What is all this commotion? Really, Mrs. Martin, I ex-pected—oh. Your Grace." Roberts joined them and looked between his fellow servant and their master. "What is wrong?"

"I'll tell you what's wrong," said Alfred with a dry mouth. "Archibald is missing."

CHAPTER TWENTY-THREE

MEREDITH KNEW IT was a dream. It could not be true. Alfred would never shout at her like that, not even if she had done all the terrible things he was now accusing her of.

"—broken all our trust!"

"No," Meredith murmured. *She had to make him understand.* She was not a bad person, and she would never have done those things. She hadn't stolen, she hadn't hurt Archibald. She would never hurt either of them.

There was a loud banging hurting her ears. The Alfred before her glaring, all affection stripped from his features. "I should never have allowed you entrance into our home—or into Rochdale! You must leave!"

"I-I cannot leave without—"

"No one wants you here," Alfred sneered, though it could not be Alfred, something about him wasn't right. "No one wants you, Meredith."

And she was crying, tears falling down her cheeks. The banging was drilling into her mind, preventing her from thinking, and Alfred was stepping toward her with fists raised.

Meredith wanted to throw herself into his arms, kiss away the mistrust and confusion, but it was not the Alfred she knew and so instead she ran from him and the pain he was causing.

"Meredith!"

She would not look back, Meredith vowed as she ran, but she did not seem to be getting any further away as she tried to put one foot before the other, trying desperately to escape him. *Her heart—was the banging she could hear the pounding from her own pulse?*

"Meredith!"

Alfred was calling her name but it sounded different now, earnest, and eager to speak to her. What was happening? Why did none of this make sense?

"Meredith, wake up!"

Meredith awoke with a start. Her sheets and pillow were damp with perspiration and there were tears on her cheeks. The banging continued—it had not been part of her dream then.

"Meredith, open the door!"

She started. Alfred's voice was whispering her name. *Was she still dreaming?*

Pinching herself and feeling the sharp sting in her arm, Meredith tried to think. She was at the King's Head. She was supposed to be leaving today, but from the little she could see in the gloom of her small chamber, today had not arrived yet.

What time was it? It must be the middle of the night, yet Alfred was here. Was he?

"Damnit, Meredith, open the door!"

Yes, he was certainly here. It was not just the remnants of the dream that was convincing her; no amount of wishful thinking would have created that.

Crash! Meredith gasped as the door of her chamber was kicked off its hinges, and a man rushed in with a bellow at the exertion of forcing his way into her room.

Clutching her bed linens to her, Meredith sat up. "Alfred?"

It was indeed Alfred, and he appeared half mad. His hair was standing up on end and there was a wildness in his eyes as he looked around the room manically.

"What on earth…" breathed Meredith.

This did not make sense. Alfred had almost thrown her from his home. He had accused her of theft, which she had not done, and not believed her when she had sworn her innocence.

Yet here he was, in the room at the inn.

And what was worse, if she was truly honest with herself, was that he did not appear to have broken her door down in a fit of passion. He had not moved toward her attempting to kiss or make love to her, or even spoken to her since he had barged his way in here.

"Alfred," Meredith hissed.

Alfred turned. "You have him, don't you? He's here? Tell me you do, Meredith!"

His words did not make any sense. "Him?"

Alfred nodded wildly. "Yes, yes, he's here, isn't he?"

Meredith could not understand him. *Him? Here? Did he believe that she merely opened up her bedchamber for any gentleman passing through?*

"Alfred, you simply cannot be here," Meredith said, trying to keep her voice down.

It was an absolute miracle no one had heard the door breaking off its hinges, but then there had been rather a lot of singing last night, from what she had heard. It was perhaps no wonder most of the inn's inhabitants were sleeping it off.

"You cannot be here," she repeated, as Alfred had given no sign he had heard her. "The scandal, if you were to be found—*you*, in my bedchamber!"

After all their concerns about what their intimacy could do to both of their reputations, it seemed ridiculous that he had decided to break into her room in the dead of night!

Meredith rubbed her eyes and looked more closely at the Duke of Rochdale. He seemed half possessed, poking into the corners of her room, pulling out the desk. Meredith's heart went cold. *Her letters—the drafted letters to Miss Clarke, they were all on that desk!*

"You have to leave," she hissed.

Alfred straightened up. "Blast it, is he here?"

"I have no comprehension of what you are talking about!"

He looked half-deranged. "Meredith, it's Archibald—is Archie with you?"

Meredith frowned. "Archibald, here? Why would he be here?"

"Because he is not at home," said Alfred, his voice cracking. "And I thought—well, he was so upset about you leaving, really took it hard. I haven't been able to get any sense out of him since you left, and I thought, maybe…"

Meredith's heart skipped a beat. *Archibald was not at home— and he was certainly not here with her. And that meant…*

"Do you mean to tell me that Archibald is missing?" she said slowly.

Alfred sagged onto the end of her bed and put his head in his hands. "I have failed him, Meredith. I have failed my only flesh and blood, and I know not where he went and I have no hope of finding him."

Meredith started getting out of bed, disentangling herself from the bedlinens which had twisted around her during her nightmare.

"My father would never forgive me this great betrayal," Alfred was saying in a muffled voice. "How can I ever forgive myself?"

"Easily," said Meredith, pulling on her gown over her night-gown.

Alfred lifted his head. "I beg your pardon?"

"Easily," Meredith repeated, pulling on her stockings as fast as her fingers could manage and then scrabbling about to find her riding boots in her open trunk.

"What…what are you doing?"

Meredith looked at him. There was the man she loved, who she had believed she would do anything for and now that was going to be put to the test.

Because he did not love her. If Alfred had loved her, he would have believed her when she told him she was not the thief in Rochdale Abbey. Not that she had believed him when he had spoken the truth about Molly Butters.

Perhaps there was too much water under the bridge for them to find happiness with each other. *But they could find Archibald.*

"What am I doing? Helping you, of course," she said lightly.

Alfred blinked. "I do not need your help!"

"Oh, really?" whispered Meredith, conscious that just a few feet in each direction, other inn dwellers were sleeping. "Then why are you here? Why come all this way, wake me and undoubtedly others up, and remove my bedchamber door?"

She looked pointedly at the door now on the floor, and Alfred had the grace to look a little sheepish.

Meredith's heart softened. He looked truly lost, unable to decide what to do next.

Archibald was missing.

Meredith sat hesitantly beside Alfred, careful to ensure space between them. "Why are you here, Your Grace?"

She watched him swallow, watched him gather his thoughts. There were plenty of wrong answers to this question, and perhaps only one right one. The trouble was, neither of them seemed sure what that was.

"I thought...I thought he might be here." It seemed to give Alfred pain to speak. "He trusts you. You know him."

Meredith knew the truth may hurt the duke, but she had to speak. "What you mean is, that in some ways, I know him better than you do."

Alfred nodded. Silence hung between them like a curtain, preventing them from speaking honestly. So much pain had occurred between them, and now Meredith knew the truth about Molly Butters, she could see much of it was of their own making.

Could they heal the hurt—or most importantly, could she help to find Archibald?

"I have servants scouring the abbey for him," Alfred said in a low voice. "I thought, maybe, he had hidden somewhere. Fallen asleep. Not realized we were looking for him."

"No, I don't think so," said Meredith thoughtfully. "No..."

Archibald. Where would he go? The boy was eight and barely knew anyone, friendless save for herself.

She could see why Alfred guessed he could be here. Clever, but wrong. Archibald was not here. It was a long way for a child to walk from the abbey to Rochdale Town, after all.

A long way to walk...

"You have searched the whole house?" Meredith said quickly as she rose to pull on her traveling cloak. "Every inch?"

"Every inch," said Alfred.

"Of the house?"

He blinked. "Yes, I said the house, what does that matter?"

But Meredith had been thinking quickly, and a wry smile crept over her face. "What is the one thing Archibald is always asking to do but cannot unless someone is with him?"

Alfred looked utterly blank. "I...I don't know. Come into town?"

Meredith worked hard to keep her face straight. It was quite clear Alfred knew as little about his brother as he did the moon. "You came by horse?"

He nodded. "Yes, but—"

"Come on," said Meredith, injecting just a little of her governess tone into her words, and seeing to her delight that Alfred immediately rose and started toward the door.

"But where are we—"

"Shh!" Meredith raised a finger to her lips as they stepped onto the landing of the King's Head. She paused, listening closely. No one else was stirring. By some sort of miracle, they would be able to leave the inn without any spying eyes.

As she hurried down the stairs, Alfred followed closely with an almost constant stream of whispered questions. "Where is he then? Do you know? Have you worked it out?"

"I don't know where," said Meredith as they let themselves out into the cold night air. "But I think I know how."

"How?"

Meredith ignored him as they raced around to the stables. There was Beauty, fast asleep with her rug carefully placed over her back. And there, still breathing heavily after the undoubted exertion to get his master here at breakneck speed, was Parker.

"Hello, Beauty," she whispered as she gently stroked her mare's nose to wake her.

The horse blinked hazily, as though unsure herself whether her mistress was a dream. Then Beauty snorted and stepped forward, pushing her nose into Meredith's hand.

"Why are we in such a hurry," said Alfred a little disgruntled, his breath blossoming out into the night air, "if you do not know where we are going?"

Meredith ignored him. "We need to get going, Beauty," she whispered, "and I know it's cold, and the middle of the night, but it's important. Out you come."

Gently encouraging her mare out of the stables, Meredith leapt up onto her back.

"You can't ride like that."

Meredith frowned. "What do you mean?"

"Well, a lady would not…you're riding bareback, in your nightgown!" he spluttered.

It was all she could do not to roll her eyes. *In the midst of a crisis, with his little brother missing, he would rather stand here and lecture her?*

"This will all go much quicker if you stop telling me things that I can and cannot do," she said curtly. "Now come on."

Gently nudging Beauty forward, within a few moments, Alfred joined her on Parker.

"You must have an idea where to start," he said as they took the road to the abbey.

"The stables."

Alfred's forehead puckered with confusion. "The stables? You think he is there?"

Meredith smiled. *Men were so predictable.* They simply couldn't look beyond what was initially there, and start to understand what could be.

"No," she said as they pushed their steeds forward to a canter. "I think he took a pony."

Alfred's face fell into an expression of understanding. "You think he's gone riding—taken Polly the pony? But he has been missing for hours, he could be anywhere!"

Meredith did not reply. She pushed Beauty into a gallop as she tried to ignore the frantic beating of her heart.

They reached the stables, and Meredith slipped down from Beauty's back and pushed open the door. A few horses, disturbed from their sleep, whinnied. Meredith paid them no attention, stepping lightly along the stalls, past the new pony still unnamed by the Rochdale heir, until she reached—

Polly's stall. It was empty.

Meredith's heart twisted. She wasn't sure whether she was glad she was right. Even a child inexpert at riding could travel a far distance on a pony. *It was usually easy to track, but would the tracks remain after so long?*

"The pony is missing! He's gone, Archie's gone," Alfred said in a low voice. "How will we ever find him now?"

Meredith swallowed and tried to slow her breathing. She needed to think.

Hay.

Looking down, she saw a thin but still evident trail of hay out of the pony's stall. It took a right, toward the main door. She smiled.

"See," she said softly. "Hay."

Alfred glanced down. "It's a stable."

Meredith did roll her eyes this time. "Yes, I know, Alfred, but think. Archibald used hay to encourage Polly out of the stall. *The pony was tired.* That means he probably did not leave until this evening. He can't have got far."

She could feel his stare on the back of her neck as she stepped forward, following the trail. "Are you coming?"

Alfred looked utterly at sea. "I have no idea who or what you are, do I?"

Meredith swallowed. She should have known revealing her skills in tracking would raise some awkward questions, but now she had been terminated from her employment, there did not seem to be much point in trying to hide her abilities.

If they found Archibald, all would be forgiven. If not...

She had never wanted Alfred to know about her past! He may think her a thief already, falsely, but how would he ever believe that if she revealed her true name?

"We need to focus on Archibald," she said shortly.

They stepped outside the stables, Alfred looking around wildly as though Archibald would magically appear before them. Meredith was more interested in the ground. *If she was right, if he had only left with Polly a few hours ago...*

"There," she said with a smile, pointing at the ground.

"What?"

"Tracks. Look, see how the curve is smaller than a horse's hoof? 'Tis a pony."

"Archie!" Alfred looked half relieved, half suspicious. "You know this because...?"

"Let's keep going," she said, stepping carefully to ensure she did not scuff the marks.

Alfred followed her. "Should we not go on horseback? What if he's miles away?"

They turned the corner toward the path to the lake. All was stillness and quiet outside, though a few muffled shouts could be heard from the house. The search still continued there, though Meredith was certain now it would be a fruitless one.

"No, we mustn't scuff the tracks," Meredith said slowly, eyes concentrating hard in the darkness. Sometimes she would go two or three feet without a mark, and her heart would sink, and then the trail would appear again. "Besides, he's only been gone an hour or so."

Alfred grabbed her arm and brought her to a halt. "No, that

can't be—I was in his bed-chamber two hours ago, and he was not there!"

Meredith looked down at his hand and he dropped her's as if burned. "He may have gone from his bedchamber," she said slowly, "but he was probably in the stable at that time. He hadn't managed to coax Polly out."

His eyes narrowed. "How do you know all this?"

Meredith swallowed. *This was not the time.* "Marks only stay in gravel for about an hour with this wind. Come on."

She had only managed to take two more steps before Alfred halted her again, and this time, he did not drop her arm as he looked deeply into her eyes.

"Before we go any further, Meredith," he said, "I need to know. You have to tell me how you know these things, how you can track him. Who...*what are you?*"

Meredith did not answer. As soon as she told him the truth, there would be no going back, though how they could be more separated from each other, she did not know. There was already so much mistrust, so many lies believed.

Alfred stepped closer, and Meredith found her heart fluttering.

"Climbing up trees," he whispered, "riding bareback, tracking a horse...you...you *are* a thief, aren't you?"

Meredith took a deep breath. "Not anymore."

"What!" Alfred's face paled in the moonlit night. "I thought Archibald was the thief, but instead you—you just hid the spoil in his desk to make it seem—"

"I am no thief, Alfred, and if you do not believe me then go back up to the house and let me find your brother on my own!" Meredith could not have believed such strong words had come out of her mouth.

"How can I believe you?"

Meredith did not know. "I...*my family* were thieves. Are thieves still, but I left that life a long time ago. I never wanted that, I wanted a normal life, a life without crime!"

Was she ruining everything by telling him this? Meredith had always hidden her connection to the Glasshand Gang so carefully. Every minute they stood here arguing they could be losing their chance to find Archibald who even now could be hurt, cold, alone.

"A criminal family?" Alfred was staring as though he had forgotten how to breathe. "A criminal family as my brother's governess?"

"You do not think people can change?" Meredith said passionately. "You do not think a good life is possible for those who finally escape iniquity and lawbreaking? Yes, my parents were wrong, and I certainly learned a great deal about horses while I was…was with them. But I turned my back on them six years ago and earn an honest living! How many people in my situation can claim such a thing?"

Alfred just stared, seemingly unable to speak. Meredith found she was breathing heavily, her lungs painful as they took in huge gulps of freezing air.

There, it was said. Now to the matter at hand.

"You are certainly a governess of great talents," he said finally. "I…I cannot think of anything else. Archibald first."

"Do you know if he took a coat?" she said, pulling herself from his grasp and looking down once more at the marks on the ground.

"I…you…no, I do not know," said Alfred, evidently deciding he would express his dislike of her later, once his brother had been found.

Men, Meredith thought as she rolled her eyes. *Utterly useless at times.*

The next five minutes were spent in silence, Meredith's concentration at its height. She knew what she was doing, had tracked horses hundreds of times, but these did not make sense. Instead of going toward the lake as she had initially supposed, the pony seemed to have gone around in circles.

Eventually they found themselves just outside the kitchen

gardens.

"Are you certain you know what you are doing?" hissed Alfred, but at that very moment, Meredith flung out an arm to stop him in his tracks.

"Quiet," she breathed.

They both fell silent, and on the air came another sound—two sounds. Quiet sobbing, and what could have been hooves on gravel.

"Archie," said Alfred as he started to run forward, but Meredith grabbed his hand and pulled him back.

"No," she said quietly. "Not yet?"

"Not yet? Not yet?" Alfred growled. "If that is Archie, then—"

"Then he will be cold, frightened, and a little embarrassed," said Meredith quietly. "Trust me. I tame children just as I tamed your horse. We go slowly."

For a moment, she was not sure whether he would obey. It was rather odd, giving orders to a duke, but Meredith held her gaze with the man she knew she still loved.

Eventually, Alfred smiled wryly. "Like a spooked horse?"

Meredith returned the smile hesitantly and nodded.

And still, she loved him. She could not magic away the feelings which had overwhelmed her weeks ago.

Stepping forward together, they came around a corner and saw—Archibald.

He was curled up in a corner of the kitchen garden, his shirt torn and his face flushed with tears. Polly, the pony, was beside him.

As they came into view in the moonlit night, Archibald stood hastily and tried to wipe his eyes.

"Alfred!"

Meredith glanced at the duke, who seemed relieved his brother had cried out his name rather than that of his governess.

"H-How did you find me?" asked the boy.

Alfred looked at Meredith for a moment before saying, "We were very worried about you, Archie. We found you as quickly as we could."

They stepped toward the boy and sat on either side of him. Archibald dropped gratefully down as though his legs would not hold him for much longer and leaned his head on Alfred's arm.

"I...I don't want you to be fighting each other."

Meredith looked at Alfred over Archibald's head. Here, in this moment, it was almost as though they were a family. She knew governesses were never supposed to be too close to the children they cared for. That was when it got complicated.

She almost laughed. *More complicated than being accused of theft by a duke with whom you had fallen in love?*

"We...we are not fighting," Alfred said softly.

Meredith smiled ruefully. "We are not?"

Her remark made Alfred shake his head before he said, "Archie, I-I found the things you had hidden in your desk. Were you...were you looking for things about Father?"

Meredith could not believe it—*she had been right!* The thief, if thief he could be called, had been Archibald all along.

Archibald nodded, looking up at his brother and his governess fearfully. "Am I in trouble?"

"Of course not," Meredith said hastily before Alfred could say anything. "We were just worried that you might have come to harm."

"But you are safe now, and that is all that matters," said Alfred quietly.

Archibald wiped his nose with his sleeve, a filthy habit Meredith had still not managed to train out of him, and then sniffed loudly.

"That is not all that matters," he said firmly. "You don't like each other."

Meredith's gaze moved from the younger to the older brother. "Well, I...I would not put it quite like that."

The cold of the gravel was seeping into her bones, but warmth stirred in Meredith's heart. Alfred had a strange expression, one she had never seen before.

"No, neither would I," he said gently, looking deep into Meredith's eyes. "Not when we are getting married."

Meredith blinked. *No, she could not have heard that correctly. Alfred would never say such a thing—would he?*

"We are?"

Alfred nodded. "We are going to be a family, Meredith, you, and me, and Archie. Perhaps more."

Meredith could hardly take it in. Only when Alfred leaned over Archibald's head and kissed her, reverentially and deeply, did she believe her own ears and her own heart.

CHAPTER TWENTY-FOUR

October 15, 1812

"I STILL DO not understand why we have to wait around like fools," Alfred muttered.

All the eyes on him were making his skin crawl. He knew he should not mind, and he knew the acceptance speech he would have to make could be short, thank God, but still. Whenever he entered the Town Hall these days, he felt a great sense of foreboding.

There was a squeeze of his hand, and Alfred's heart slowed thanks to the comfort of the woman beside him. The woman who would never leave him. The woman he had been fortunate to have a second chance to win.

"Don't fuss," Meredith said quietly by his side. "It is a pleasant enough day, and we only have to be here another hour at the most. Besides, the people like to see you."

Alfred looked out across the room. Yes, there were plenty of people there; he could espy the Hemmings, the Johnsons, even the Reverend Michaels and the entire Walker clan, which was saying something. Everyone who was anyone was here to celebrate his win. There was even tea and cake being passed round by the Walkers, their servants wandering around with teapots offering more tea to those with cups.

He sighed heavily. *It was going to be just like last time.* The results would be announced, everyone would feign surprise that the Duke of Rochdale had won again, and then he would be forced to leave the place he loved and descend to London.

At least it would be over soon. *It could not be much longer before the result would be announced, would it?*

"Think of it as a celebration," came the murmured words from the woman he loved.

Meredith was beaming, eyes bright and gown accentuating her loveliness more than ever. Alfred's stomach lurched. *How was it possible that he had managed to win her in the end?* It did not seem possible. Not after all the foolish mistakes they had both made.

"There is Mr. and Mrs. Walker," said Meredith with a smile. "Goodness, they look pleased, don't they?"

Pleased with themselves, was Alfred's less than charitable thought, but he pushed it aside. True, the couple had their heads held high as though they were going to be announced the winner, rosettes of the Carmichael blue carefully pinned to their fronts.

But then, Alfred reminded himself, *they had done most, if not all of the hard work of the election, bar giving the speeches—and they had been written by Mr. Walker in most cases.*

No, he should give them their dues, and Mr. Hemming, who was somewhere in the bustling crowd.

"So much of my life builds up to this moment," he said in a low voice so that only Meredith could hear, "and now I am here, again, 'tis nothing like what I had expected."

Meredith raised an eyebrow. "You thought there would be trumpets to herald you, crowds to throw flowers at you?"

Alfred chuckled, despite the anxiety balled in his chest. He would make a speech, even if it was short, and in all the kerfuffle of the last week—the accusations of theft, Meredith leaving, Archibald going missing, his proposal—he had completely neglected to write one.

"Not exactly," he said. "More…I do not know. I have won this seat before, and I will surely win it again after today. But it is different. I think—"

"Can I go and play over there?"

Both Alfred and Meredith turned to look down at Archibald's beseeching face.

"Play?" said Alfred rather hesitantly. After Archibald's runaway attempt, he had trodden rather carefully around the boy. He had no wish to spark another moment of rebellion. "Play where? With whom?"

It was only then that he caught Meredith's silencing look.

"Archibald," said Meredith, lowering herself down to her haunches so she could look into the boy's eyes. "Tell me what you would like to do."

The child hesitated, still looking up at Alfred as he spoke. "I…I want to go to the other corner, away from the stage, and play tig with the other children."

The two Carmichael brothers and Meredith peered over. There were several children, mostly clean though none as smartly dressed as Archibald, giggling away in a corner of the Town Hall playing tig. One of the chairs had been pulled away from the rows and was 'home'.

"I'm not sure if…" began Alfred.

"Make sure you stay within the Town Hall, do you hear me, Archibald Carmichael?" said Meredith sternly.

Archibald looked at his brother.

"Listen to your gov—to Miss Hubert," amended Alfred with a grin. "Go on with you."

A look of surprise and delight suffused over the boy's face before he muttered a 'thank you' and scampered off to play with the other children.

Alfred watched his brother approach them slowly. A few words were spoken on both sides, and within an instant, Archibald was giggling with delight as he leaned out of the way of whoever it was being tig.

"What are you thinking?" Meredith asked softly.

Alfred hardly knew. The last week had been such a whirlwind he had almost forgotten, truth be told, that the ruddy election was to be announced so soon. Its importance had paled into insignificance when he looked at Meredith Hubert.

He did so now, and she blushed prettily. Here she was, a woman who would continue to challenge him right into their old age. Encourage him, surprise him—teach him things he did not even know he did not know.

He was the most fortunate of men, and whenever he tried not to notice just how beautiful she was, or what she did to his body when he was near her...

Well. They had been careful. Rochdale Abbey was large enough for two people to do almost anything without being found out, after all.

Keeping their hands off each other had proved utterly impossible. Alfred would just have to hope no one caught them before...

"I said, what you are thinking?" she repeated.

Alfred smiled wryly. "Truthfully?"

She nodded.

"I am not entirely sure how I managed to land you," said Alfred, almost laughing. "After all the confusion between us— after I had accused you of a crime!"

He could hardly believe it. They would be married, and he would be the happiest of men.

But Meredith did not look overly impressed with the praise. "Land me? You forget, Your Grace, it was you who chose me in the first place. You picked me out of a catalog!"

That made Alfred chuckle. "I mean, in the fullest sense of the word, I suppose I did. I was sent the details of all the governesses available at the Bureau, and you seemed the most proficient. I could never have imagined you would have so many great talents. You have far surpassed your description! Besides," he said more softly now, "you are perfect for me."

Meredith raised a quizzical eyebrow. "Not perfect, just perfect for you? Where is your flattery, Your Grace?"

Alfred's heart soared. *Well, he would never be bored whenever he was with Meredith, that was certain.* "Absolutely perfect, *and* perfect for me."

Meredith squeezed his arm and was about to say something when she faltered, her mouth closing and her eyes fixed on something just behind Alfred.

He turned to see Miss Wilhelmina Talbot walking past haughtily, sniffing as she glanced at them before she returned to her brother's side.

Alfred looked back at Meredith and saw the shine had gone.

"You should have married her," she said quietly. "That is what she thinks, anyway."

"And yet not what I think, and surely 'tis my opinion that matters here," said Alfred with a dry smile. "Miss Talbot is accustomed to getting whatever she wants. She will have to learn that that doesn't extend to people."

Yet despite his warm words, Meredith did not appear consoled. Her cheeks flushed, and her gaze had dropped, though she had not mercifully dropped his arm.

Alfred squeezed her hand. "Ignore her."

Meredith gave him a swift smile. "You must have noticed, though, Alfred."

He waited for more, but when it did not come, prompted, "Noticed?"

Meredith nodded. "No one has approached you—no one at all. Wouldn't you expect your supporters to be congratulating you on your campaign? Gentlemen and ladies to approach for the honor of speaking to their duke? Even tenants, interested in settling a grievance or getting a decision from you?"

It was only now she mentioned it that Alfred realized: no, no one had. He and Meredith had been able to chatter away quite happily without interruption, but only now did he see how odd that was.

"I suppose they do not wish to disturb us," he said bracingly.

Meredith's smile was too knowing. "'Tis because of me, Alfred. Look. *Really look.*"

Alfred did so, though he was not entirely sure what he was supposed to be looking for. Only when he concentrated did he spot it.

No one would meet his eyes.

Whenever he looked at someone, their gaze would slide over to someone else, or the floor, or in some rare occasions, the ceiling. Worse, there were a few people—the Hemmings over there, and the Talbots of course—who were glaring. They looked genuinely angry as they beheld him and Meredith standing near the stage.

Alfred swallowed. It was a rather unusual experience for a duke, not to be universally beloved and applauded. He had never noticed it before, but now it was absent. It was rather unsettling.

"Well, let them stare, let them ignore us," he said heartily. "If they do so because I am in love with you and will be marrying you in two weeks, then so be it."

Meredith's cheeks darkened. "This was exactly what I was afraid of, why we held back for so long. You have...you have lost your standing, Alfred. Your reputation."

"I may have done something wild and radical, but I am happy," said Alfred fiercely. *He had to make sure she understood.* "I regret nothing, Meredith, for if I lost their affection by merely securing your own, it was not worth having. I tell you I am happy, and as long as you are, that is all that matters."

The hot flush lessened in Meredith's face, and she smiled. "I do love you."

Alfred kissed her on the cheek, ignoring the shock of those around them, and tightened his grip on her arm.

He had known this would happen, of course. Meredith was right. This was precisely why the idea of professing their love to each other had been such a radical idea.

Dukes did not marry governesses.

Except this one did. Alfred smiled. He had always done what he had been told, his whole life. Even this damned election was because he was following the wishes of his father, now long gone from this world.

But not with love. Love could not be dictated in that way, and so he would marry Meredith, blast them all!

"And I will even represent them properly in Parliament with no malice," he whispered to her, seeing her smile, "even though they are being downright rude! After all, 'tis not as though—careful, Archie!"

Archibald, giggling loudly and cheeks flushed, rocketed past them as the game of tig started to break the boundaries of that little corner.

Alfred stepped forward to go after him, but Meredith held him back.

"Let him play," she said softly. "He gets so few opportunities to do so, and besides, the announcement will be made soon."

"I thought they would have done by now," Alfred said, his temper rising. "It's past twelve."

"They will announce it when it is ready," said Meredith patiently, as only a governess could. "I...I hope you do not blame me if our engagement announcement has lost you votes."

Alfred sighed. Mr. Walker had been adamant it would, and they had argued over it five days ago when Alfred had shown him the announcement he was sending to The Times.

"You cannot possibly mean to—wait a week, Your Grace," Mr. Walker had pleaded, while Meredith had sat quietly in the drawing room, saying nothing. "A week is all I ask, and then you can announce whatsoever you wish."

"A week?" Alfred had not understood in that moment. "Why a week?"

And Mr. Walker had glanced awkwardly at 'the governess', as he had called her that entire conversation, and Meredith had laughed.

"To ensure you win the election, of course," she had said

lightly. "Mr. Walker knows there will be those who would never vote for a duke who could so forget his place in society as to marry a *servant!*"

The Town Hall was growing louder as more people joined the throng. Alfred sighed and shook his head.

"I never wished to run in this damned election," he said under his breath so only Meredith could hear. "You know that, Meredith. You knew that about me almost as soon as you first met me. I am far more interested in being your husband—which will happen *when*, by the way?"

Meredith seemed to glow with pleasure at his words. "You are a very impatient man, Alfred Carmichael! I told you, two weeks is the fastest we could possibly marry, and you have already waited half that time. You just need to be patient."

Lowering his head to whisper in her ear, he murmured, "You will need to teach me that."

Alfred turned around and saw the official counter enter the Town Hall in his ceremonial red robes. He was moving toward the stage. *This was it.*

Stomach dropping, Alfred tried to swallow but found he could not. In just a few short minutes, his election to Parliament would be announced, and he would have only enough time to complete his packing, marry his beloved, and wave goodbye to Archibald before returning to London.

Crowded, dirty London. It did not bear thinking about.

But, Alfred thought as John Talbot stepped to the stage in the wake of the official, *he was a Rochdale*. This was his duty.

"You know," whispered Meredith as the volume of the chatter rose. "We could take in some of the children from other gentry families—for lessons, you know. Archibald would be happier then, and it would bring greater education to the area."

Alfred tried to grin, but his heart was beating too quickly. "Yes, we could charge them, too—think of the fortune we could make."

Meredith laughed and started to speak, but her words were

drowned out.

"Quiet!" bellowed the official.

A hush fell across the room. This was the moment they had been waiting for. Weeks of campaigning, miles upon miles of meeting with voters, hustings, speeches...it all came down to this moment.

Alfred was not entirely sure he could feel his feet. How he was still standing, he could not tell. Only Meredith holding onto his arm brought him relief, and when Archibald scampered over to them, standing on Alfred's other side, he placed a hand on his shoulder.

"Archibald! Don't you want to play with your friends?" Meredith whispered as the official cleared his throat.

The boy shook his head. "When Alfred wins, we all have to go up onto the stage."

Meredith stared. "We—we all do?"

Alfred nodded. He did not trust his voice. Any moment now, he would have to go up there and make a speech thanking everyone for voting him in. He felt nauseous just thinking about it.

"I have here the results of the October eighteen twelve election of Rochdale," said the official in a loud, clear voice into the silence. "These results have been ratified by myself, the chamberlain of the..."

Alfred tried to concentrate, but the words just seemed to wash over him. This was the moment that dedicated him to servitude for the next goodness knows how many years. And then there would be another election and another...

"—and so do declare the winner, thusly," said the official. He hesitated, looked down at his paper again, and then said, "The member of Parliament for Rochdale, as chosen by its electorate in a free and fair campaign, is the Right Honorable John Talbot!"

Gasps echoed around the Town Hall, and there was the sound of breaking china.

Alfred looked around and saw Mr. Walker standing in a daze

that mirrored how he felt. A smashed teacup was scattered around his feet.

"My goodness," murmured Meredith.

Alfred stood still, trying to understand what had just happened.

"The member of Parliament for Rochdale, as chosen by its electorate in a free and fair campaign, is the Right Honorable John Talbot!"

The words were clear, but they had not sunk in.

John Talbot. *John Talbot?*

And then there was cheering from his right, and Talbot stepped forward with wide eyes and a broad grin. Forcing his way past Alfred and Meredith, almost knocking Archibald to the floor, he stepped onto the stage and looked out at the crowd.

Applause started, and was taken up by the rest of the crowd.

"Why thank you, thank you," said Talbot sycophantically, bowing low. "Oh, what a day! I must thank a great number of people who made this possible—who made it possible for I, John Talbot, to represent the great people of Rochdale in our noble city! First, my sister, whose words of encouragement..."

Alfred stared up at the man as he continued to spout nonsense. John Talbot. *Talbot had won the election.*

Something—no, someone was squeezing his arm. Alfred blinked, and Meredith swam into view.

"Are you quite well, Alfred?"

Her voice was quiet, obviously concerned. Alfred was hardly sure. He could barely comprehend his feelings, let alone express them. They were complex, to be sure, but one overriding emotion was drowning out all the others, and he could not yet discern it.

It was only when he focused on Meredith and allowed the pretentious speech of Talbot to disappear that he realized.

Relief.

A huge wave of relief had washed over him, leaving him standing on the shore of his life with so much more before him than he could ever have imagined.

He had not won. He was not the member of Parliament for Rochdale. He would not have to leave his land, his people, Archibald—he would not have to live in smokey London.

He was free. Finally, he was free to do something different with his life, to make his own decisions.

"Alfred?" Meredith was clearly a little alarmed by his utter silence.

There was a tug on his frockcoat, and Alfred looked down to see Archibald's face, a little concerned. "Does...does this mean we have let Father down?"

Alfred opened his mouth, but no words came out. It was a question he had never had to consider before. He had always done what he had been told, always obeyed the rules of the Carmichaels.

"Alfred?" said Archibald, a little fearfully now. "Have we let Father down? Would he be angry with us?"

"No," said a voice firmly.

Alfred was not sure how he had managed to say it until he realized he had not. Meredith had removed her arm from his and was once again leaning on her haunches, looking into Archibald's serious face with an expression just as serious, though with more warmth.

"Your Father loved being in Parliament," she said quietly as Talbot's speech continued on. "He served his people that way, and it made him happy. Now we will find our own ways of serving our people, and that will make us happy. Do you understand?"

Alfred watched with love twisting in his heart as Archibald carefully considered her words and then nodded solemnly.

"In that case," he said slowly, "can I go back and play tig with my new friends?"

Meredith smiled, and Alfred cuffed him gently around the ear. "Of course you can."

"Just don't wander off," Meredith added. "I don't want to track you down again!"

Archibald grinned. "Yes, Miss Hubert. And no matter what happens, I am proud of you, Alfred."

Hugging his older brother swiftly, he disappeared off into the crowd.

Meredith rose as Alfred blinked away hot tears. He had lost today, but he had gained so much. Some of it he had always had. He had just never realized how precious it was.

"—so you can always depend on your new member of Parliament, John Talbot!" finished the newly crowned politician to raucous applause from his gaggle of followers.

There was polite applause from the rest of the Town Hall, and even Alfred managed to clap a few times. *Much good may it do him.* Taking his seat at Parliament had never brought him much joy, but perhaps he was simply not suited to it. *Perhaps Talbot was.*

Chatter was growing as people discussed the rather shocking results. Alfred could feel the stares on the back of his neck. Everyone wanted to see how he would react.

Meredith slipped her hand in his, and much of the discomfort dislodged from his heart. *How could he imagine being happier than this?* He had Archibald restored to him, Meredith was to be his bride—what could be better?

He kissed Meredith hard on the mouth, ignoring the gasps from those around them. "You aren't disappointed?"

Meredith shook her head. "Disappointed? I can already see the weight lifted from you, and I would rather marry a happy duke than a miserable member of Parliament."

Alfred laughed and kissed her again, utterly ignoring the pointed looks of disapproval being cast their way. *He had managed it, though goodness knows how.*

"On the other hand," said Meredith delicately, "I think there is someone there who is greatly disappointed and would benefit from speaking with you."

Alfred turned and groaned. Mr. Walker had not moved an inch since the result had been announced, and his teacup had evidently slipped from his fingers. Mrs. Walker was fussing around him, instructing one of their maids to clean it all up.

"I will have to go over and comfort Mr. Walker," said Alfred ruefully. "I don't think he has taken the news at all well. I will be but a moment."

Regretfully relinquishing Meredith's arm and hating being parted from her, Alfred started to push through the crowd toward Mr. Walker.

And then someone took his arm.

"And where do you think you are going?" Meredith said with a mock frown on her face. "We go together. We come as a pair now, Alfred, whether you want to or not."

The knot of pain disappeared, and Alfred squeezed her hand. "Together, then."

EPILOGUE

October 30, 1812

THERE WAS DEFINITELY a winter chill in the air as Meredith looked up at the imposing building. She sighed, her breath blossoming before her as the church's tower clock chimed eleven o'clock.

The cold, frosty morning had been a surprise as she had awoken that morning, but after spending months in the north, London felt warm. It was strange to see Jack Frost's fingers scratched across the glass windows when it felt so warm.

The pavement around Meredith was bustling, people moving around her as she continued to look up at the building.

She knew what she had to do. She needed to step forward and face up to what she had done, but she couldn't. Something held her back.

Meredith sighed again. "She will be unhappy with me."

"Probably," said her husband cheerfully by her side.

"I did send Miss Clarke a letter in the end," said Meredith, assiduously ignoring Alfred's unhelpful remarks. "Perhaps...I mean, I did not receive a reply. Perhaps it would be easier, better not to go in at all."

She glanced into Alfred's caring eyes and felt the courage she knew she did not have.

"Yes, we could not go in," he said gently, "but this is the last tie to the past. I am not sure whether I want to meet your family, for example."

"I suppose so," she said hesitantly.

Alfred looked up at the building. Meredith had always considered it a rather austere building; gray stone, no embellishments or adornments.

"Though now you mention it, I am not entirely sure whether a second letter would have done just as well as a visit," said Alfred with a sigh. "I did not wish to come to London in the first place, 'twas you who insisted."

Meredith smiled. She was the most fortunate woman in the world and well aware of that fact. No longer Meredith Hubert, or even Meredith Glasshand: she was Meredith Carmichael, Duchess of Rochdale. Married to the best man she had ever met—and sister-in-law to one just as fine!

Alfred had made her happier in the last week since they married than…well, she could ever remember. A real home, a real husband, a real life. They were things she had believed beyond her reach when trapped living a life of iniquity with her family.

Now she had a man who loved her, no matter her past. He had looked beyond what would have cowed even some of the best of men, and saw instead…*her*.

Meredith. As she was, not as a governess or a criminal or a servant. And he loved what he saw.

"Well, I suppose the sooner we go in, the sooner we can leave."

Buoyed by this thought, Meredith stepped forward and knocked on the front door of the Governess Bureau.

It was opened almost immediately, and a maid appeared, looking at them inquiringly.

Meredith smiled. She had to remember everything was different now, particularly since the last time she was here. It was time to face what she had done, and she would not feel at ease with herself until she had looked Miss Clarke in the eyes.

"I have an appointment," she said quietly. "To see Miss Clarke."

The maid looked at her curiously. Her gaze was a little too penetrating, but the servant did not seem able to place her face, no matter how much she attempted it. Well, she looked very different than three months ago. New coat, new gown, new bonnet.

New name.

"An appointment?"

"Yes," said Alfred gruffly. "And it is cold out here. Rochdale's the name."

The girl looked abashed at his words. There was also something about the way Alfred spoke. Meredith had never been able to place it, not exactly, but being a duke was not just in the blood, but in the voice, too. He had a way of commanding people without actually making any commands.

"Yes, of course," said the maid, dropping into a hasty curtsey. "Come this way, Miss Clarke is expecting you."

Meredith was careful as they entered the waiting room in the wake of the maid, not to catch the eye of any of the governesses there. Miss Patrick had her nose buried in a book, and there was Miss Fletcher, with whom Meredith had shared a few pleasant evenings.

Neither of them looked up at the splendidly dressed woman; however, a fur stole around her neck, diamonds peeking out from her pelisse, and feathers in her bonnet.

Meredith almost laughed. *It was hard to believe this was her life now.*

"Miss Clarke," said the maid, bobbing another curtsey and immediately disappearing as another knock echoed from the front door.

The study door opened, and Meredith took a deep breath. This was the moment she would be forced to have a conversation with Miss Clarke she simply did not want to have.

Alfred took off his top hat and stepped around Meredith. "Ah, Miss Clarke."

Meredith could no longer hesitate. As she entered Miss Clarke's study, the proprietress of the Governess Bureau was standing behind her desk just rising from a curtsey.

"Your Grace," she said demurely, "and—oh. Miss Hubert. I do apologize, there has clearly been a misunderstanding."

Meredith tried to smile as she stepped to Alfred's side. He had not taken one of the seats before the desk and was evidently waiting for her to explain.

How could she find the words?

"A-A misunderstanding, Miss Clarke?" was all she could manage.

"Yes," said Miss Clarke with a brisk smile. "I was told the Duke of Rochdale and the duchess wanted to see me. I have to admit I was not aware there was a duchess, but now I can see the mistake. It is the duke and his governess. Please, sit down."

Alfred grinned at Meredith as he sat. She did not return his smile. *This was intolerable, she had to say something immediately. But how could she find the words?*

Slowly lowering herself onto the chair, she resolved to say something—and quickly, before this misunderstanding continued.

"Yes, I thought I might have a visit from you, Miss Hubert," said Miss Clarke, affixing her with a stern look. "I have not received a report for the last month. I hope all is in order?"

She had spoken to Alfred rather than Meredith and sat waiting patiently for his response. Alfred did not speak, however, and looked pointedly at Meredith.

Meredith swallowed, her throat dry. "Miss Clarke, there are some facts which you need to be informed of."

The glare Miss Clarke subjected her to was fierce indeed. "Excuse me, Miss Hubert, but I was speaking to your employer."

It was the perfect opening, but even then, Meredith almost

did not take it. Only Alfred's subtle nod encouraged her onward.

Meredith took a deep breath. "No, not my employer. My husband."

Alfred reached out with a smile and took her hand in his. Meredith did not look at him. Her eyes were transfixed on Miss Clarke.

For a moment, it appeared Miss Clarke had been frozen solid. She moved not one inch, her gaze on Meredith.

Meredith wondered whether she should say more. After all, that was hardly an explanation, was it! If she could just explain how they had fallen in love without any intention of doing ill on either side—surely then, the owner of the Governess Bureau would not be so angry with her!

Miss Clarke carefully removed her glasses, cleaned them with a scrap of silk, and replaced them before saying quietly, "You know the rules, Miss Hubert."

"I know," said Meredith, "and I broke them. I would only have done it if I...I truly fell in love."

This simple statement seemed to render Miss Clarke speechless. Her gaze flickered between Meredith and Alfred, still hand in hand, her expression moving from astonishment to outrage.

"There are but three rules of the Governess Bureau," she said with a quiet fury. "Three rules. I have those rules to protect the reputation of the Governess Bureau—goodness, no one would ever hire one of our girls if they thought she was going to make eyes at the master!"

Meredith did not know what to say. She may be a duchess now, but Miss Clarke was still the woman who had given her a second chance. She had taken her on, without references.

And she had betrayed that trust.

"This is the first time this has ever happened. I am very disappointed, Miss Hubert!"

Meredith fought the instinct to hang her head in shame. She would never permit anyone to make her feel guilty for loving Alfred—for finding a shared love with him.

"Actually," she said quietly, "it's 'Your Grace'."

Miss Clarke gaped and then looked to Alfred. "I do apologize for my outburst, Your Grace, but you must be able to see this from my perspective. I have a business to run!"

"Meredith was such a wonderful governess to my brother, thanks undoubtedly to your excellent tutelage," said Alfred smoothly, "I just had to secure her for all our future children."

Meredith almost laughed. *He did have a way with words.* Put him on a stage, and he would fall to pieces, but place him before a lioness like Miss Clarke, and he was magnificent.

"You can be assured we wish for no scandal, Miss Clarke," continued the duke. "We want to live a quiet life with my half-brother, and…and any children we have ourselves."

Meredith flushed at these words.

"We are not looking for gossip," Alfred reiterated, "nor to bring you into disrepute."

Whether it was his calming tone or the content of his words, Meredith was not sure. Either way, Miss Clarke appeared to be mollified by these statements.

"Well," she said. "Well, all I can say is I hope I shall never have to endure this sort of news again. Why, I have a meeting with the Earl of Clarcton in ten minutes, and he would certainly not want to hear such things!"

The poor woman did look very upset, and guilt crept into Meredith's heart. It was her fault Miss Clarke was so flustered, so concerned for the reputation of the Governess Bureau.

But what could she do? She would never compromise her feelings for Alfred just to keep someone else happy.

Taking a deep breath, Miss Clarke looked once more at Meredith. "How…how did this happen? I will need to know, to see how I can prevent it from happening again."

"Never fear, Miss Clarke," said Alfred. "I am not looking for a second governess nor wife!"

Meredith laughed, but stopped abruptly at the sight of Miss Clarke. "Alfred is joking, Miss Clarke."

The proprietress nodded. "Ah. I see."

A rather uncomfortable silence followed this, and Meredith felt obliged to fill it. "'Tis hard to remember exactly how it happened, in truth."

"It was an instant attraction, I am afraid," said Alfred with a roguish grin. "But every day has taught me more about you, and each bit of knowledge I loved."

Meredith felt a lurch in her stomach and looked at Miss Clarke, who had gone pink.

"I cannot create rules against that, I suppose," she said hesitantly as a bell rang in the distance. "Ah, the earl is early. You...you will not say anything to him, will you?"

"Of course not," said Alfred as he rose to his feet, Meredith mirroring him. "And thank you, Miss Clarke. Though you did not intend to give me such happiness in this precise way, I can assure you, you have."

Meredith saw something strange flicker across Miss Clarke's face; something like regret, or bitterness perhaps. Before she could examine it in any detail, it was gone.

They were bustled out of the room before they could say any more, and Meredith saw to her surprise and delight that they had been shown the servants' door. Evidently, Miss Clarke would do anything to prevent the earl from meeting with a governess turned duchess.

"Goodness, the servants' way out!" Meredith giggled. "I think that's probably the first time a duke has stepped through it!"

And they were out, into the freezing air. Meredith breathed it in as though she had been underwater all this time. The day felt fresh, new, somehow. The alleyway around the side of the Governess Bureau was empty. They were alone.

She had done it. She had told Miss Clarke, and she had no more secrets to share.

Now there was nothing anyone could do to prevent her from being happy.

"Hallo, Meredith—I thought you were up north with some

duke?"

Meredith turned to see Miss Anne Gilbert, brilliant ginger hair shining in the wintery sun, a broad smile on her face. They had both been chosen as candidates for the Earl of Marnmouth, and in the three days trial which the old man had given both of them, she had grown fond of the other woman. She was an excellent governess if a little loud and flamboyant.

"Goodness, are you it?" Miss Gilbert said, stepping forward to take a closer look at Alfred.

He laughed. "Why yes, I am it."

Meredith was not entirely sure how it happened, but before she knew it, Miss Gilbert had thrown her arms around her, giggling wildly.

"The gossip is true then! You really did marry him?"

"She really did," said Alfred with a laugh. "Goodness, don't strangle my wife, please, Miss."

Meredith was released, and Miss Gilbert beamed. "Well, I don't mind saying how pleased I am, Meredith, I really don't. I'm heading in now to find out my next charge. Apparently, the master's just arrived!"

"Ah, you'll be for the Earl of Clarcton, then," said Meredith with a smile. It was strange to think that only a few months ago, she was in this same position. Waiting for her next assignment, wondering what the children would be like when she arrived there.

And now...

"Oh, another earl!" Miss Gilbert nodded impressively. "Well, you know more than I do, then. Better dash, Miss Clarke is a stickler for punctuality, as you know. Good luck!"

Meredith smiled as Miss Gilbert disappeared into the Governess Bureau with a flurry of goodbyes.

Alfred kissed her neck as he came up and hugged her from behind. "Right, is that it? Can we go back to Rochdale Abbey now?"

Meredith smiled and pulled herself out of his arms as she said seriously, "No. I am afraid we have one more appointment."

Alfred groaned as they stepped toward the bustling street before them. "Meredith, you know I hate London! Can't you go and do whatever it is near home? In Rochdale?"

Home. The word had never meant much to her as a child. They were always on the move, always looking for the next big score. As a governess, one learned not to take too seriously the masters and mistresses who encouraged you to treat the place like your home. Sooner or later, you would be leaving, on to start with a new family.

But not anymore.

"No," she said decidedly. "The doctor I want to see is here."

Alfred froze as he said urgently, "Doctor? You're not ill, are you?"

Another rush of nausea threatened to overwhelm her, but Meredith just smiled. *Perhaps this was the best time to tell him.* She would have to tell him when they arrived at Harley Street, anyway.

"No," she said quietly, "but I think... I think I am pregnant."

For a moment, Alfred said nothing, merely staring as though she had announced she was on her way to the moon.

Then he pulled her into a tight embrace, kissing her wildly until he finally said, "Are—you are sure?"

"No," said Meredith with a laugh, heart soaring at his joy. "As sure as I can be without seeing the doctor!"

"A baby," said Alfred, half in wonder, half in shock. "A baby— our baby, Meredith!"

"Come on," she said with a grin. "We don't want to be late for this next great adventure."

And they walked away from the Governess Bureau arm in arm.

About Emily E K Murdoch

If you love falling in love, then you've come to the right place.

I am a historian and writer and have a varied career to date: from examining medieval manuscripts to designing museum exhibitions, to working as a researcher for the BBC to working for the National Trust.

My books range from England 1050 to Texas 1848, and I can't wait for you to fall in love with my heroes and heroines!

Follow me on twitter and instagram @emilyekmurdoch, find me on facebook at facebook.com/theemilyekmurdoch, and read my blog at www.emilyekmurdoch.com.

www.ingramcontent.com/pod-product-compliance
Lightning Source LLC
Chambersburg PA
CBHW070753190726
48292CB00002B/522